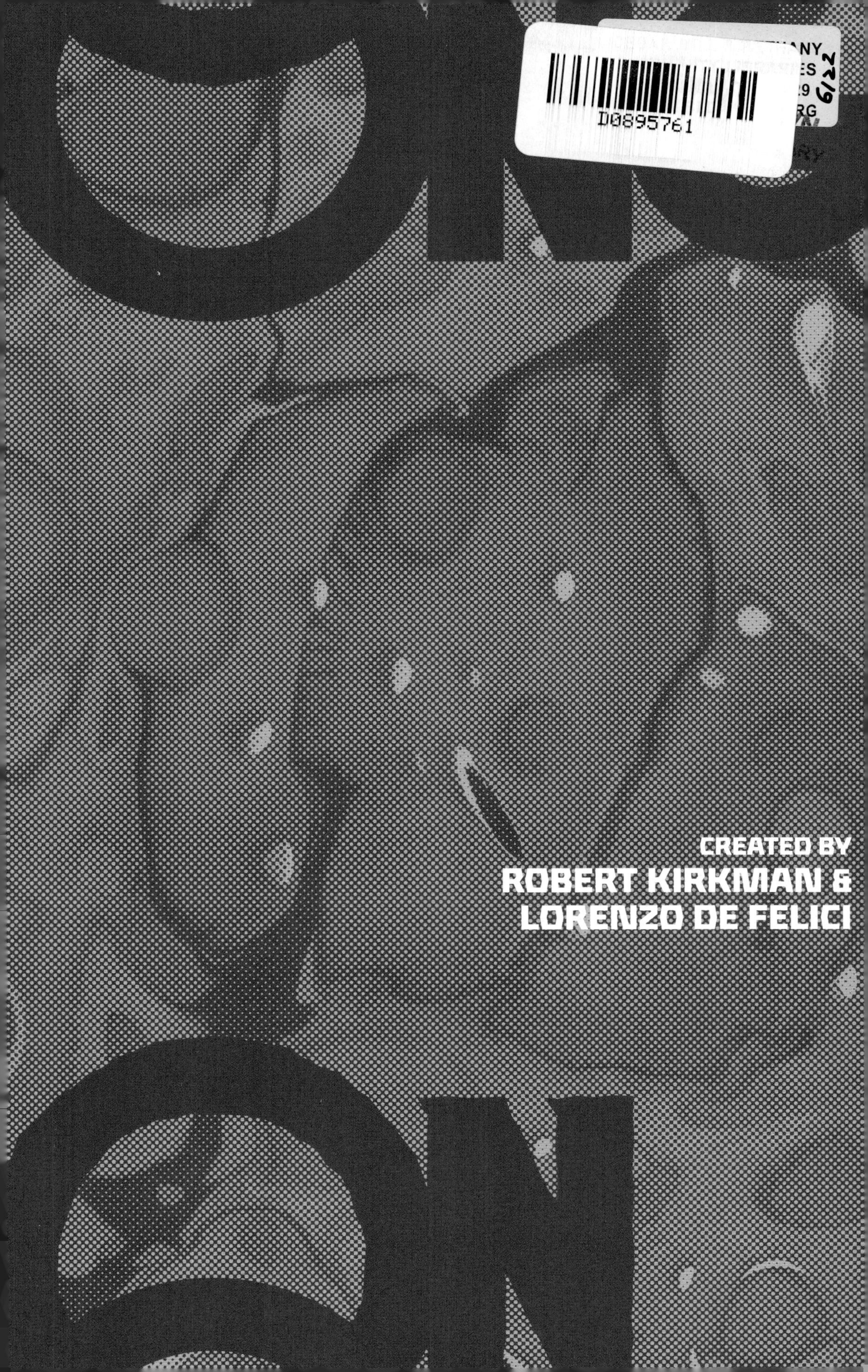
CREATED BY
ROBERT KIRKMAN &
LORENZO DE FELICI

ROBERT KIRKMAN
WRITER/CREATOR

LORENZO DE FELICI
ARTIST/CREATOR

ANNALISA LEONI
COLORIST/BONUS STORY ARTIST

RUS WOOTON
LETTERER

SEAN MACKIEWICZ
EDITOR

LORENZO DE FELICI
COVER

ANDRES JUAREZ
LOGO & PRODUCTION DESIGN

CARINA TAYLOR
PRODUCTION

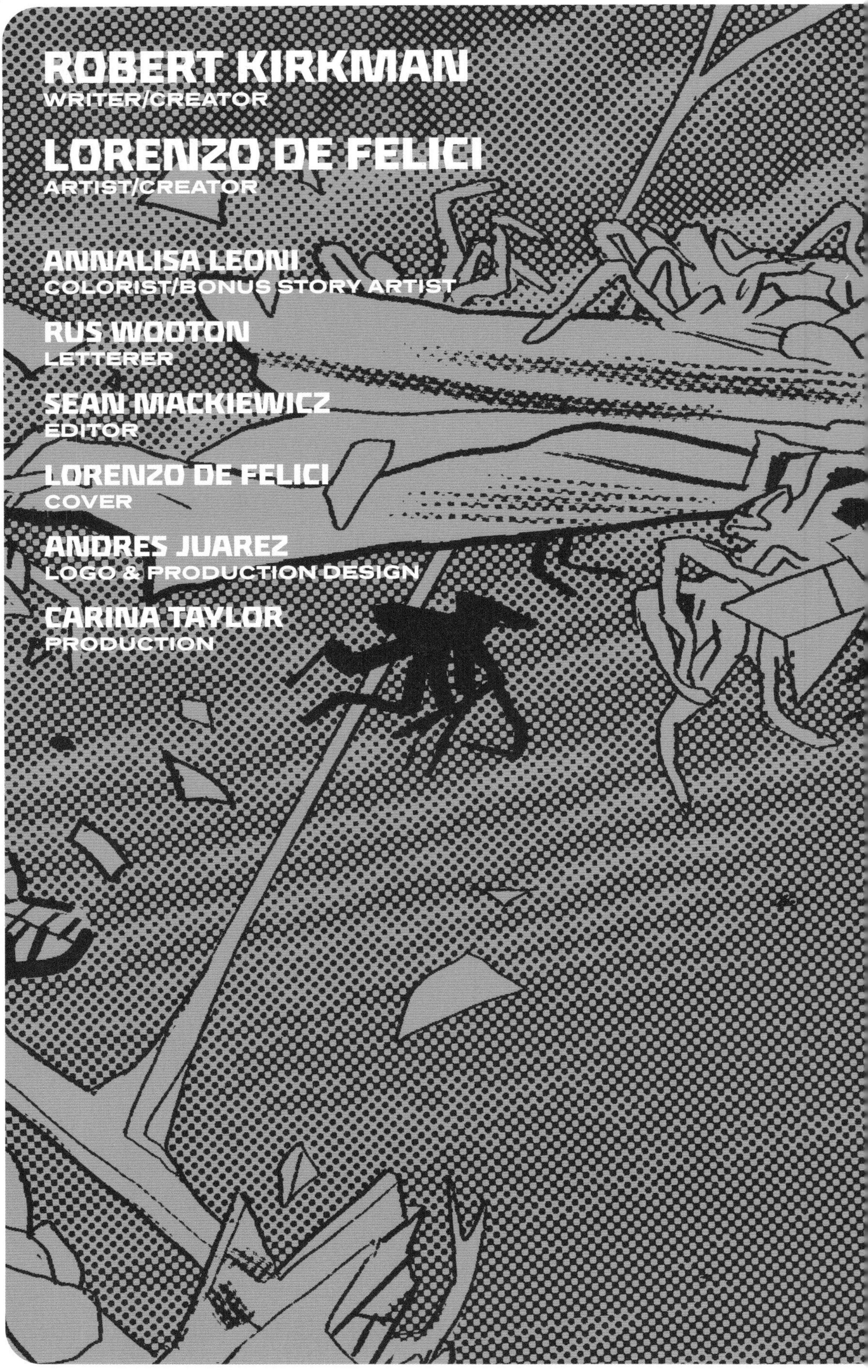

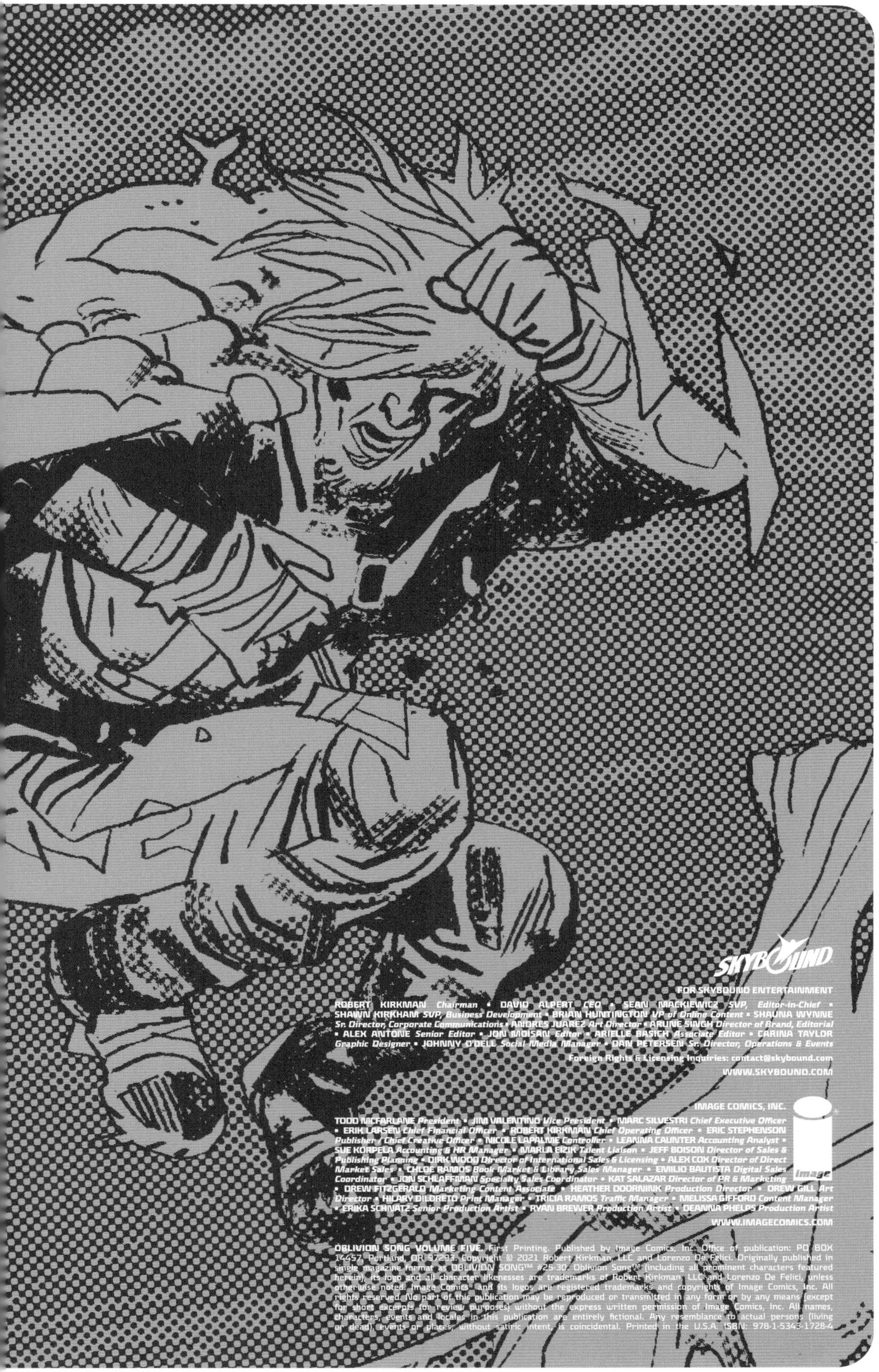

FOR SKYBOUND ENTERTAINMENT

ROBERT KIRKMAN *Chairman* • DAVID ALPERT *CEO* • SEAN MACKIEWICZ *SVP, Editor-in-Chief* • SHAWN KIRKHAM *SVP, Business Development* • BRIAN HUNTINGTON *VP of Online Content* • SHAUNA WYNNE *Sr. Director, Corporate Communications* • ANDRES JUAREZ *Art Director* • ARUNE SINGH *Director of Brand, Editorial* • ALEX ANTONE *Senior Editor* • JON MOISAN *Editor* • ARIELLE BASICH *Associate Editor* • CARINA TAYLOR *Graphic Designer* • JOHNNY O'DELL *Social Media Manager* • DAN PETERSEN *Sr. Director, Operations & Events*

Foreign Rights & Licensing Inquiries: contact@skybound.com

WWW.SKYBOUND.COM

IMAGE COMICS, INC.

TODD MCFARLANE *President* • JIM VALENTINO *Vice President* • MARC SILVESTRI *Chief Executive Officer* • ERIK LARSEN *Chief Financial Officer* • ROBERT KIRKMAN *Chief Operating Officer* • ERIC STEPHENSON *Publisher / Chief Creative Officer* • NICOLE LAPALME *Controller* • LEANNA CAUNTER *Accounting Analyst* • SUE KORPELA *Accounting & HR Manager* • MARLA EIZIK *Talent Liaison* • JEFF BOISON *Director of Sales & Publishing Planning* • DIRK WOOD *Director of International Sales & Licensing* • ALEX COX *Director of Direct Market Sales* • CHLOE RAMOS *Book Market & Library Sales Manager* • EMILIO BAUTISTA *Digital Sales Coordinator* • JON SCHLAFFMAN *Specialty Sales Coordinator* • KAT SALAZAR *Director of PR & Marketing* • DREW FITZGERALD *Marketing Content Associate* • HEATHER DOORNINK *Production Director* • DREW GILL *Art Director* • HILARY DILORETO *Print Manager* • TRICIA RAMOS *Traffic Manager* • MELISSA GIFFORD *Content Manager* • ERIKA SCHNATZ *Senior Production Artist* • RYAN BREWER *Production Artist* • DEANNA PHELPS *Production Artist*

WWW.IMAGECOMICS.COM

OBLIVION SONG VOLUME FIVE. First Printing. Published by Image Comics, Inc. Office of publication: PO BOX 14457, Portland, OR 97293. Printed in the U.S.A. ISBN: 978-1-5343-1728-4

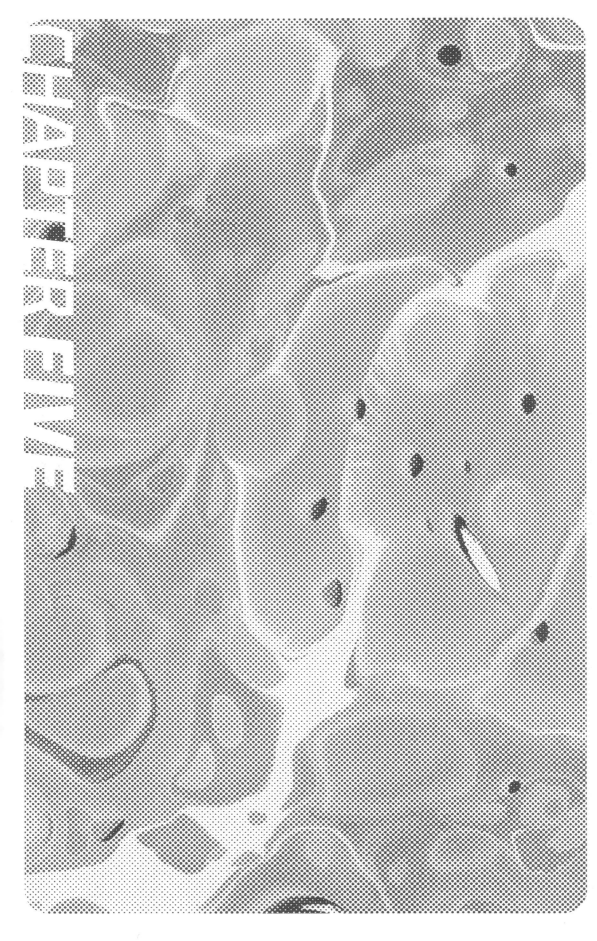

CHAPTER FIVE

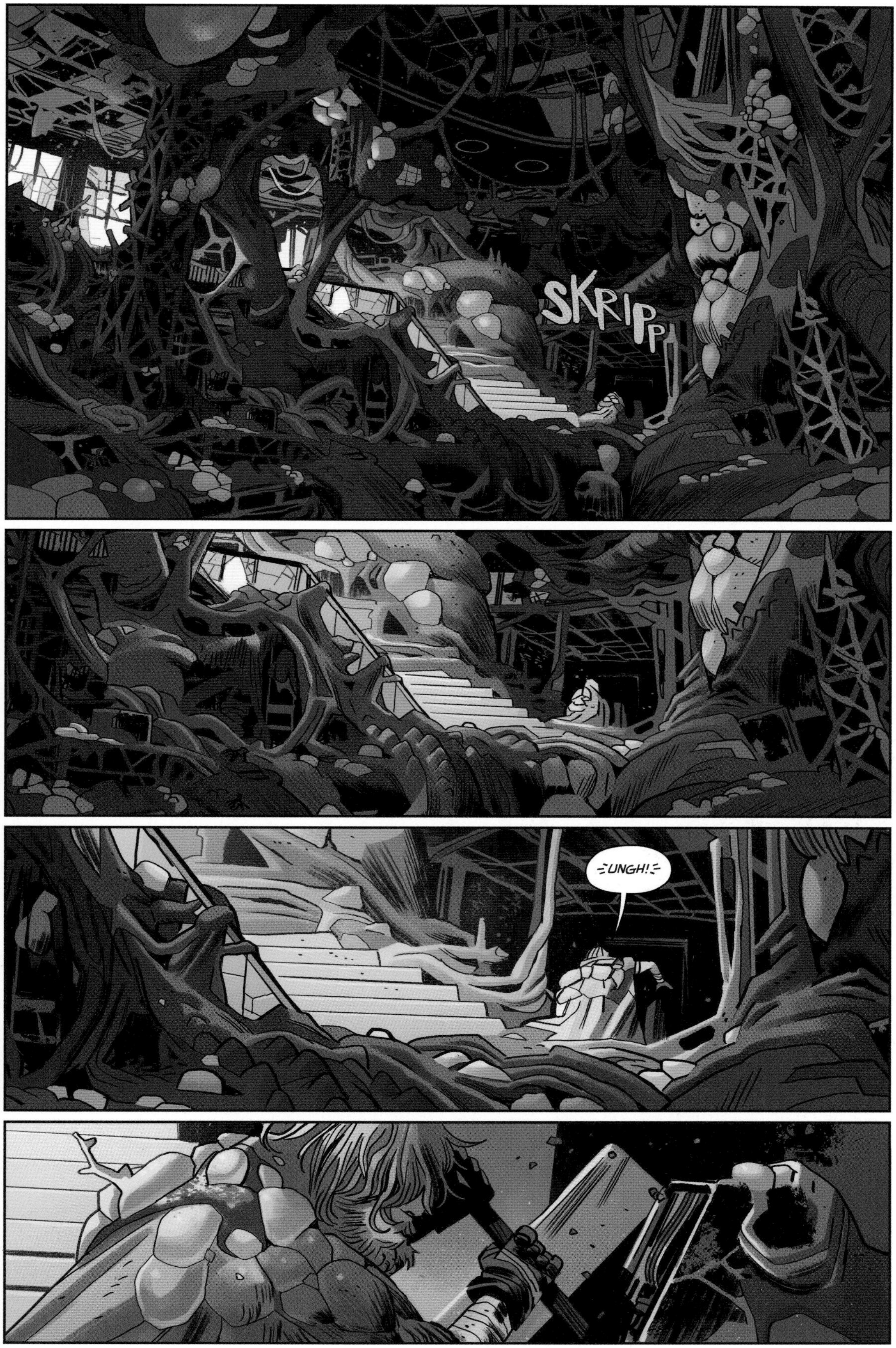
SKRIPP
UNGH!

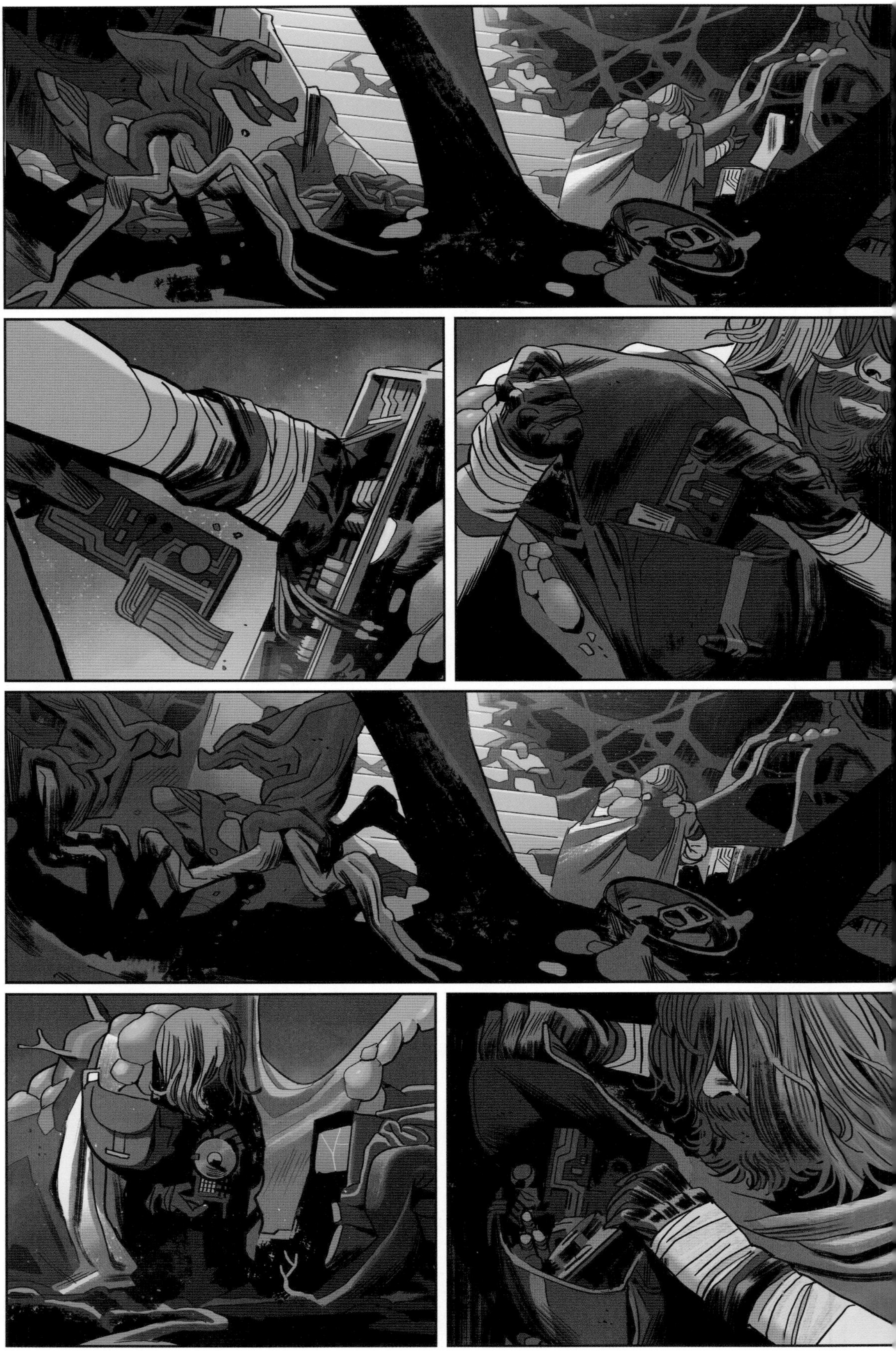

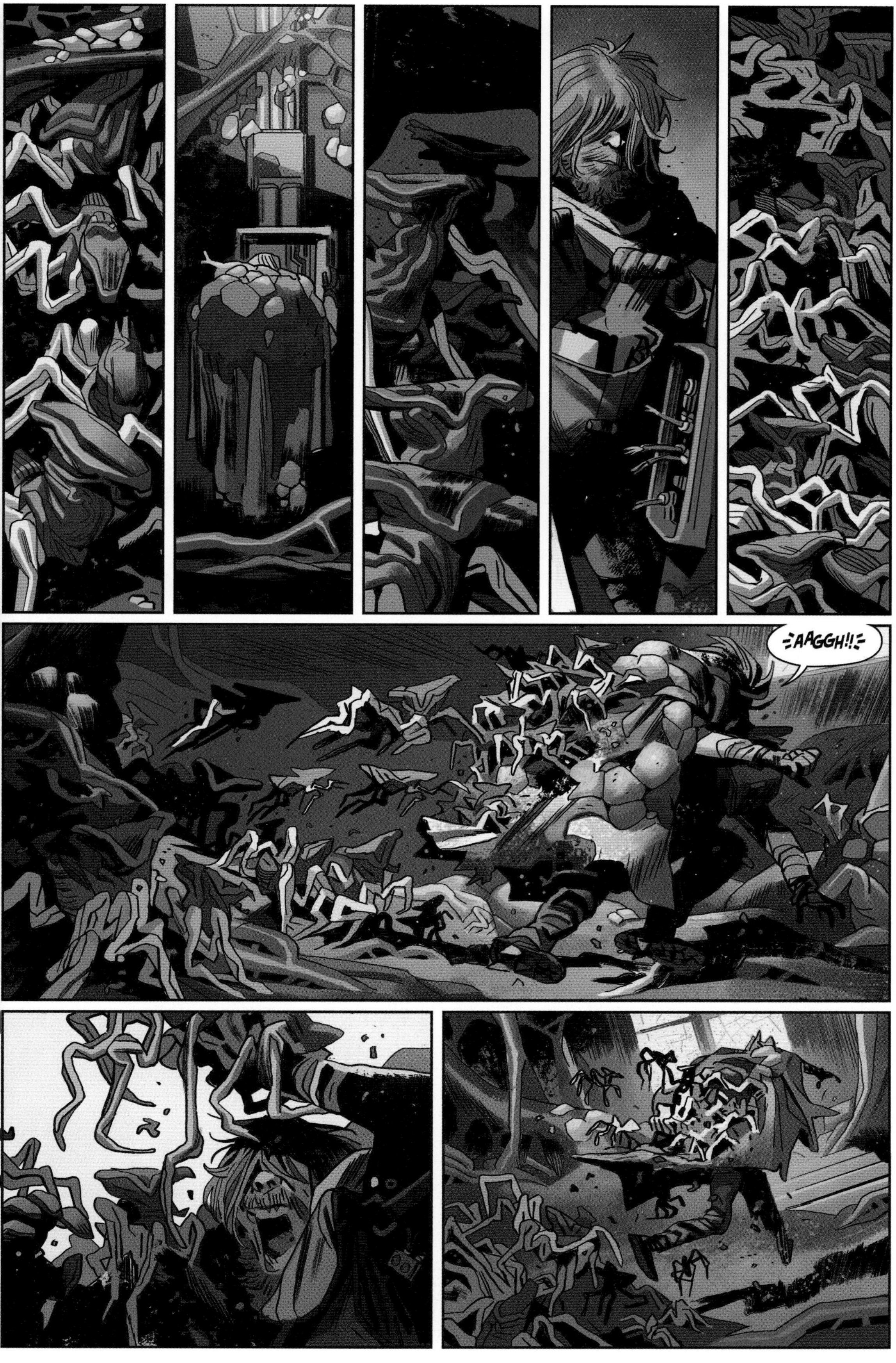
AAGGH!!

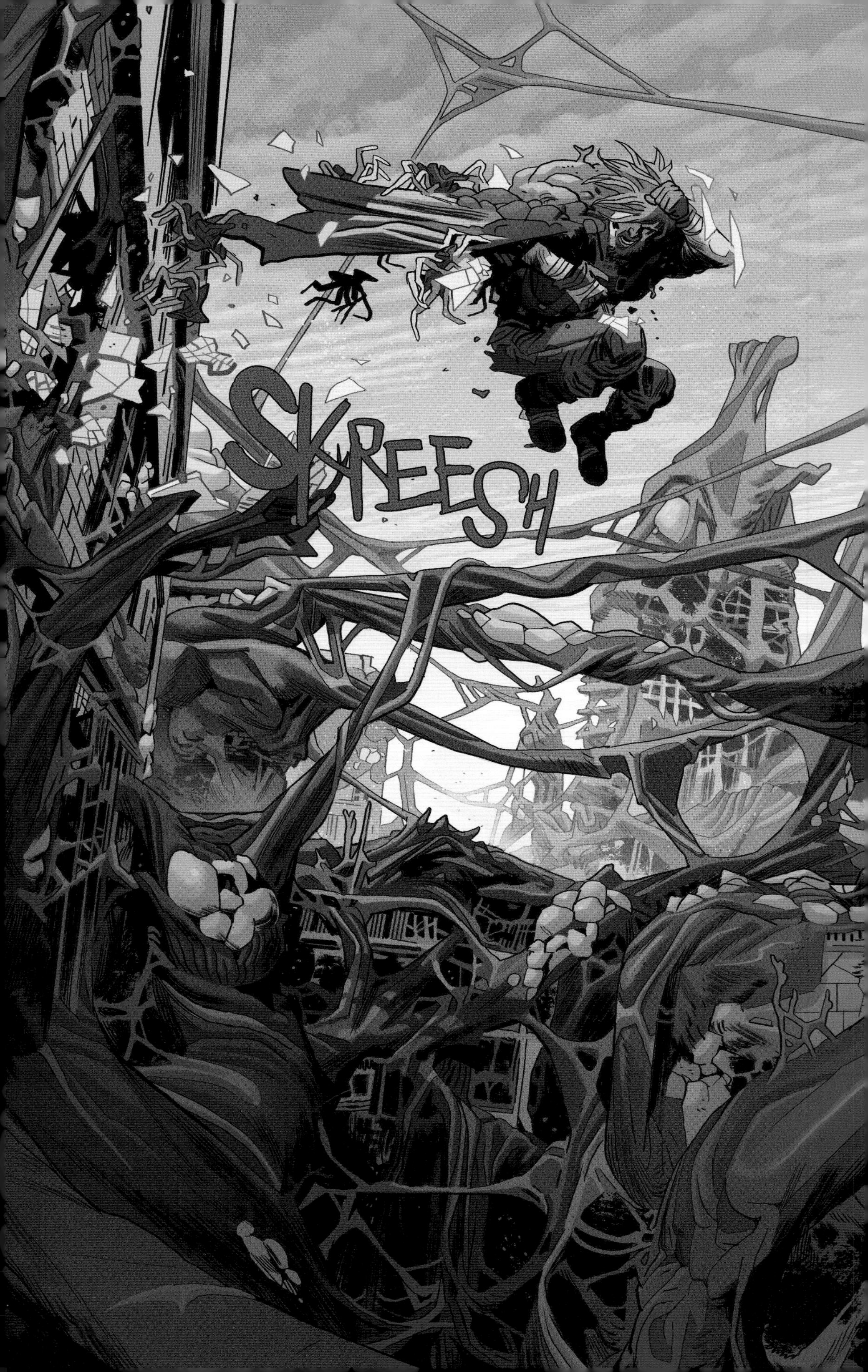
SKREESH

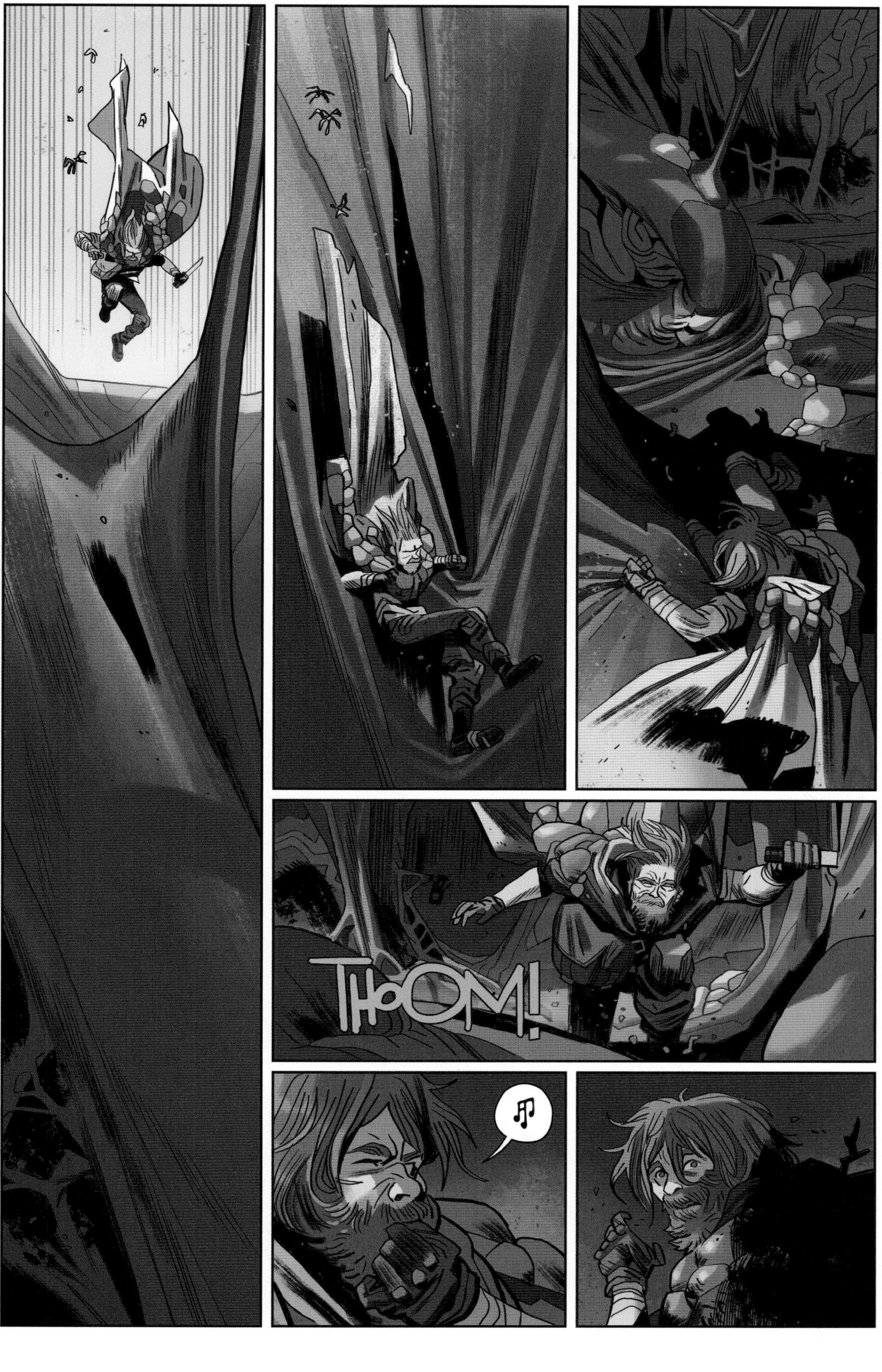
THOOM!

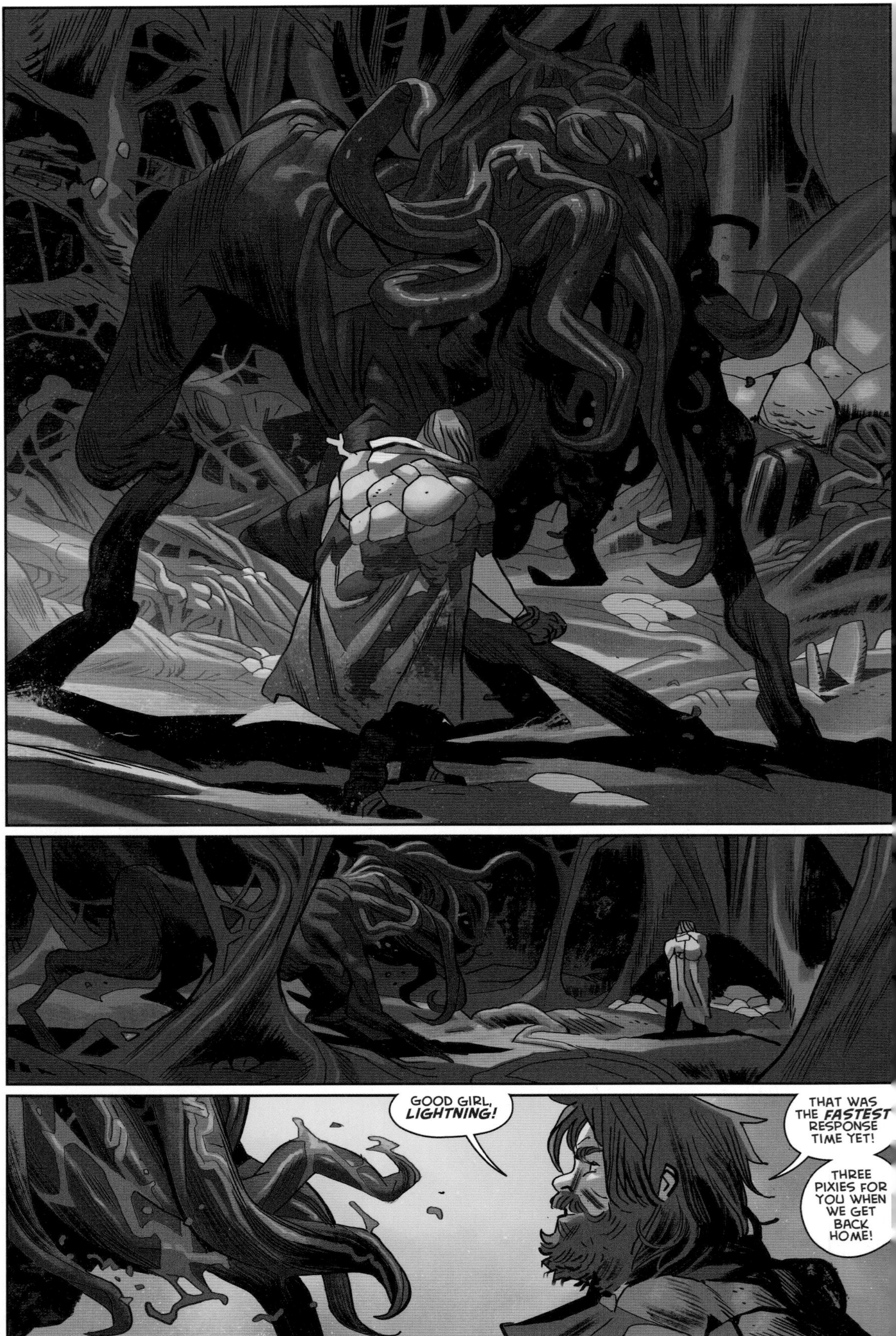
GOOD GIRL, LIGHTNING!
THAT WAS THE FASTEST RESPONSE TIME YET!
THREE PIXIES FOR YOU WHEN WE GET BACK HOME!

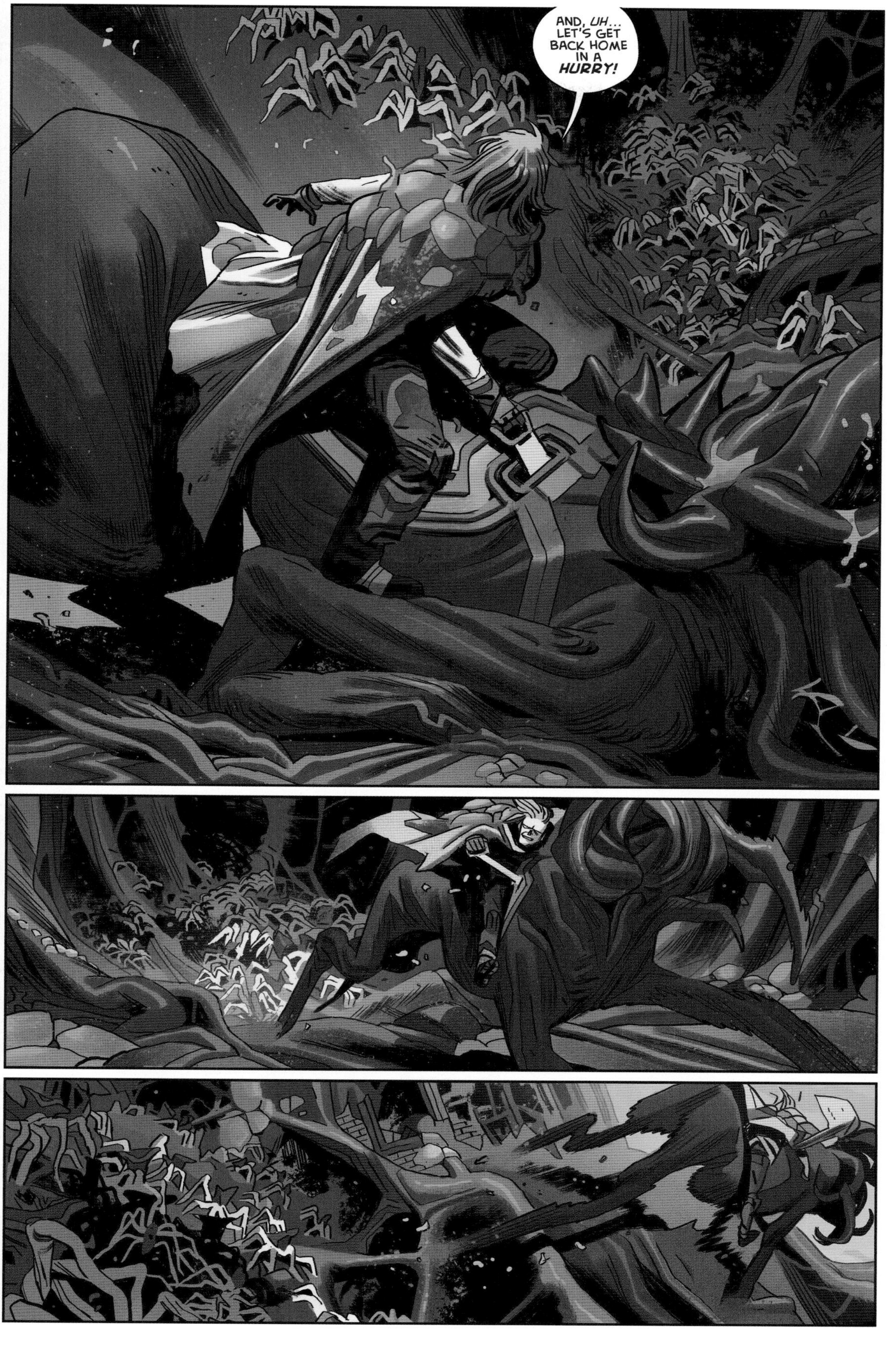
AND, UH... LET'S GET BACK HOME IN A HURRY!

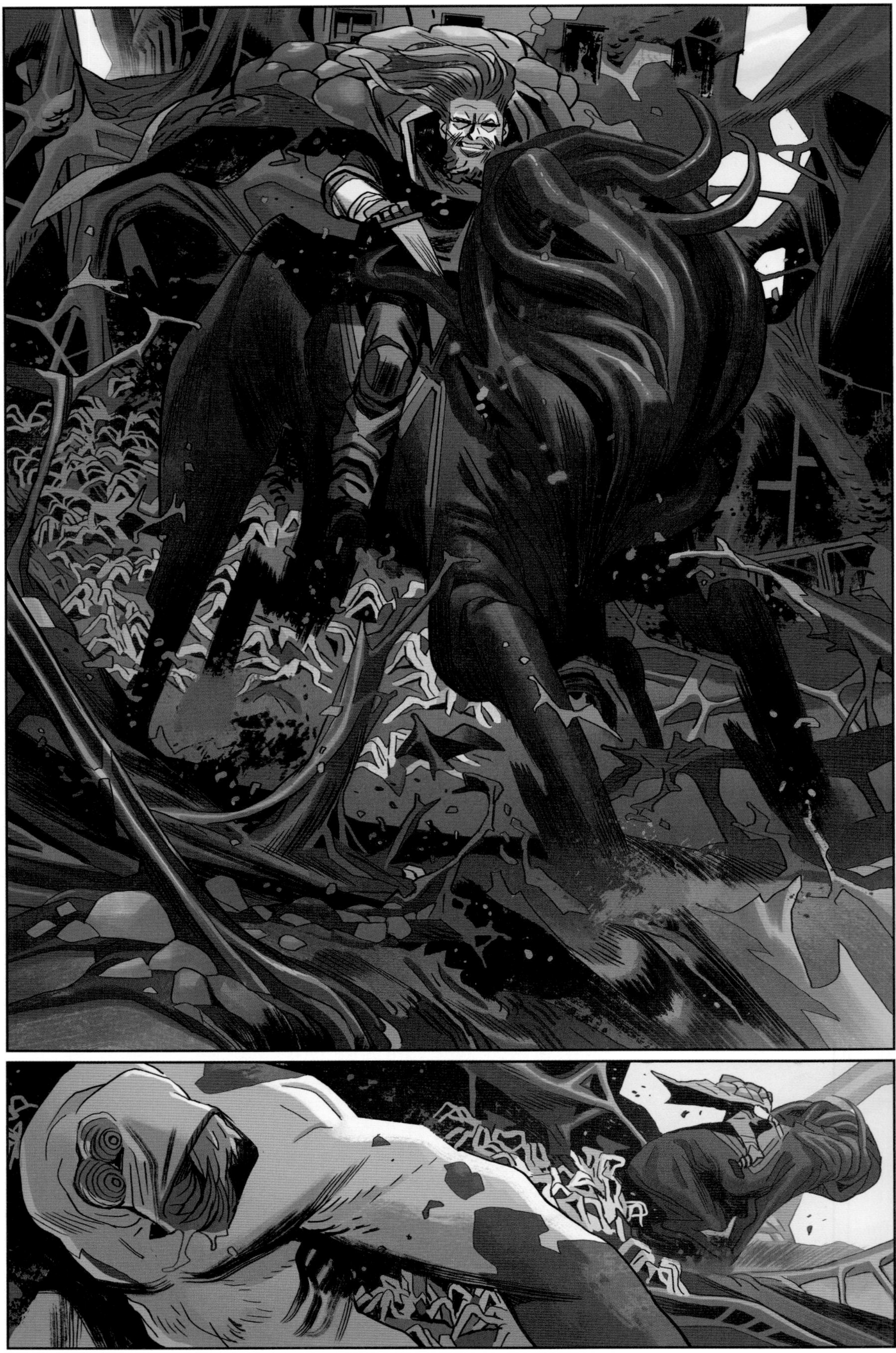

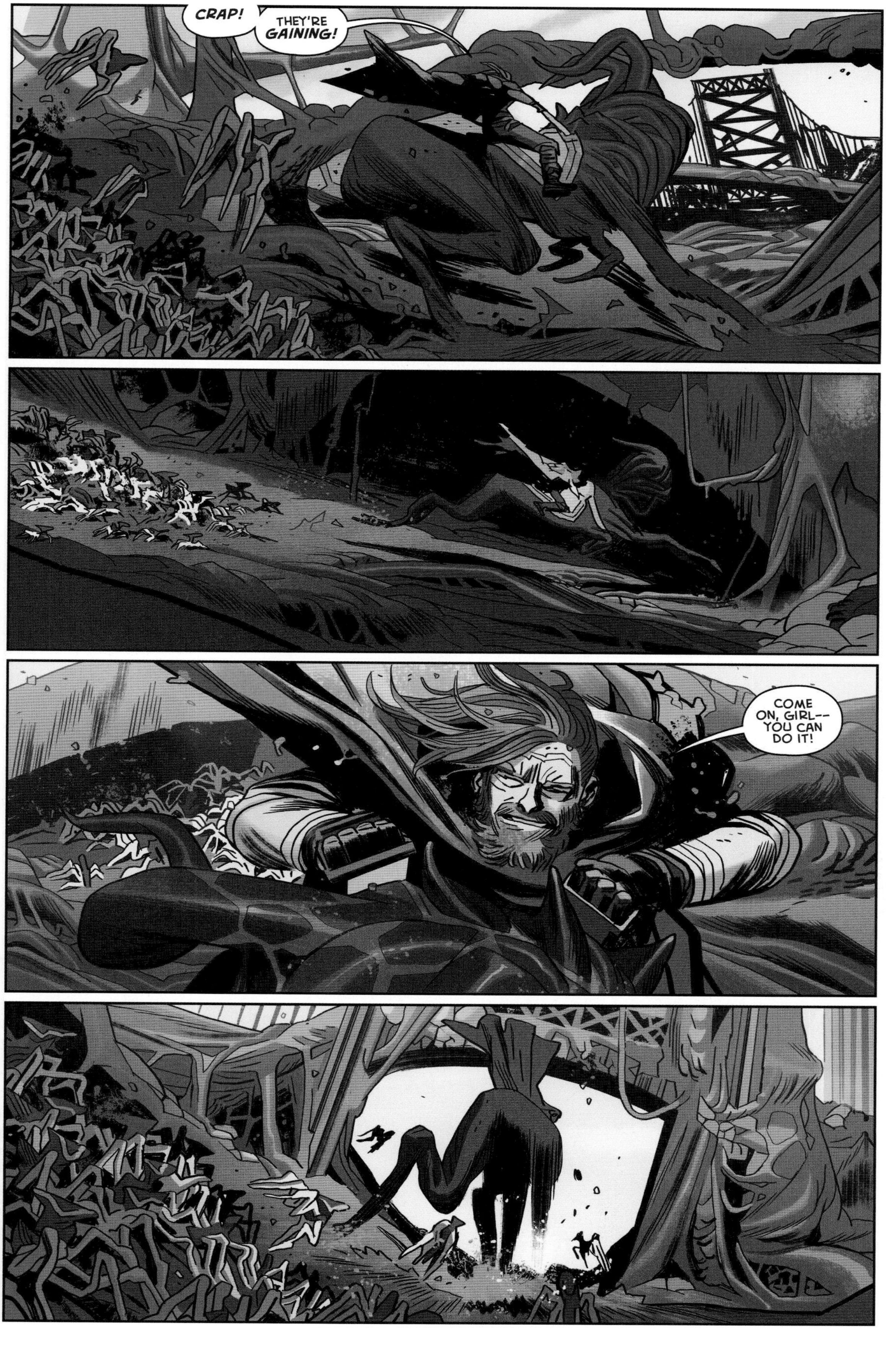

CRAP!
THEY'RE GAINING!
COME ON, GIRL-- YOU CAN DO IT!

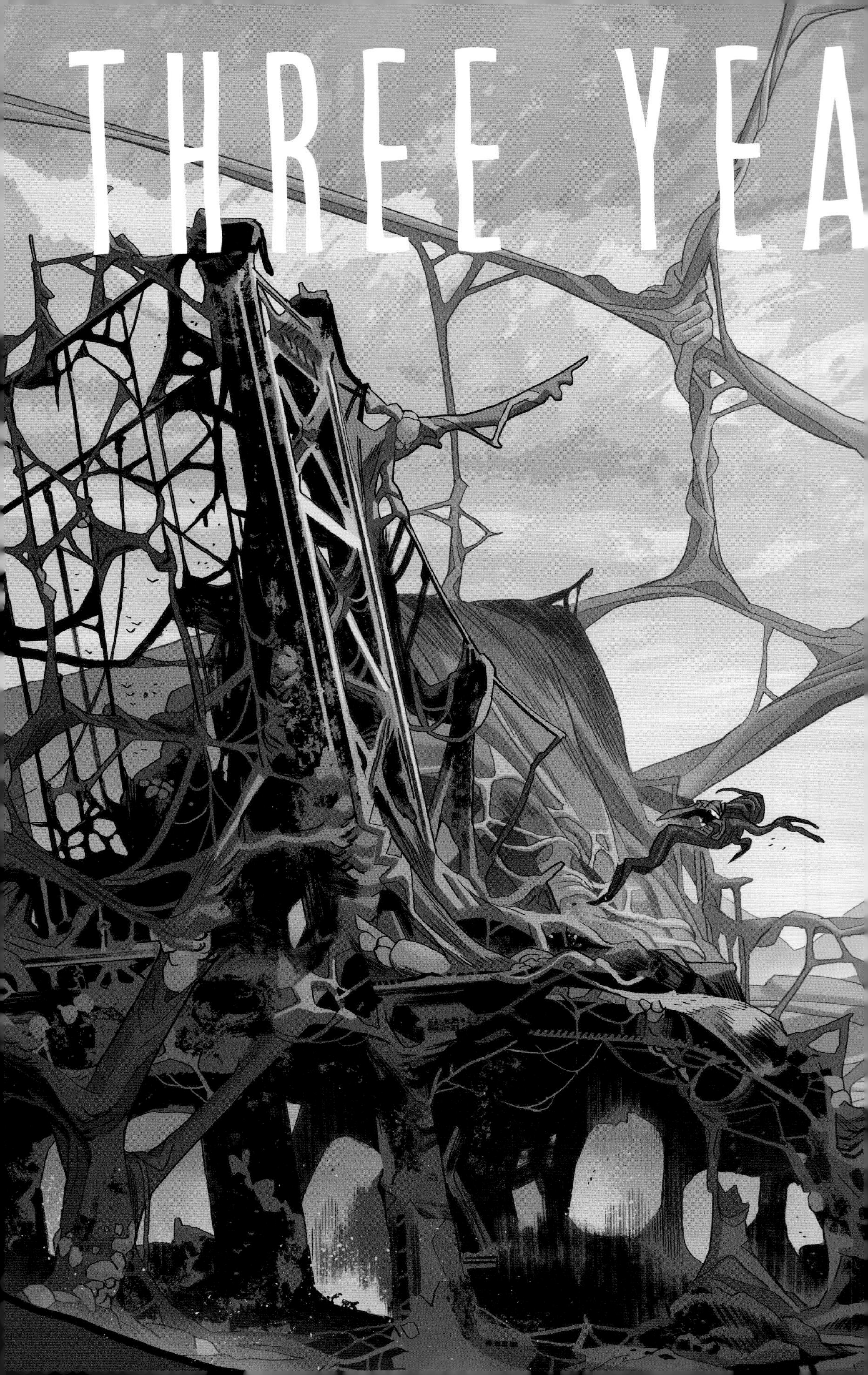
THREE YEA

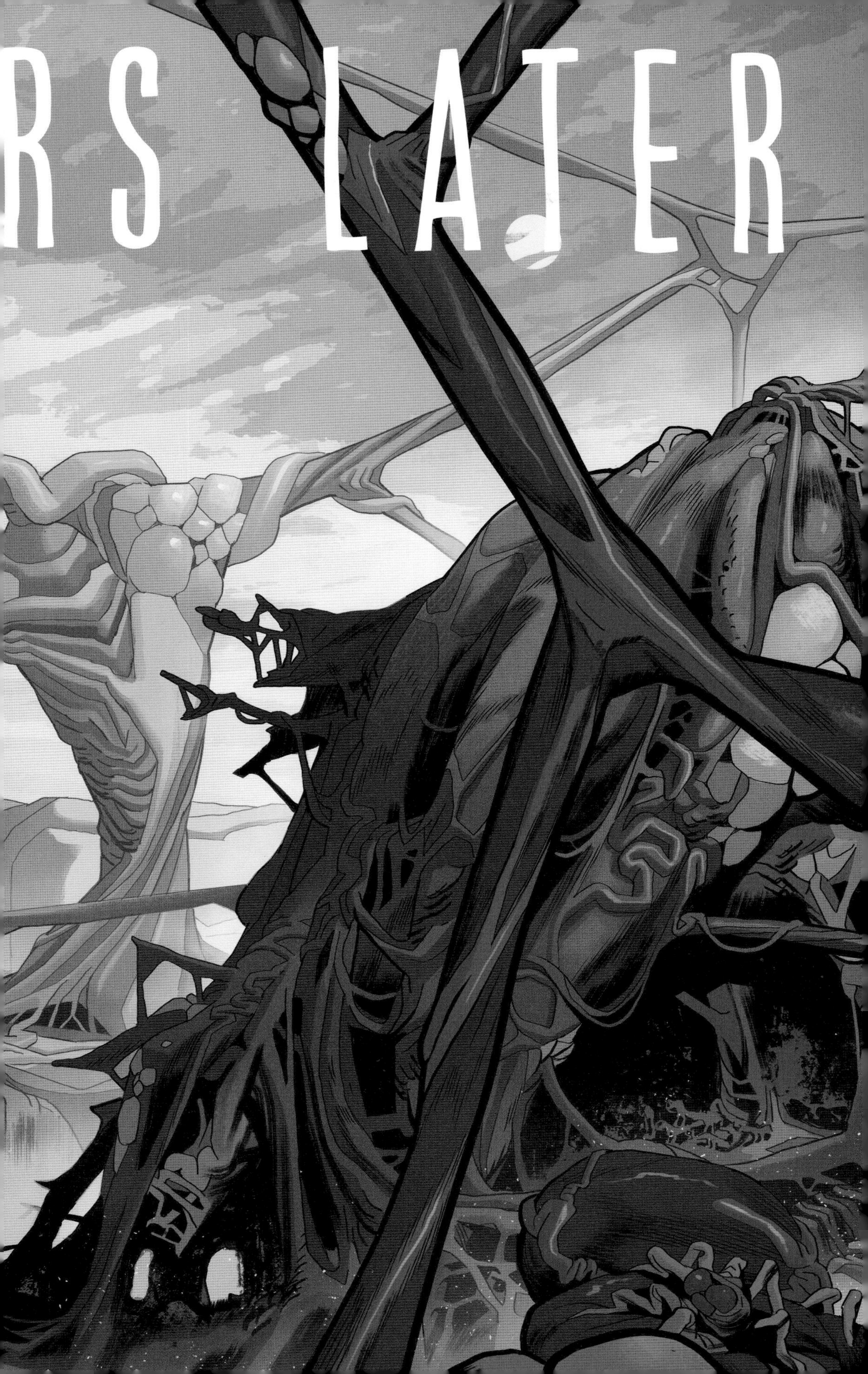
RS LATER

THUDD

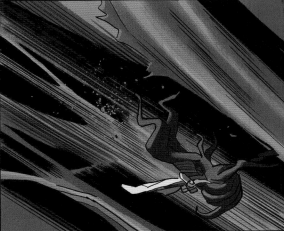

I THINK
WE LOST
THEM...

HEY!

I *SAID* WE LOST THEM!

OKAY, SHOWOFF.

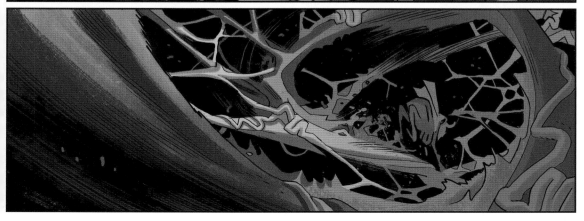

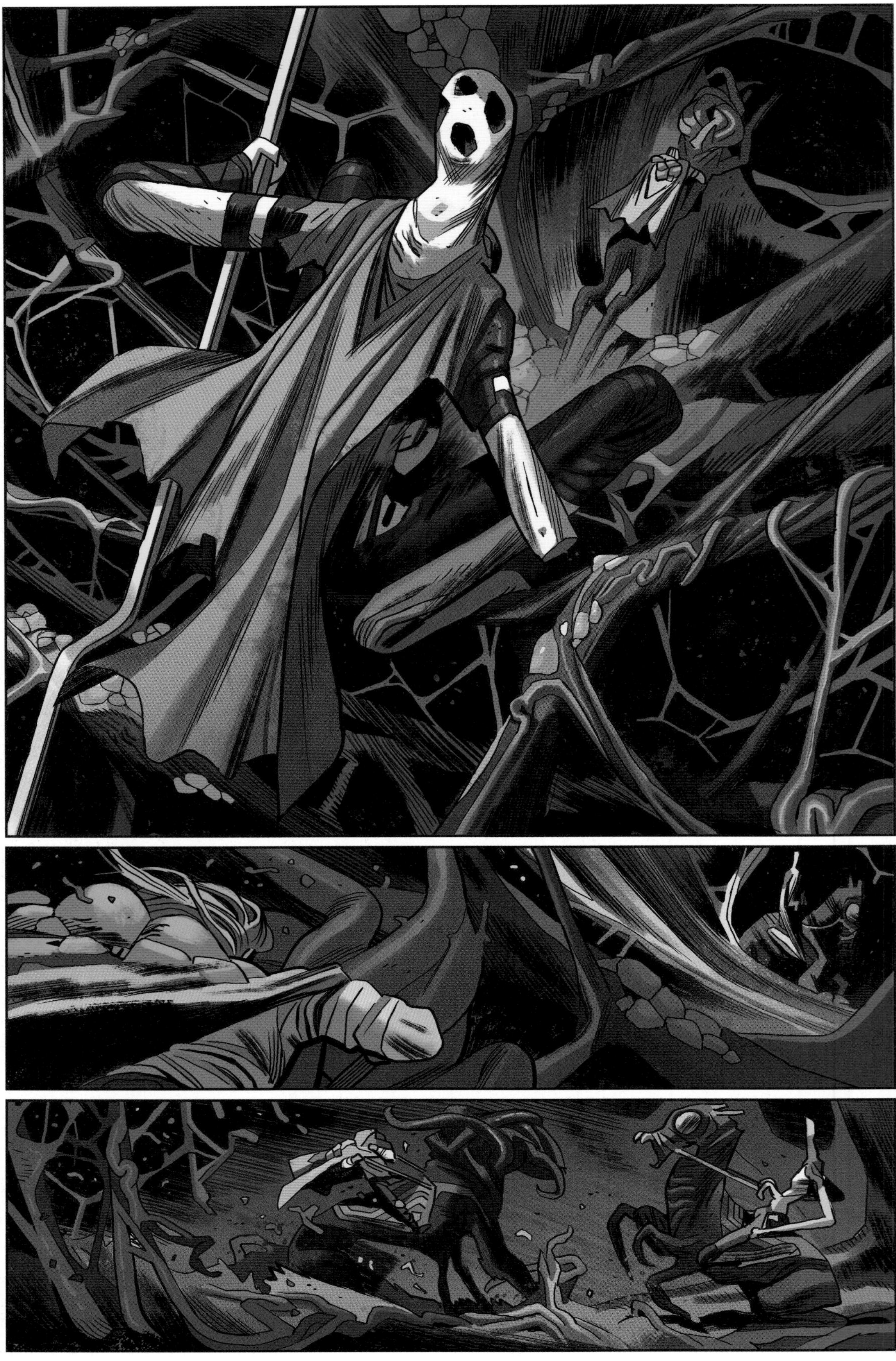

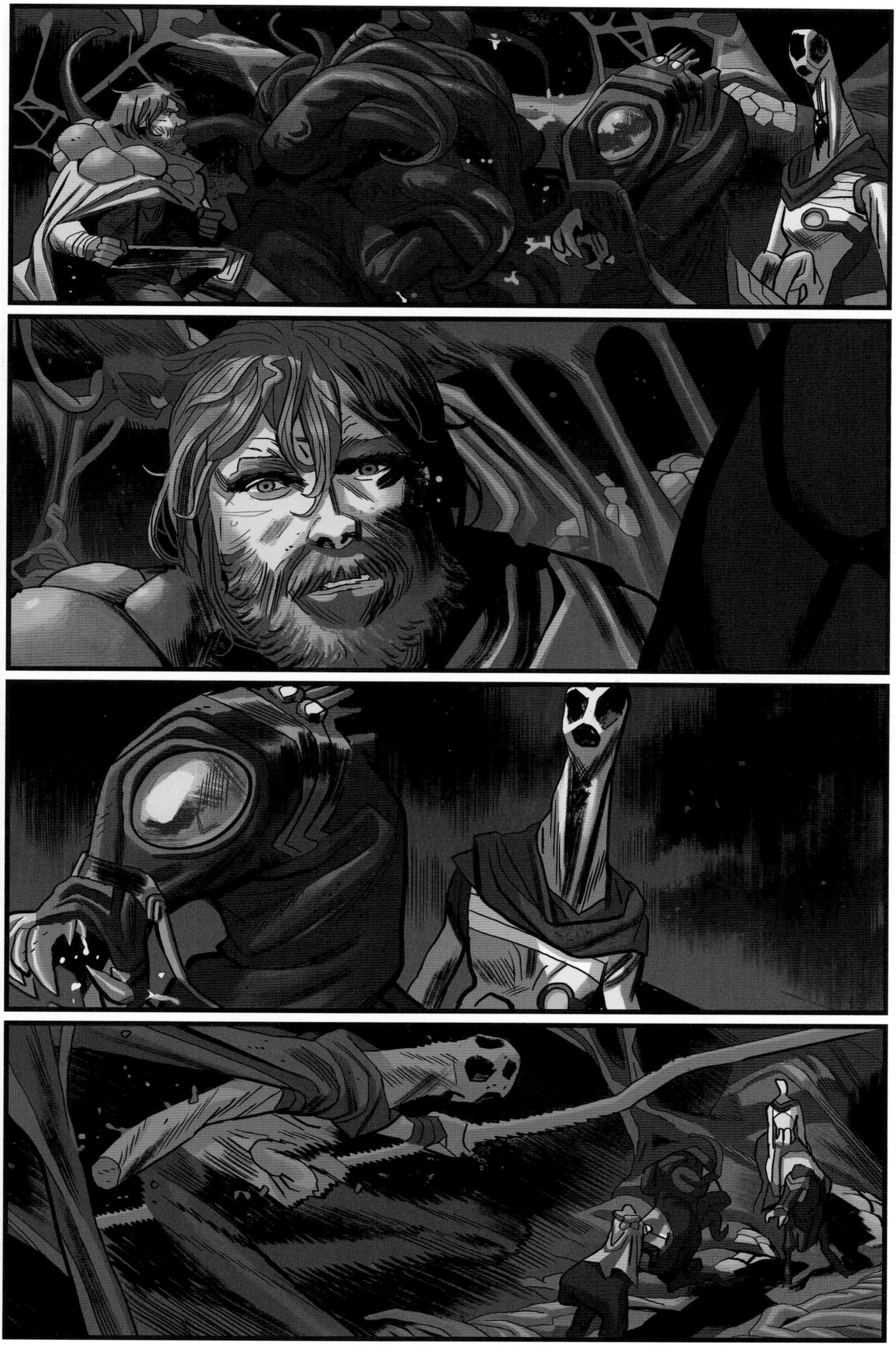

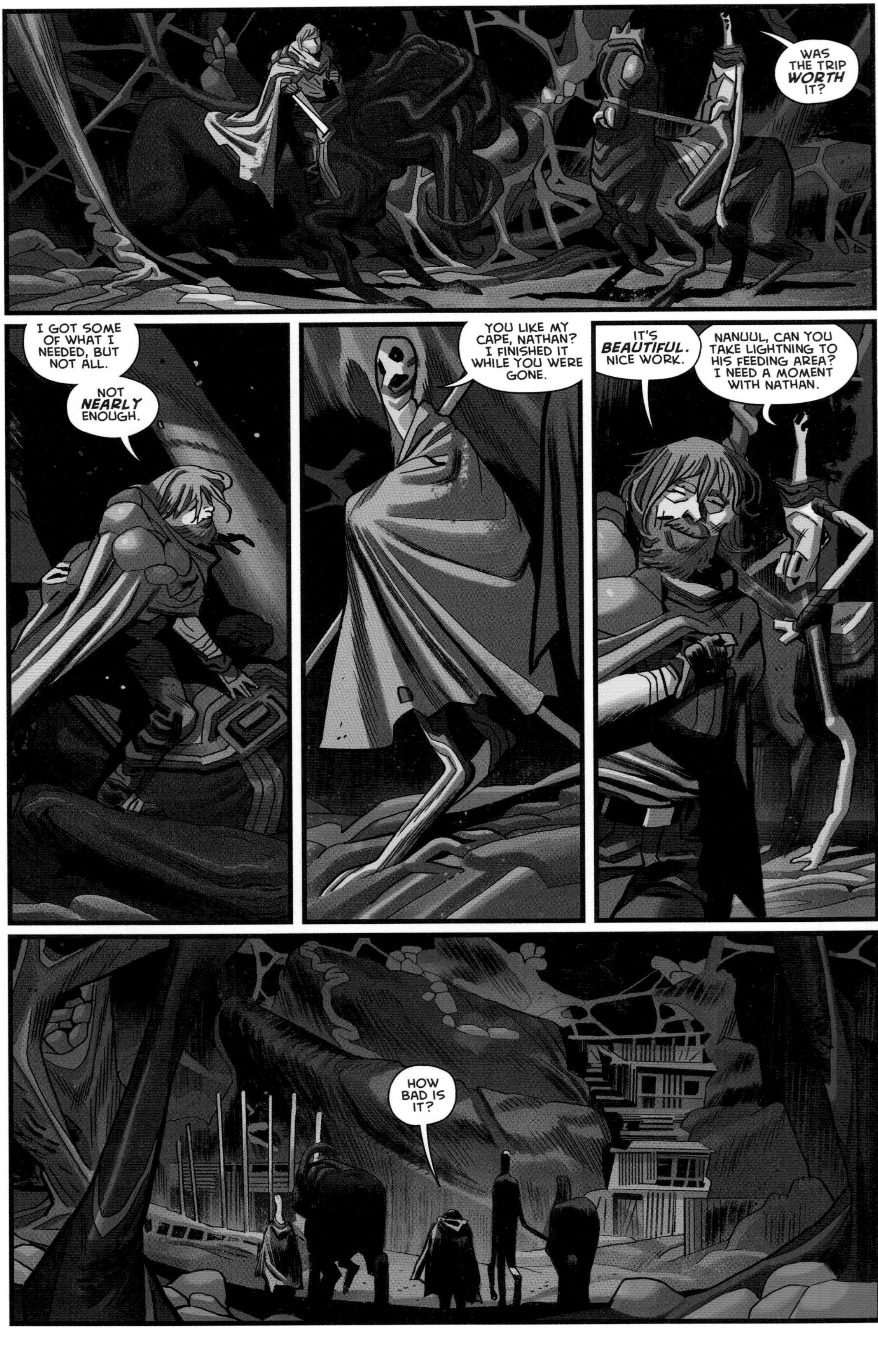
WAS THE TRIP WORTH IT?
I GOT SOME OF WHAT I NEEDED, BUT NOT ALL.
NOT NEARLY ENOUGH.
YOU LIKE MY CAPE, NATHAN? I FINISHED IT WHILE YOU WERE GONE.
IT'S BEAUTIFUL. NICE WORK.
NANUUL, CAN YOU TAKE LIGHTNING TO HIS FEEDING AREA? I NEED A MOMENT WITH NATHAN.
HOW BAD IS IT?

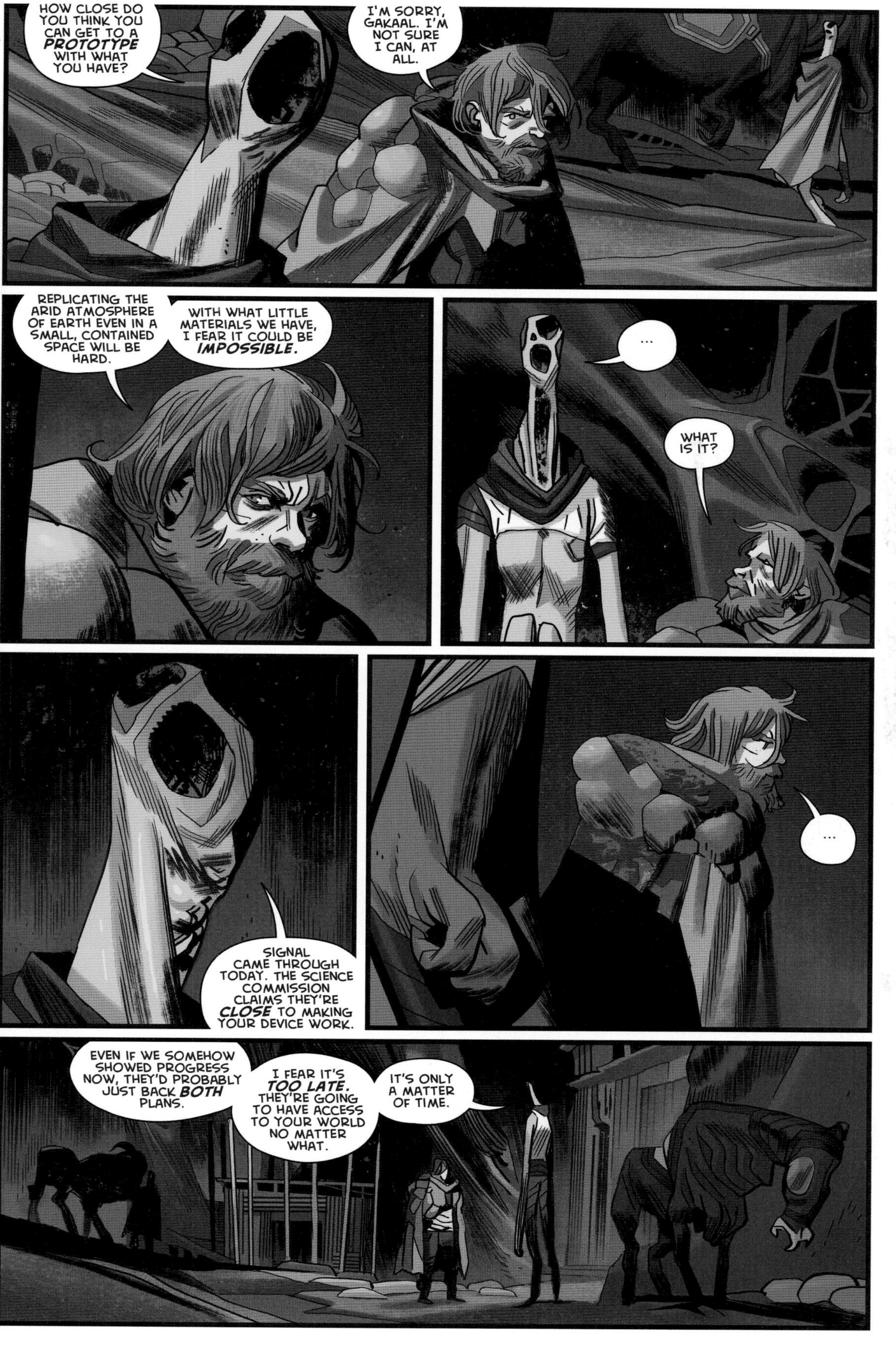
HOW CLOSE DO YOU THINK YOU CAN GET TO A *PROTOTYPE* WITH WHAT YOU HAVE?
I'M SORRY, GAKAAL. I'M NOT SURE I CAN, AT ALL.
REPLICATING THE ARID ATMOSPHERE OF EARTH EVEN IN A SMALL, CONTAINED SPACE WILL BE HARD.
WITH WHAT LITTLE MATERIALS WE HAVE, I FEAR IT COULD BE *IMPOSSIBLE.*
...
WHAT IS IT?
SIGNAL CAME THROUGH TODAY. THE SCIENCE COMMISSION CLAIMS THEY'RE *CLOSE* TO MAKING YOUR DEVICE WORK.
...
EVEN IF WE SOMEHOW SHOWED PROGRESS NOW, THEY'D PROBABLY JUST BACK *BOTH* PLANS.
I FEAR IT'S *TOO LATE.* THEY'RE GOING TO HAVE ACCESS TO YOUR WORLD NO MATTER WHAT.
IT'S ONLY A MATTER OF TIME.

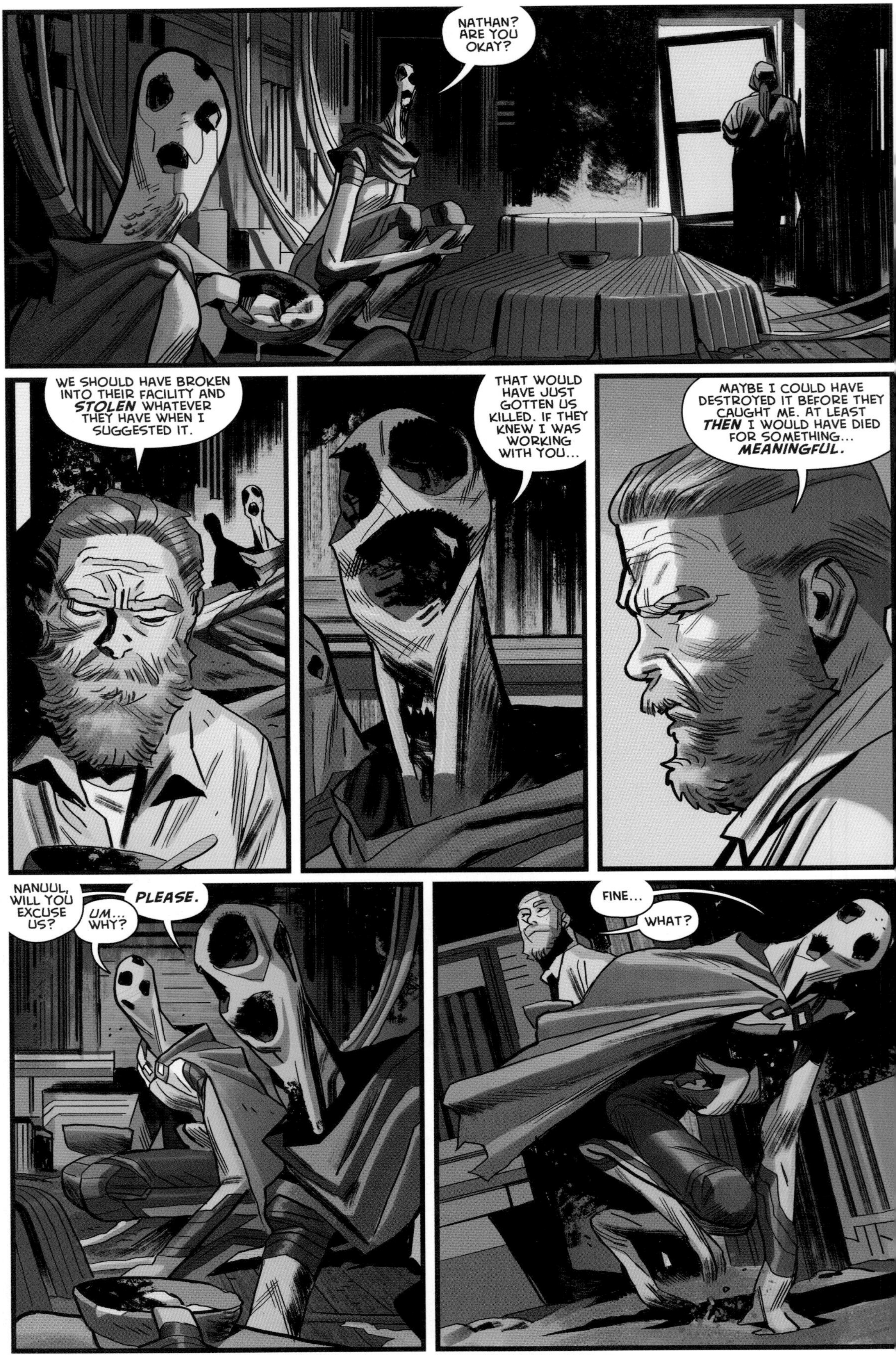
NATHAN? ARE YOU OKAY?
WE SHOULD HAVE BROKEN INTO THEIR FACILITY AND STOLEN WHATEVER THEY HAVE WHEN I SUGGESTED IT.
THAT WOULD HAVE JUST GOTTEN US KILLED. IF THEY KNEW I WAS WORKING WITH YOU...
MAYBE I COULD HAVE DESTROYED IT BEFORE THEY CAUGHT ME. AT LEAST THEN I WOULD HAVE DIED FOR SOMETHING... MEANINGFUL.
NANUUL, WILL YOU EXCUSE US?
UM... WHY?
PLEASE.
FINE...
WHAT?

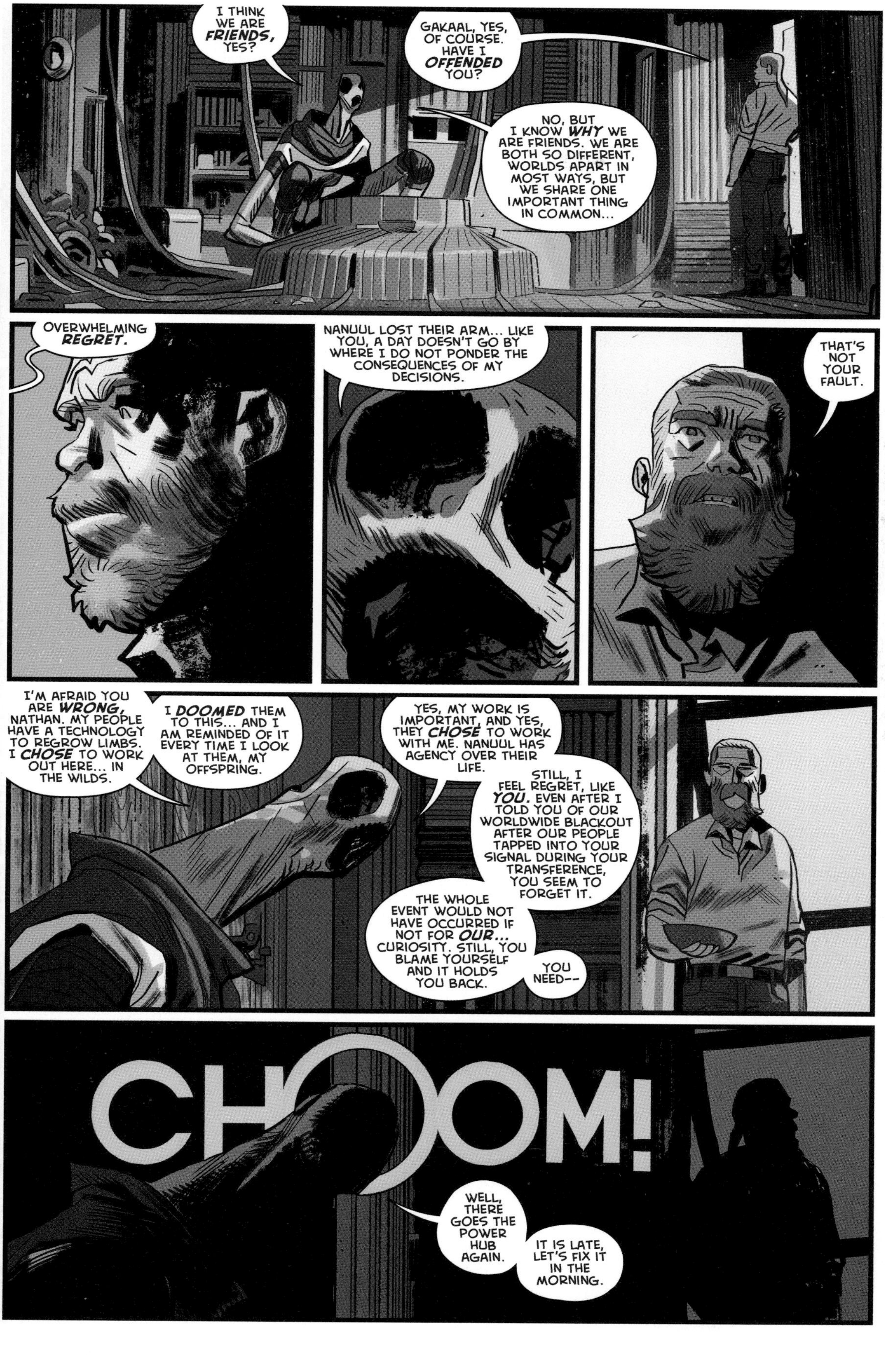
I THINK WE ARE FRIENDS, YES?
GAKAAL, YES, OF COURSE. HAVE I OFFENDED YOU?
NO, BUT I KNOW WHY WE ARE FRIENDS. WE ARE BOTH SO DIFFERENT, WORLDS APART IN MOST WAYS, BUT WE SHARE ONE IMPORTANT THING IN COMMON...
OVERWHELMING REGRET.
NANUUL LOST THEIR ARM... LIKE YOU, A DAY DOESN'T GO BY WHERE I DO NOT PONDER THE CONSEQUENCES OF MY DECISIONS.
THAT'S NOT YOUR FAULT.
I'M AFRAID YOU ARE WRONG, NATHAN. MY PEOPLE HAVE A TECHNOLOGY TO REGROW LIMBS. I CHOSE TO WORK OUT HERE... IN THE WILDS.
I DOOMED THEM TO THIS... AND I AM REMINDED OF IT EVERY TIME I LOOK AT THEM, MY OFFSPRING.
YES, MY WORK IS IMPORTANT, AND YES, THEY CHOSE TO WORK WITH ME. NANUUL HAS AGENCY OVER THEIR LIFE.
STILL, I FEEL REGRET, LIKE YOU. EVEN AFTER I TOLD YOU OF OUR WORLDWIDE BLACKOUT AFTER OUR PEOPLE TAPPED INTO YOUR SIGNAL DURING YOUR TRANSFERENCE, YOU SEEM TO FORGET IT.
THE WHOLE EVENT WOULD NOT HAVE OCCURRED IF NOT FOR OUR... CURIOSITY. STILL, YOU BLAME YOURSELF AND IT HOLDS YOU BACK.
YOU NEED--
CHOOM!
WELL, THERE GOES THE POWER HUB AGAIN.
IT IS LATE, LET'S FIX IT IN THE MORNING.

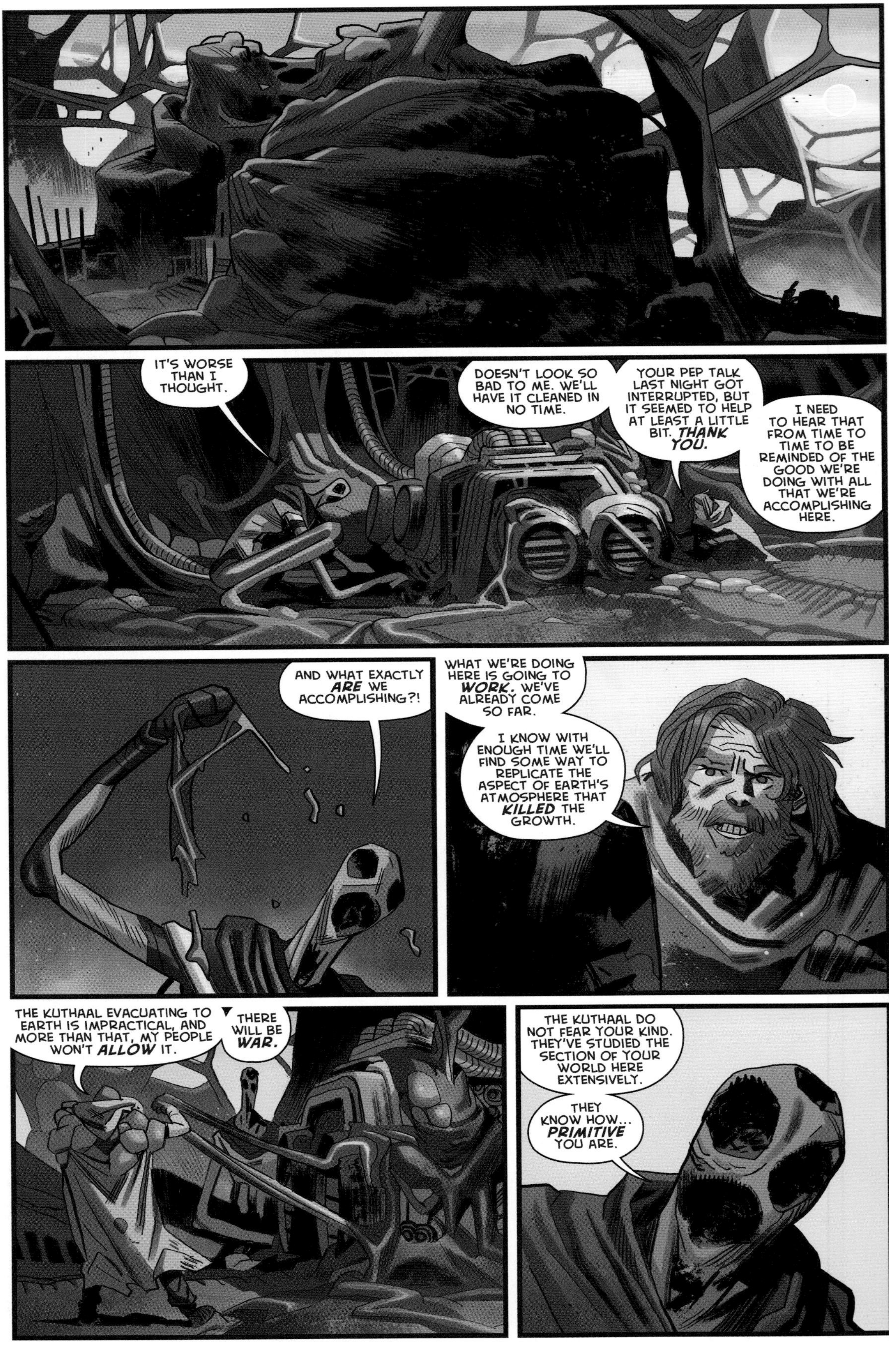
IT'S WORSE THAN I THOUGHT.
DOESN'T LOOK SO BAD TO ME. WE'LL HAVE IT CLEANED IN NO TIME.
YOUR PEP TALK LAST NIGHT GOT INTERRUPTED, BUT IT SEEMED TO HELP AT LEAST A LITTLE BIT. **THANK YOU.**
I NEED TO HEAR THAT FROM TIME TO TIME TO BE REMINDED OF THE GOOD WE'RE DOING WITH ALL THAT WE'RE ACCOMPLISHING HERE.
AND WHAT EXACTLY **ARE** WE ACCOMPLISHING?!
WHAT WE'RE DOING HERE IS GOING TO **WORK.** WE'VE ALREADY COME SO FAR.
I KNOW WITH ENOUGH TIME WE'LL FIND SOME WAY TO REPLICATE THE ASPECT OF EARTH'S ATMOSPHERE THAT **KILLED** THE GROWTH.
THE KUTHAAL EVACUATING TO EARTH IS IMPRACTICAL, AND MORE THAN THAT, MY PEOPLE WON'T **ALLOW** IT.
THERE WILL BE **WAR.**
THE KUTHAAL DO NOT FEAR YOUR KIND. THEY'VE STUDIED THE SECTION OF YOUR WORLD HERE EXTENSIVELY.
THEY KNOW HOW... **PRIMITIVE** YOU ARE.

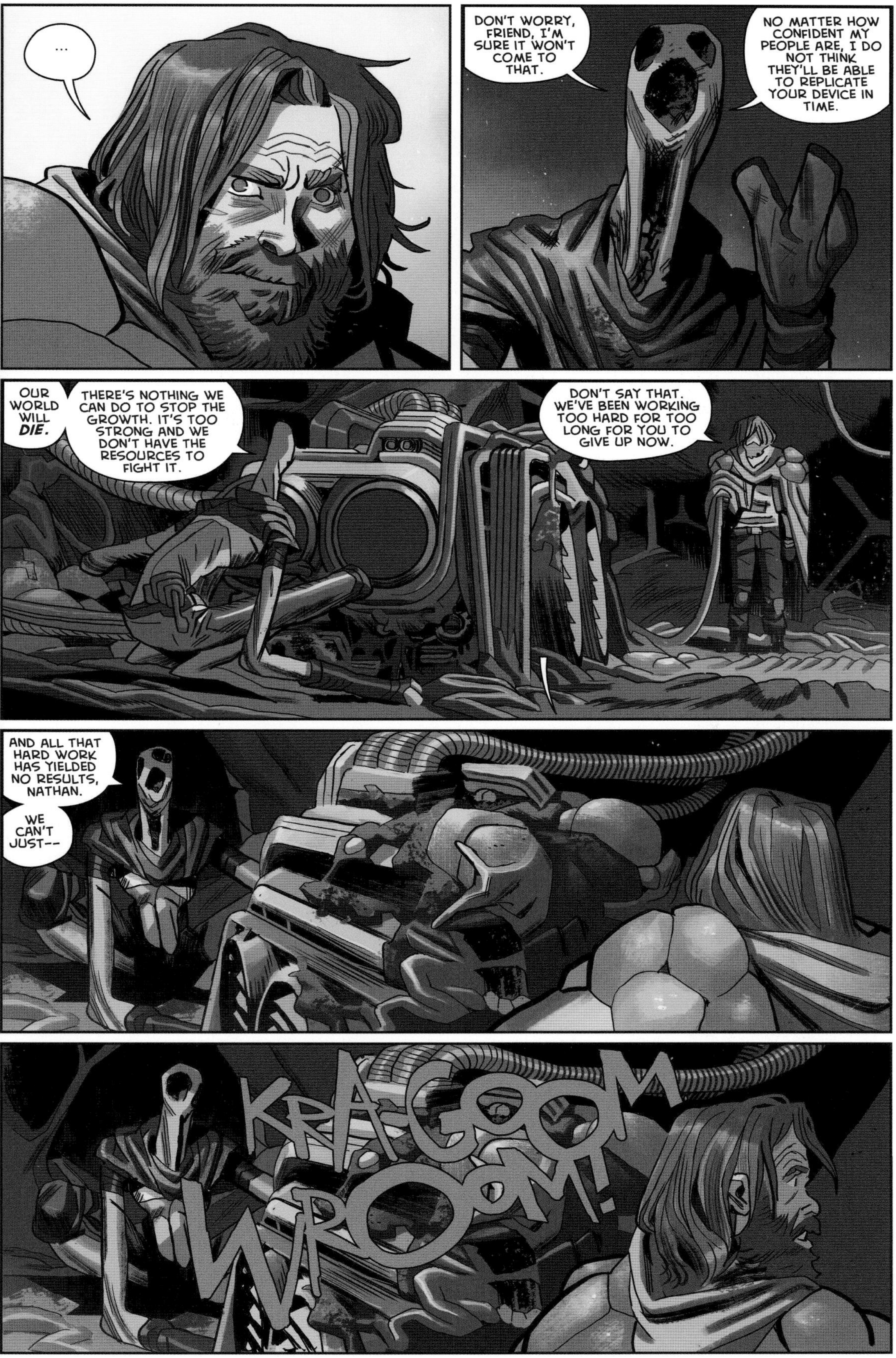
...
DON'T WORRY, FRIEND, I'M SURE IT WON'T COME TO THAT.
NO MATTER HOW CONFIDENT MY PEOPLE ARE, I DO NOT THINK THEY'LL BE ABLE TO REPLICATE YOUR DEVICE IN TIME.
OUR WORLD WILL *DIE.*
THERE'S NOTHING WE CAN DO TO STOP THE GROWTH. IT'S TOO STRONG AND WE DON'T HAVE THE RESOURCES TO FIGHT IT.
DON'T SAY THAT. WE'VE BEEN WORKING TOO HARD FOR TOO LONG FOR YOU TO GIVE UP NOW.
AND ALL THAT HARD WORK HAS YIELDED NO RESULTS, NATHAN.
WE CAN'T JUST--
KRA-GOOM
WROOM!

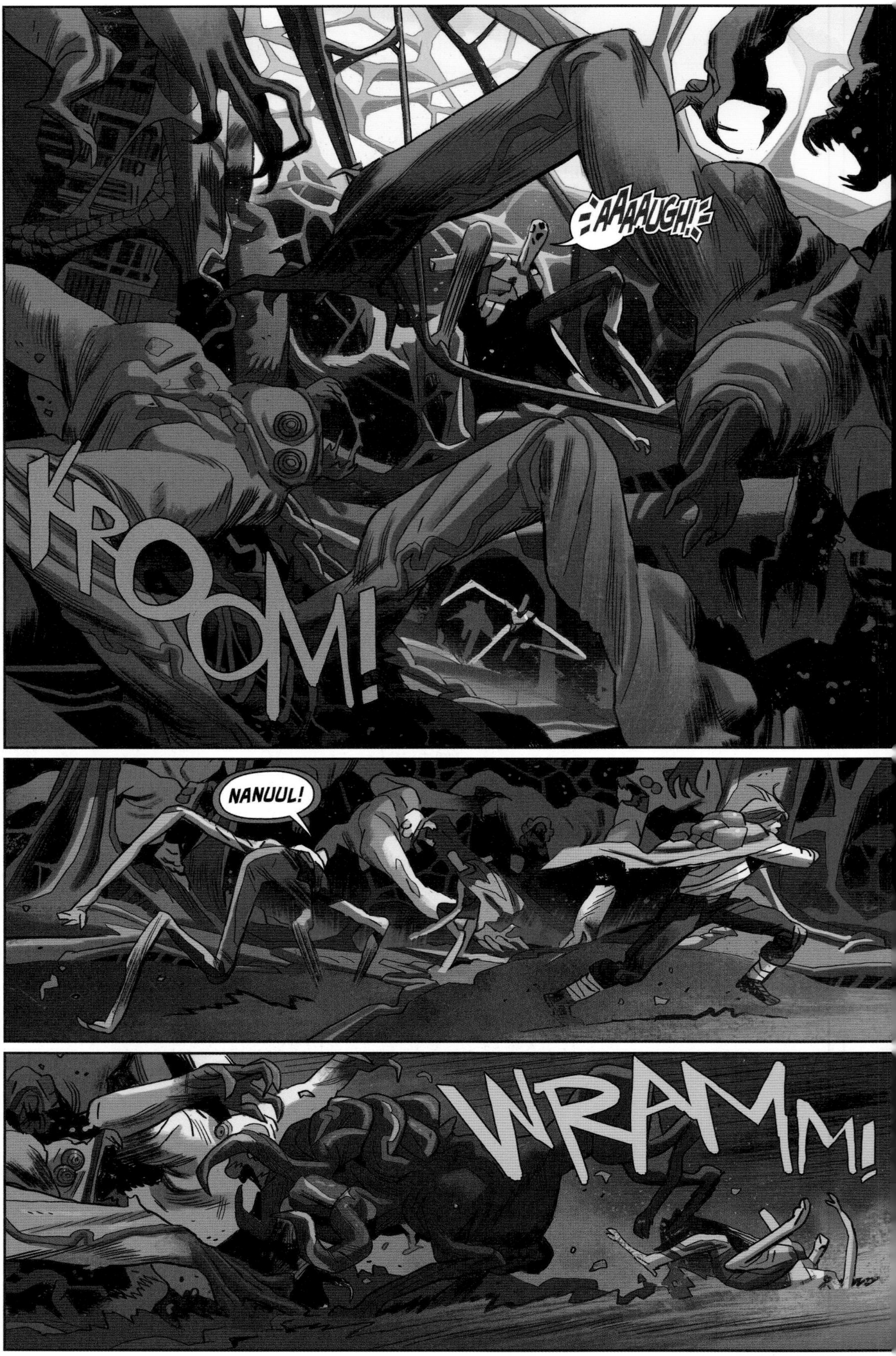
AAAAUGH!
KROOOM!
NANUUL!
WRAMM!

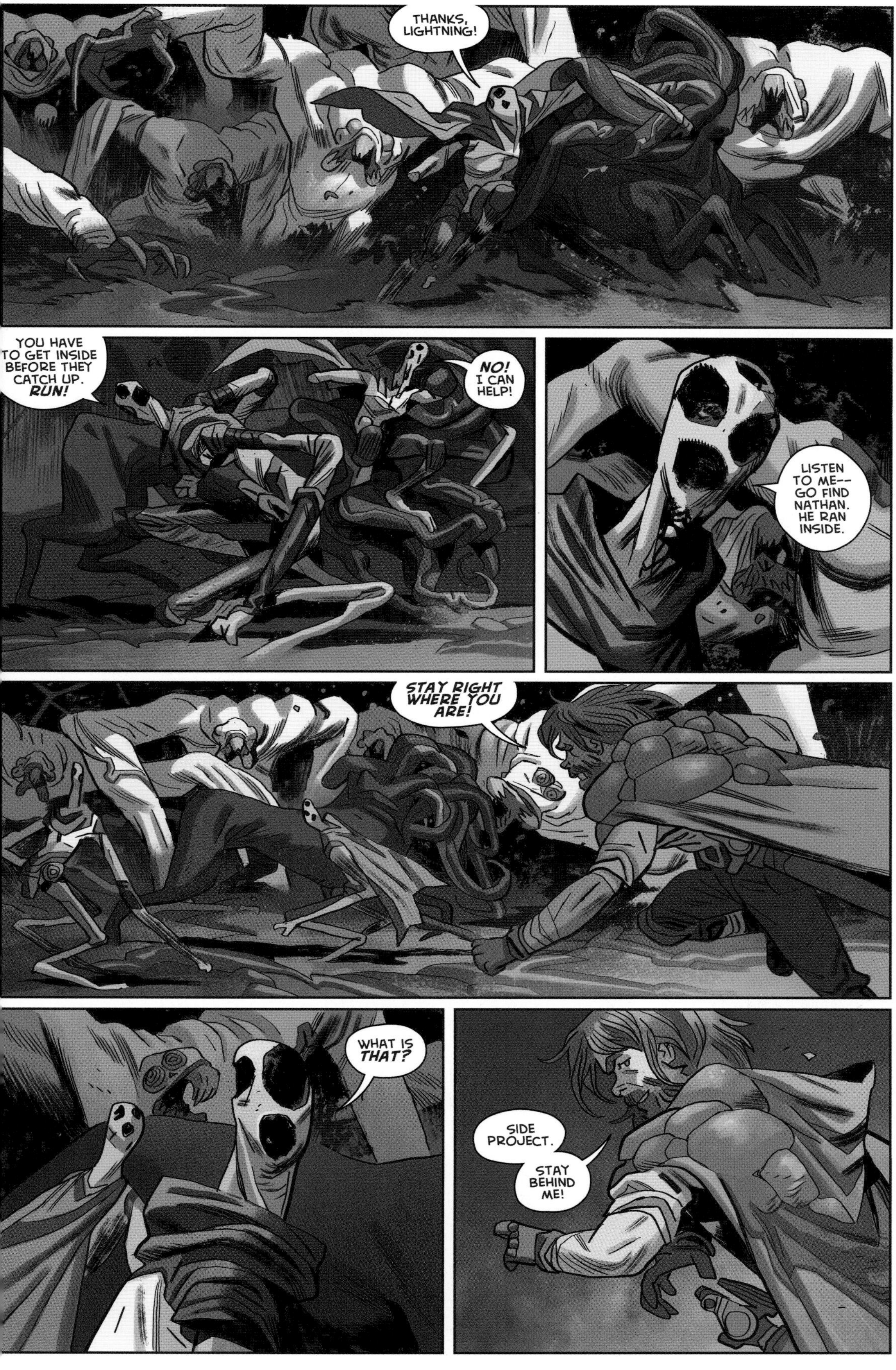
THANKS, LIGHTNING!
YOU HAVE TO GET INSIDE BEFORE THEY CATCH UP. *RUN!*
NO! I CAN HELP!
LISTEN TO ME-- GO FIND NATHAN. HE RAN INSIDE.
STAY RIGHT WHERE YOU ARE!
WHAT IS *THAT?*
SIDE PROJECT.
STAY BEHIND ME!

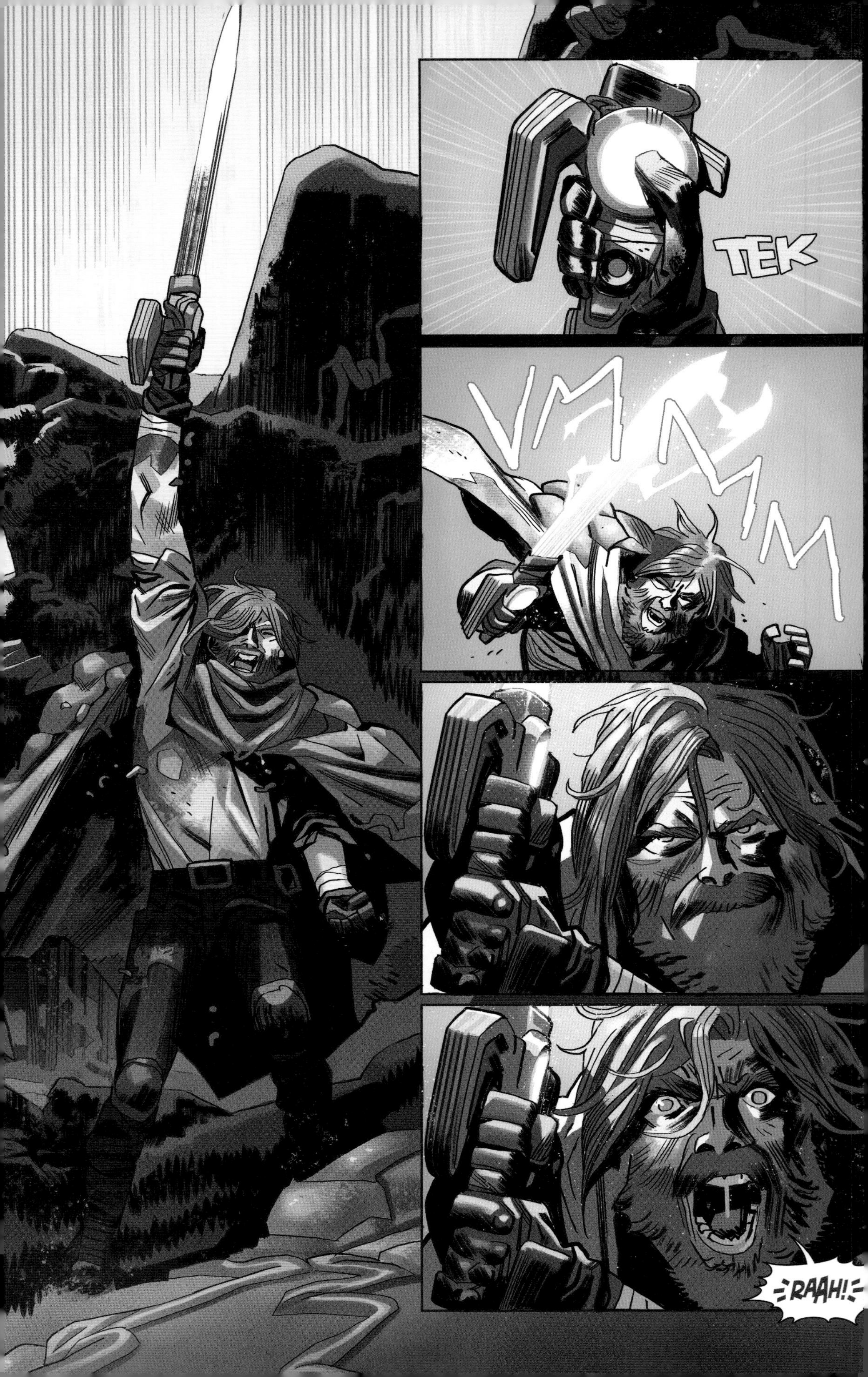
TEK
VMMMM
RAAH!

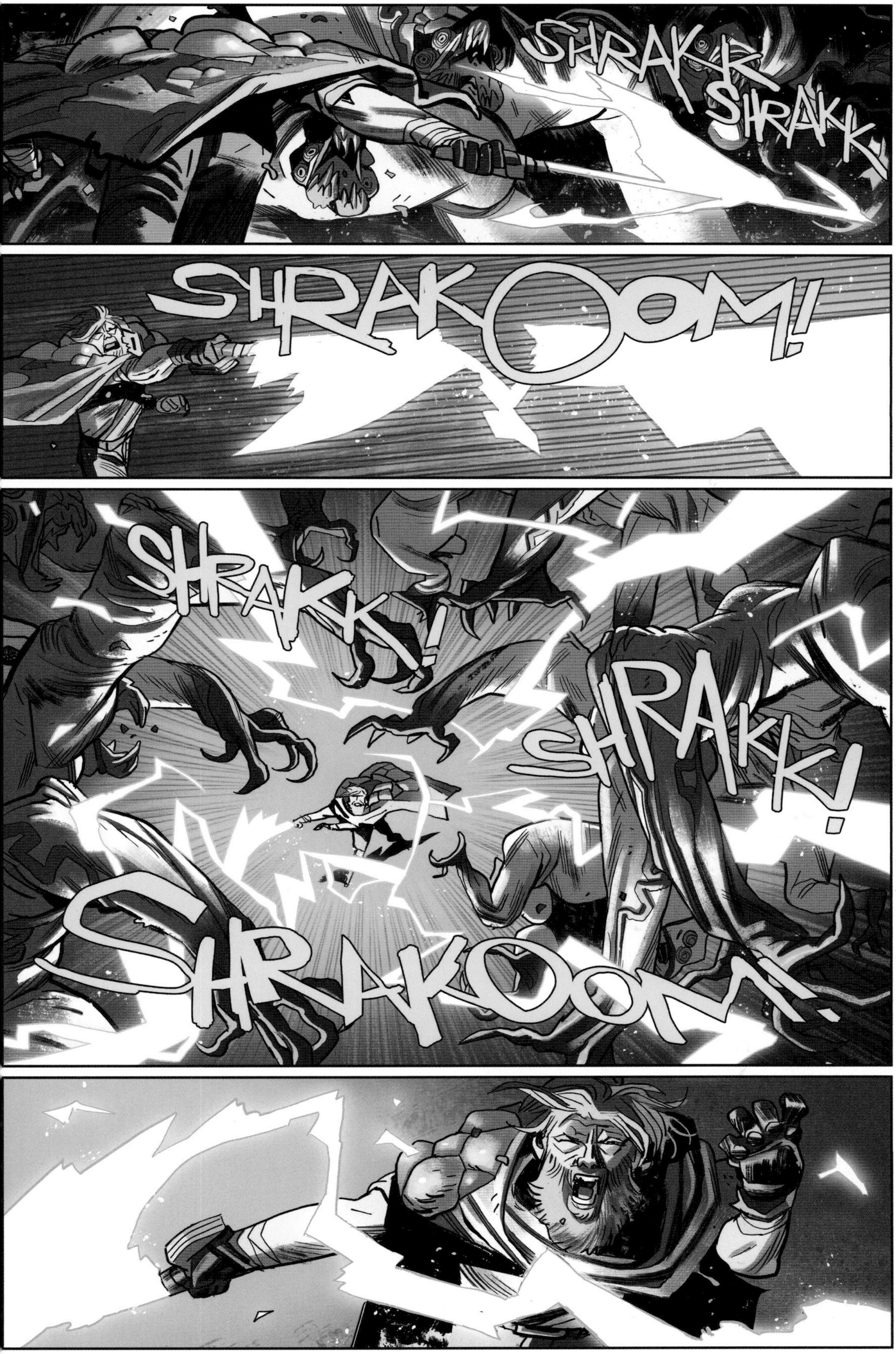
SHRAKKK
SHRAKK
SHRAKOOM!
SHRAKK!
SHRAKK!
SHRAKOOM!

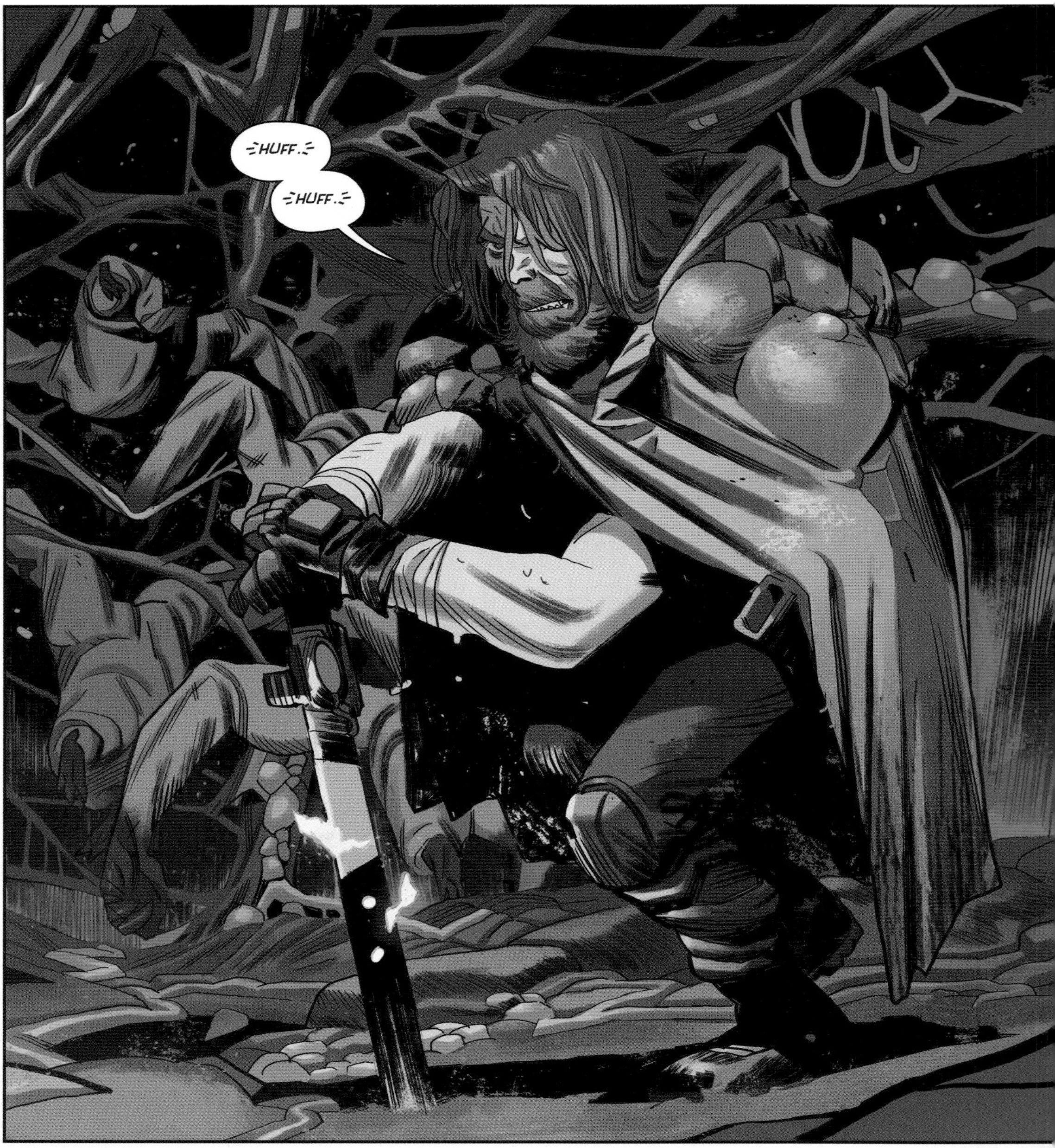
HUFF.
HUFF.
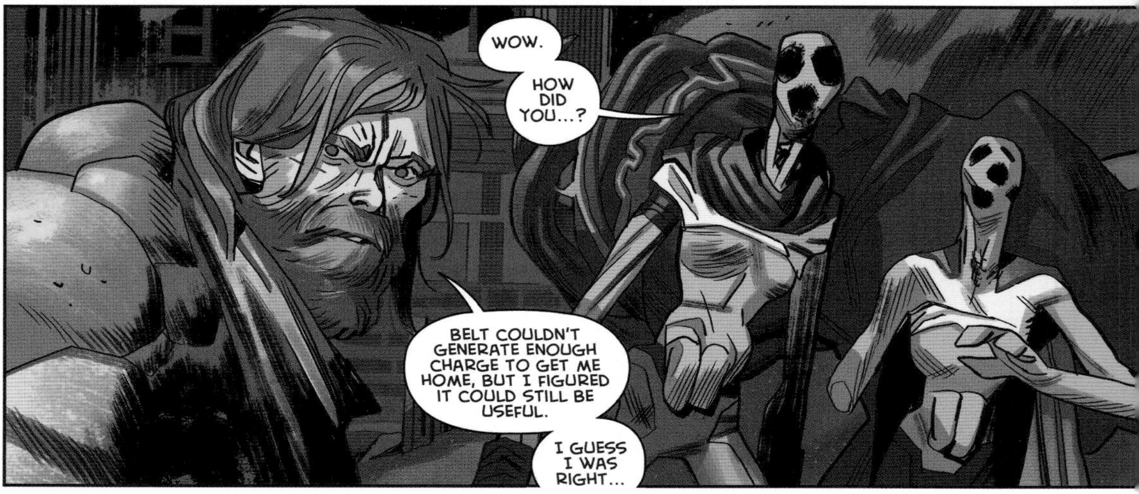
WOW.
HOW DID YOU...?
BELT COULDN'T GENERATE ENOUGH CHARGE TO GET ME HOME, BUT I FIGURED IT COULD STILL BE USEFUL.
I GUESS I WAS RIGHT...

OKAY. THERE.

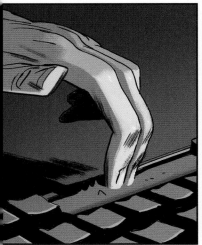

WHIRRRRRRRR

C'MON.

C'MON...

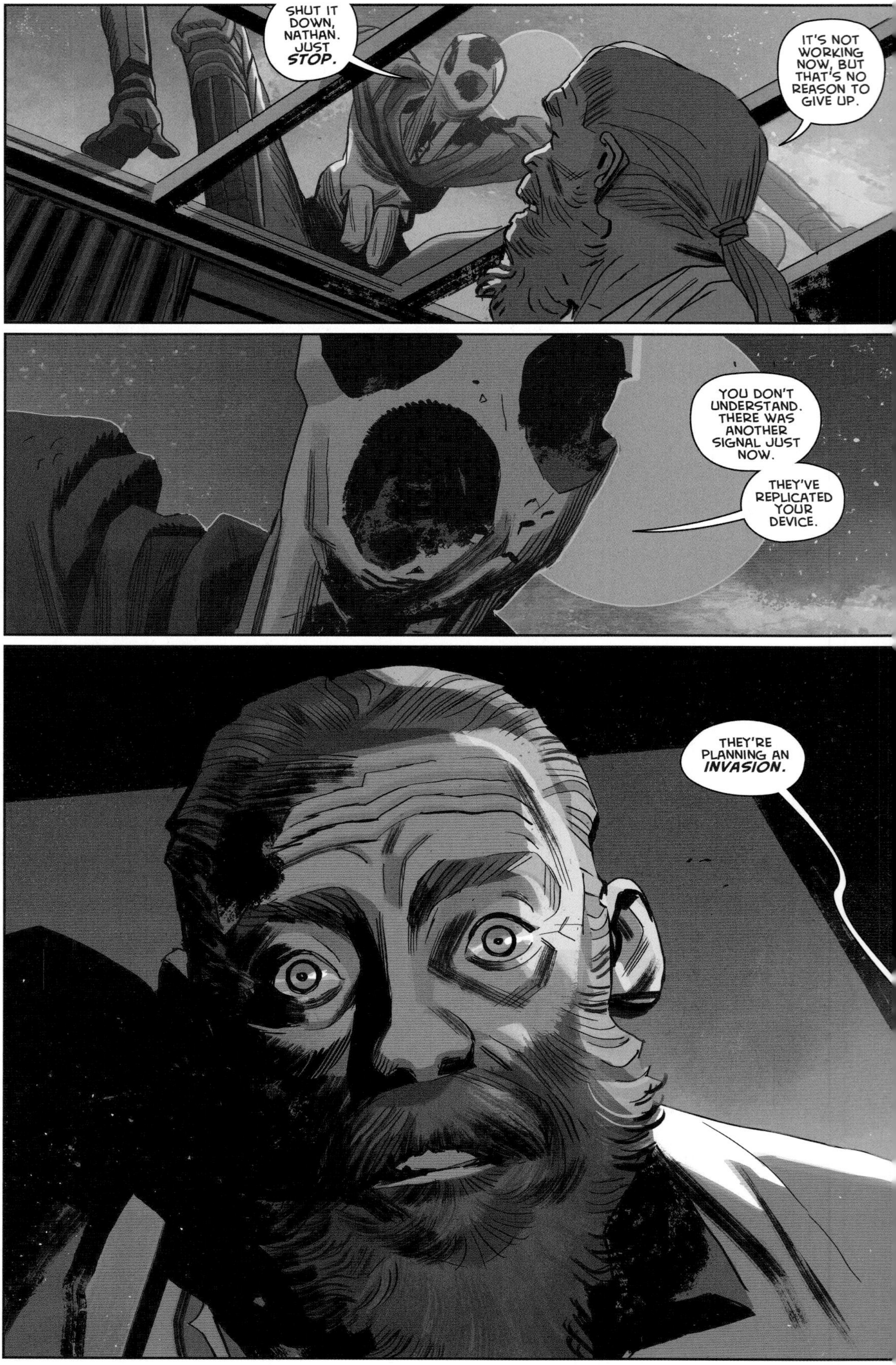
SHUT IT DOWN, NATHAN. JUST *STOP.*
IT'S NOT WORKING NOW, BUT THAT'S NO REASON TO GIVE UP.
YOU DON'T UNDERSTAND. THERE WAS ANOTHER SIGNAL JUST NOW.
THEY'VE REPLICATED YOUR DEVICE.
THEY'RE PLANNING AN *INVASION.*

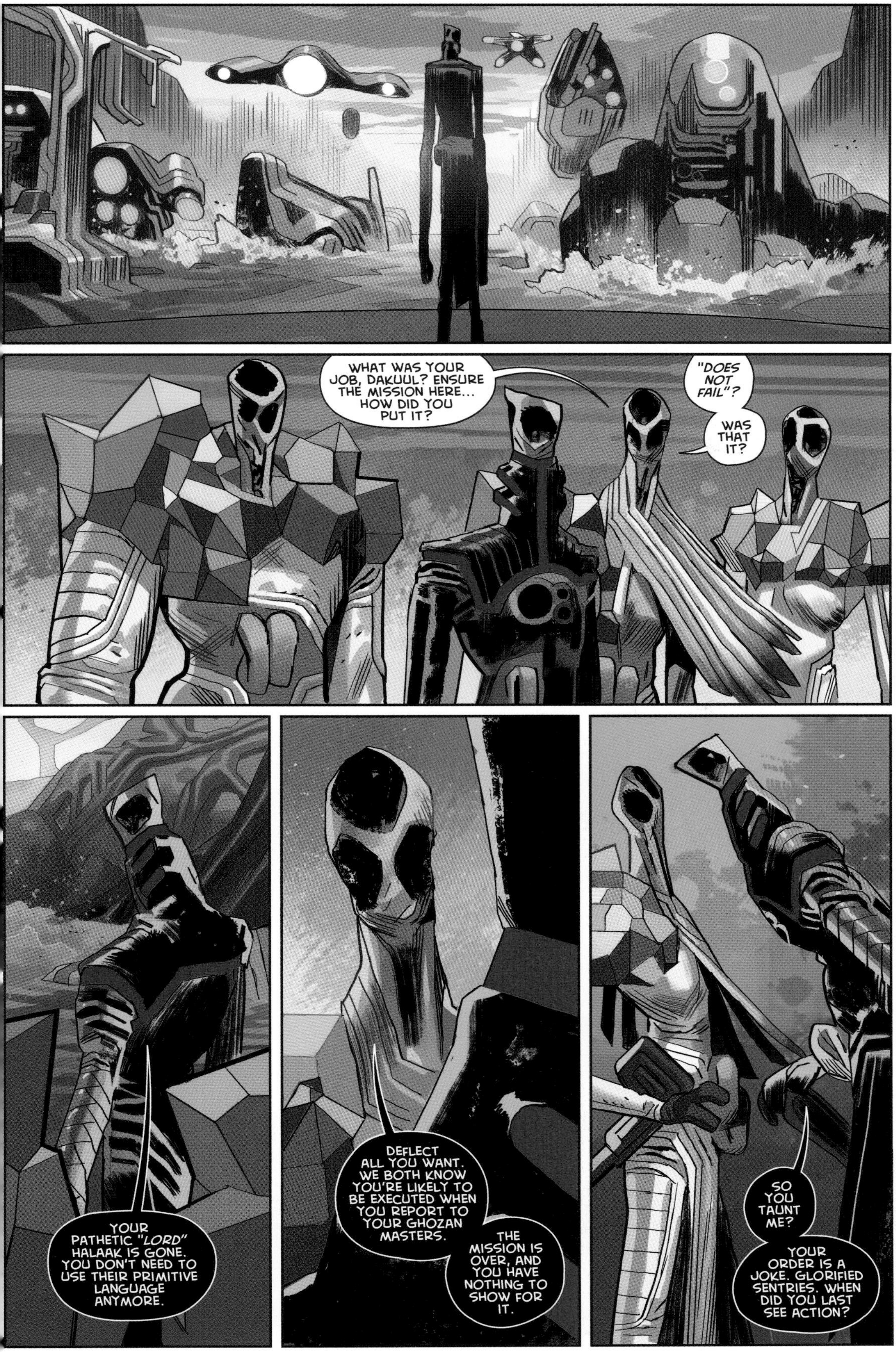
WHAT WAS YOUR JOB, DAKUUL? ENSURE THE MISSION HERE... HOW DID YOU PUT IT?
"DOES NOT FAIL"?
WAS THAT IT?
YOUR PATHETIC "LORD" HALAAK IS GONE. YOU DON'T NEED TO USE THEIR PRIMITIVE LANGUAGE ANYMORE.
DEFLECT ALL YOU WANT. WE BOTH KNOW YOU'RE LIKELY TO BE EXECUTED WHEN YOU REPORT TO YOUR GHOZAN MASTERS.
THE MISSION IS OVER, AND YOU HAVE NOTHING TO SHOW FOR IT.
SO YOU TAUNT ME?
YOUR ORDER IS A JOKE. GLORIFIED SENTRIES. WHEN DID YOU LAST SEE ACTION?

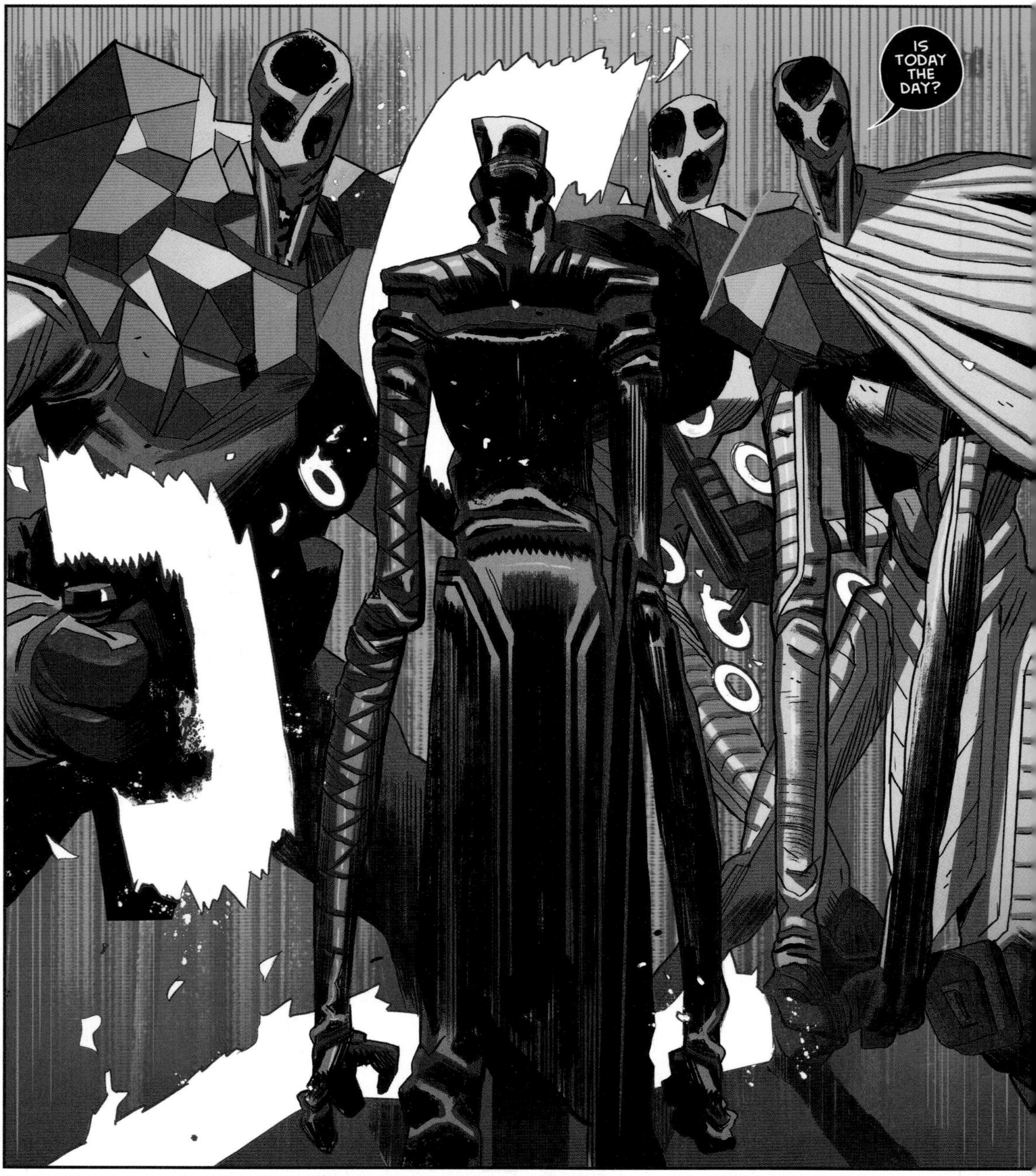
IS TODAY THE DAY?

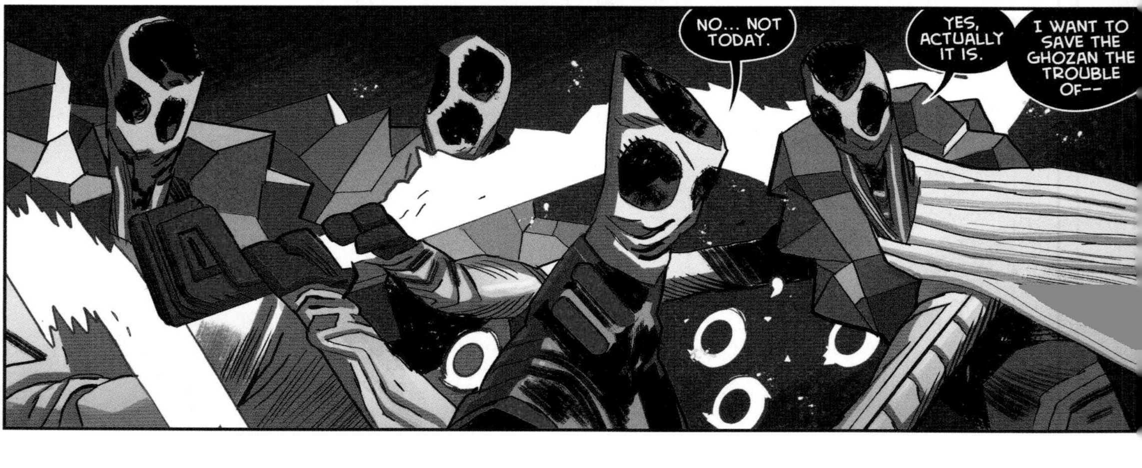
NO... NOT TODAY.
YES, ACTUALLY IT IS.
I WANT TO SAVE THE GHOZAN THE TROUBLE OF--

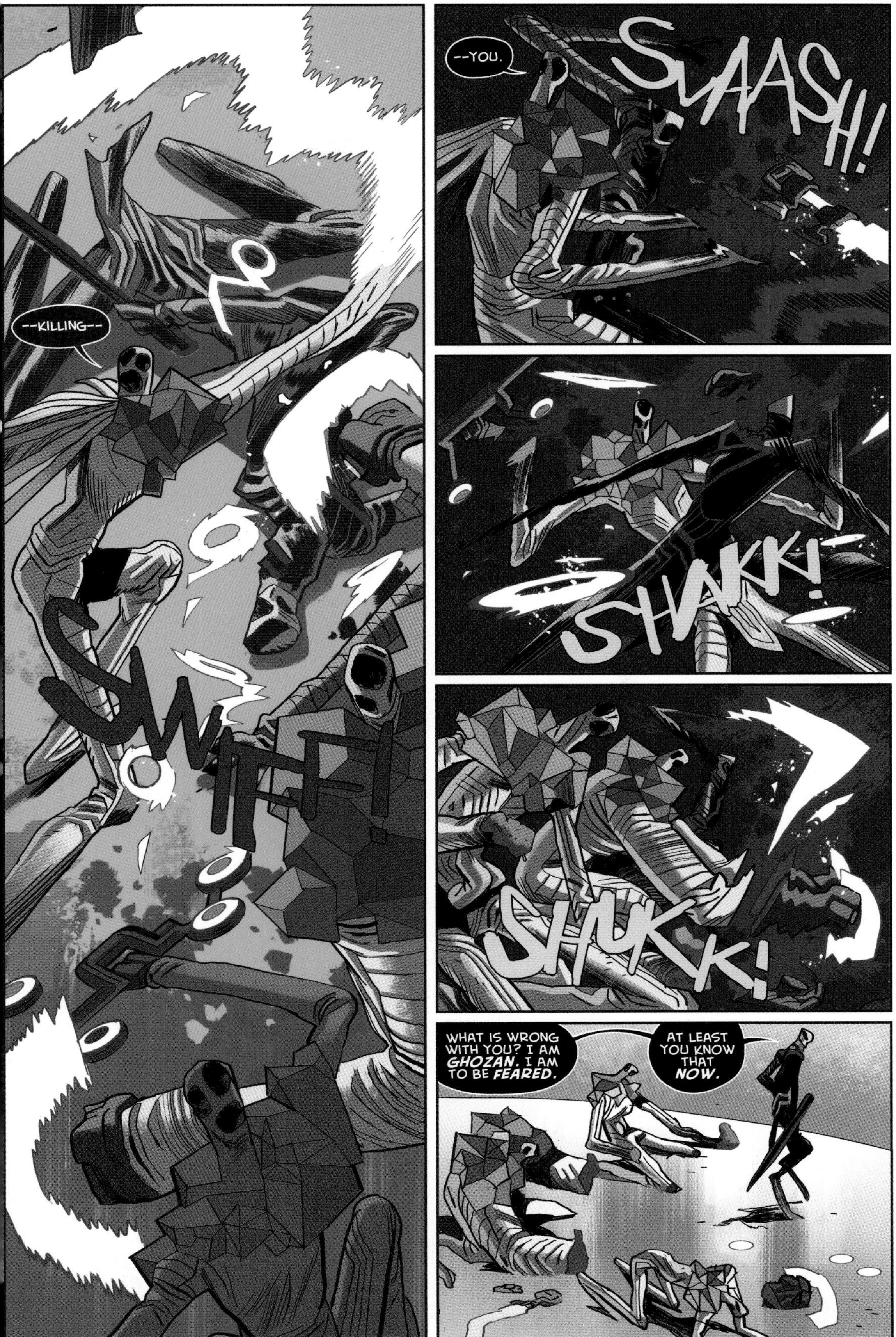
--KILLING--
SWIFF!
--YOU.
SWAASH!
SHAKK!
SHUKK!
WHAT IS WRONG WITH YOU? I AM GHOZAN. I AM TO BE FEARED.
AT LEAST YOU KNOW THAT NOW.

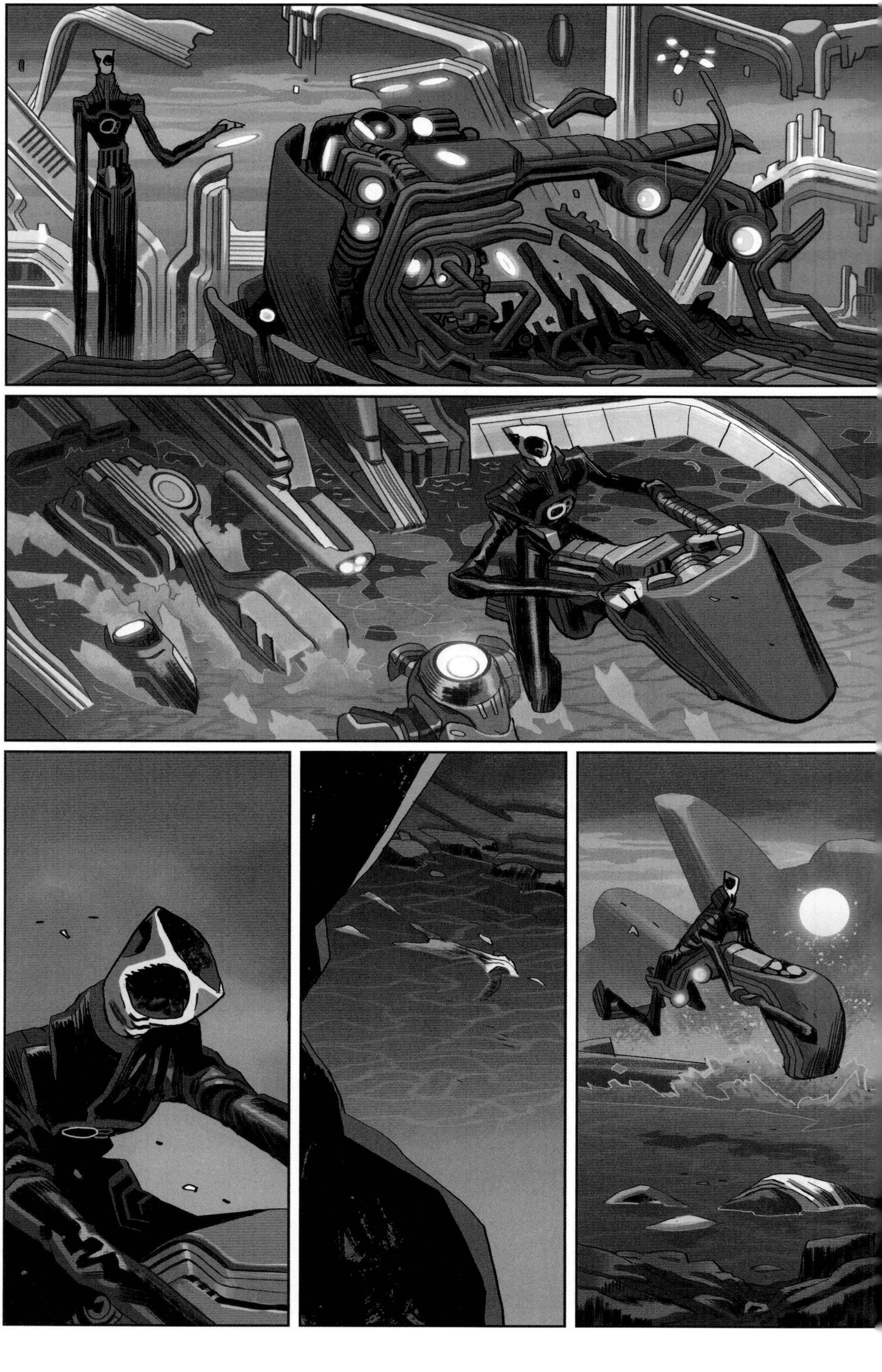

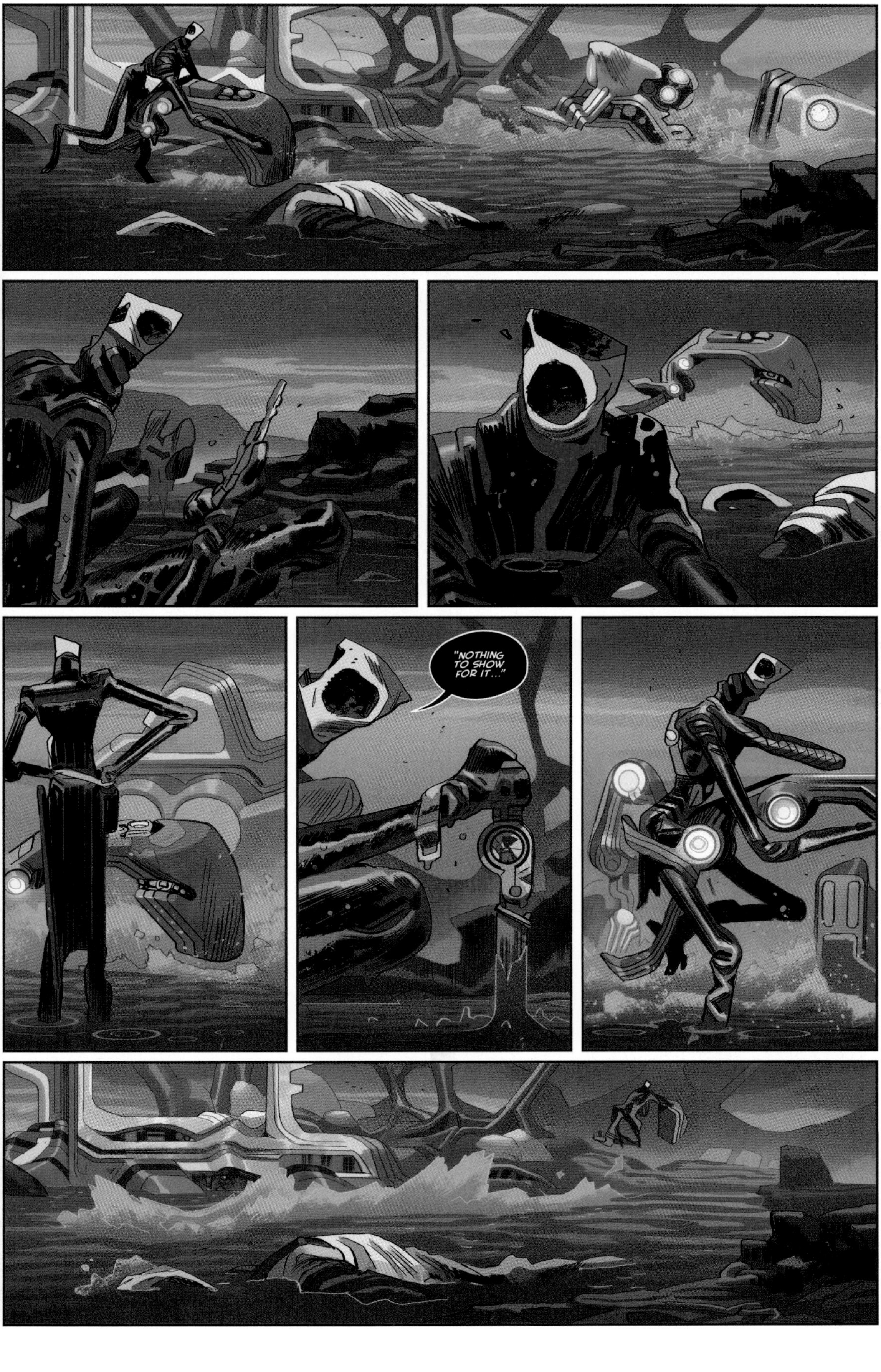
"NOTHING TO SHOW FOR IT..."

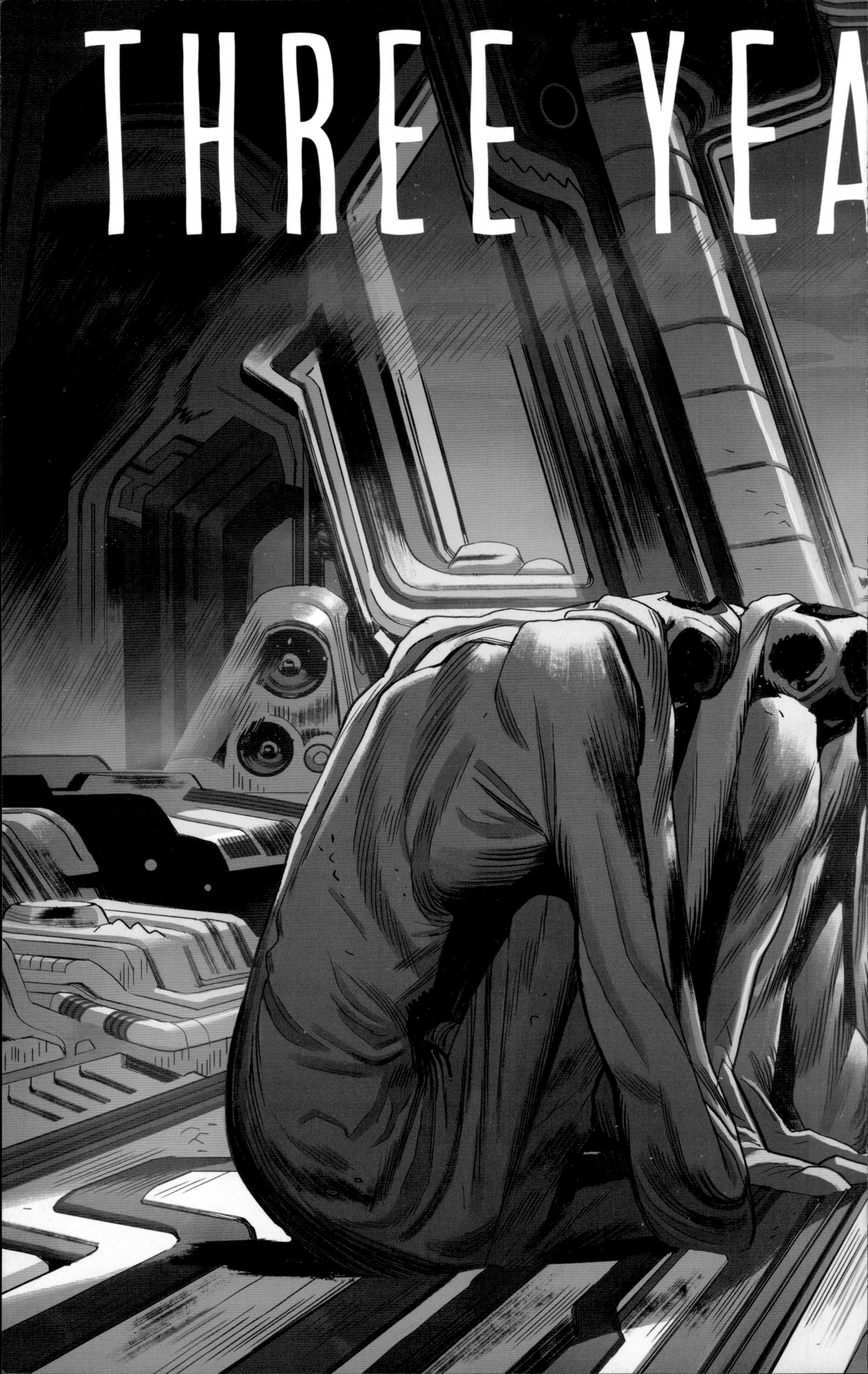
THREE YEA

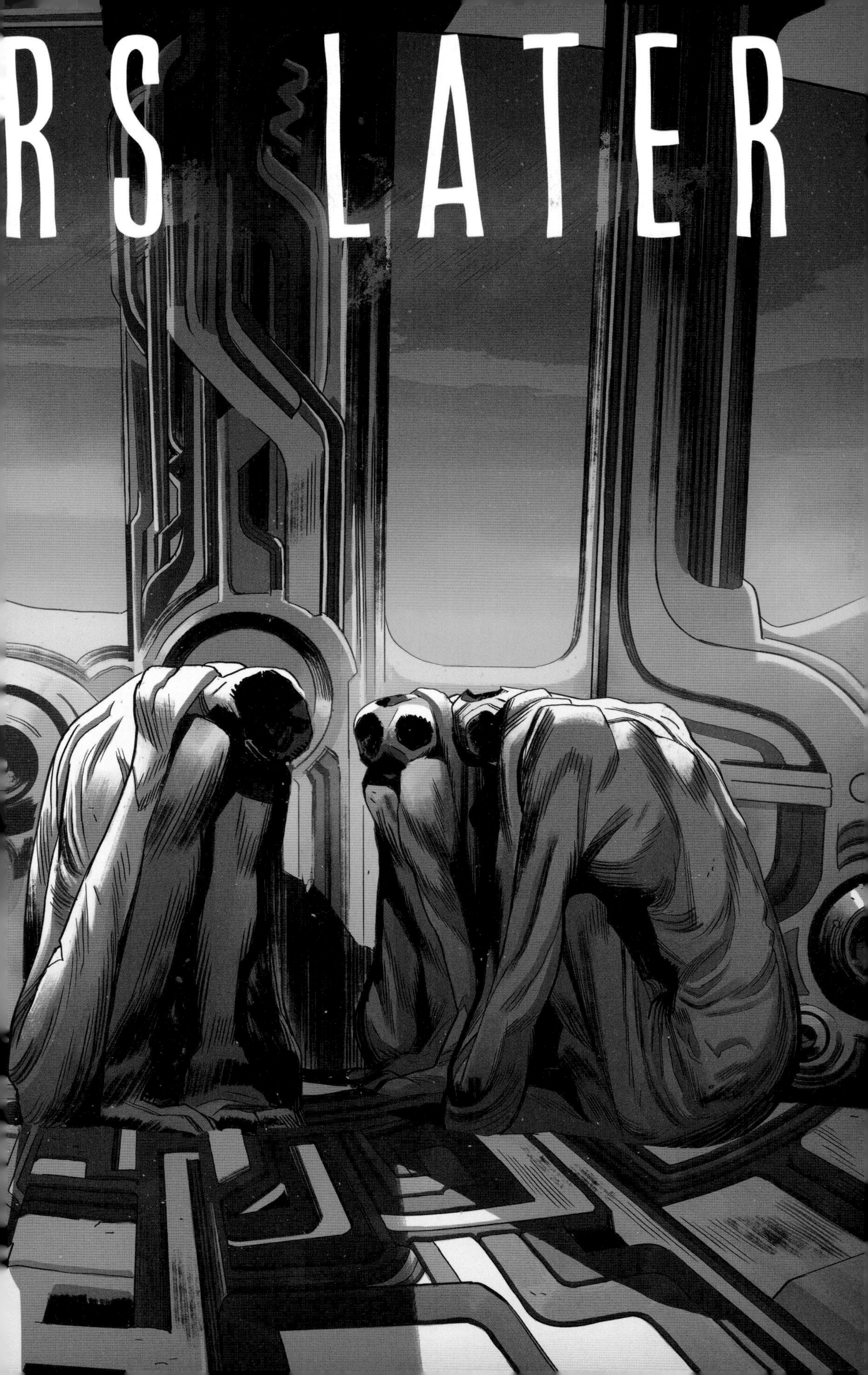
RS LATER

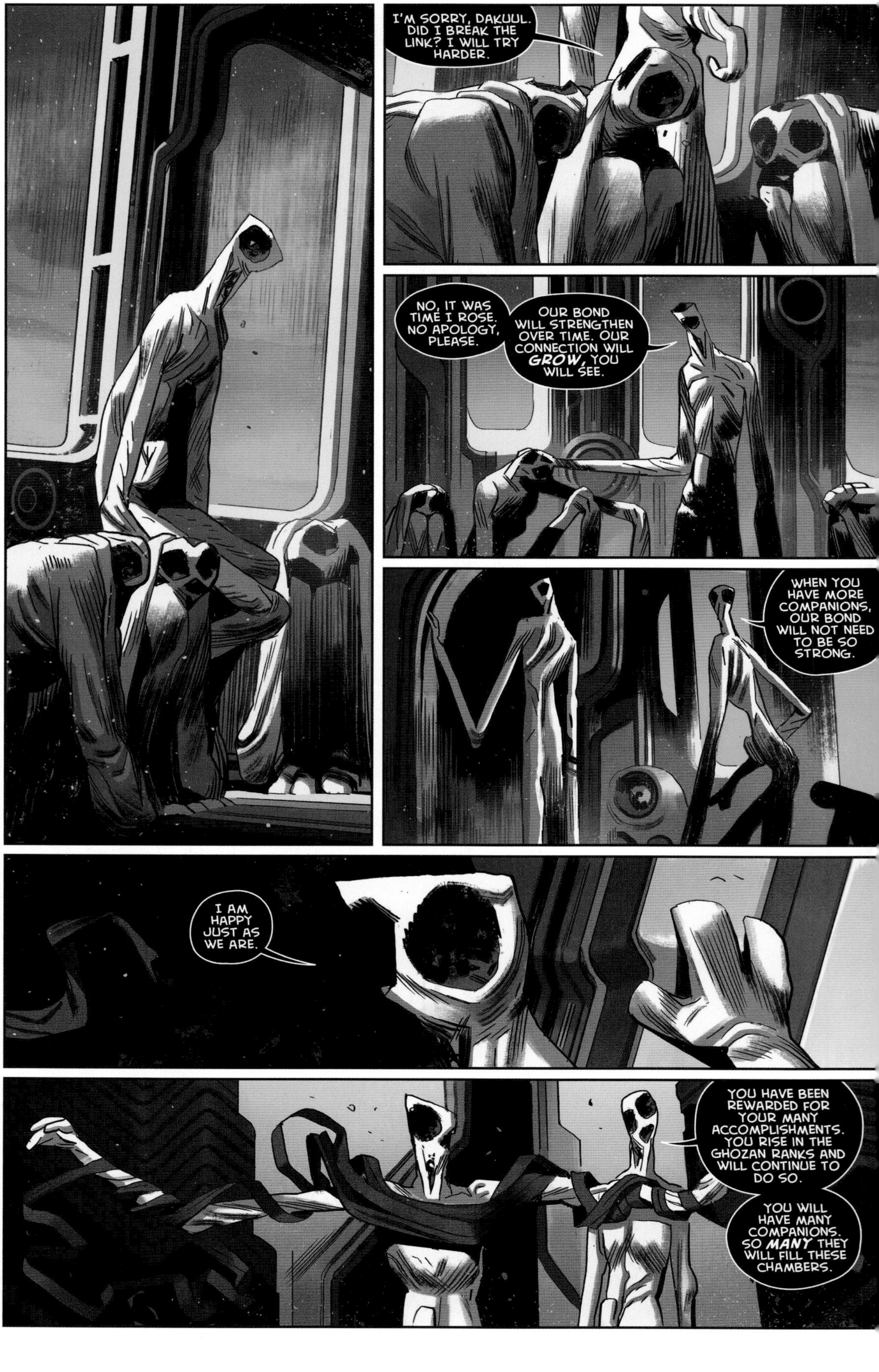
I'M SORRY, DAKUUL. DID I BREAK THE LINK? I WILL TRY HARDER.
NO, IT WAS TIME I ROSE. NO APOLOGY, PLEASE.
OUR BOND WILL STRENGTHEN OVER TIME. OUR CONNECTION WILL GROW, YOU WILL SEE.
WHEN YOU HAVE MORE COMPANIONS, OUR BOND WILL NOT NEED TO BE SO STRONG.
I AM HAPPY JUST AS WE ARE.
YOU HAVE BEEN REWARDED FOR YOUR MANY ACCOMPLISHMENTS. YOU RISE IN THE GHOZAN RANKS AND WILL CONTINUE TO DO SO.
YOU WILL HAVE MANY COMPANIONS. SO MANY THEY WILL FILL THESE CHAMBERS.

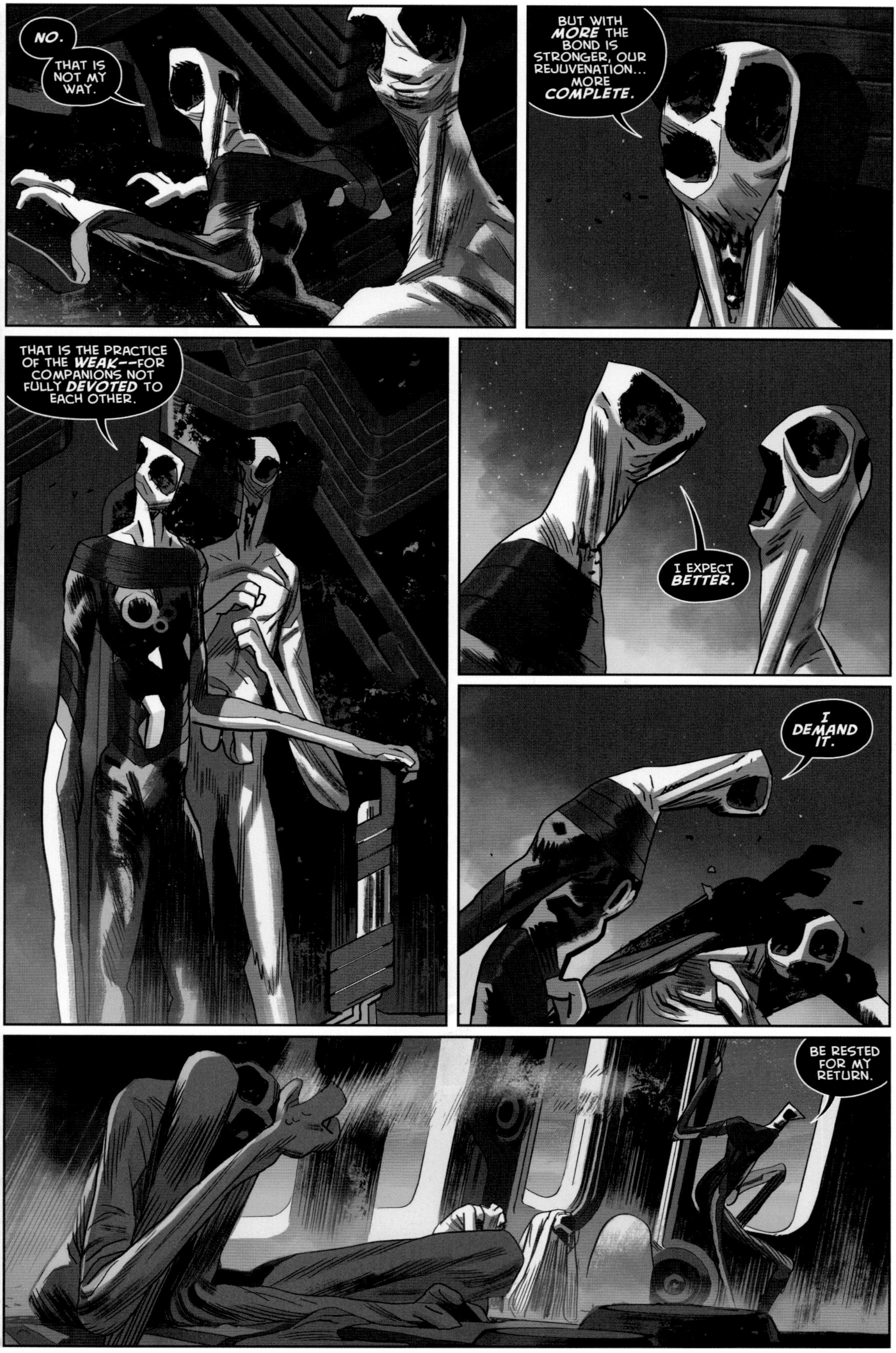
NO.
THAT IS NOT MY WAY.
BUT WITH MORE THE BOND IS STRONGER, OUR REJUVENATION... MORE COMPLETE.
THAT IS THE PRACTICE OF THE WEAK--FOR COMPANIONS NOT FULLY DEVOTED TO EACH OTHER.
I EXPECT BETTER.
I DEMAND IT.
BE RESTED FOR MY RETURN.

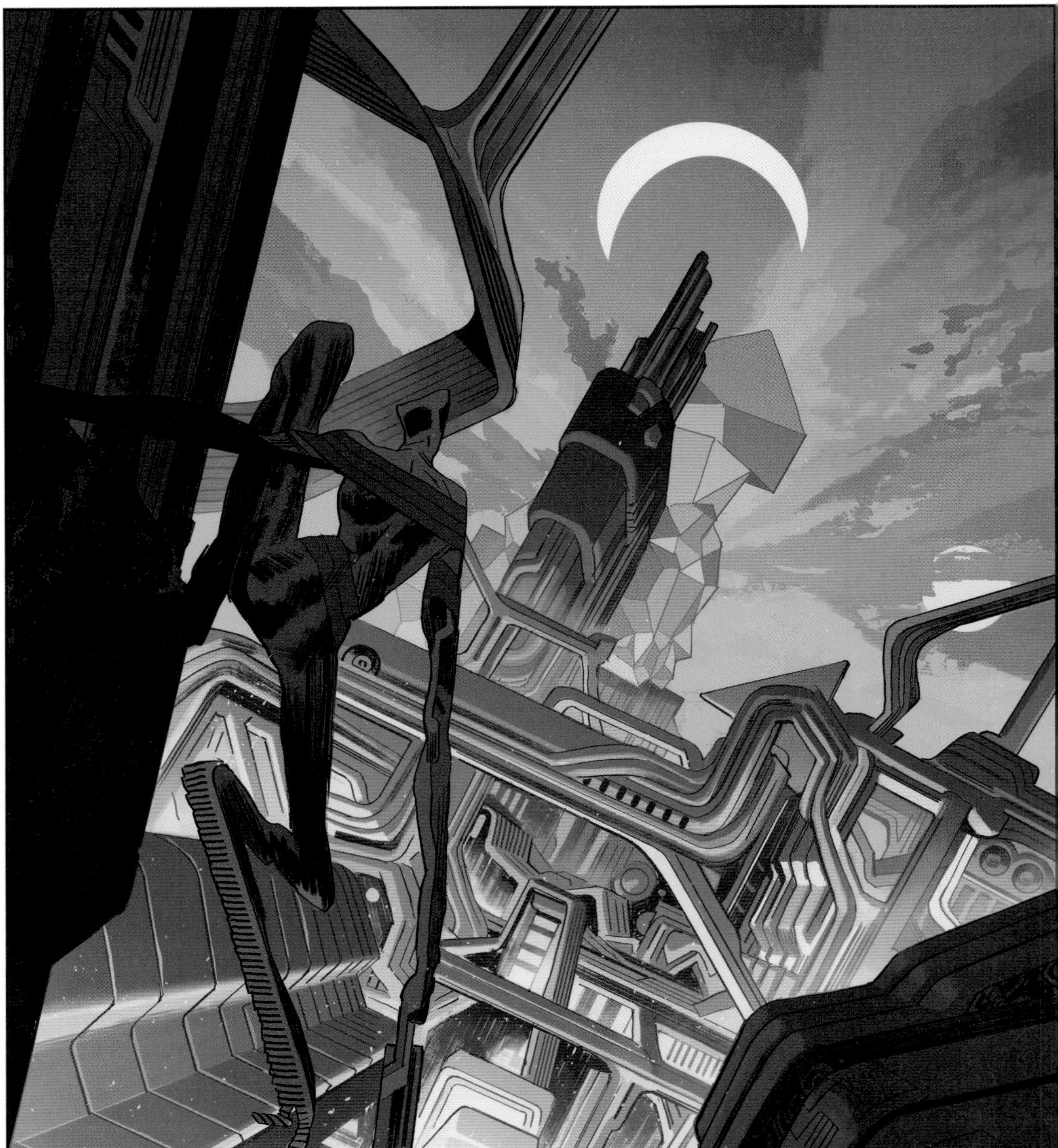

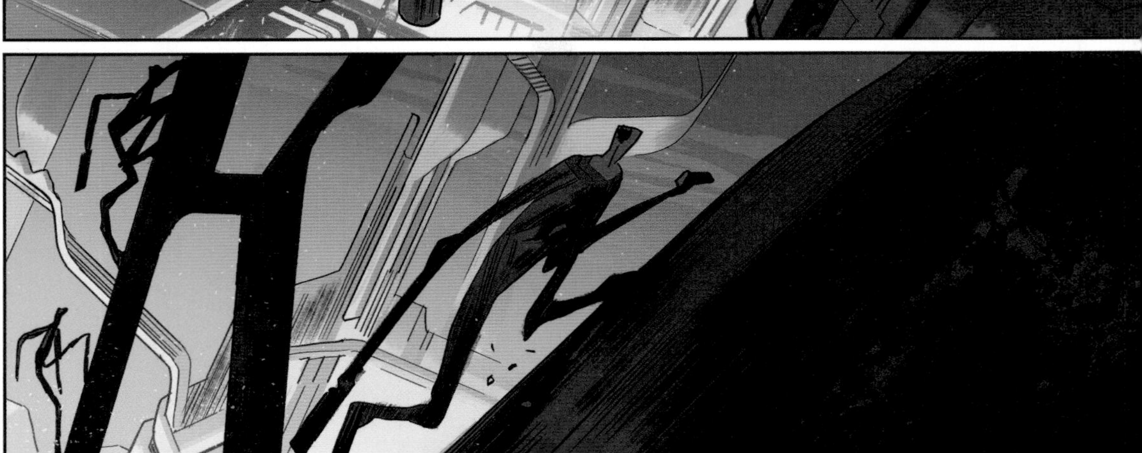

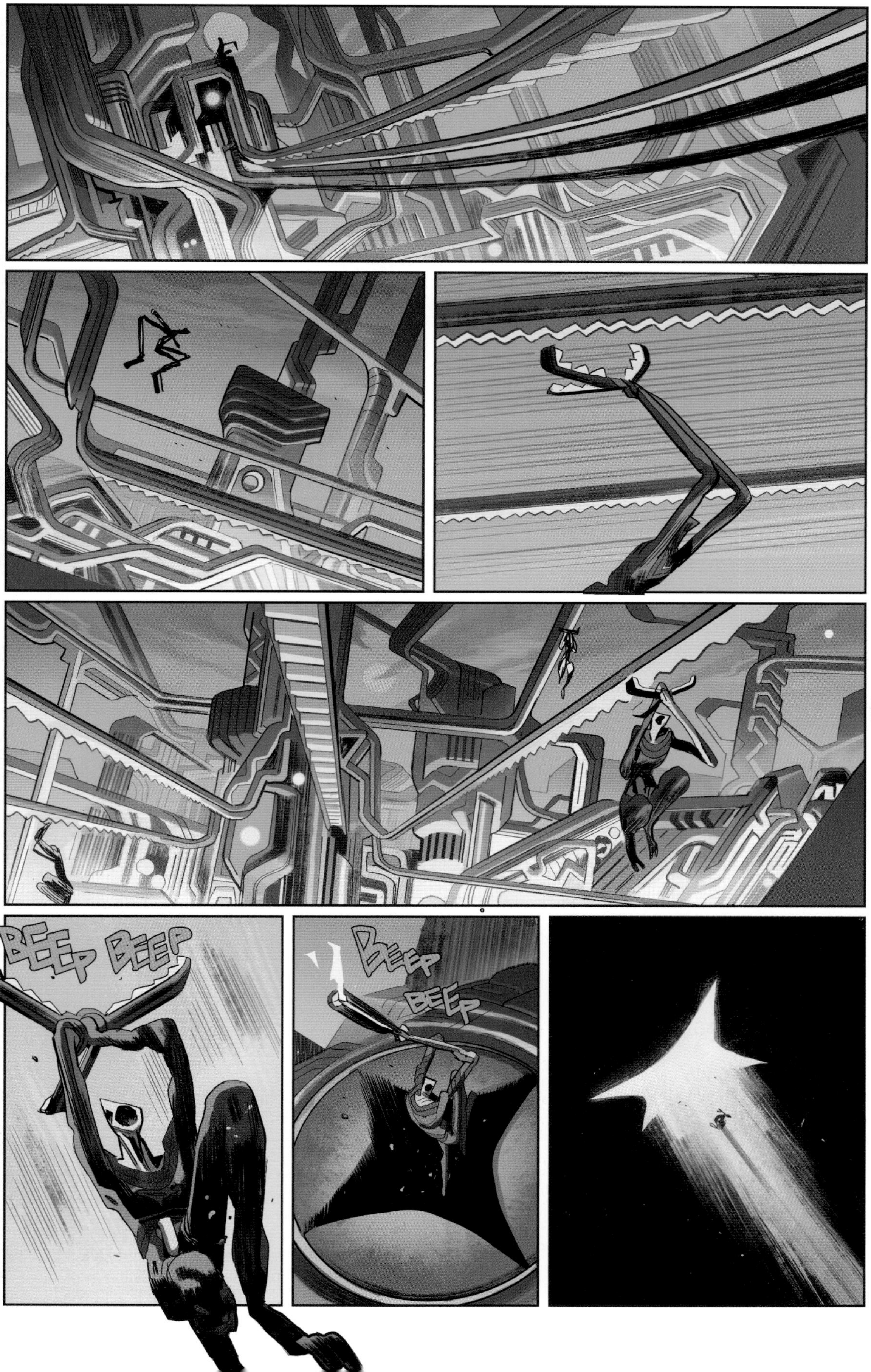
BEEP BEEP
BEEP
BEEP

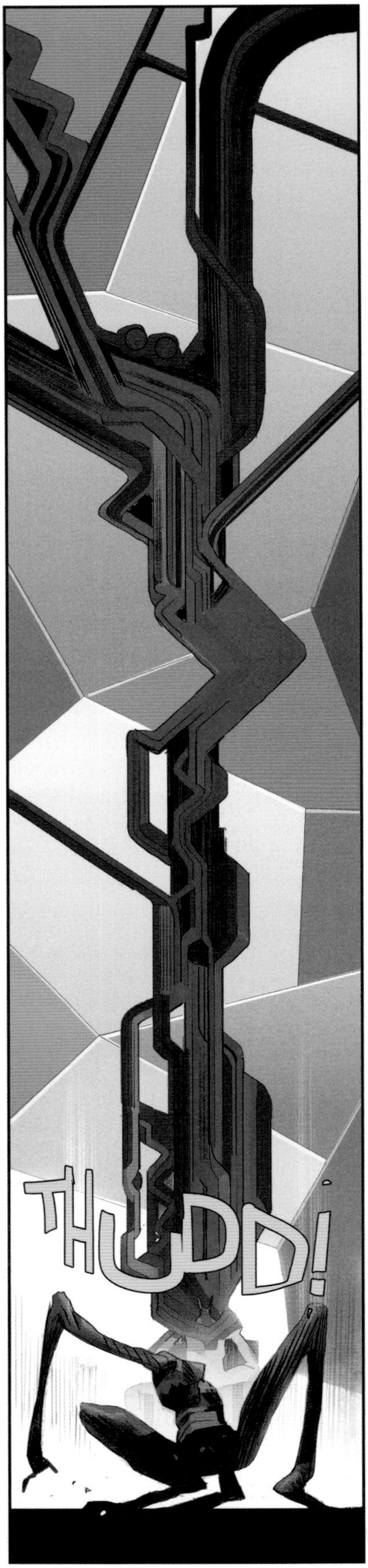
THUDD!

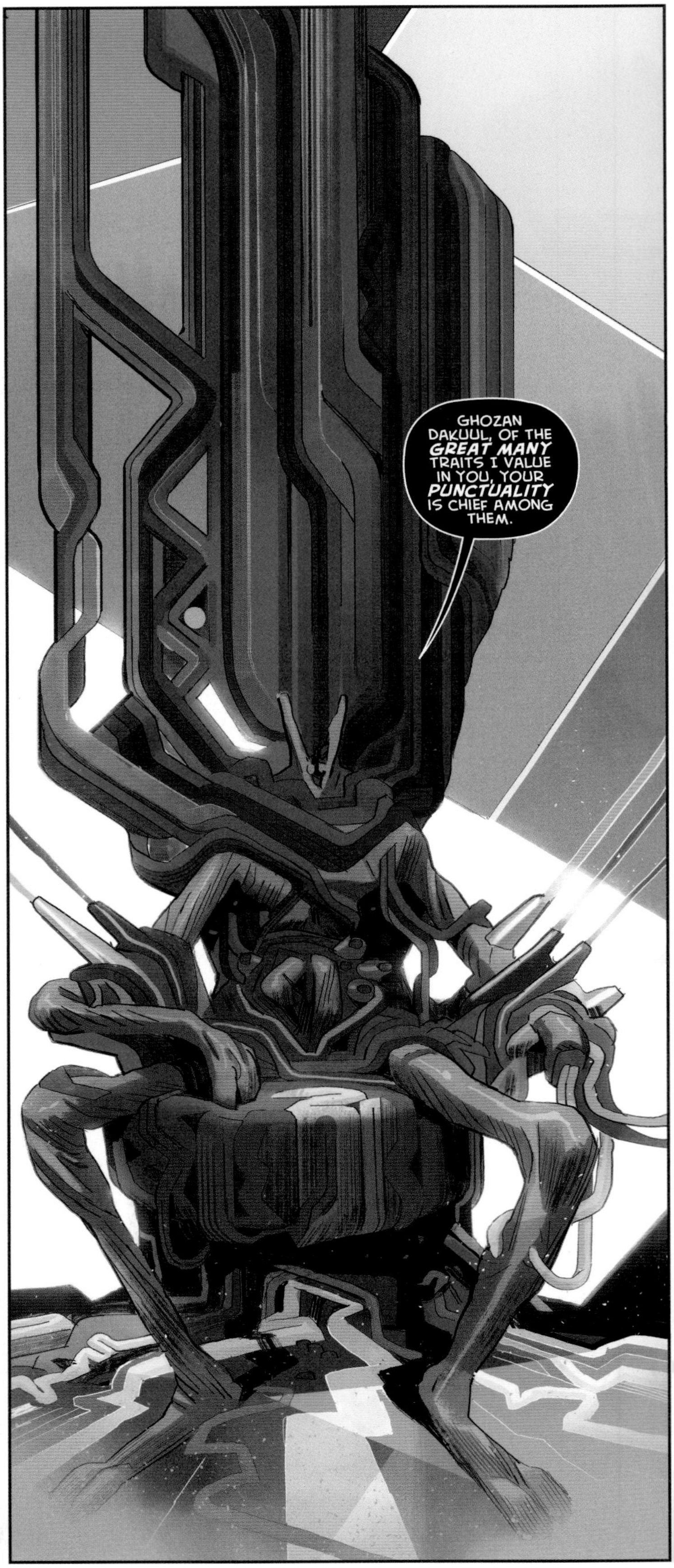
GHOZAN DAKUUL, OF THE ***GREAT MANY*** TRAITS I VALUE IN YOU, YOUR ***PUNCTUALITY*** IS CHIEF AMONG THEM.

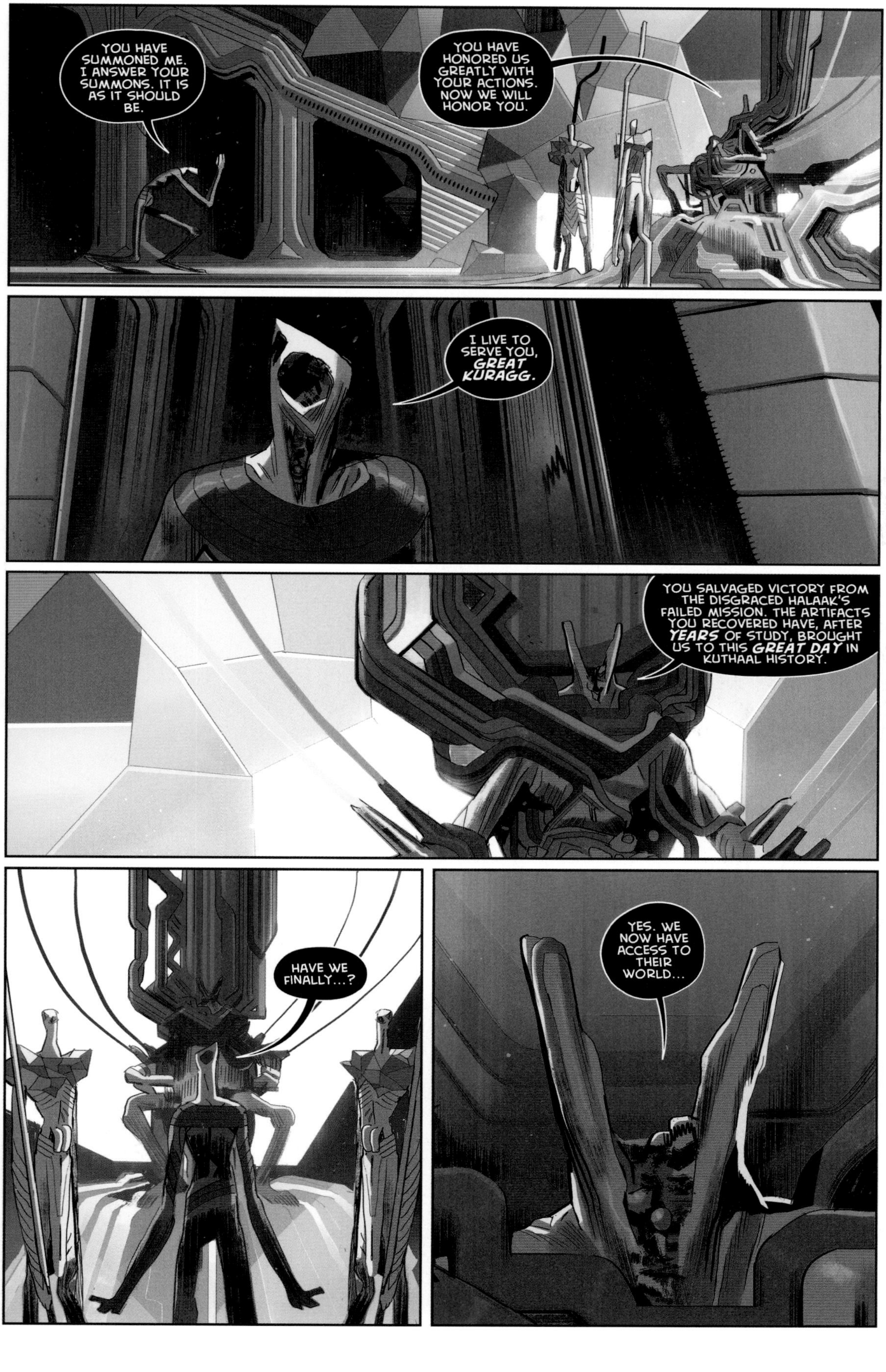
YOU HAVE SUMMONED ME. I ANSWER YOUR SUMMONS. IT IS AS IT SHOULD BE.
YOU HAVE HONORED US GREATLY WITH YOUR ACTIONS. NOW WE WILL HONOR YOU.
I LIVE TO SERVE YOU, GREAT KURAGG.
YOU SALVAGED VICTORY FROM THE DISGRACED HALAAK'S FAILED MISSION. THE ARTIFACTS YOU RECOVERED HAVE, AFTER YEARS OF STUDY, BROUGHT US TO THIS GREAT DAY IN KUTHAAL HISTORY.
HAVE WE FINALLY...?
YES. WE NOW HAVE ACCESS TO THEIR WORLD...

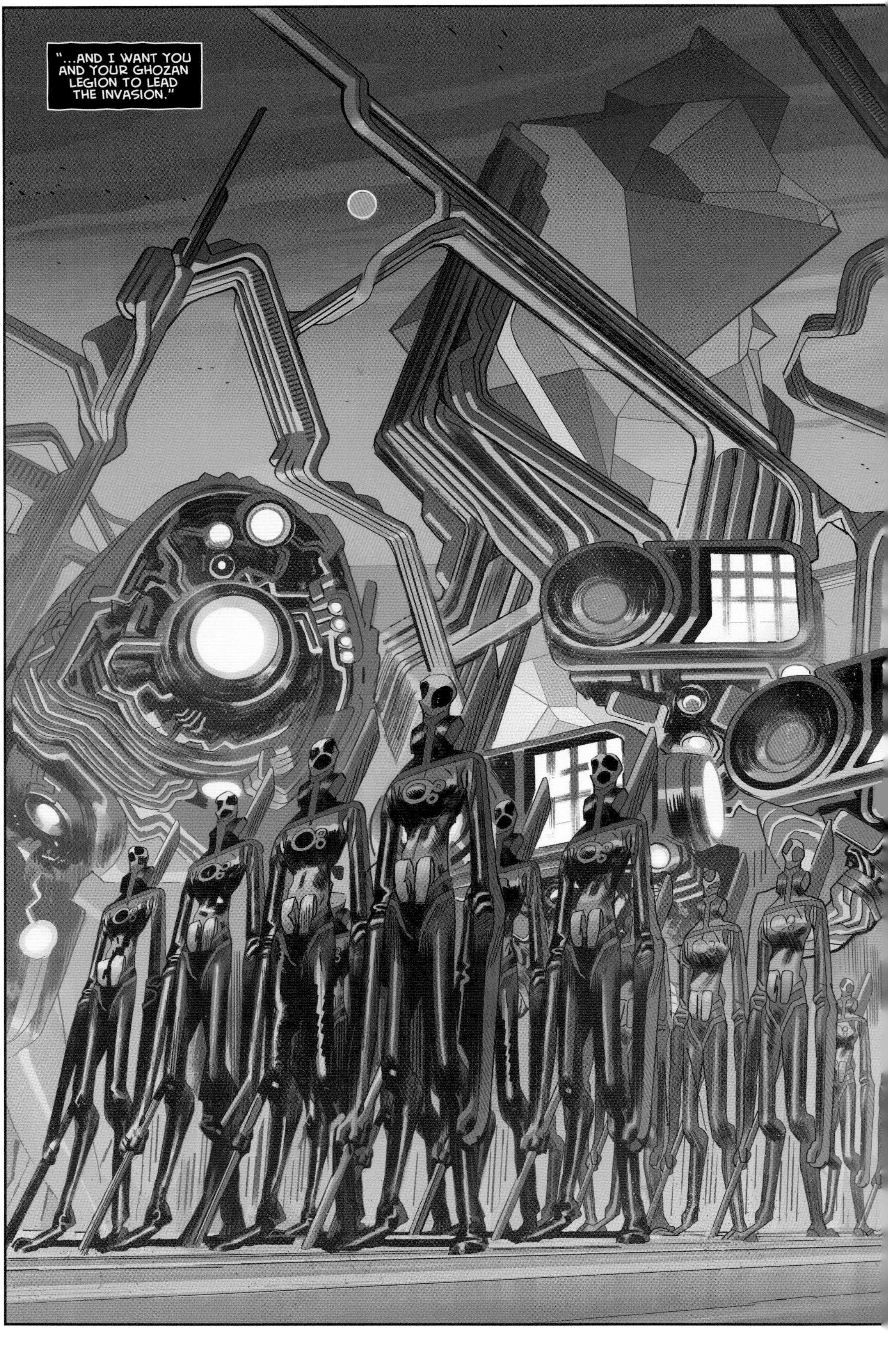
"...AND I WANT YOU AND YOUR GHOZAN LEGION TO LEAD THE INVASION."

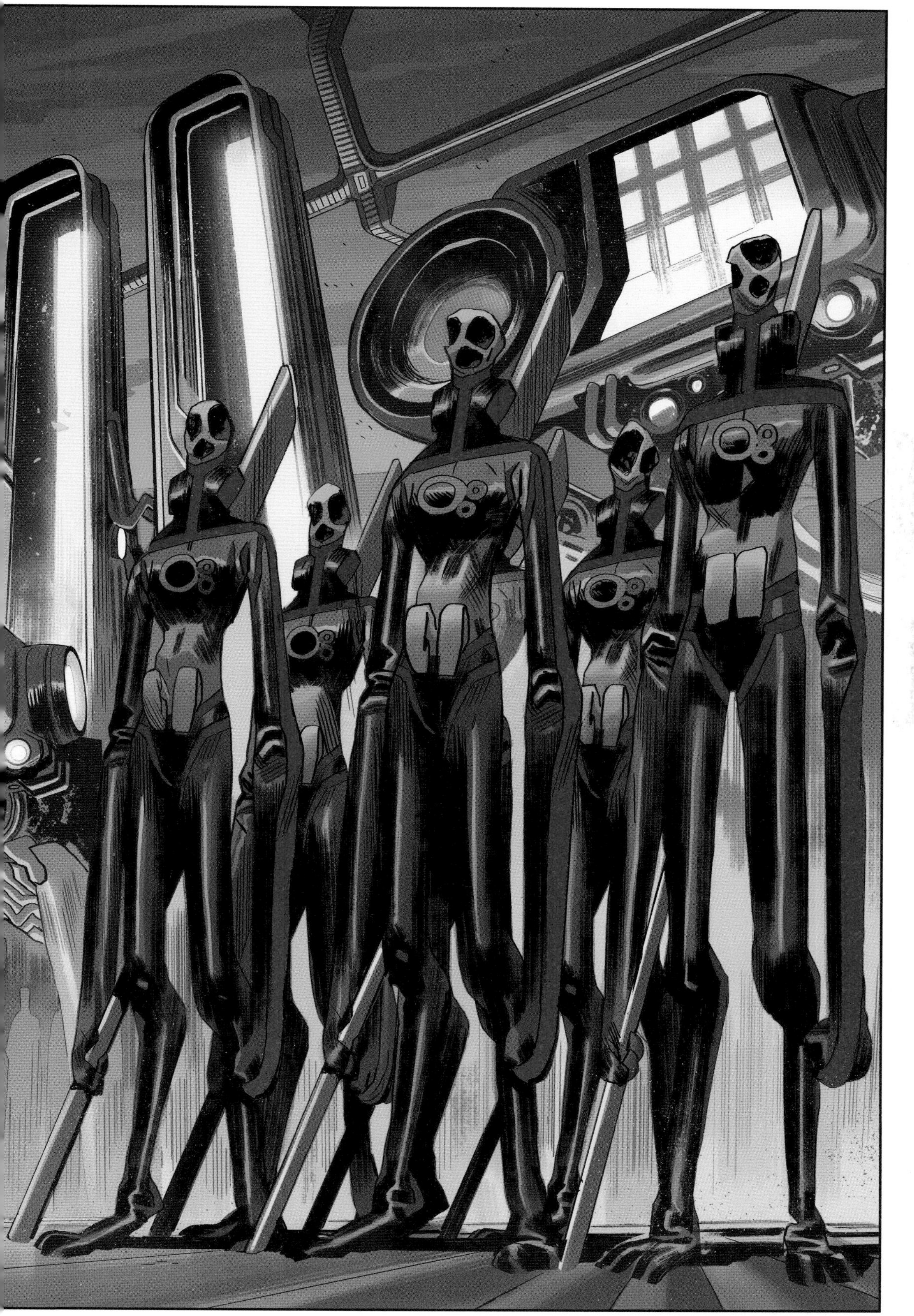

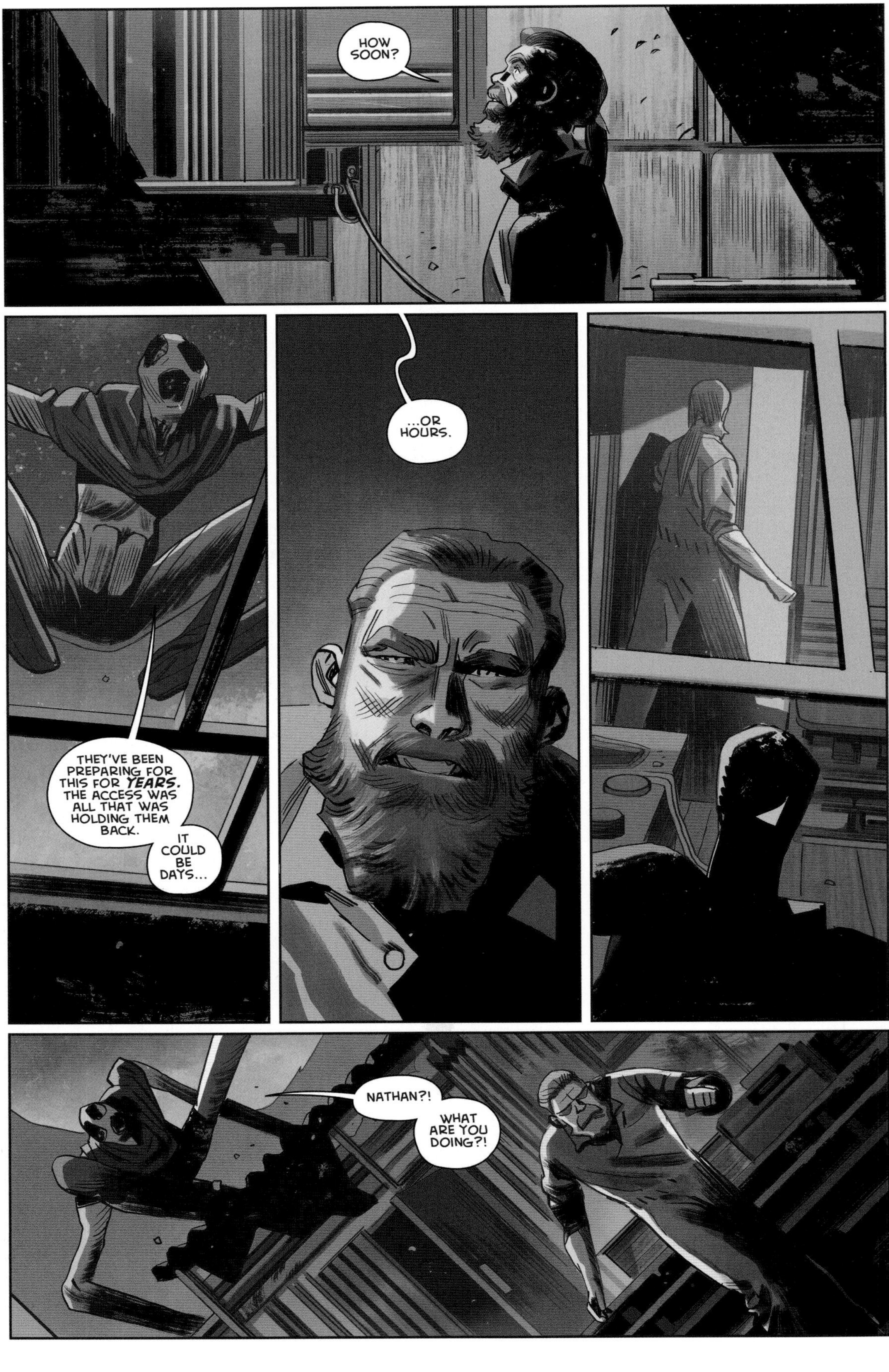
HOW SOON?
THEY'VE BEEN PREPARING FOR THIS FOR YEARS. THE ACCESS WAS ALL THAT WAS HOLDING THEM BACK.
IT COULD BE DAYS...
...OR HOURS.
NATHAN?!
WHAT ARE YOU DOING?!

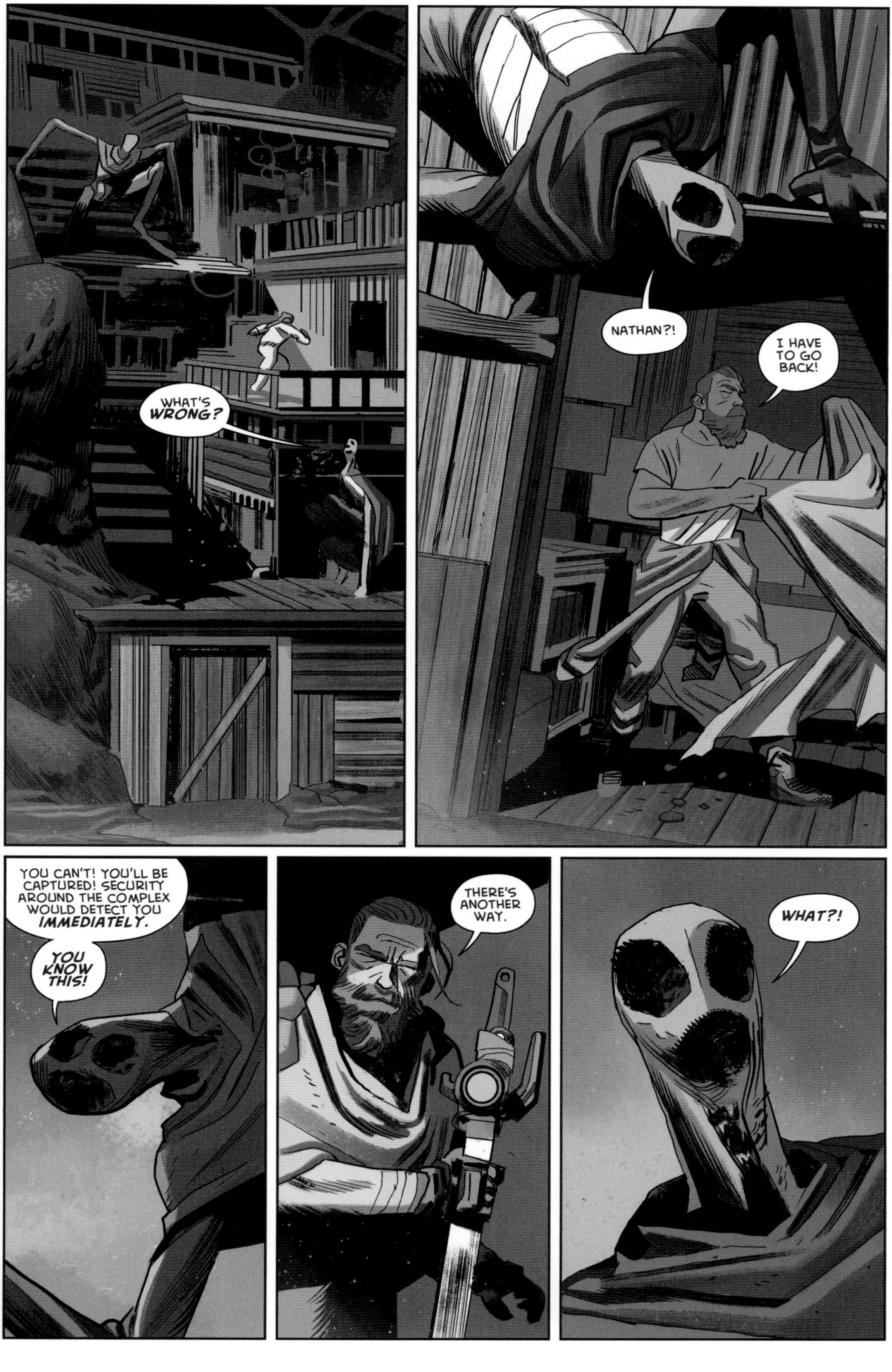
WHAT'S *WRONG?*
NATHAN?!
I HAVE TO GO BACK!
YOU CAN'T! YOU'LL BE CAPTURED! SECURITY AROUND THE COMPLEX WOULD DETECT YOU *IMMEDIATELY.*
YOU KNOW THIS!
THERE'S ANOTHER WAY.
WHAT?!

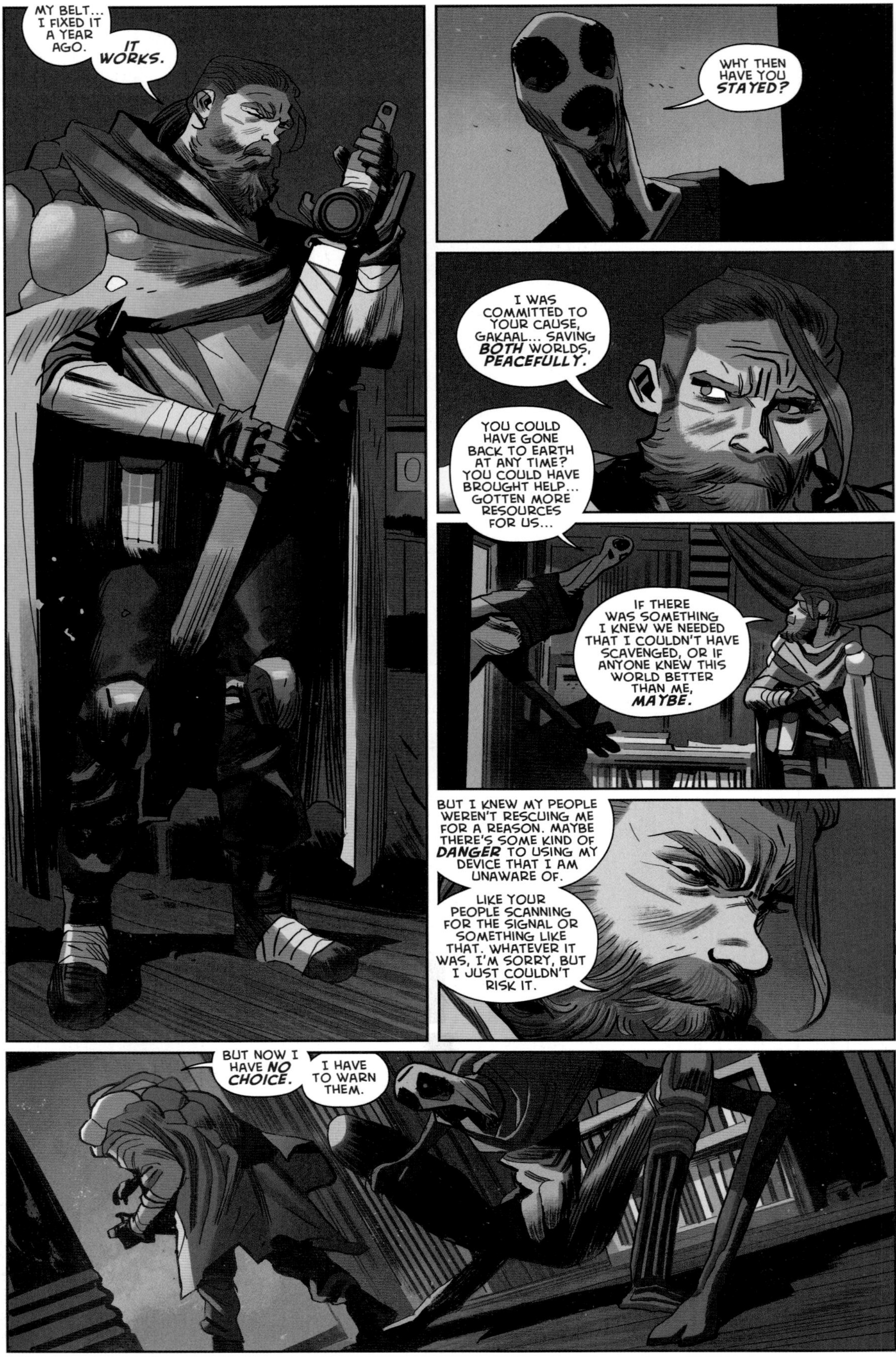
MY BELT... I FIXED IT A YEAR AGO.
IT WORKS.
WHY THEN HAVE YOU STAYED?
I WAS COMMITTED TO YOUR CAUSE, GAKAAL... SAVING BOTH WORLDS, PEACEFULLY.
YOU COULD HAVE GONE BACK TO EARTH AT ANY TIME? YOU COULD HAVE BROUGHT HELP... GOTTEN MORE RESOURCES FOR US...
IF THERE WAS SOMETHING I KNEW WE NEEDED THAT I COULDN'T HAVE SCAVENGED, OR IF ANYONE KNEW THIS WORLD BETTER THAN ME, MAYBE.
BUT I KNEW MY PEOPLE WEREN'T RESCUING ME FOR A REASON. MAYBE THERE'S SOME KIND OF DANGER TO USING MY DEVICE THAT I AM UNAWARE OF.
LIKE YOUR PEOPLE SCANNING FOR THE SIGNAL OR SOMETHING LIKE THAT. WHATEVER IT WAS, I'M SORRY, BUT I JUST COULDN'T RISK IT.
BUT NOW I HAVE NO CHOICE.
I HAVE TO WARN THEM.

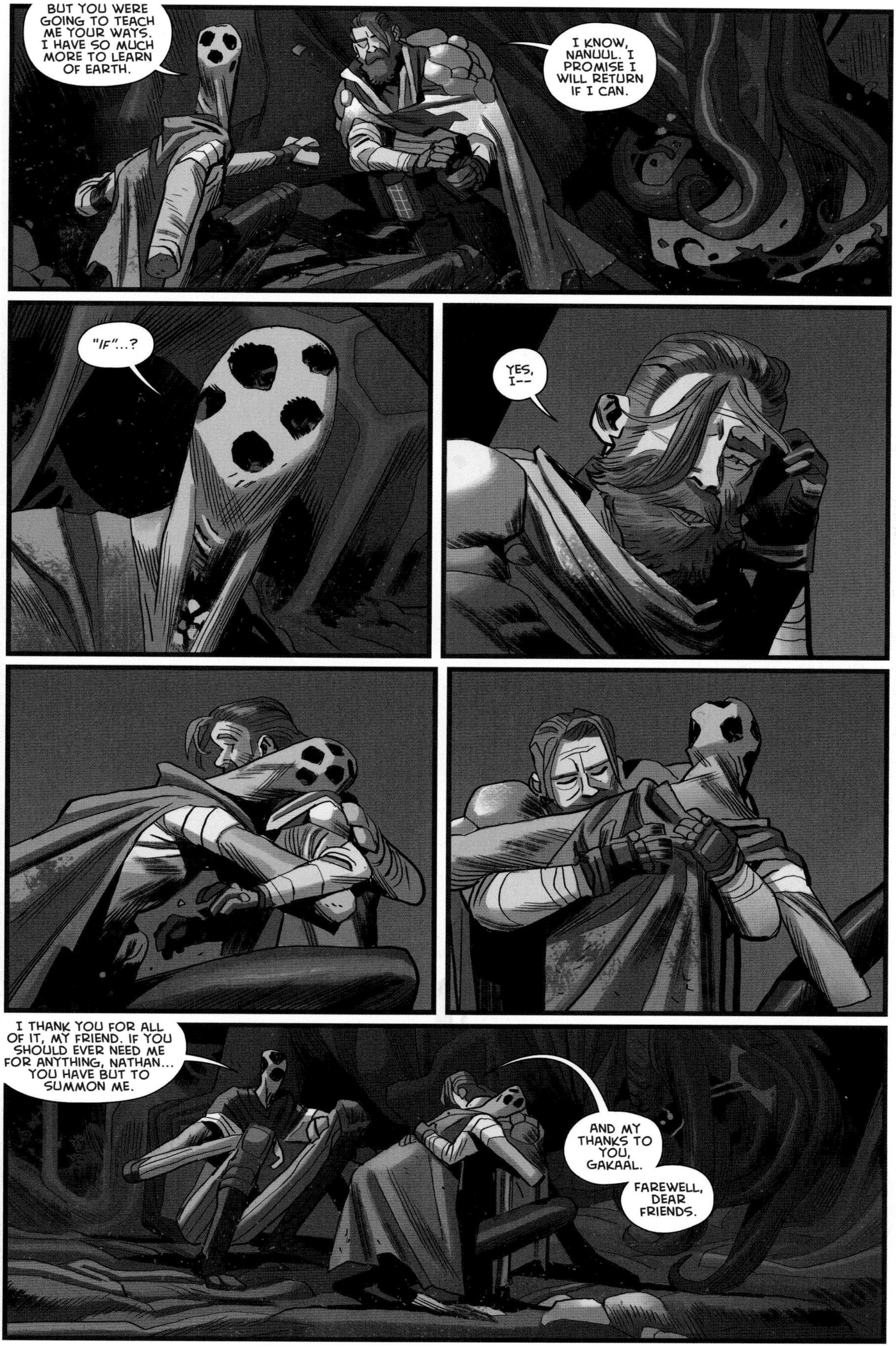
BUT YOU WERE GOING TO TEACH ME YOUR WAYS. I HAVE SO MUCH MORE TO LEARN OF EARTH.
I KNOW, NANUUL. I PROMISE I WILL RETURN IF I CAN.
"IF"...?
YES, I--
I THANK YOU FOR ALL OF IT, MY FRIEND. IF YOU SHOULD EVER NEED ME FOR ANYTHING, NATHAN... YOU HAVE BUT TO SUMMON ME.
AND MY THANKS TO YOU, GAKAAL.
FAREWELL, DEAR FRIENDS.

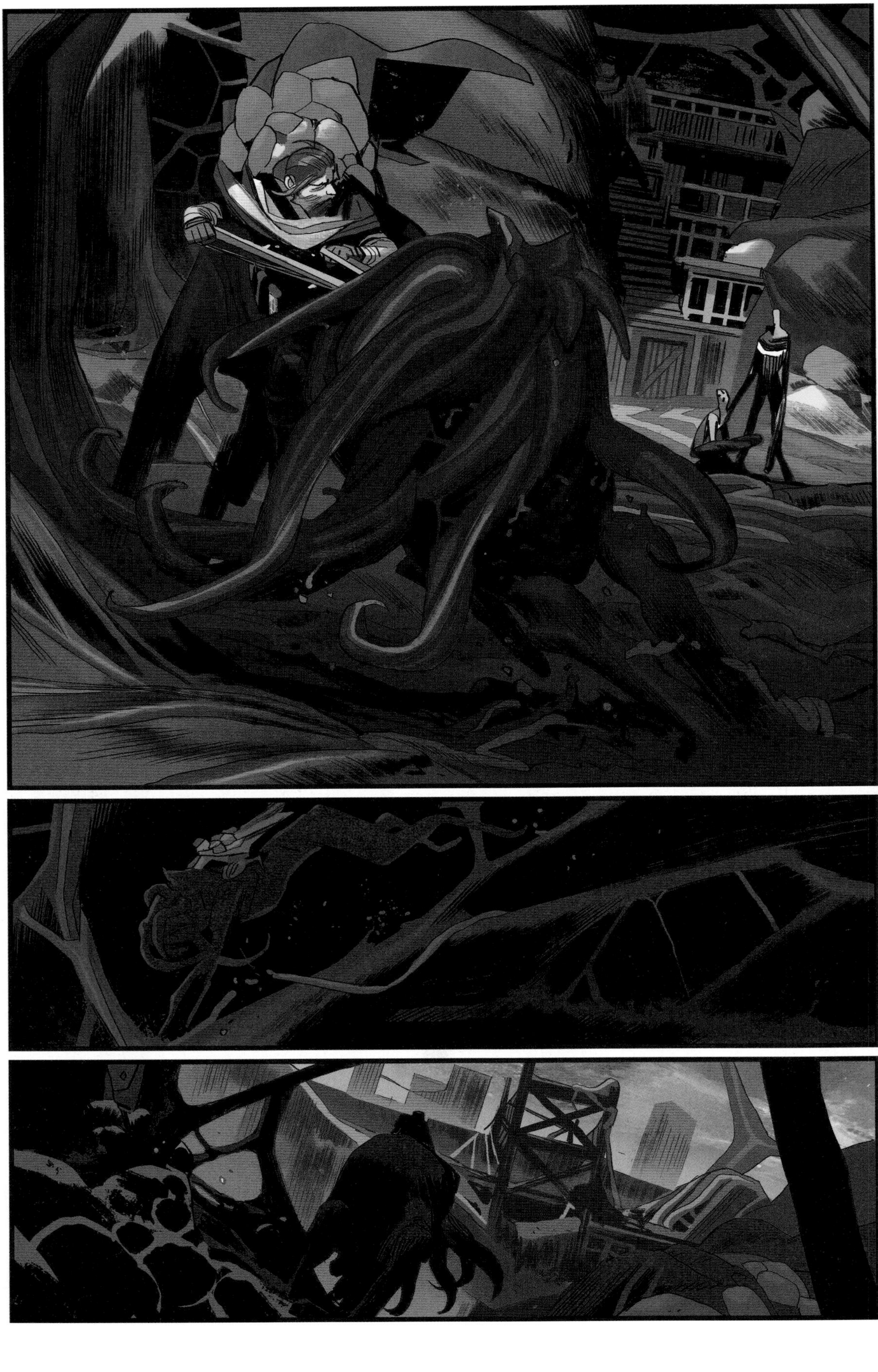

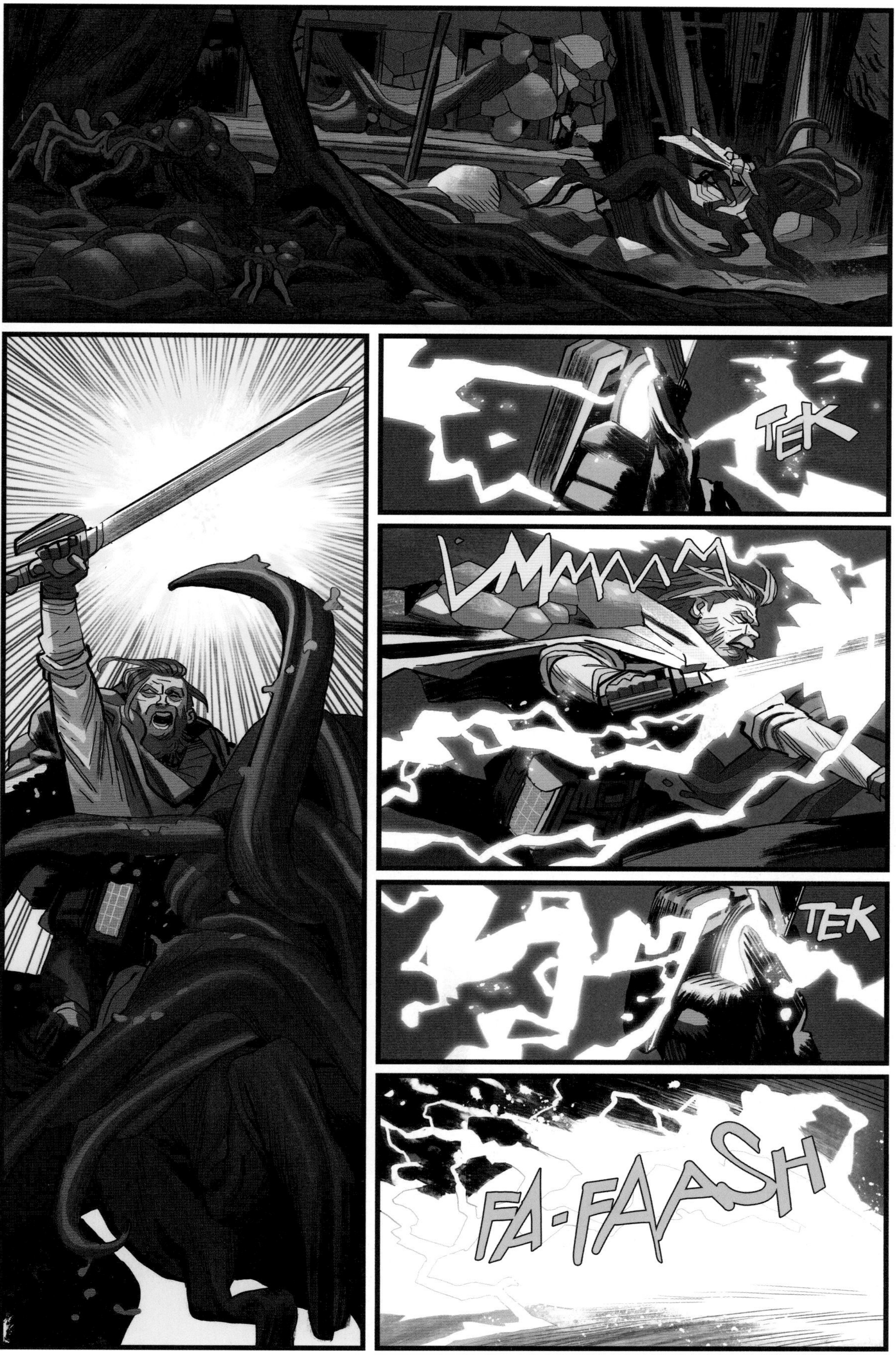
TEK
TEK
FA-FAASH

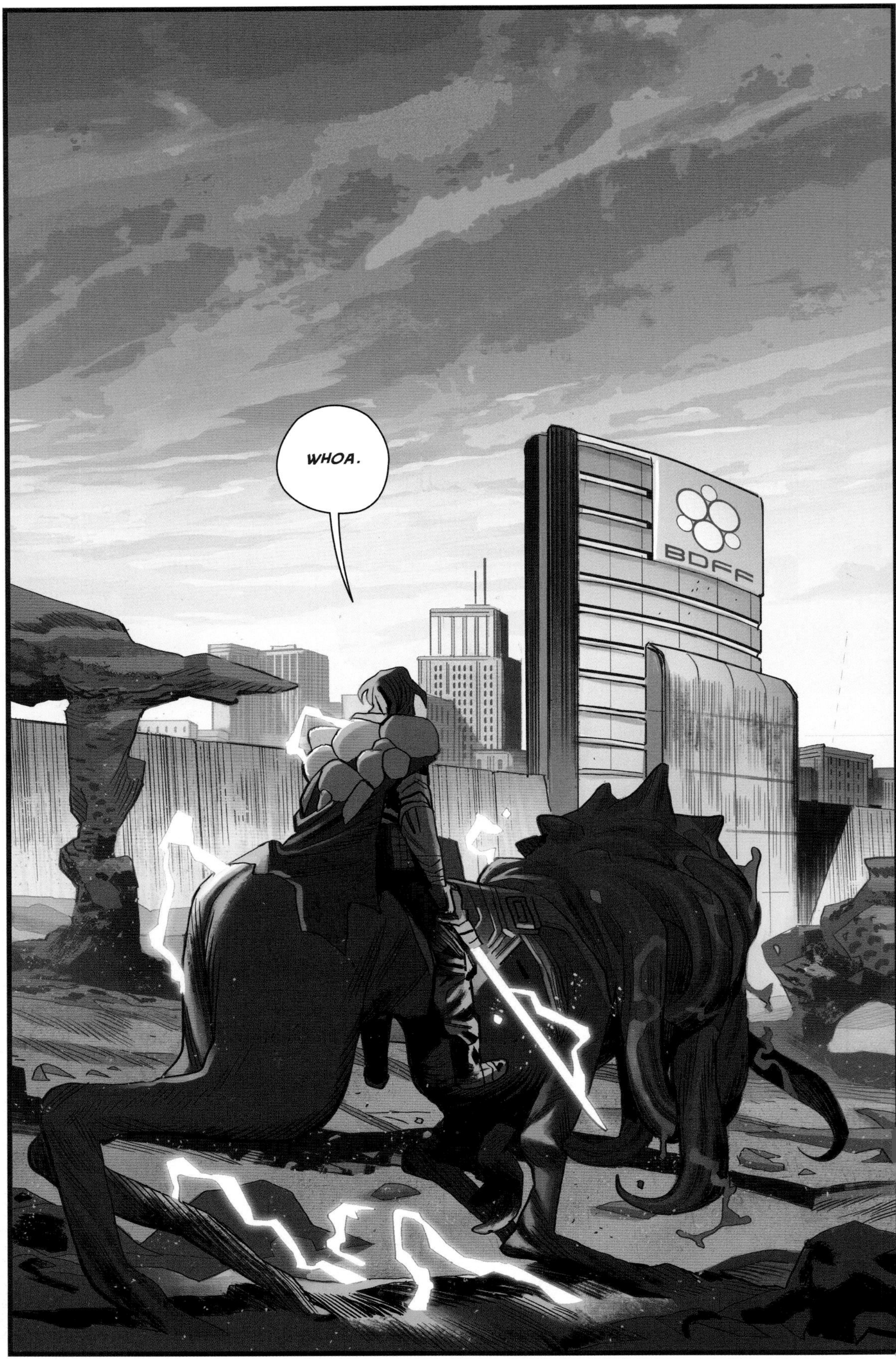
WHOA.
BDFF

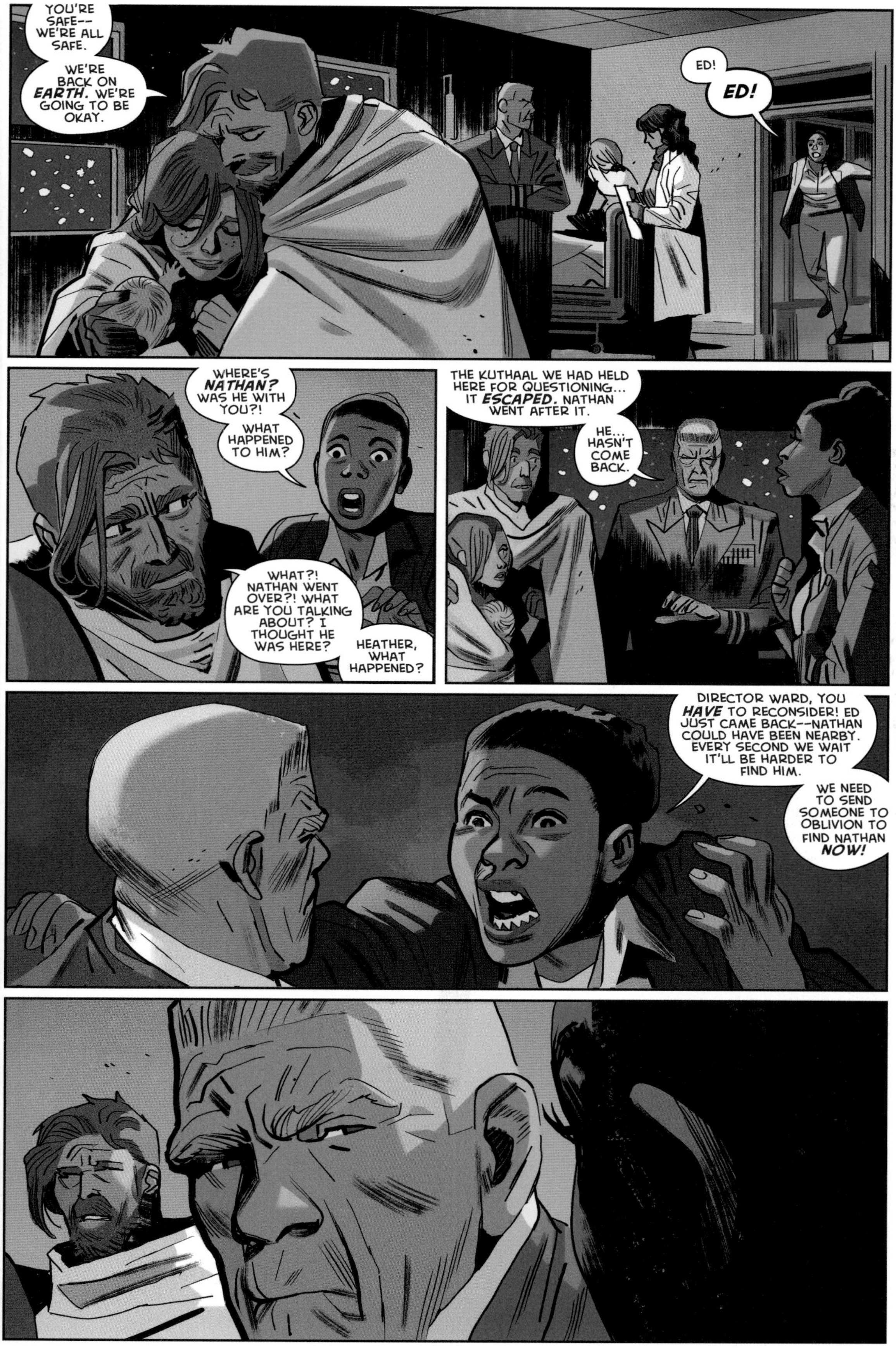
YOU'RE SAFE-- WE'RE ALL SAFE.
WE'RE BACK ON EARTH. WE'RE GOING TO BE OKAY.
ED!
ED!
WHERE'S NATHAN? WAS HE WITH YOU?!
WHAT HAPPENED TO HIM?
WHAT?! NATHAN WENT OVER?! WHAT ARE YOU TALKING ABOUT? I THOUGHT HE WAS HERE?
HEATHER, WHAT HAPPENED?
THE KUTHAAL WE HAD HELD HERE FOR QUESTIONING... IT ESCAPED. NATHAN WENT AFTER IT.
HE... HASN'T COME BACK.
DIRECTOR WARD, YOU HAVE TO RECONSIDER! ED JUST CAME BACK--NATHAN COULD HAVE BEEN NEARBY. EVERY SECOND WE WAIT IT'LL BE HARDER TO FIND HIM.
WE NEED TO SEND SOMEONE TO OBLIVION TO FIND NATHAN NOW!

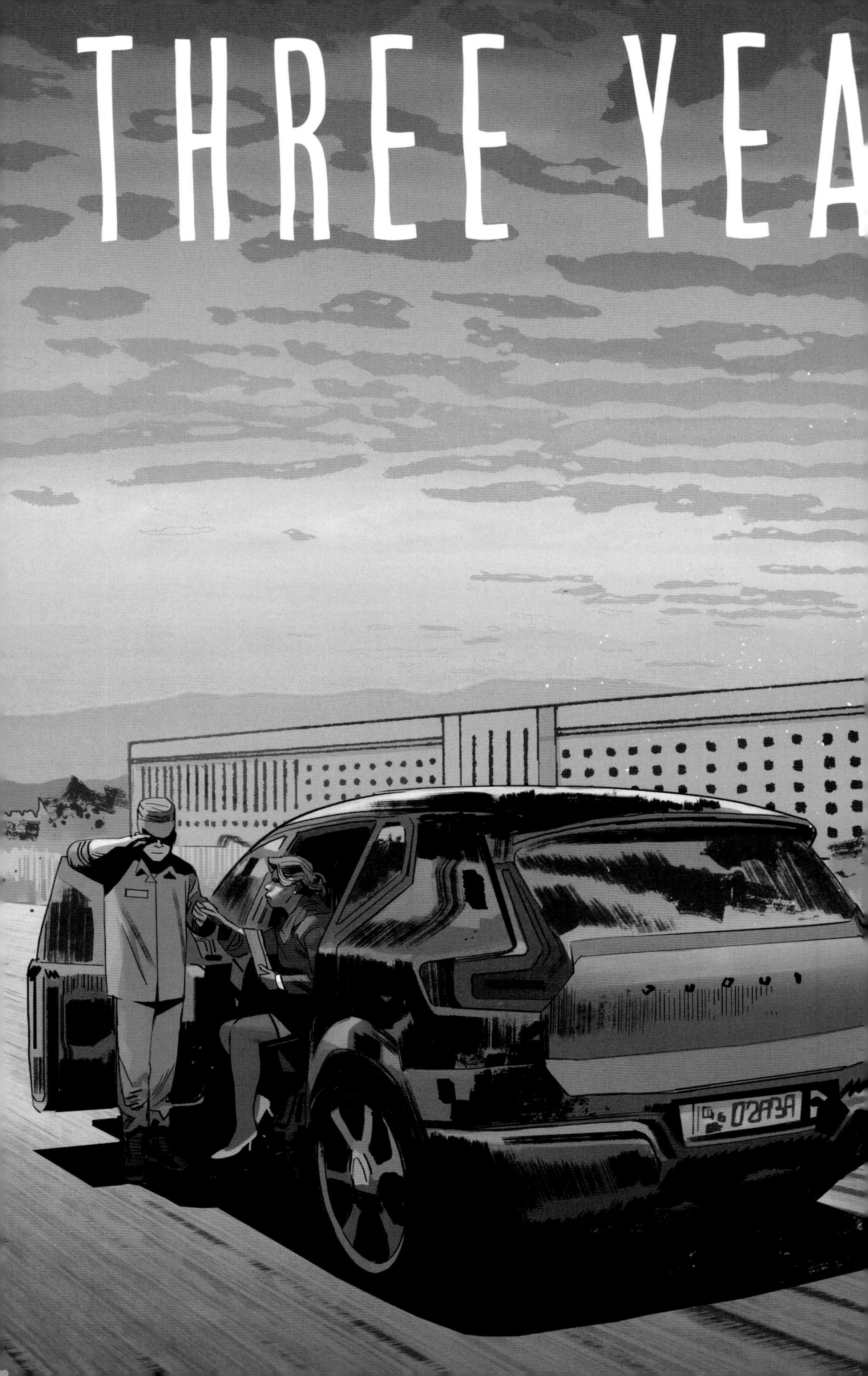
THREE YEA

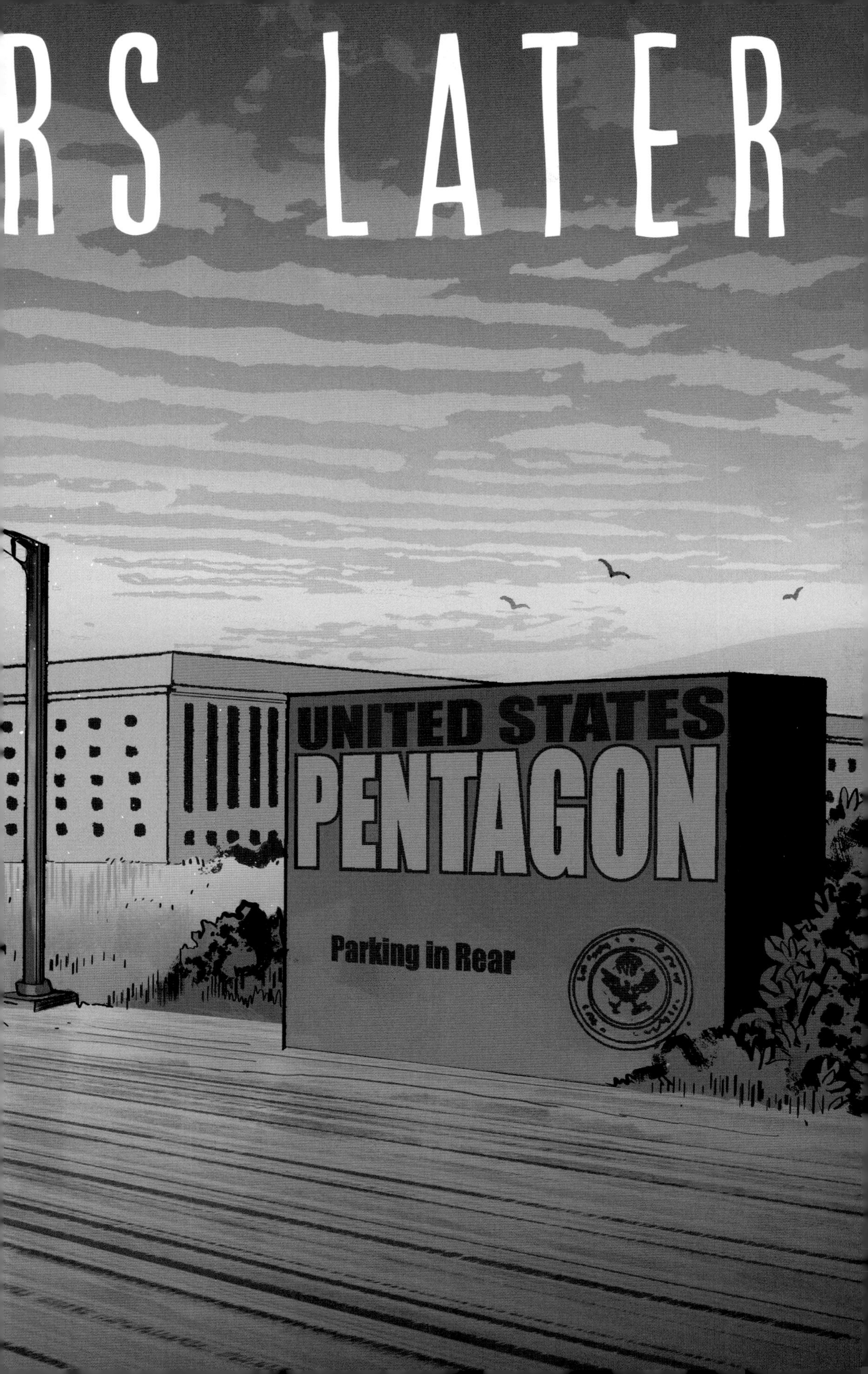
RS LATER
UNITED STATES
PENTAGON
Parking in Rear

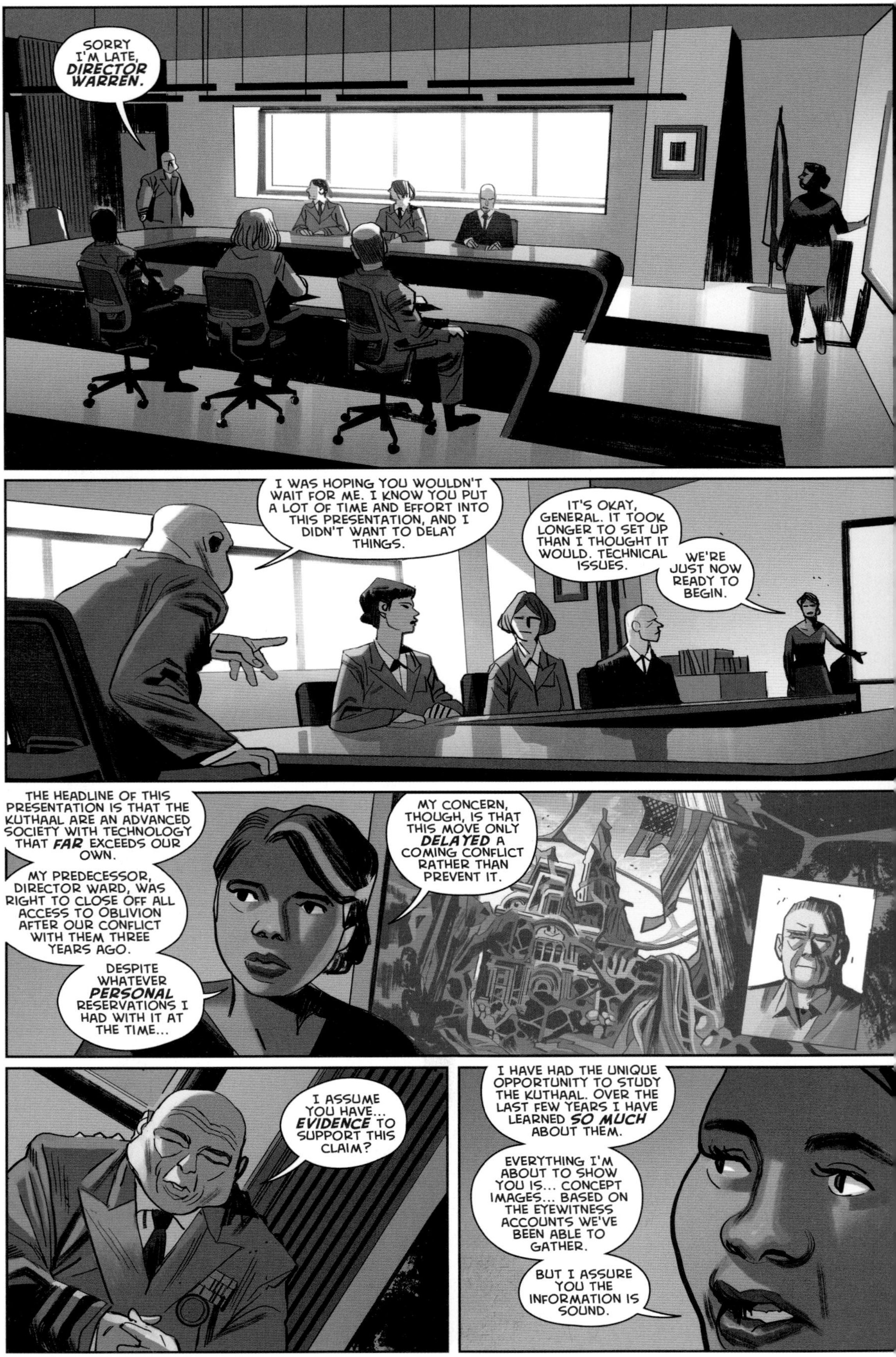
SORRY I'M LATE, DIRECTOR WARREN.
I WAS HOPING YOU WOULDN'T WAIT FOR ME. I KNOW YOU PUT A LOT OF TIME AND EFFORT INTO THIS PRESENTATION, AND I DIDN'T WANT TO DELAY THINGS.
IT'S OKAY, GENERAL. IT TOOK LONGER TO SET UP THAN I THOUGHT IT WOULD. TECHNICAL ISSUES.
WE'RE JUST NOW READY TO BEGIN.
THE HEADLINE OF THIS PRESENTATION IS THAT THE KUTHAAL ARE AN ADVANCED SOCIETY WITH TECHNOLOGY THAT FAR EXCEEDS OUR OWN.
MY PREDECESSOR, DIRECTOR WARD, WAS RIGHT TO CLOSE OFF ALL ACCESS TO OBLIVION AFTER OUR CONFLICT WITH THEM THREE YEARS AGO.
DESPITE WHATEVER PERSONAL RESERVATIONS I HAD WITH IT AT THE TIME...
MY CONCERN, THOUGH, IS THAT THIS MOVE ONLY DELAYED A COMING CONFLICT RATHER THAN PREVENT IT.
I ASSUME YOU HAVE... EVIDENCE TO SUPPORT THIS CLAIM?
I HAVE HAD THE UNIQUE OPPORTUNITY TO STUDY THE KUTHAAL. OVER THE LAST FEW YEARS I HAVE LEARNED SO MUCH ABOUT THEM.
EVERYTHING I'M ABOUT TO SHOW YOU IS... CONCEPT IMAGES... BASED ON THE EYEWITNESS ACCOUNTS WE'VE BEEN ABLE TO GATHER.
BUT I ASSURE YOU THE INFORMATION IS SOUND.

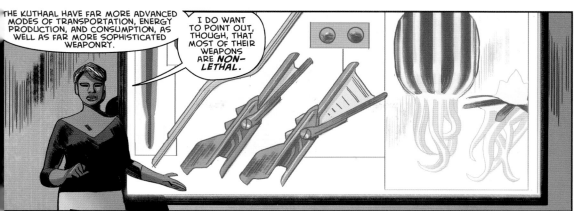

THE KUTHAAL HAVE FAR MORE ADVANCED MODES OF TRANSPORTATION, ENERGY PRODUCTION, AND CONSUMPTION, AS WELL AS FAR MORE SOPHISTICATED WEAPONRY.

I DO WANT TO POINT OUT, THOUGH, THAT MOST OF THEIR WEAPONS ARE *NON-LETHAL.*

WELL, THAT'S GOOD NEWS.

NEUTRAL AT BEST, I'M SORRY TO SAY.

AND WHY DO YOU SAY THAT?

IT DOESN'T MATTER IF THEIR WEAPONS DON'T KILL US IF THEY ARE EFFECTIVE ENOUGH TO INCAPACITATE US *IMMEDIATELY* IN WAYS WE HAVE NO DEFENSE FOR.

I CAN GLEAN *NO ADVANTAGE* FROM THE INFORMATION I'VE GATHERED.

A HEAD-TO-HEAD CONFLICT WOULD *NOT* GO OUR WAY.

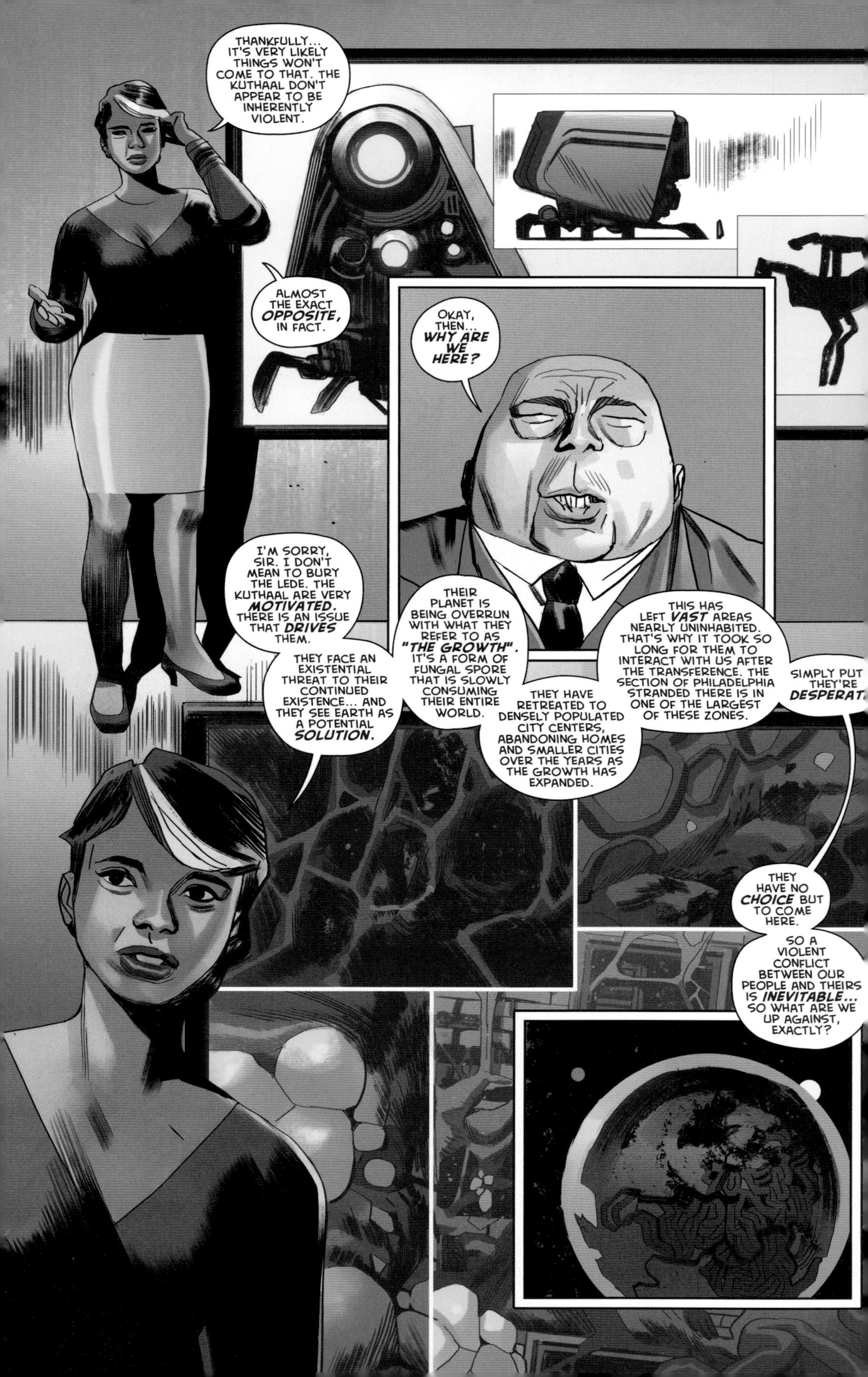
THANKFULLY... IT'S VERY LIKELY THINGS WON'T COME TO THAT. THE KUTHAAL DON'T APPEAR TO BE INHERENTLY VIOLENT.
ALMOST THE EXACT OPPOSITE, IN FACT.
OKAY, THEN... WHY ARE WE HERE?
I'M SORRY, SIR. I DON'T MEAN TO BURY THE LEDE. THE KUTHAAL ARE VERY MOTIVATED. THERE IS AN ISSUE THAT DRIVES THEM.
THEY FACE AN EXISTENTIAL THREAT TO THEIR CONTINUED EXISTENCE... AND THEY SEE EARTH AS A POTENTIAL SOLUTION.
THEIR PLANET IS BEING OVERRUN WITH WHAT THEY REFER TO AS "THE GROWTH". IT'S A FORM OF FUNGAL SPORE THAT IS SLOWLY CONSUMING THEIR ENTIRE WORLD.
THEY HAVE RETREATED TO DENSELY POPULATED CITY CENTERS, ABANDONING HOMES AND SMALLER CITIES OVER THE YEARS AS THE GROWTH HAS EXPANDED.
THIS HAS LEFT VAST AREAS NEARLY UNINHABITED. THAT'S WHY IT TOOK SO LONG FOR THEM TO INTERACT WITH US AFTER THE TRANSFERENCE. THE SECTION OF PHILADELPHIA STRANDED THERE IS IN ONE OF THE LARGEST OF THESE ZONES.
SIMPLY PUT THEY'RE DESPERAT
THEY HAVE NO CHOICE BUT TO COME HERE.
SO A VIOLENT CONFLICT BETWEEN OUR PEOPLE AND THEIRS IS INEVITABLE... SO WHAT ARE WE UP AGAINST, EXACTLY?

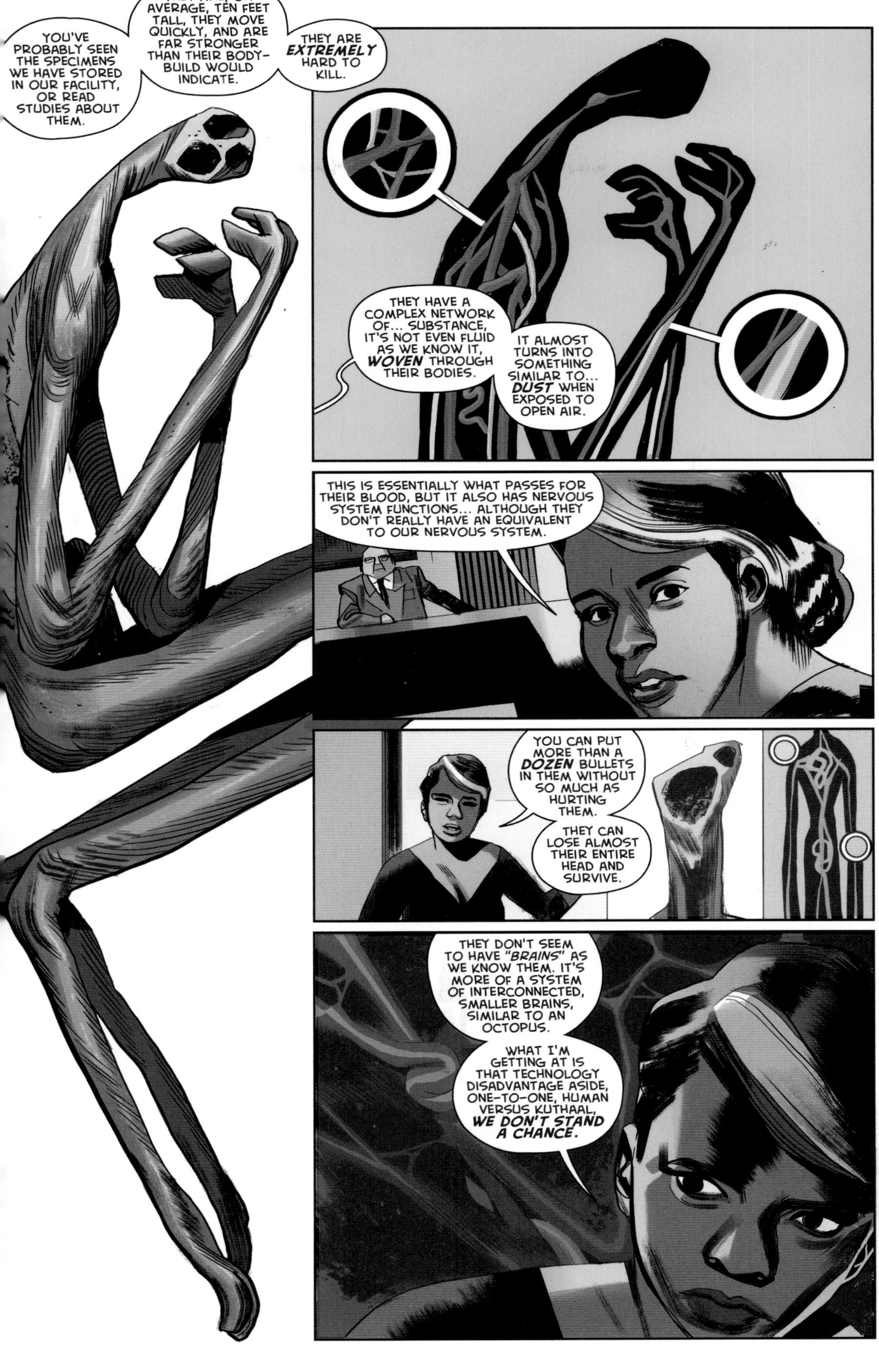
YOU'VE PROBABLY SEEN THE SPECIMENS WE HAVE STORED IN OUR FACILITY, OR READ STUDIES ABOUT THEM.
THEY ARE, ON AVERAGE, TEN FEET TALL, THEY MOVE QUICKLY, AND ARE FAR STRONGER THAN THEIR BODY-BUILD WOULD INDICATE.
THEY ARE *EXTREMELY* HARD TO KILL.
THEY HAVE A COMPLEX NETWORK OF... SUBSTANCE, IT'S NOT EVEN FLUID AS WE KNOW IT, *WOVEN* THROUGH THEIR BODIES.
IT ALMOST TURNS INTO SOMETHING SIMILAR TO... *DUST* WHEN EXPOSED TO OPEN AIR.
THIS IS ESSENTIALLY WHAT PASSES FOR THEIR BLOOD, BUT IT ALSO HAS NERVOUS SYSTEM FUNCTIONS... ALTHOUGH THEY DON'T REALLY HAVE AN EQUIVALENT TO OUR NERVOUS SYSTEM.
YOU CAN PUT MORE THAN A *DOZEN* BULLETS IN THEM WITHOUT SO MUCH AS HURTING THEM.
THEY CAN LOSE ALMOST THEIR ENTIRE HEAD AND SURVIVE.
THEY DON'T SEEM TO HAVE "*BRAINS*" AS WE KNOW THEM. IT'S MORE OF A SYSTEM OF INTERCONNECTED, SMALLER BRAINS, SIMILAR TO AN OCTOPUS.
WHAT I'M GETTING AT IS THAT TECHNOLOGY DISADVANTAGE ASIDE, ONE-TO-ONE, HUMAN VERSUS KUTHAAL, ***WE DON'T STAND A CHANCE.***

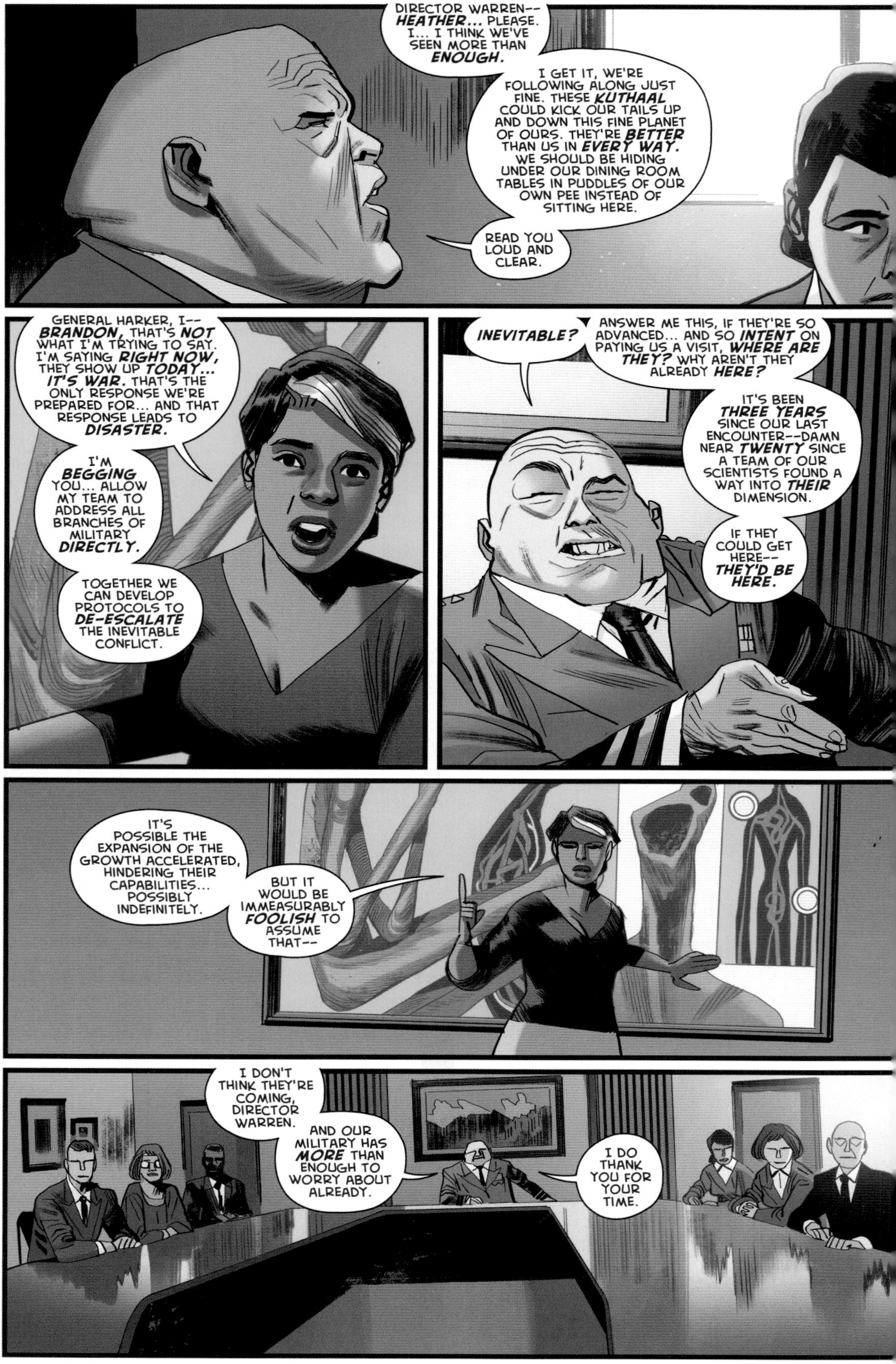
DIRECTOR WARREN-- HEATHER... PLEASE. I... I THINK WE'VE SEEN MORE THAN ENOUGH.
I GET IT, WE'RE FOLLOWING ALONG JUST FINE. THESE KUTHAAL COULD KICK OUR TAILS UP AND DOWN THIS FINE PLANET OF OURS. THEY'RE BETTER THAN US IN EVERY WAY. WE SHOULD BE HIDING UNDER OUR DINING ROOM TABLES IN PUDDLES OF OUR OWN PEE INSTEAD OF SITTING HERE.
READ YOU LOUD AND CLEAR.
GENERAL HARKER, I-- BRANDON, THAT'S NOT WHAT I'M TRYING TO SAY. I'M SAYING RIGHT NOW, THEY SHOW UP TODAY... IT'S WAR. THAT'S THE ONLY RESPONSE WE'RE PREPARED FOR... AND THAT RESPONSE LEADS TO DISASTER.
I'M BEGGING YOU... ALLOW MY TEAM TO ADDRESS ALL BRANCHES OF MILITARY DIRECTLY.
TOGETHER WE CAN DEVELOP PROTOCOLS TO DE-ESCALATE THE INEVITABLE CONFLICT.
INEVITABLE?
ANSWER ME THIS, IF THEY'RE SO ADVANCED... AND SO INTENT ON PAYING US A VISIT, WHERE ARE THEY? WHY AREN'T THEY ALREADY HERE?
IT'S BEEN THREE YEARS SINCE OUR LAST ENCOUNTER--DAMN NEAR TWENTY SINCE A TEAM OF OUR SCIENTISTS FOUND A WAY INTO THEIR DIMENSION.
IF THEY COULD GET HERE-- THEY'D BE HERE.
IT'S POSSIBLE THE EXPANSION OF THE GROWTH ACCELERATED, HINDERING THEIR CAPABILITIES... POSSIBLY INDEFINITELY.
BUT IT WOULD BE IMMEASURABLY FOOLISH TO ASSUME THAT--
I DON'T THINK THEY'RE COMING, DIRECTOR WARREN.
AND OUR MILITARY HAS MORE THAN ENOUGH TO WORRY ABOUT ALREADY.
I DO THANK YOU FOR YOUR TIME.

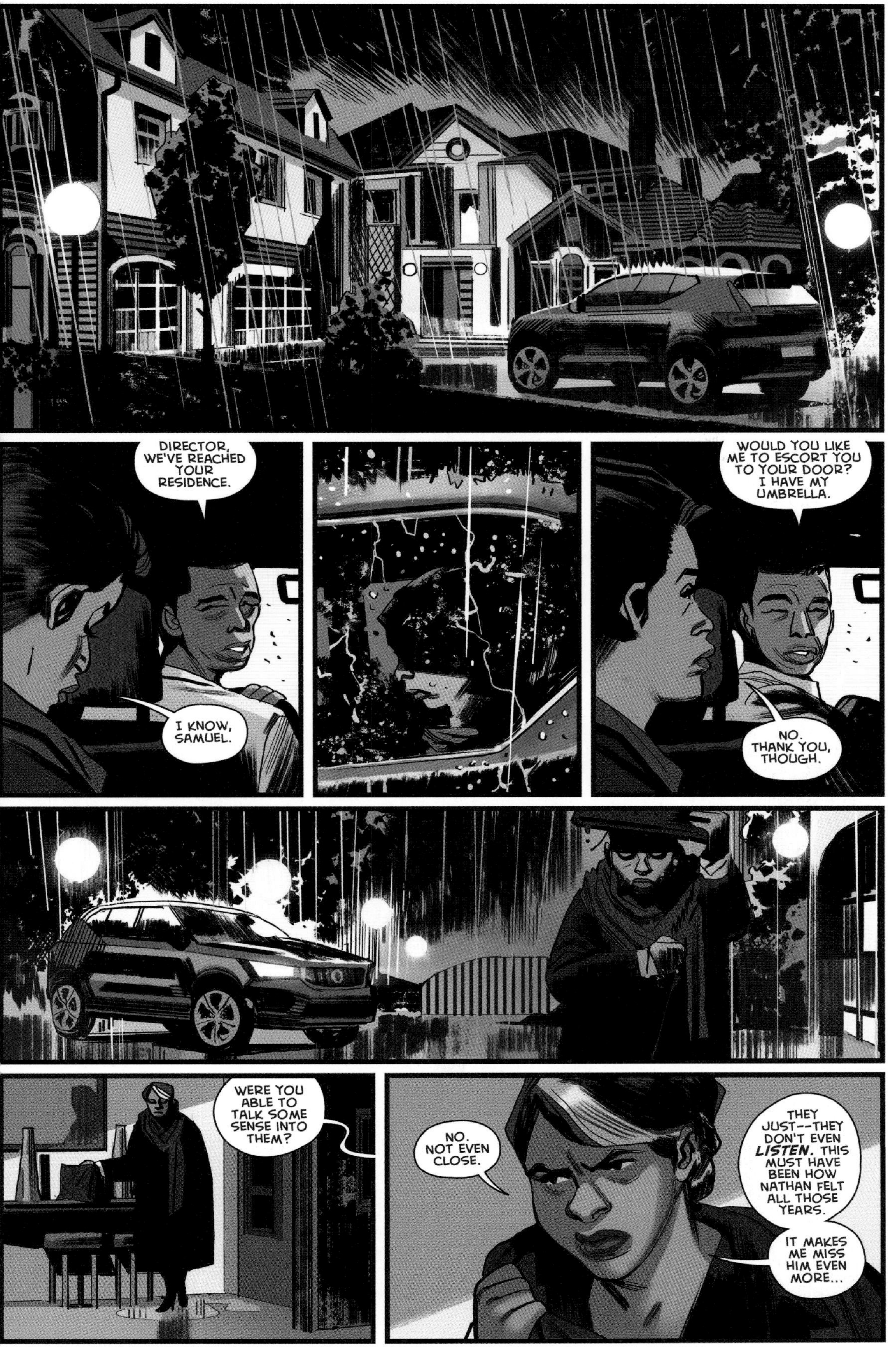
DIRECTOR, WE'VE REACHED YOUR RESIDENCE.
I KNOW, SAMUEL.
WOULD YOU LIKE ME TO ESCORT YOU TO YOUR DOOR? I HAVE MY UMBRELLA.
NO. THANK YOU, THOUGH.
WERE YOU ABLE TO TALK SOME SENSE INTO THEM?
NO. NOT EVEN CLOSE.
THEY JUST--THEY DON'T EVEN *LISTEN.* THIS MUST HAVE BEEN HOW NATHAN FELT ALL THOSE YEARS.
IT MAKES ME MISS HIM EVEN MORE...

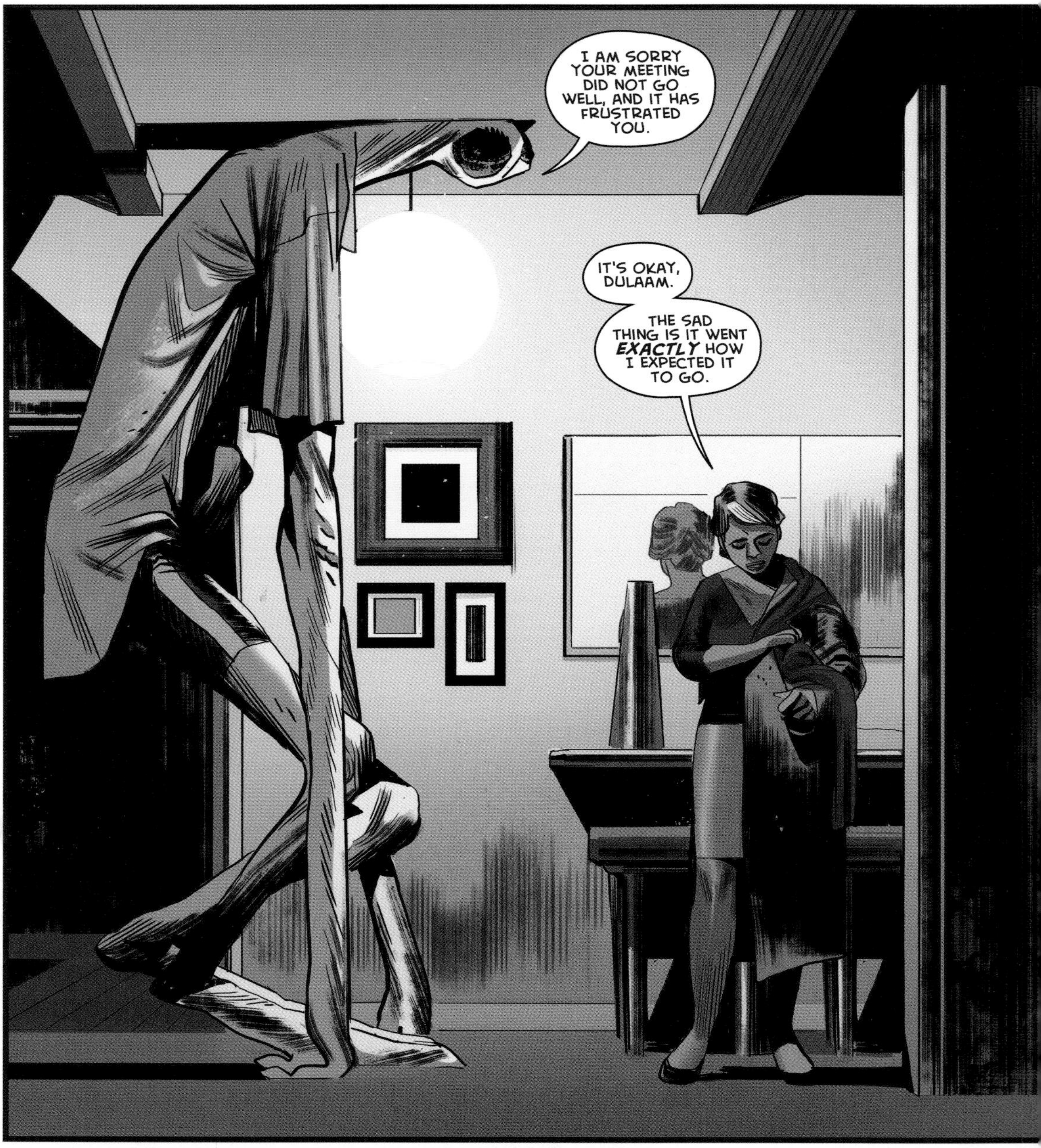
I AM SORRY YOUR MEETING DID NOT GO WELL, AND IT HAS FRUSTRATED YOU.
IT'S OKAY, DULAAM.
THE SAD THING IS IT WENT EXACTLY HOW I EXPECTED IT TO GO.

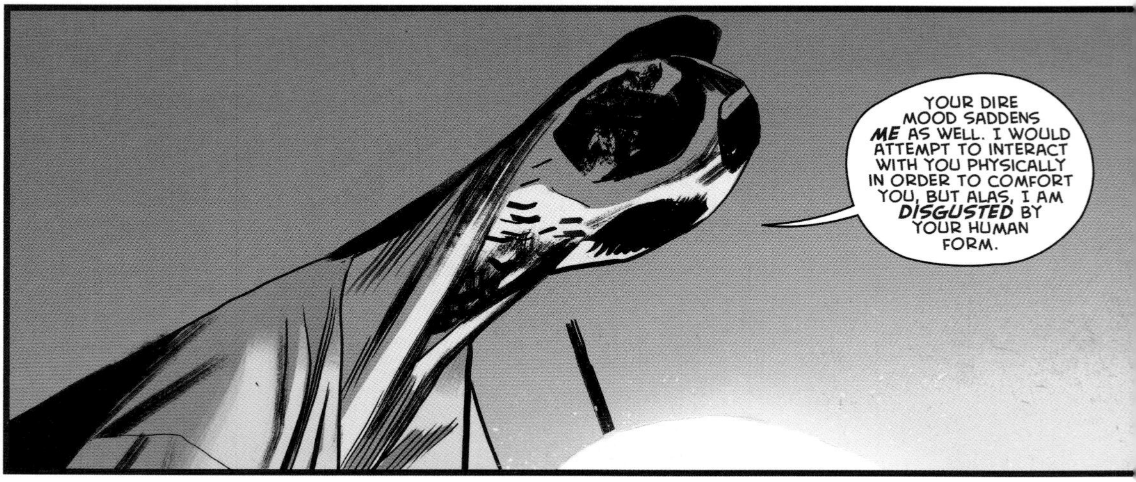
YOUR DIRE MOOD SADDENS ME AS WELL. I WOULD ATTEMPT TO INTERACT WITH YOU PHYSICALLY IN ORDER TO COMFORT YOU, BUT ALAS, I AM DISGUSTED BY YOUR HUMAN FORM.

DID MY ATTEMPT AT EARTH HUMOR AMUSE YOU?

A LITTLE BIT. *YEAH.*

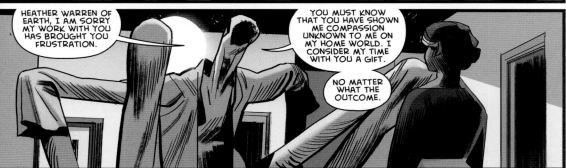

HEATHER WARREN OF EARTH, I AM SORRY MY WORK WITH YOU HAS BROUGHT YOU FRUSTRATION.

YOU MUST KNOW THAT YOU HAVE SHOWN ME COMPASSION UNKNOWN TO ME ON MY HOME WORLD. I CONSIDER MY TIME WITH YOU A GIFT.

NO MATTER WHAT THE OUTCOME.

AND YOU, DULAAM, HAVE TAUGHT ME MORE THAN I COULD HAVE LEARNED IN A LIFETIME ON MY OWN.

THIS IS A SETBACK, NOT THE END. OUR WORK WILL SAVE *BOTH* OUR WORLDS.

YOU SPEAK ALMOST AS WELL AS ONE OF MY KIND NOW. *VERY* IMPRESSIVE.

I WOULD VERY MUCH LIKE TO WATCH THE HOUSEWIVES IN THE TELEVISION NOW.

SAME.

I'LL MAKE POPCORN.

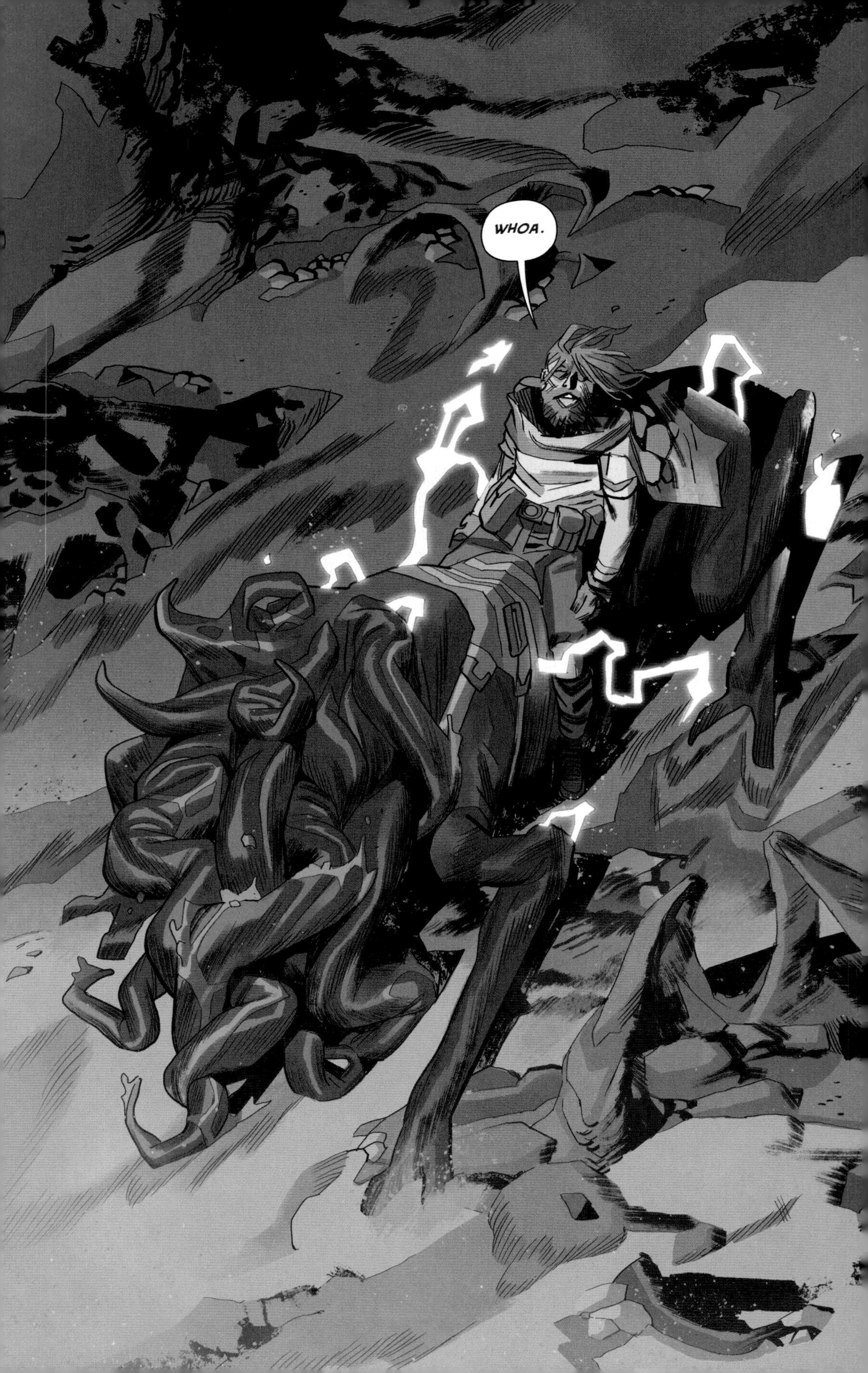
WHOA.

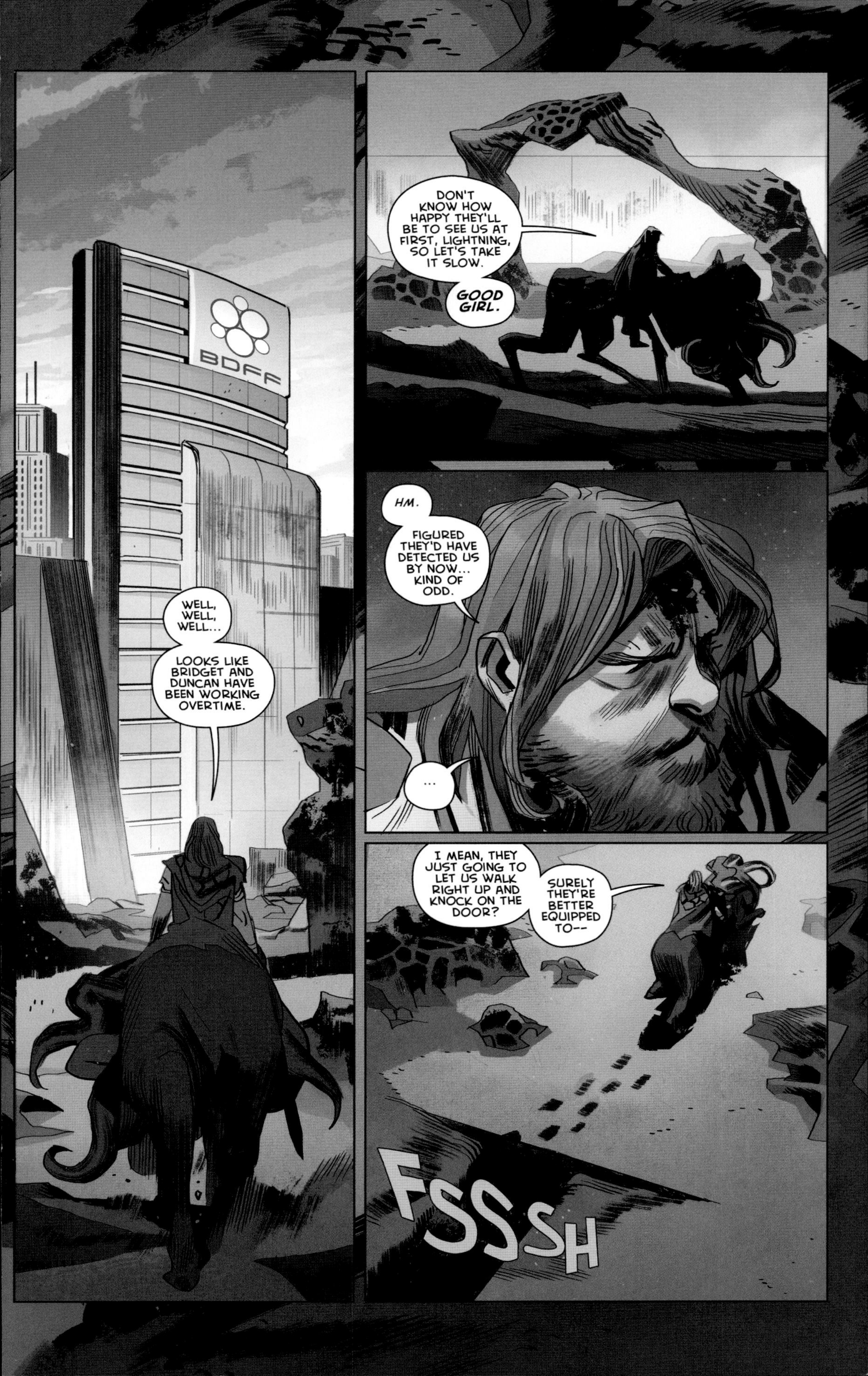
WELL, WELL, WELL...
LOOKS LIKE BRIDGET AND DUNCAN HAVE BEEN WORKING OVERTIME.
BDFF
DON'T KNOW HOW HAPPY THEY'LL BE TO SEE US AT FIRST, LIGHTNING, SO LET'S TAKE IT SLOW.
GOOD GIRL.
HM.
FIGURED THEY'D HAVE DETECTED US BY NOW... KIND OF ODD.
...
I MEAN, THEY JUST GOING TO LET US WALK RIGHT UP AND KNOCK ON THE DOOR?
SURELY THEY'RE BETTER EQUIPPED TO--
FSSSH

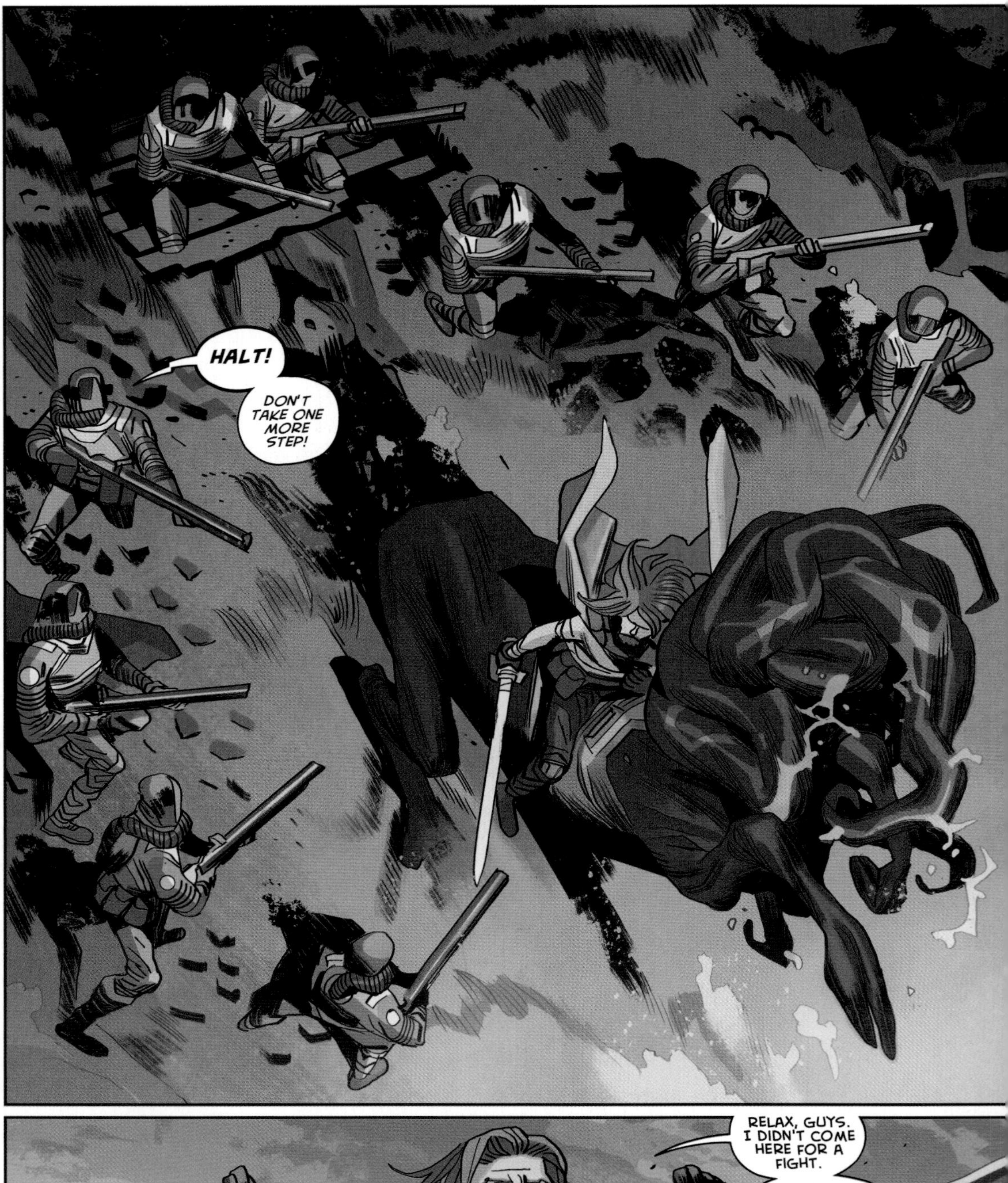
HALT!
DON'T TAKE ONE MORE STEP!

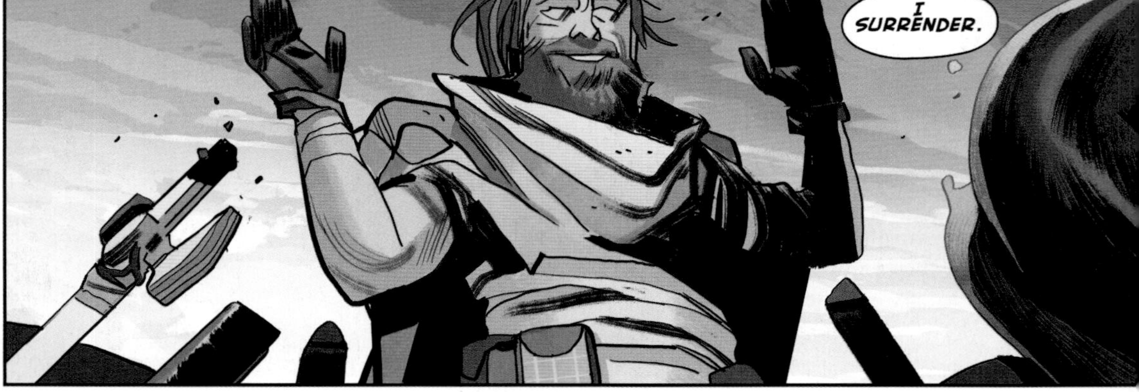
RELAX, GUYS. I DIDN'T COME HERE FOR A FIGHT.
I SURRENDER.

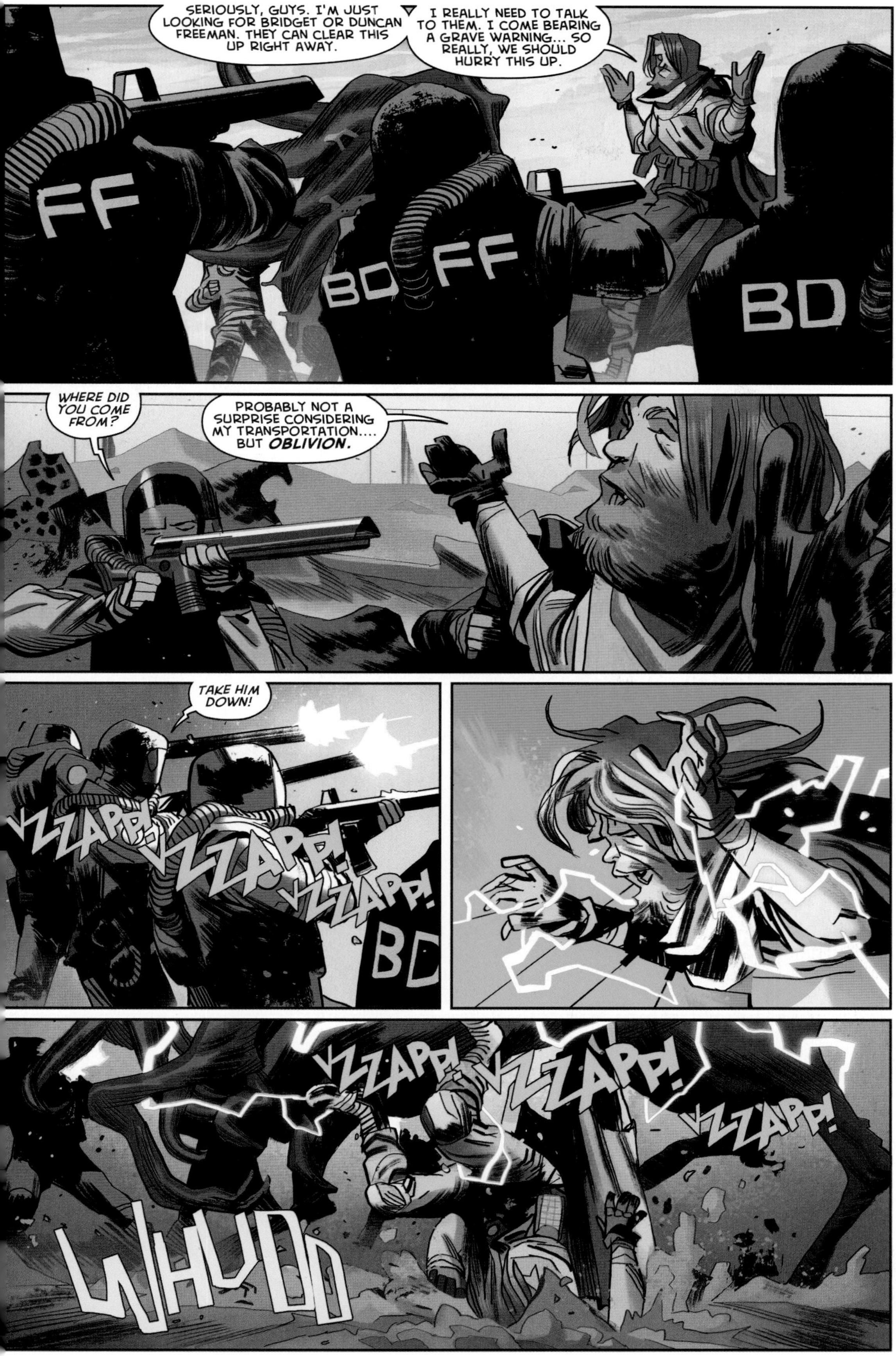
SERIOUSLY, GUYS. I'M JUST LOOKING FOR BRIDGET OR DUNCAN FREEMAN. THEY CAN CLEAR THIS UP RIGHT AWAY.
I REALLY NEED TO TALK TO THEM. I COME BEARING A GRAVE WARNING... SO REALLY, WE SHOULD HURRY THIS UP.
FF
BD
FF
BD
WHERE DID YOU COME FROM?
PROBABLY NOT A SURPRISE CONSIDERING MY TRANSPORTATION.... BUT *OBLIVION.*
TAKE HIM DOWN!
VZZAPP!
VZZAPP!
VZZAPP!
BD
VZZAPP!
VZZAPP!
VZZAPP!
WHUDD

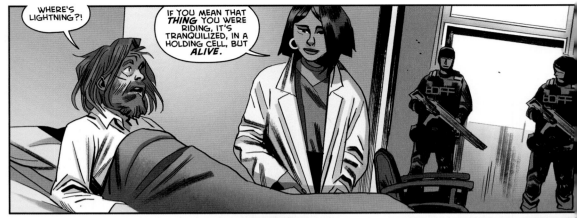

WHERE'S LIGHTNING?!

IF YOU MEAN THAT **THING** YOU WERE RIDING, IT'S TRANQUILIZED, IN A HOLDING CELL, BUT **ALIVE.**

BRIDGET.

YOU'VE CERTAINLY LOOKED BETTER, NATHAN COLE.

I'M SO HAPPY TO SEE YOU ALIVE.

LIGHTNING, HER SPECIES, THEY'RE SMARTER THAN DOLPHINS, ALMOST TO THE LEVEL OF A HUMAN CHILD.

SHE CAN BE REASONED WITH. PLEASE, DON'T HURT HER.

DON'T WORRY... "SHE'S" FINE. I'M MORE WORRIED ABOUT **YOU**. IT LOOKS LIKE DURING YOUR TIME IN OBLIVION YOU'VE GONE NATIVE.

I NEED TO DETERMINE **HOW** NATIVE.

JESUS CHRIST, BRIDGET. I'M NOT WORKING FOR THE **KUTHAAL** IF THAT'S WHAT YOU MEAN!

I'VE COME HERE TO **WARN** YOU! THEY HAVE MY TECHNOLOGY, THEY'RE COMING HERE!

IF THEY HAVE YOUR TECHNOLOGY... WHO **GAVE** IT TO THEM?

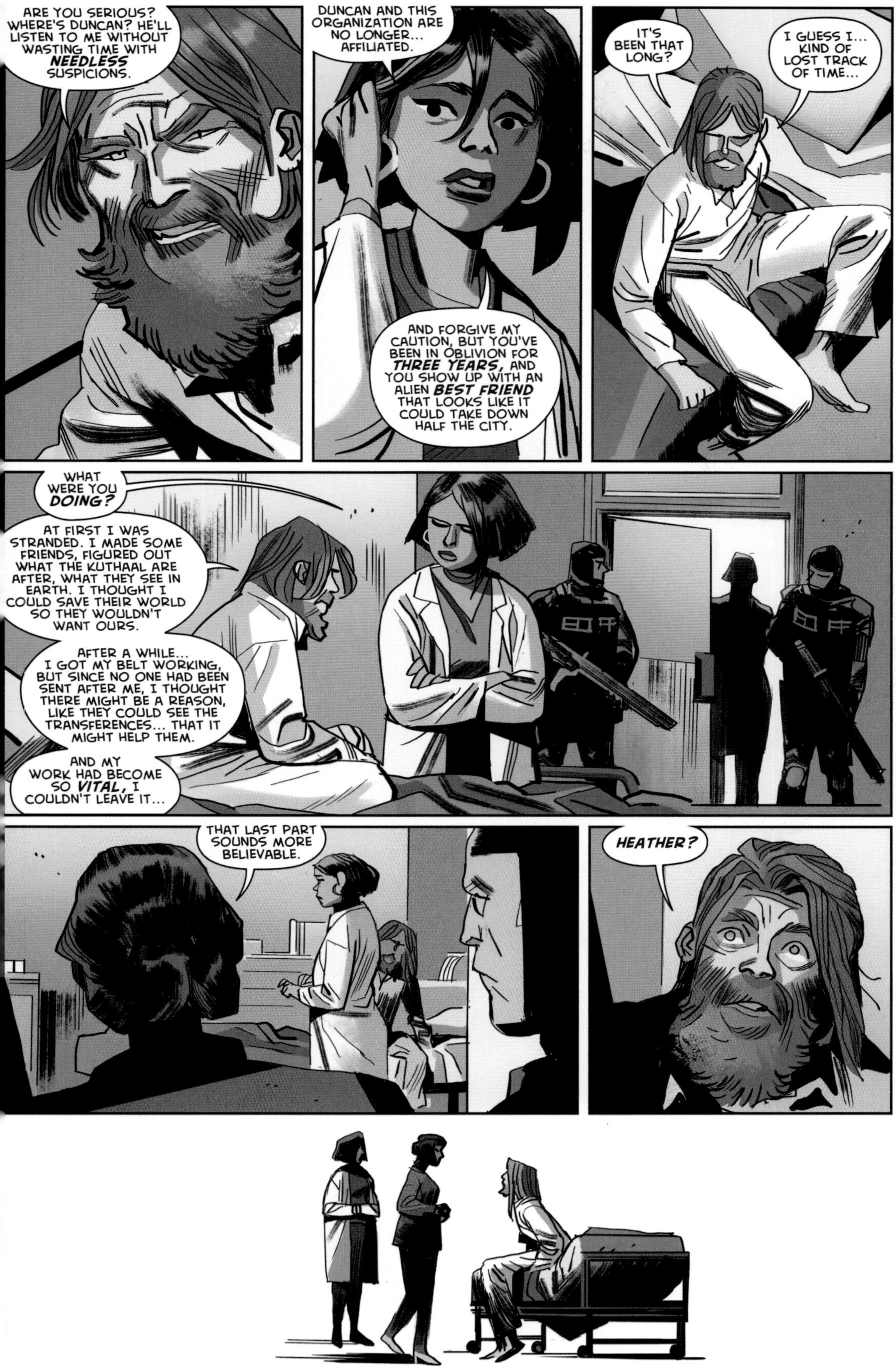
ARE YOU SERIOUS? WHERE'S DUNCAN? HE'LL LISTEN TO ME WITHOUT WASTING TIME WITH NEEDLESS SUSPICIONS.
DUNCAN AND THIS ORGANIZATION ARE NO LONGER... AFFILIATED.
AND FORGIVE MY CAUTION, BUT YOU'VE BEEN IN OBLIVION FOR THREE YEARS, AND YOU SHOW UP WITH AN ALIEN BEST FRIEND THAT LOOKS LIKE IT COULD TAKE DOWN HALF THE CITY.
IT'S BEEN THAT LONG?
I GUESS I... KIND OF LOST TRACK OF TIME...
WHAT WERE YOU DOING?
AT FIRST I WAS STRANDED. I MADE SOME FRIENDS, FIGURED OUT WHAT THE KUTHAAL ARE AFTER, WHAT THEY SEE IN EARTH. I THOUGHT I COULD SAVE THEIR WORLD SO THEY WOULDN'T WANT OURS.
AFTER A WHILE... I GOT MY BELT WORKING, BUT SINCE NO ONE HAD BEEN SENT AFTER ME, I THOUGHT THERE MIGHT BE A REASON, LIKE THEY COULD SEE THE TRANSFERENCES... THAT IT MIGHT HELP THEM.
AND MY WORK HAD BECOME SO VITAL, I COULDN'T LEAVE IT...
THAT LAST PART SOUNDS MORE BELIEVABLE.
HEATHER?

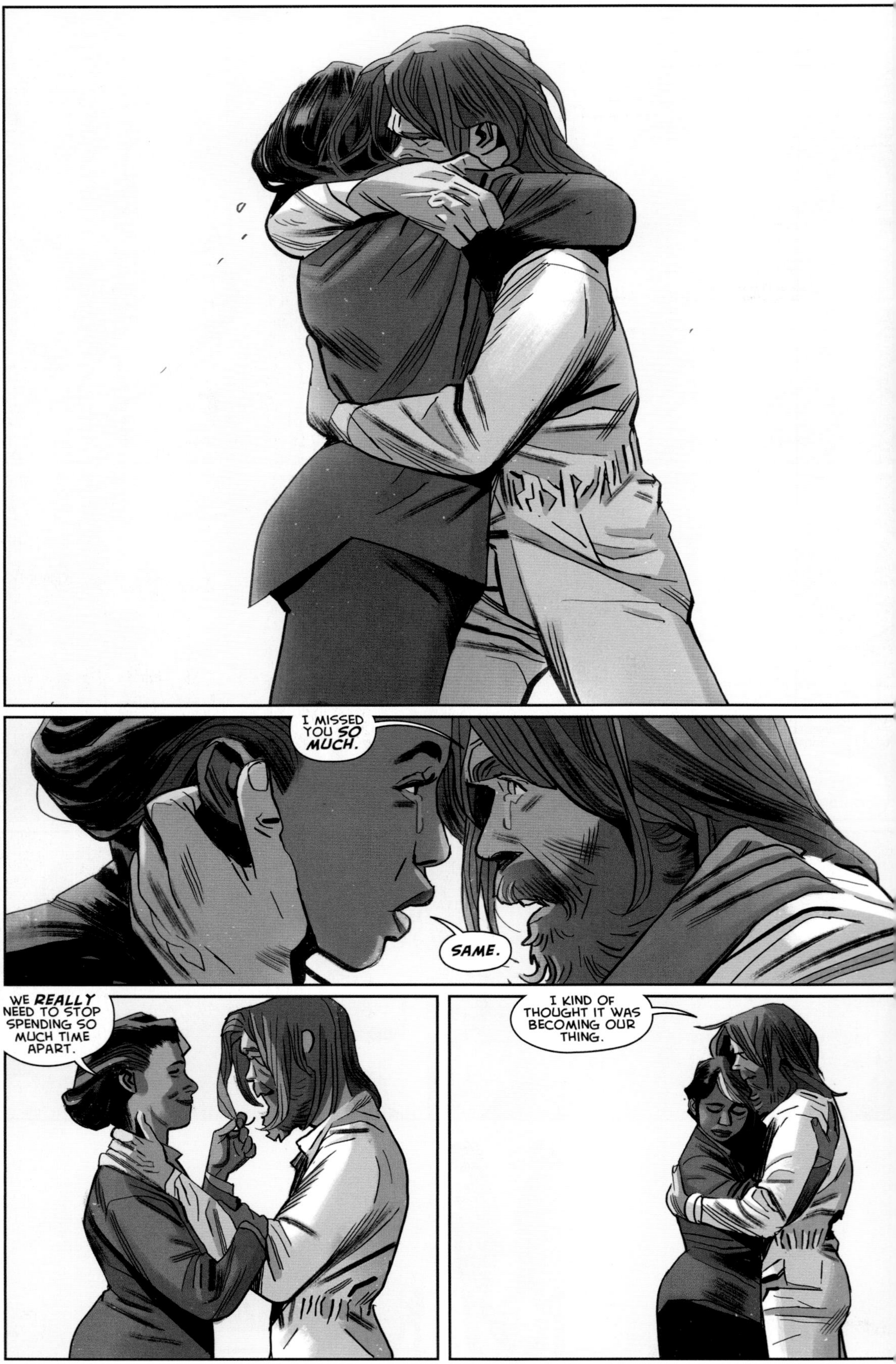
I MISSED YOU SO MUCH.
SAME.
WE REALLY NEED TO STOP SPENDING SO MUCH TIME APART.
I KIND OF THOUGHT IT WAS BECOMING OUR THING.

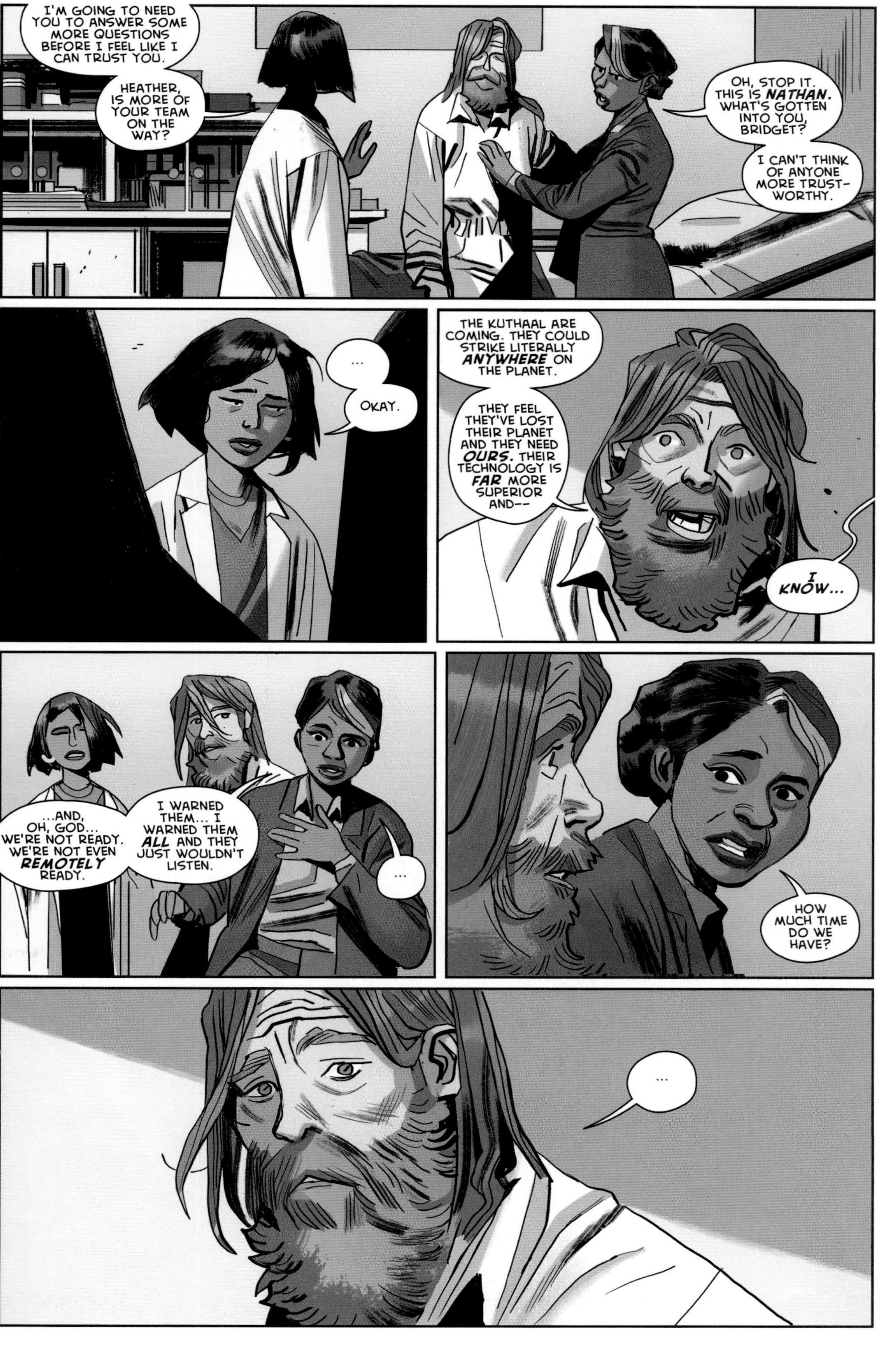
I'M GOING TO NEED YOU TO ANSWER SOME MORE QUESTIONS BEFORE I FEEL LIKE I CAN TRUST YOU.
HEATHER, IS MORE OF YOUR TEAM ON THE WAY?
OH, STOP IT. THIS IS NATHAN. WHAT'S GOTTEN INTO YOU, BRIDGET?
I CAN'T THINK OF ANYONE MORE TRUST-WORTHY.
...
OKAY.
THE KUTHAAL ARE COMING. THEY COULD STRIKE LITERALLY ANYWHERE ON THE PLANET.
THEY FEEL THEY'VE LOST THEIR PLANET AND THEY NEED OURS. THEIR TECHNOLOGY IS FAR MORE SUPERIOR AND--
I KNOW...
...AND, OH, GOD... WE'RE NOT READY. WE'RE NOT EVEN REMOTELY READY.
I WARNED THEM... I WARNED THEM ALL AND THEY JUST WOULDN'T LISTEN.
...
HOW MUCH TIME DO WE HAVE?
...

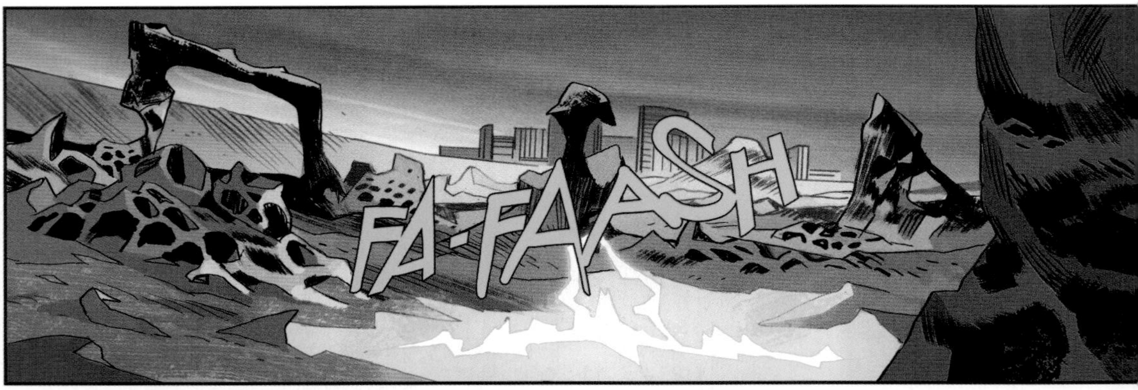
FA-FASH

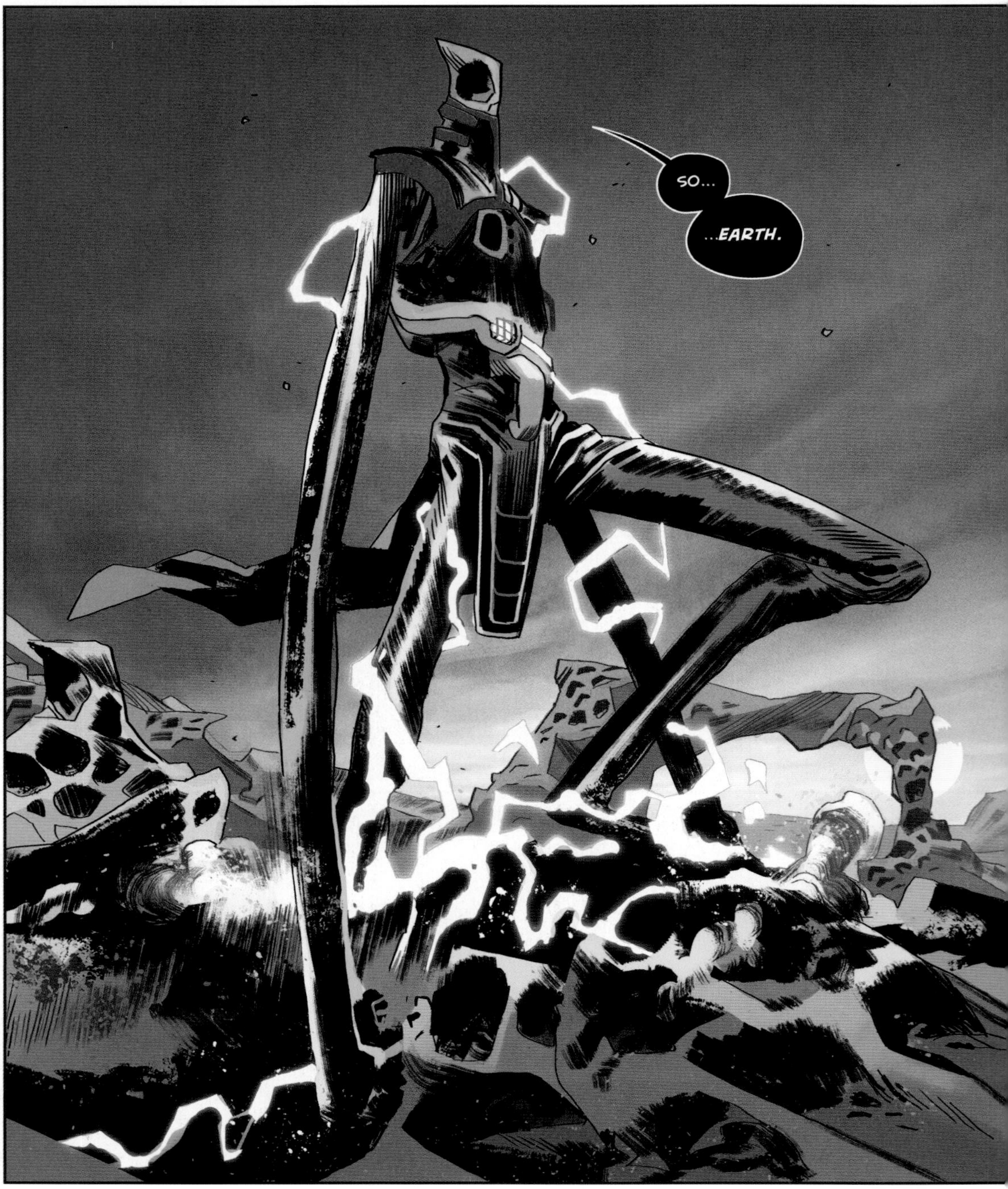
SO...
...EARTH.

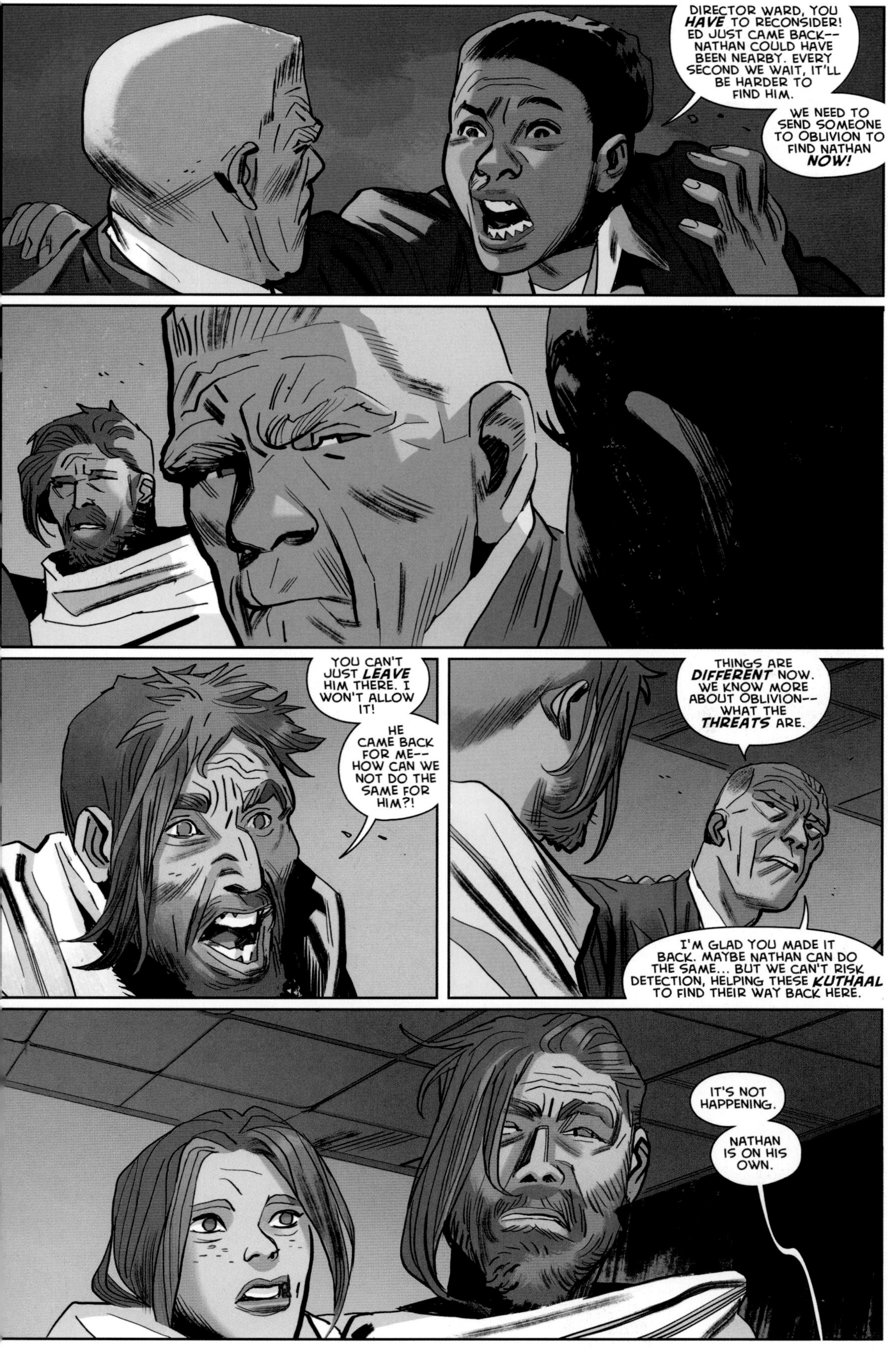
DIRECTOR WARD, YOU HAVE TO RECONSIDER! ED JUST CAME BACK-- NATHAN COULD HAVE BEEN NEARBY. EVERY SECOND WE WAIT, IT'LL BE HARDER TO FIND HIM.
WE NEED TO SEND SOMEONE TO OBLIVION TO FIND NATHAN NOW!
YOU CAN'T JUST LEAVE HIM THERE. I WON'T ALLOW IT!
HE CAME BACK FOR ME-- HOW CAN WE NOT DO THE SAME FOR HIM?!
THINGS ARE DIFFERENT NOW. WE KNOW MORE ABOUT OBLIVION-- WHAT THE THREATS ARE.
I'M GLAD YOU MADE IT BACK. MAYBE NATHAN CAN DO THE SAME... BUT WE CAN'T RISK DETECTION, HELPING THESE KUTHAAL TO FIND THEIR WAY BACK HERE.
IT'S NOT HAPPENING.
NATHAN IS ON HIS OWN.

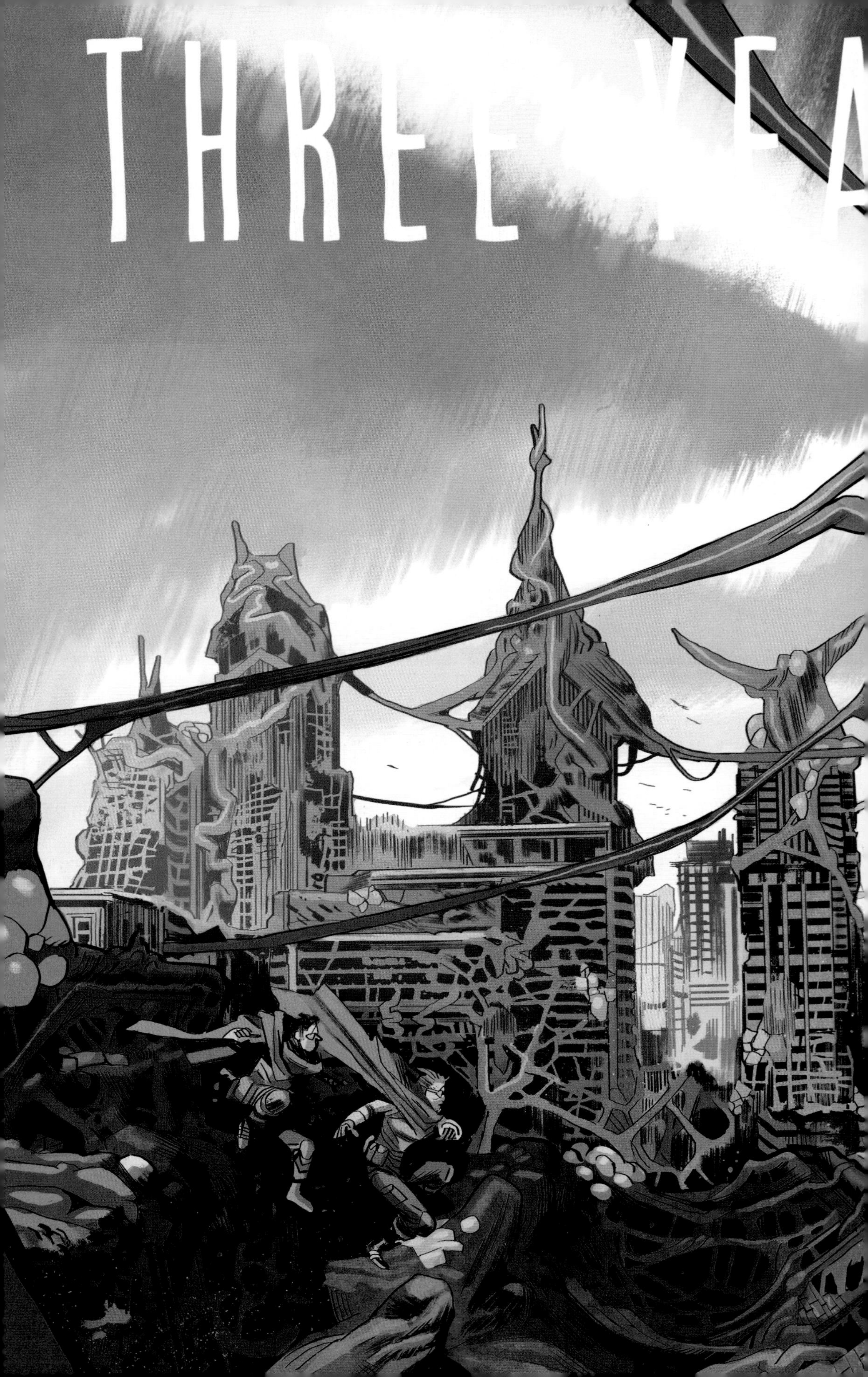
THREE YEA

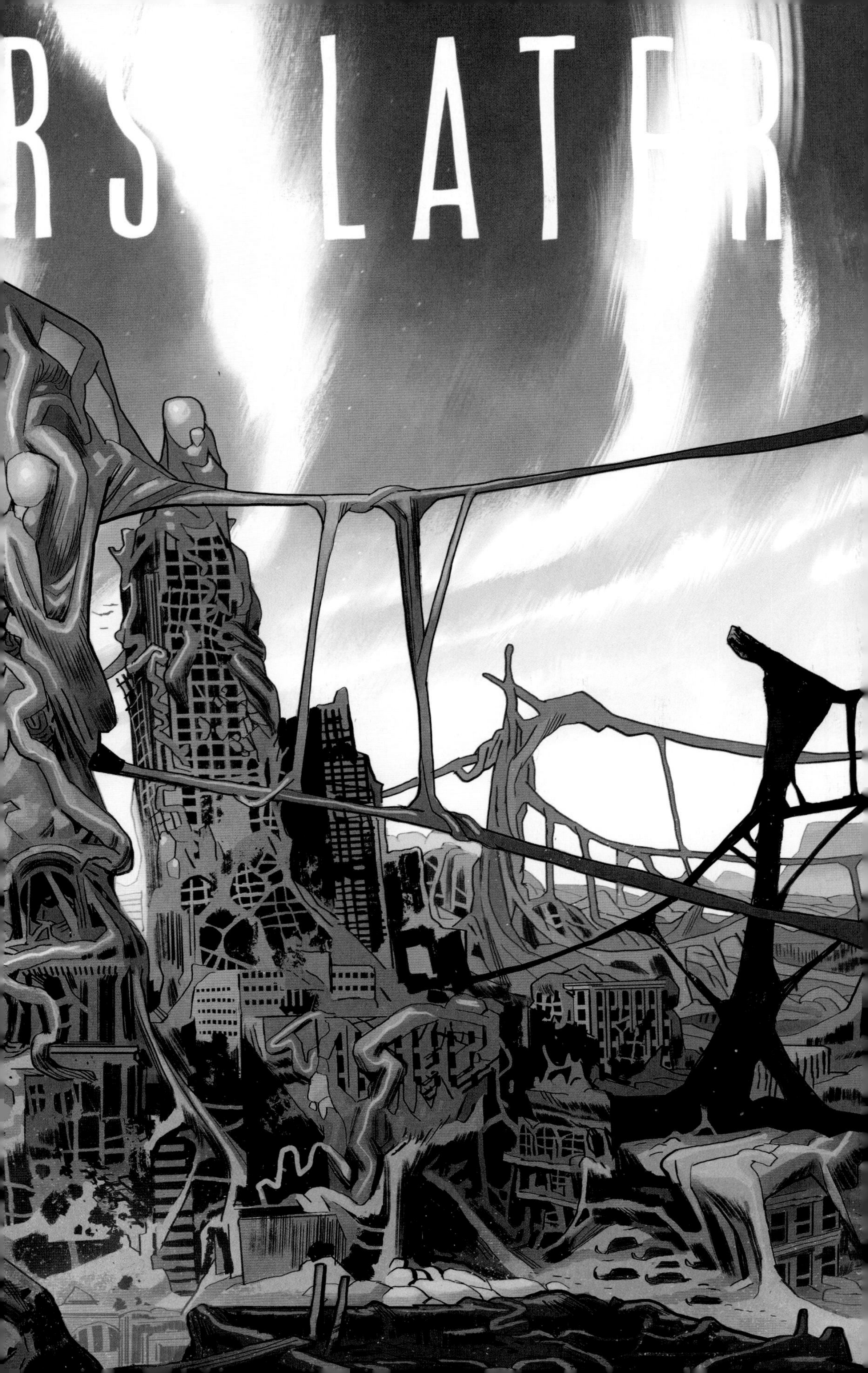
RS LATER

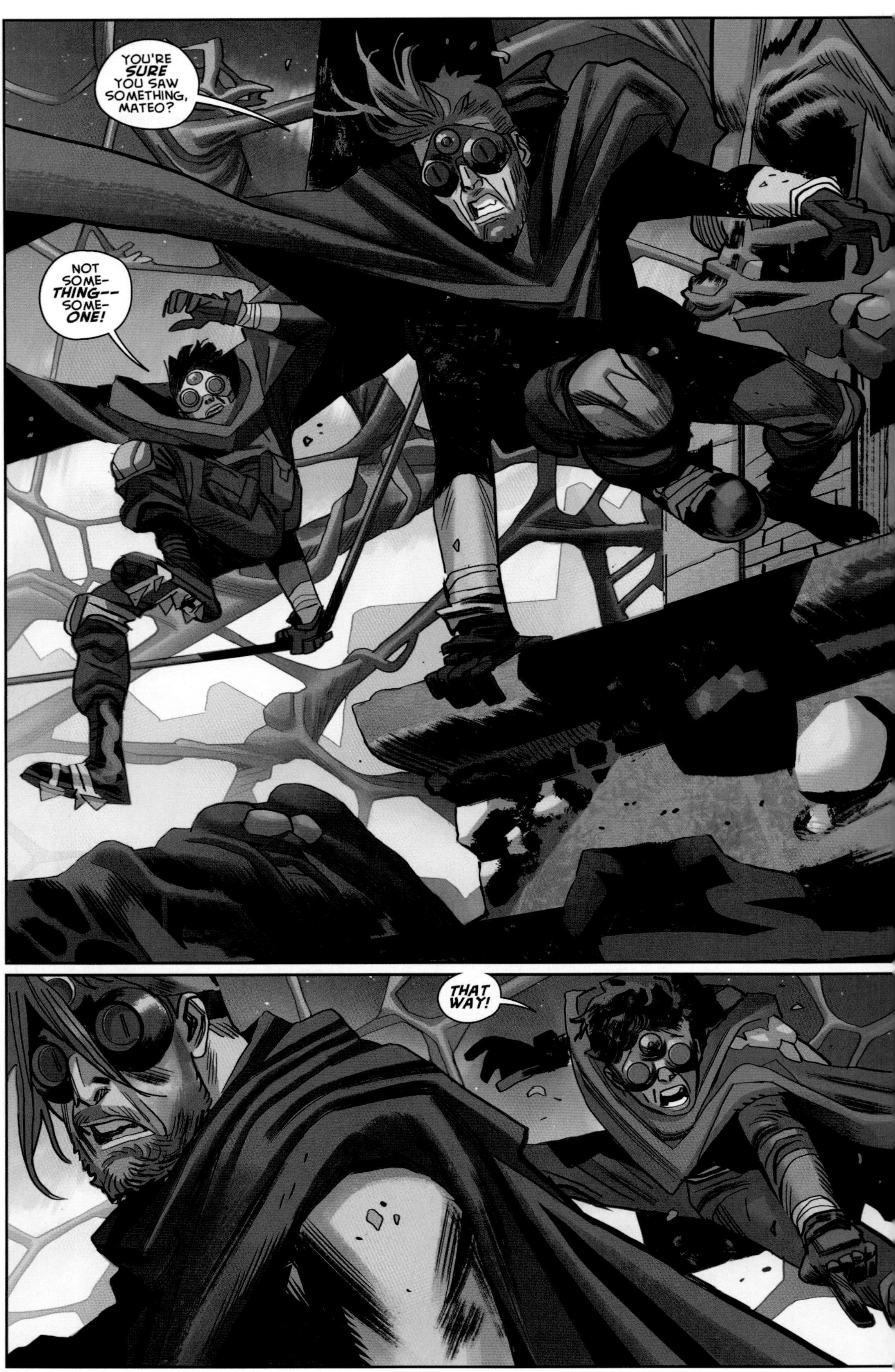
YOU'RE SURE YOU SAW SOMETHING, MATEO?
NOT SOME-THING-- SOME-ONE!
THAT WAY!

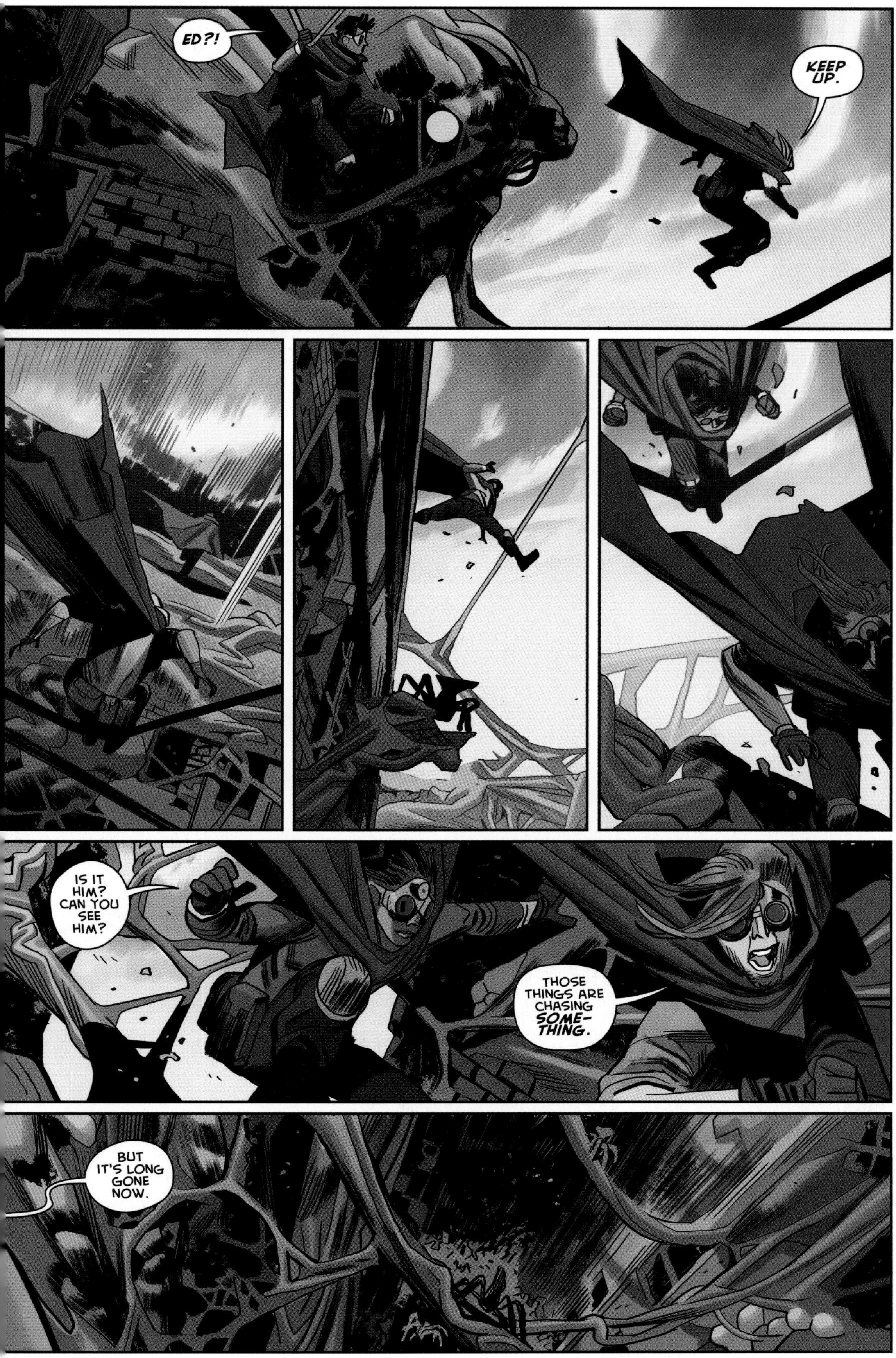
ED?!
KEEP UP.
IS IT HIM? CAN YOU SEE HIM?
THOSE THINGS ARE CHASING SOME-THING.
BUT IT'S LONG GONE NOW.

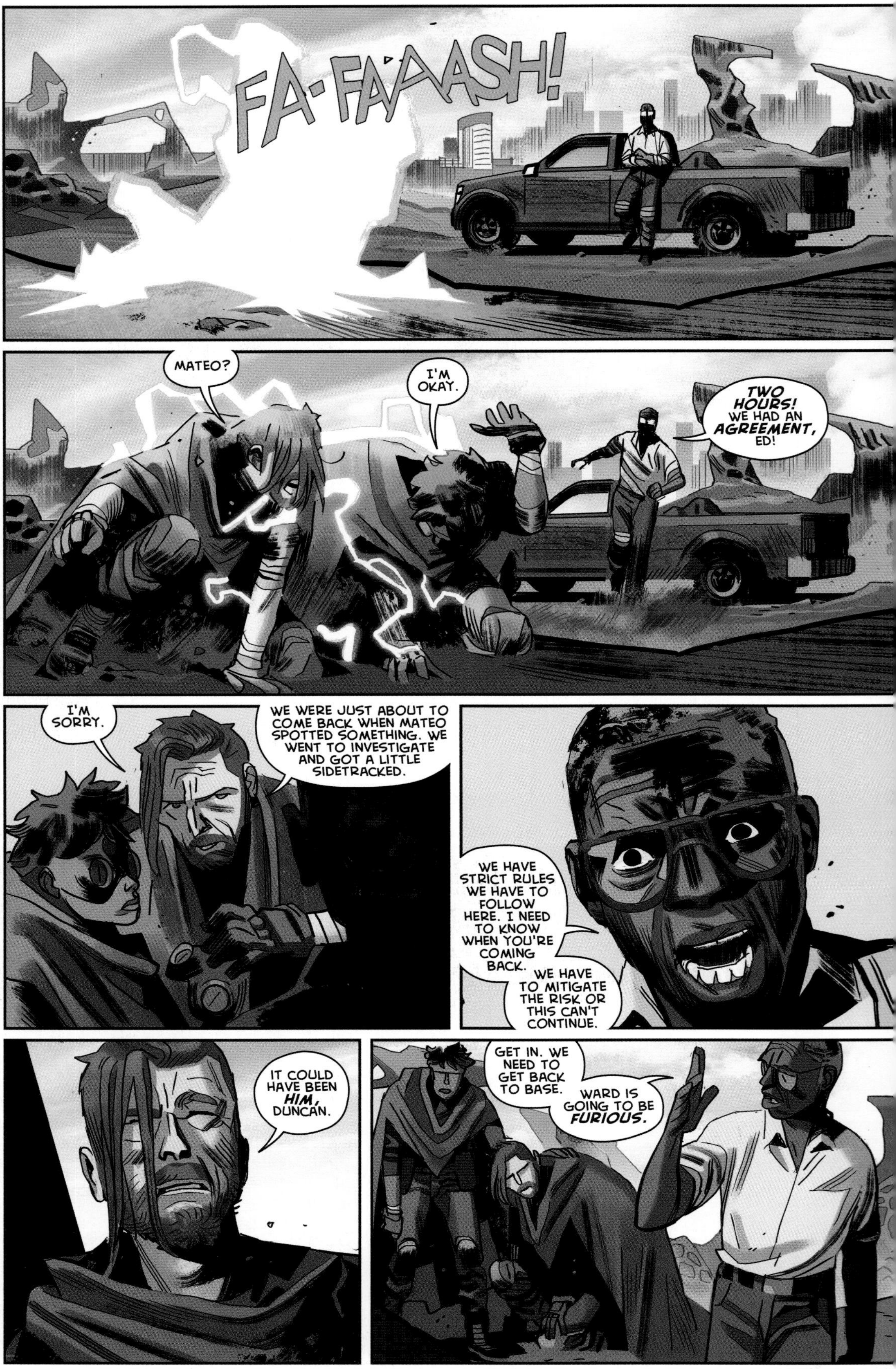
FA-FAAASH!
MATEO?
I'M OKAY.
TWO HOURS! WE HAD AN AGREEMENT, ED!
I'M SORRY.
WE WERE JUST ABOUT TO COME BACK WHEN MATEO SPOTTED SOMETHING. WE WENT TO INVESTIGATE AND GOT A LITTLE SIDETRACKED.
WE HAVE STRICT RULES WE HAVE TO FOLLOW HERE. I NEED TO KNOW WHEN YOU'RE COMING BACK.
WE HAVE TO MITIGATE THE RISK OR THIS CAN'T CONTINUE.
IT COULD HAVE BEEN HIM, DUNCAN.
GET IN. WE NEED TO GET BACK TO BASE.
WARD IS GOING TO BE FURIOUS.

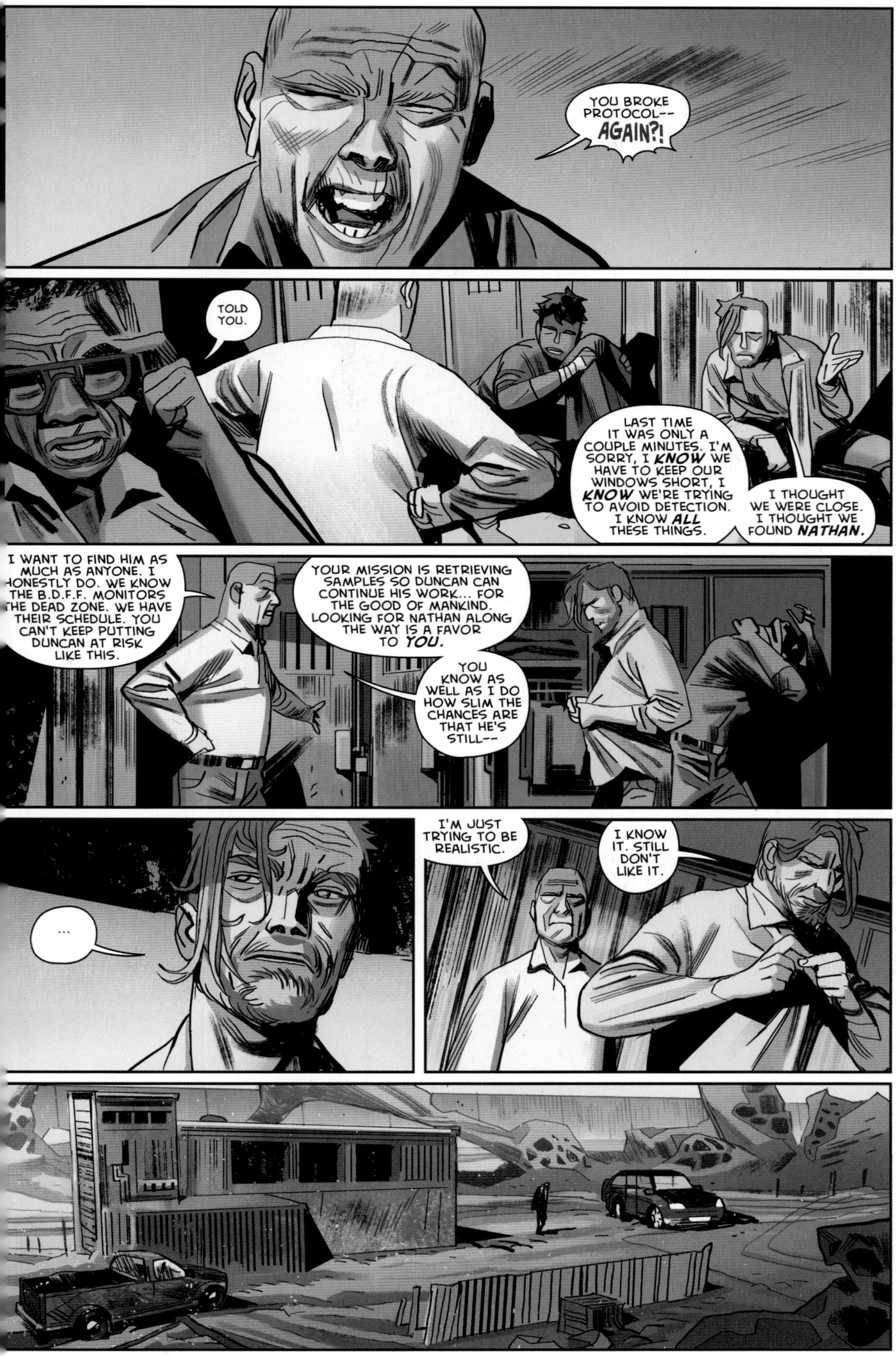
YOU BROKE PROTOCOL-- AGAIN?!
TOLD YOU.
LAST TIME IT WAS ONLY A COUPLE MINUTES. I'M SORRY, I KNOW WE HAVE TO KEEP OUR WINDOWS SHORT, I KNOW WE'RE TRYING TO AVOID DETECTION. I KNOW ALL THESE THINGS.
I THOUGHT WE WERE CLOSE. I THOUGHT WE FOUND NATHAN.
I WANT TO FIND HIM AS MUCH AS ANYONE. I HONESTLY DO. WE KNOW THE B.D.F.F. MONITORS THE DEAD ZONE. WE HAVE THEIR SCHEDULE. YOU CAN'T KEEP PUTTING DUNCAN AT RISK LIKE THIS.
YOUR MISSION IS RETRIEVING SAMPLES SO DUNCAN CAN CONTINUE HIS WORK... FOR THE GOOD OF MANKIND. LOOKING FOR NATHAN ALONG THE WAY IS A FAVOR TO YOU.
YOU KNOW AS WELL AS I DO HOW SLIM THE CHANCES ARE THAT HE'S STILL--
...
I'M JUST TRYING TO BE REALISTIC.
I KNOW IT. STILL DON'T LIKE IT.

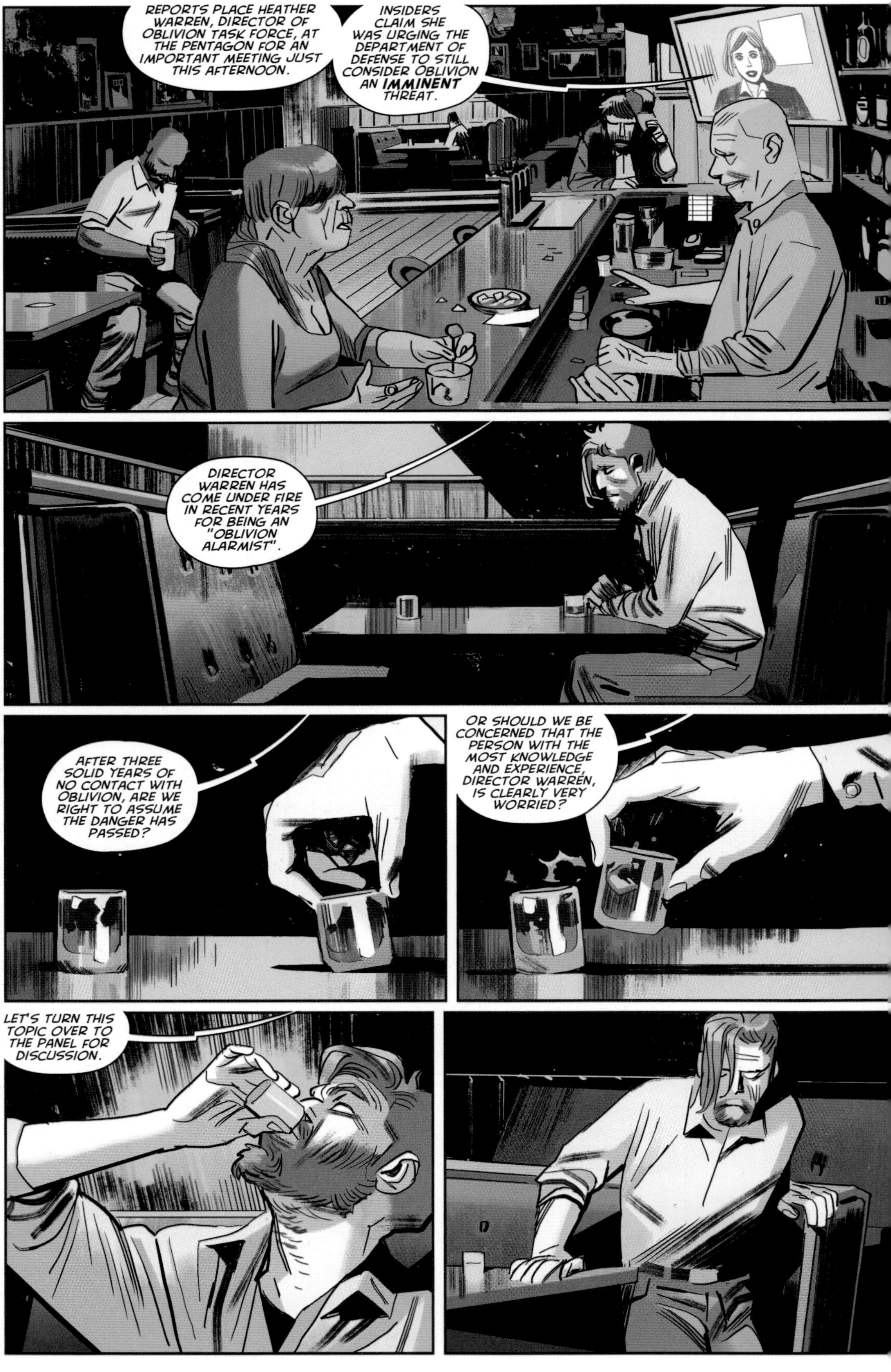
REPORTS PLACE HEATHER WARREN, DIRECTOR OF OBLIVION TASK FORCE, AT THE PENTAGON FOR AN IMPORTANT MEETING JUST THIS AFTERNOON.
INSIDERS CLAIM SHE WAS URGING THE DEPARTMENT OF DEFENSE TO STILL CONSIDER OBLIVION AN **IMMINENT** THREAT.
DIRECTOR WARREN HAS COME UNDER FIRE IN RECENT YEARS FOR BEING AN "OBLIVION ALARMIST".
AFTER THREE SOLID YEARS OF NO CONTACT WITH OBLIVION, ARE WE RIGHT TO ASSUME THE DANGER HAS PASSED?
OR SHOULD WE BE CONCERNED THAT THE PERSON WITH THE MOST KNOWLEDGE AND EXPERIENCE, DIRECTOR WARREN, IS CLEARLY VERY WORRIED?
LET'S TURN THIS TOPIC OVER TO THE PANEL FOR DISCUSSION.

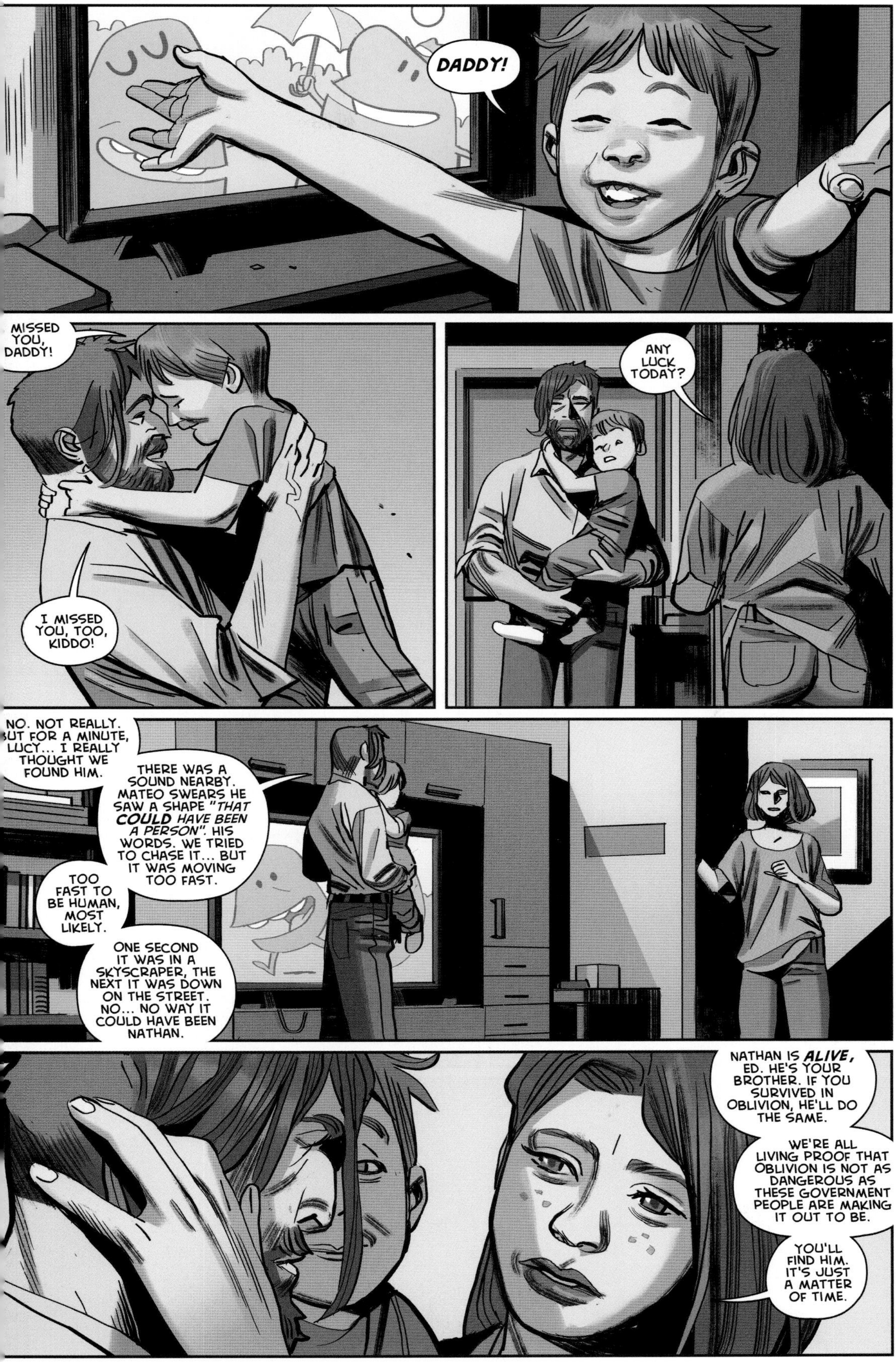
DADDY!
MISSED YOU, DADDY!
I MISSED YOU, TOO, KIDDO!
ANY LUCK TODAY?
NO. NOT REALLY. BUT FOR A MINUTE, LUCY... I REALLY THOUGHT WE FOUND HIM.
THERE WAS A SOUND NEARBY. MATEO SWEARS HE SAW A SHAPE "THAT COULD HAVE BEEN A PERSON". HIS WORDS. WE TRIED TO CHASE IT... BUT IT WAS MOVING TOO FAST.
TOO FAST TO BE HUMAN, MOST LIKELY.
ONE SECOND IT WAS IN A SKYSCRAPER, THE NEXT IT WAS DOWN ON THE STREET. NO... NO WAY IT COULD HAVE BEEN NATHAN.
NATHAN IS ALIVE, ED. HE'S YOUR BROTHER. IF YOU SURVIVED IN OBLIVION, HE'LL DO THE SAME.
WE'RE ALL LIVING PROOF THAT OBLIVION IS NOT AS DANGEROUS AS THESE GOVERNMENT PEOPLE ARE MAKING IT OUT TO BE.
YOU'LL FIND HIM. IT'S JUST A MATTER OF TIME.

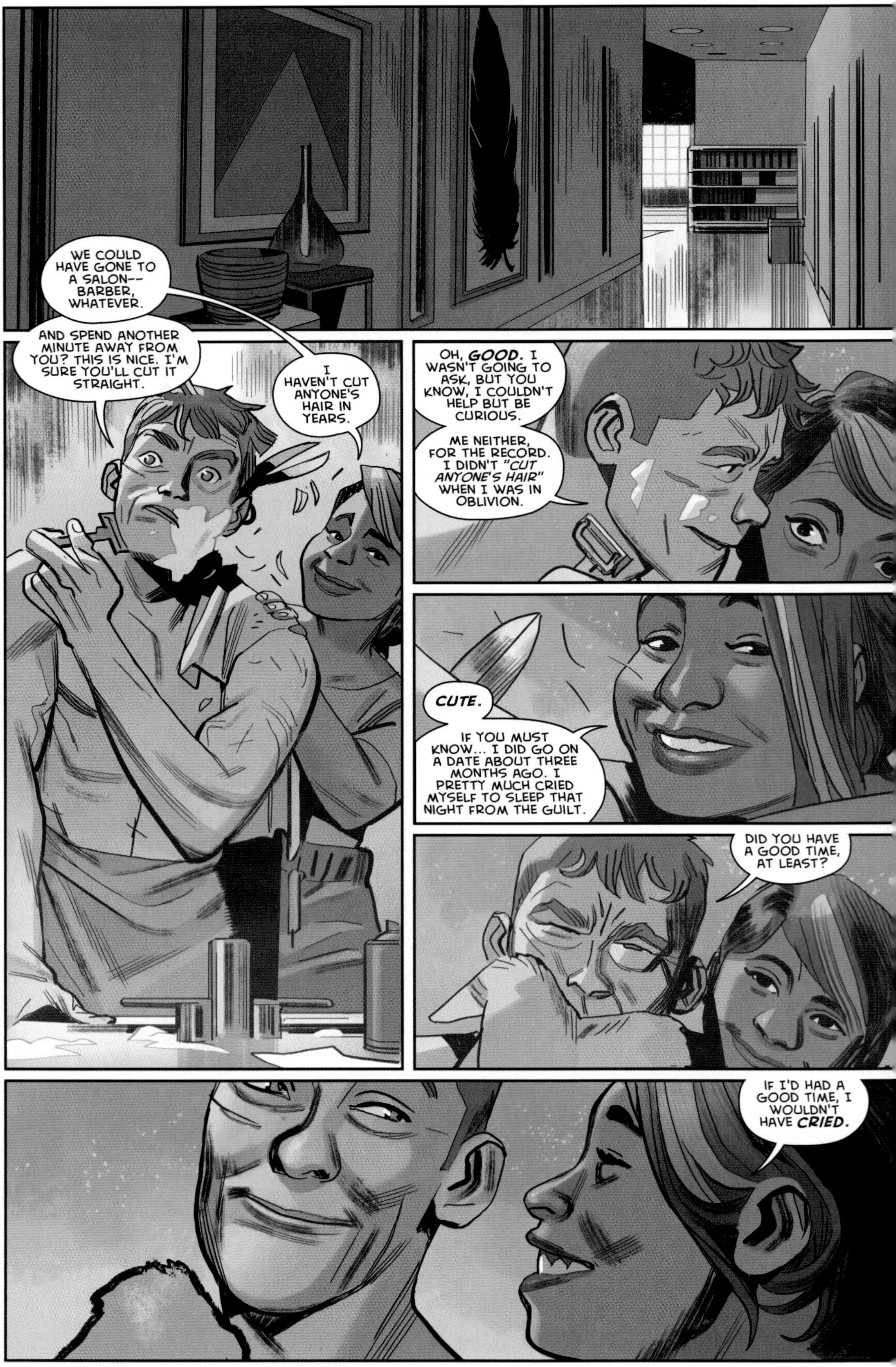
WE COULD HAVE GONE TO A SALON-- BARBER, WHATEVER.
AND SPEND ANOTHER MINUTE AWAY FROM YOU? THIS IS NICE. I'M SURE YOU'LL CUT IT STRAIGHT.
I HAVEN'T CUT ANYONE'S HAIR IN YEARS.
OH, GOOD. I WASN'T GOING TO ASK, BUT YOU KNOW, I COULDN'T HELP BUT BE CURIOUS.
ME NEITHER, FOR THE RECORD. I DIDN'T "CUT ANYONE'S HAIR" WHEN I WAS IN OBLIVION.
CUTE.
IF YOU MUST KNOW... I DID GO ON A DATE ABOUT THREE MONTHS AGO. I PRETTY MUCH CRIED MYSELF TO SLEEP THAT NIGHT FROM THE GUILT.
DID YOU HAVE A GOOD TIME, AT LEAST?
IF I'D HAD A GOOD TIME, I WOULDN'T HAVE CRIED.

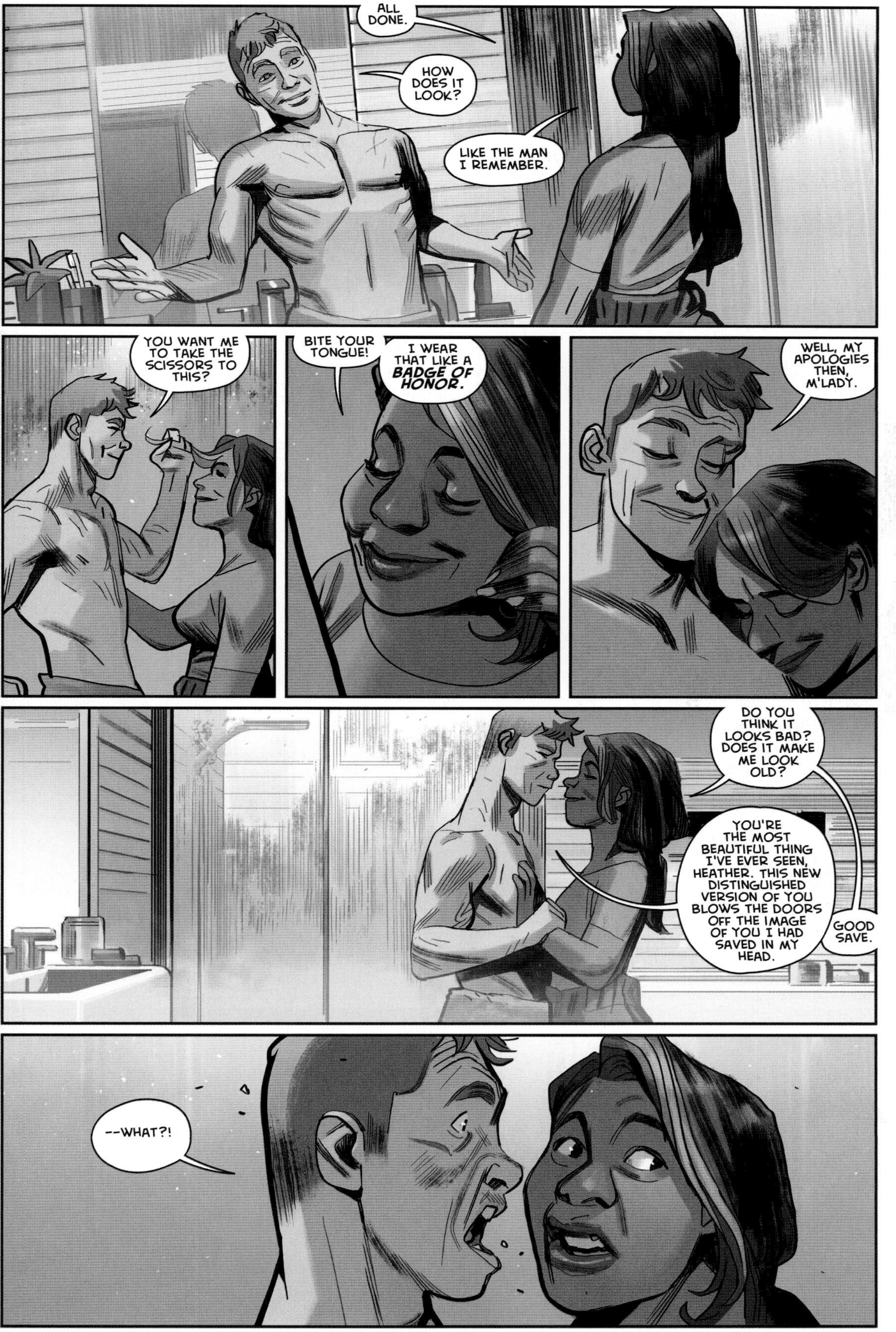
ALL DONE.
HOW DOES IT LOOK?
LIKE THE MAN I REMEMBER.
YOU WANT ME TO TAKE THE SCISSORS TO THIS?
BITE YOUR TONGUE!
I WEAR THAT LIKE A BADGE OF HONOR.
WELL, MY APOLOGIES THEN, M'LADY.
DO YOU THINK IT LOOKS BAD? DOES IT MAKE ME LOOK OLD?
YOU'RE THE MOST BEAUTIFUL THING I'VE EVER SEEN, HEATHER. THIS NEW DISTINGUISHED VERSION OF YOU BLOWS THE DOORS OFF THE IMAGE OF YOU I HAD SAVED IN MY HEAD.
GOOD SAVE.
--WHAT?!

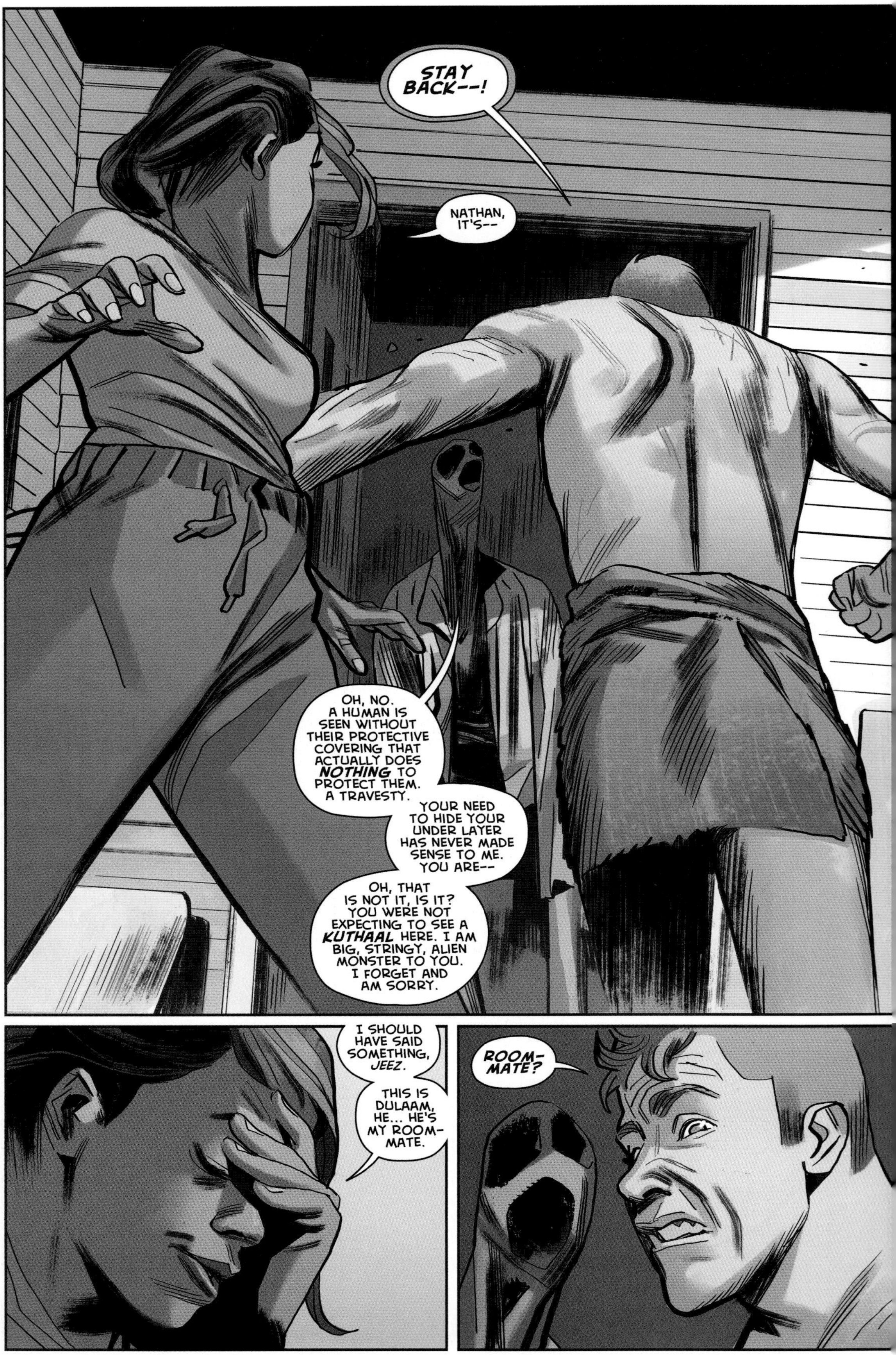
STAY BACK--!
NATHAN, IT'S--
OH, NO. A HUMAN IS SEEN WITHOUT THEIR PROTECTIVE COVERING THAT ACTUALLY DOES NOTHING TO PROTECT THEM. A TRAVESTY.
YOUR NEED TO HIDE YOUR UNDER LAYER HAS NEVER MADE SENSE TO ME. YOU ARE--
OH, THAT IS NOT IT, IS IT? YOU WERE NOT EXPECTING TO SEE A KUTHAAL HERE. I AM BIG, STRINGY, ALIEN MONSTER TO YOU. I FORGET AND AM SORRY.
I SHOULD HAVE SAID SOMETHING, JEEZ.
THIS IS DULAAM, HE... HE'S MY ROOM-MATE.
ROOM-MATE?

DULAAM WAS ONE OF THE KUTHAAL WHO WERE STRANDED HERE DURING THE RESCUE OF ED'S PEOPLE. WE ORIGINALLY THOUGHT HE FELL TO HIS DEATH.

WARD AND I WERE PRETTY MUCH THE ONLY PEOPLE WHO KNEW DULAAM SURVIVED. WE KEPT HIM HIDDEN, TRYING TO GET AS MUCH INFORMATION FROM HIM AS WE COULD.

HE WENT FROM COOPERATIVE TO FRIENDLY AND EVENTUALLY... LONG STORY... I HAD TO HIDE HIM HERE.

WE WATCH THE HOUSEWIVES TOGETHER. THEIR FIGHTING BRINGS US JOY. IT IS *WEIRD.*

I MADE MY OWN KUTHAAL FRIENDS, IN OBLIVION.

GAKAAL AND HIS OFFSPRING, NANU--

GAKAAL THE GHOZAN COMMANDER?!

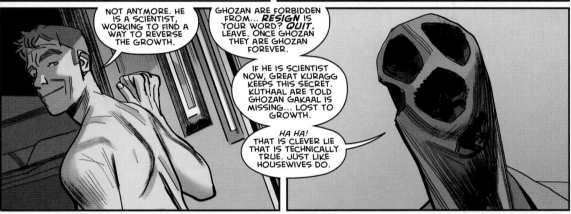

NOT ANYMORE. HE IS A SCIENTIST, WORKING TO FIND A WAY TO REVERSE THE GROWTH.

GHOZAN ARE FORBIDDEN FROM... *RESIGN* IS YOUR WORD? *QUIT.* LEAVE. ONCE GHOZAN THEY ARE GHOZAN FOREVER.

IF HE IS SCIENTIST NOW, GREAT KURAGG KEEPS THIS SECRET. KUTHAAL ARE TOLD GHOZAN GAKAAL IS MISSING... LOST TO GROWTH.

HA HA! THAT IS CLEVER LIE THAT IS TECHNICALLY TRUE. JUST LIKE HOUSEWIVES DO.

YOU ARE AN UNUSUAL KUTHAAL, DULAAM.

HE GROWS ON YOU.

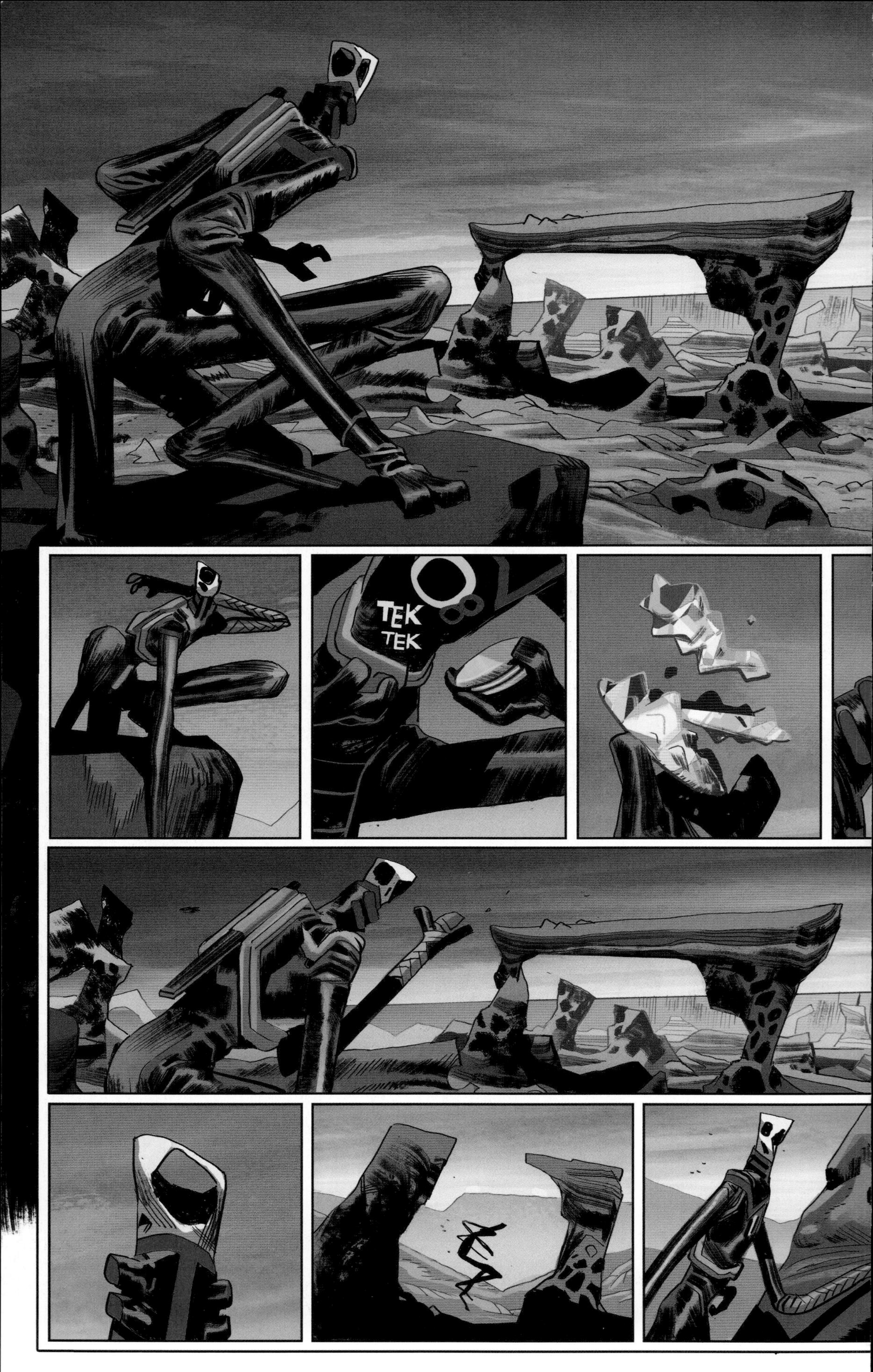
TEK
TEK

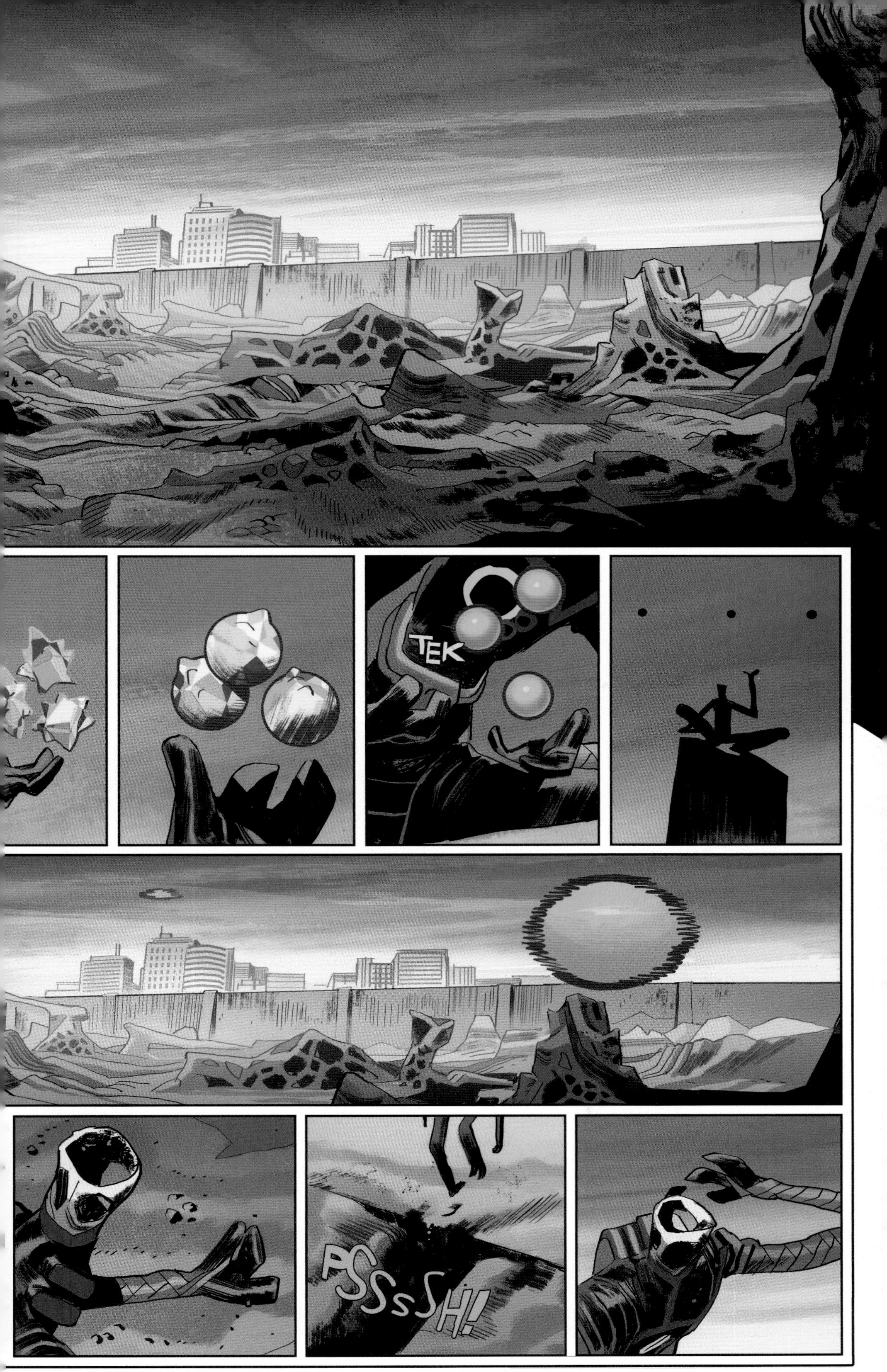
TEK
. . .
PSSsSH!

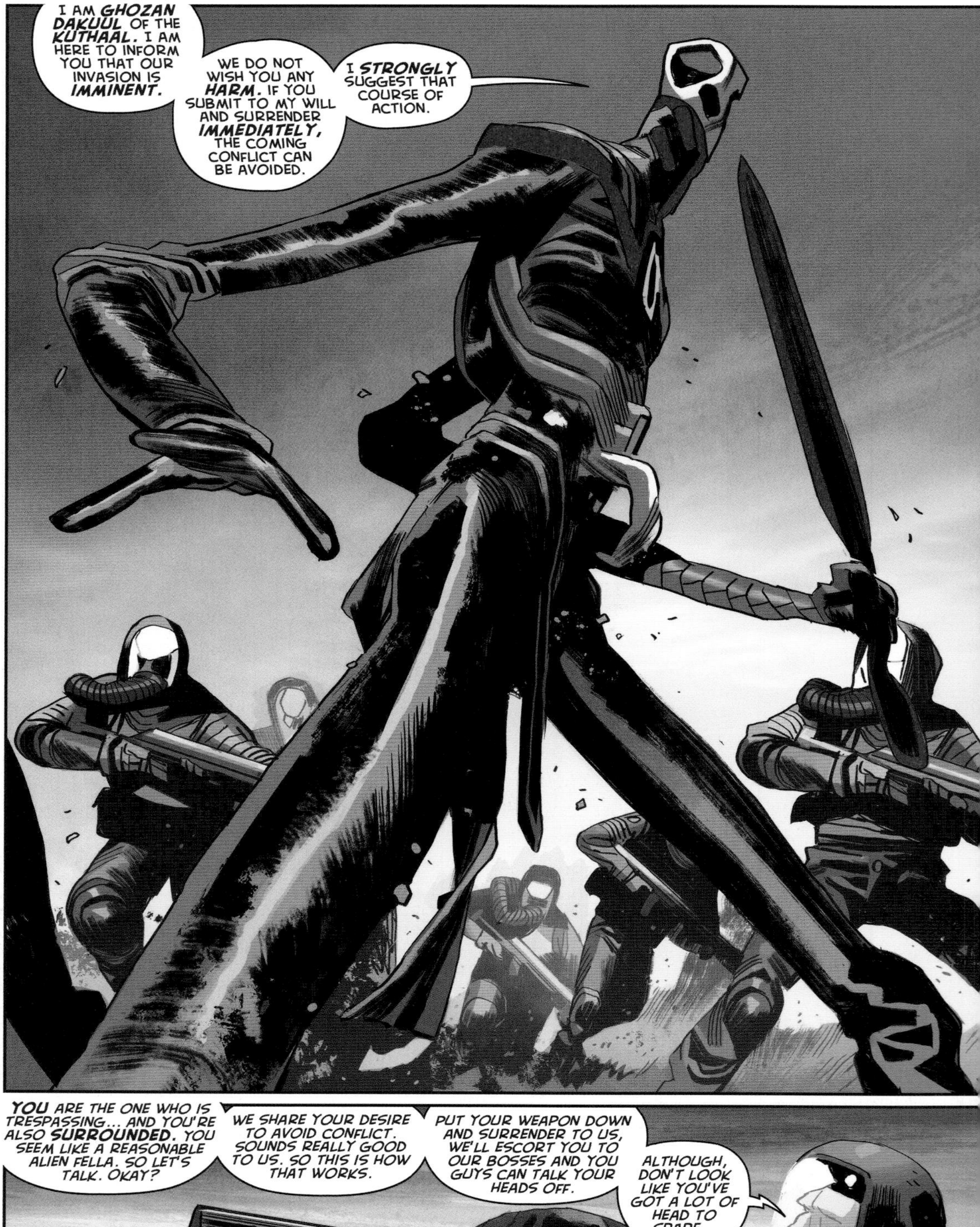
I AM GHOZAN DAKUUL OF THE KUTHAAL. I AM HERE TO INFORM YOU THAT OUR INVASION IS IMMINENT.
WE DO NOT WISH YOU ANY HARM. IF YOU SUBMIT TO MY WILL AND SURRENDER IMMEDIATELY, THE COMING CONFLICT CAN BE AVOIDED.
I STRONGLY SUGGEST THAT COURSE OF ACTION.

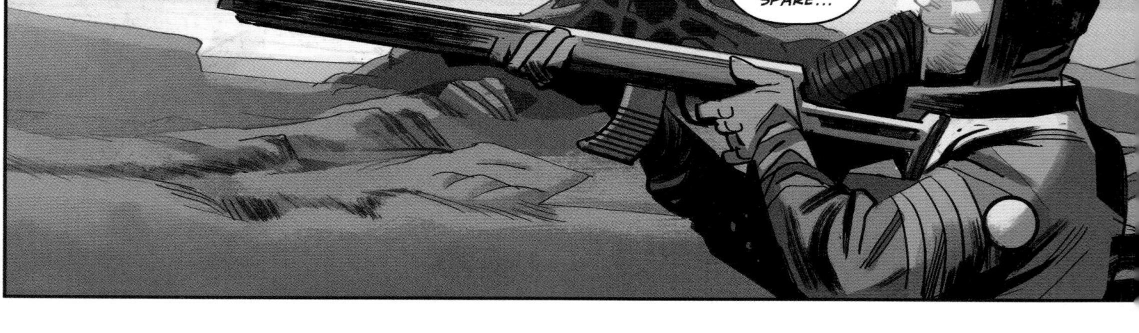
YOU ARE THE ONE WHO IS TRESPASSING... AND YOU'RE ALSO SURROUNDED. YOU SEEM LIKE A REASONABLE ALIEN FELLA. SO LET'S TALK. OKAY?
WE SHARE YOUR DESIRE TO AVOID CONFLICT. SOUNDS REALLY GOOD TO US. SO THIS IS HOW THAT WORKS.
PUT YOUR WEAPON DOWN AND SURRENDER TO US, WE'LL ESCORT YOU TO OUR BOSSES AND YOU GUYS CAN TALK YOUR HEADS OFF.
ALTHOUGH, DON'T LOOK LIKE YOU'VE GOT A LOT OF HEAD TO SPARE...

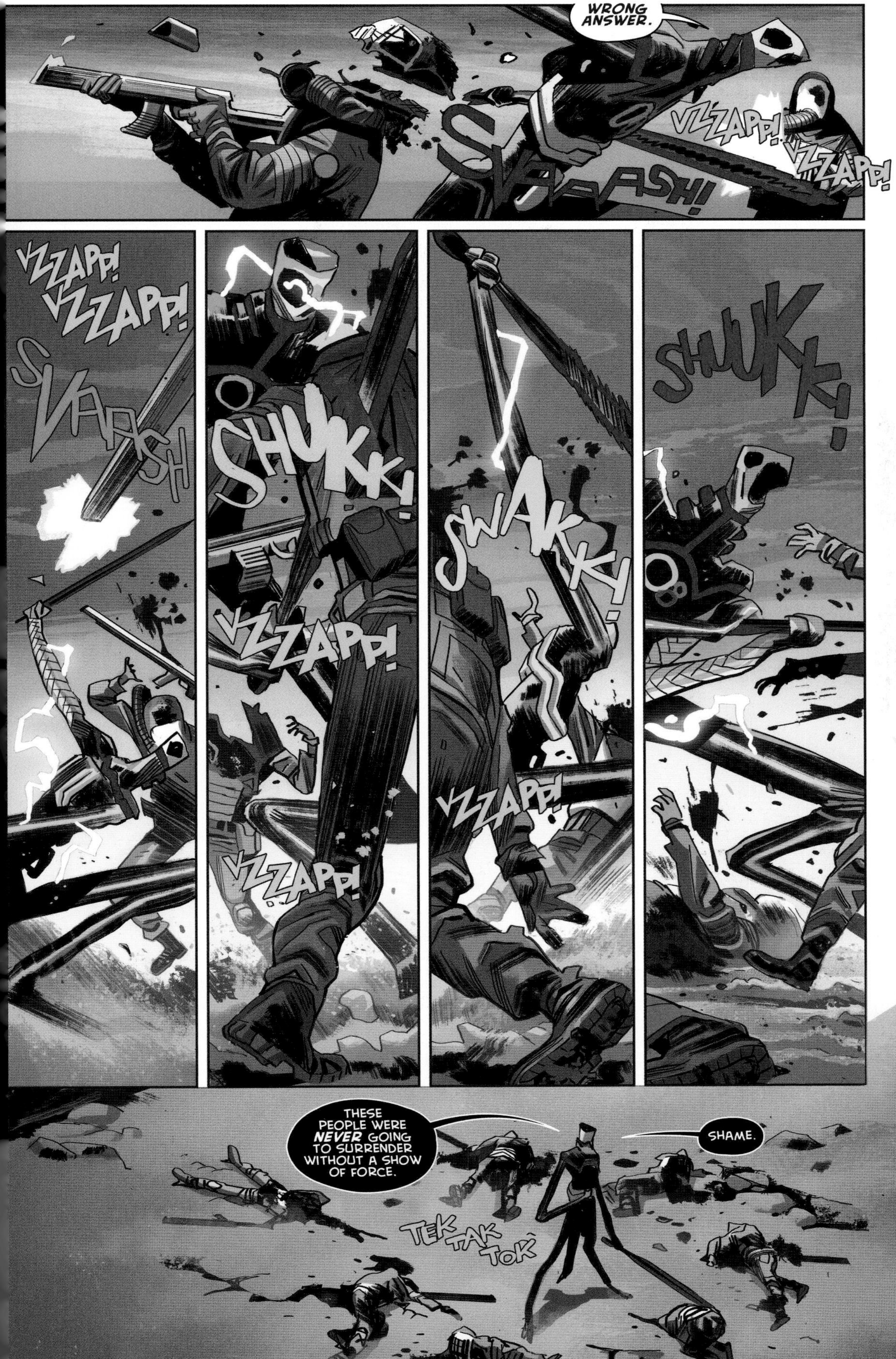
WRONG ANSWER.
SVAAASH!
VZZAPP!
VZZAPP!
VZZAPP!
VZZAPP!
SVARSH
SHUKK!
VZZAPP!
VZZAPP!
SWAKKK!
VZZAPP!
SHUUKK!
THESE PEOPLE WERE NEVER GOING TO SURRENDER WITHOUT A SHOW OF FORCE.
SHAME.
TEK TAK TOK

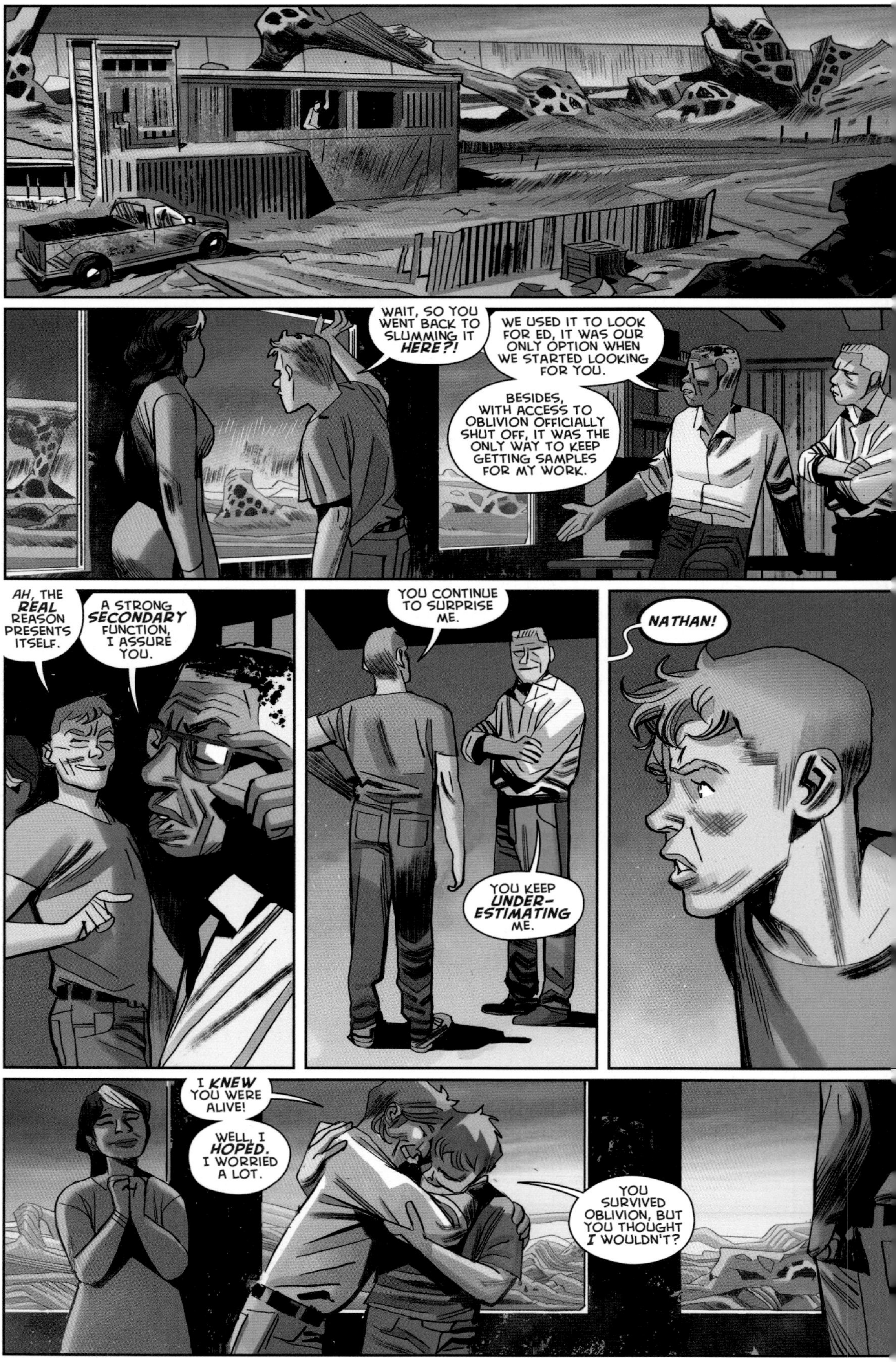
WAIT, SO YOU WENT BACK TO SLUMMING IT HERE?!
WE USED IT TO LOOK FOR ED, IT WAS OUR ONLY OPTION WHEN WE STARTED LOOKING FOR YOU.
BESIDES, WITH ACCESS TO OBLIVION OFFICIALLY SHUT OFF, IT WAS THE ONLY WAY TO KEEP GETTING SAMPLES FOR MY WORK.
AH, THE REAL REASON PRESENTS ITSELF.
A STRONG SECONDARY FUNCTION, I ASSURE YOU.
YOU CONTINUE TO SURPRISE ME.
YOU KEEP UNDER-ESTIMATING ME.
NATHAN!
I KNEW YOU WERE ALIVE!
WELL, I HOPED. I WORRIED A LOT.
YOU SURVIVED OBLIVION, BUT YOU THOUGHT I WOULDN'T?

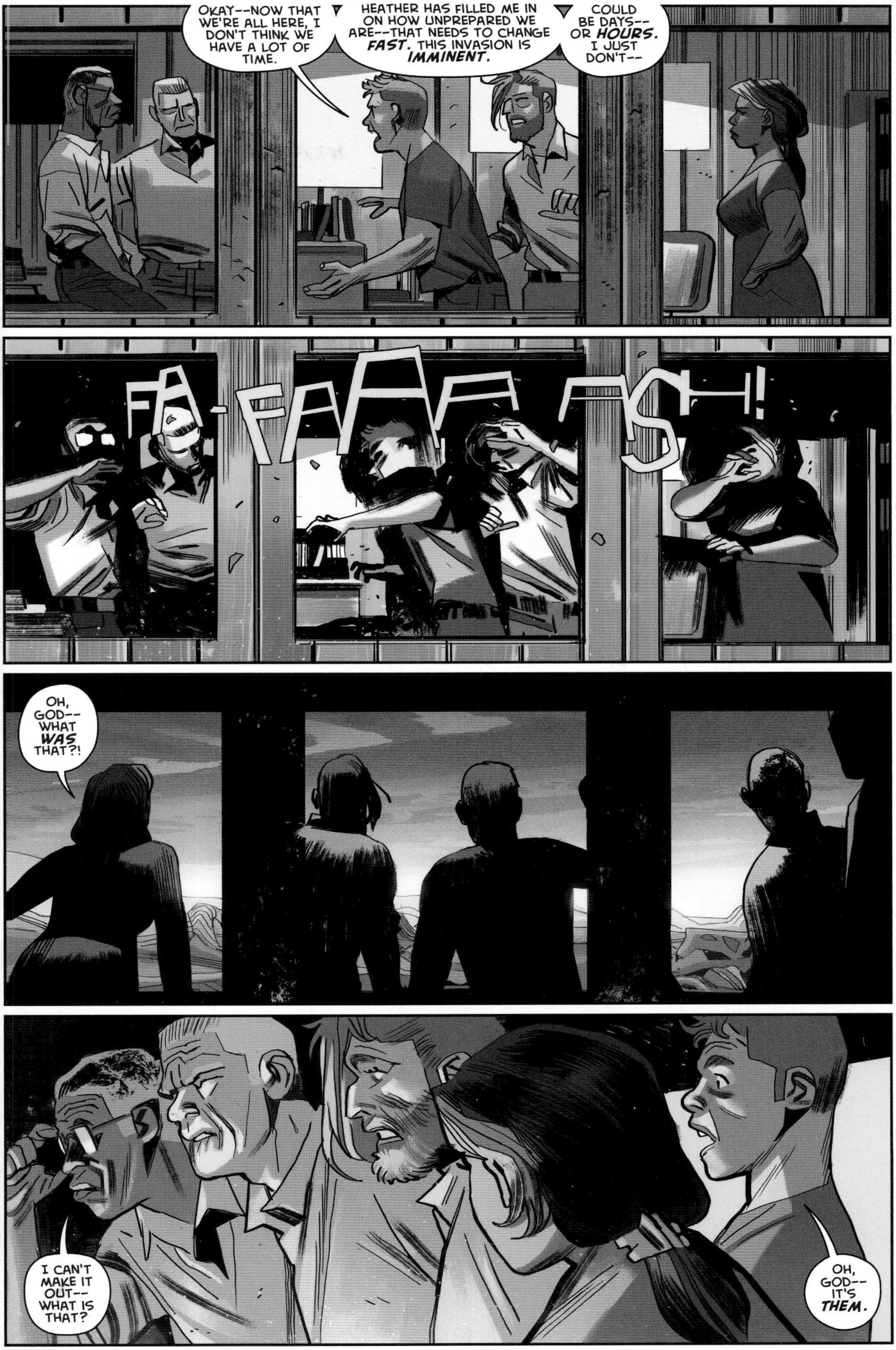
OKAY--NOW THAT WE'RE ALL HERE, I DON'T THINK WE HAVE A LOT OF TIME.
HEATHER HAS FILLED ME IN ON HOW UNPREPARED WE ARE--THAT NEEDS TO CHANGE FAST. THIS INVASION IS IMMINENT.
COULD BE DAYS-- OR HOURS. I JUST DON'T--
FA-FAAAA-ASH!
OH, GOD-- WHAT WAS THAT?!
I CAN'T MAKE IT OUT-- WHAT IS THAT?
OH, GOD-- IT'S THEM.

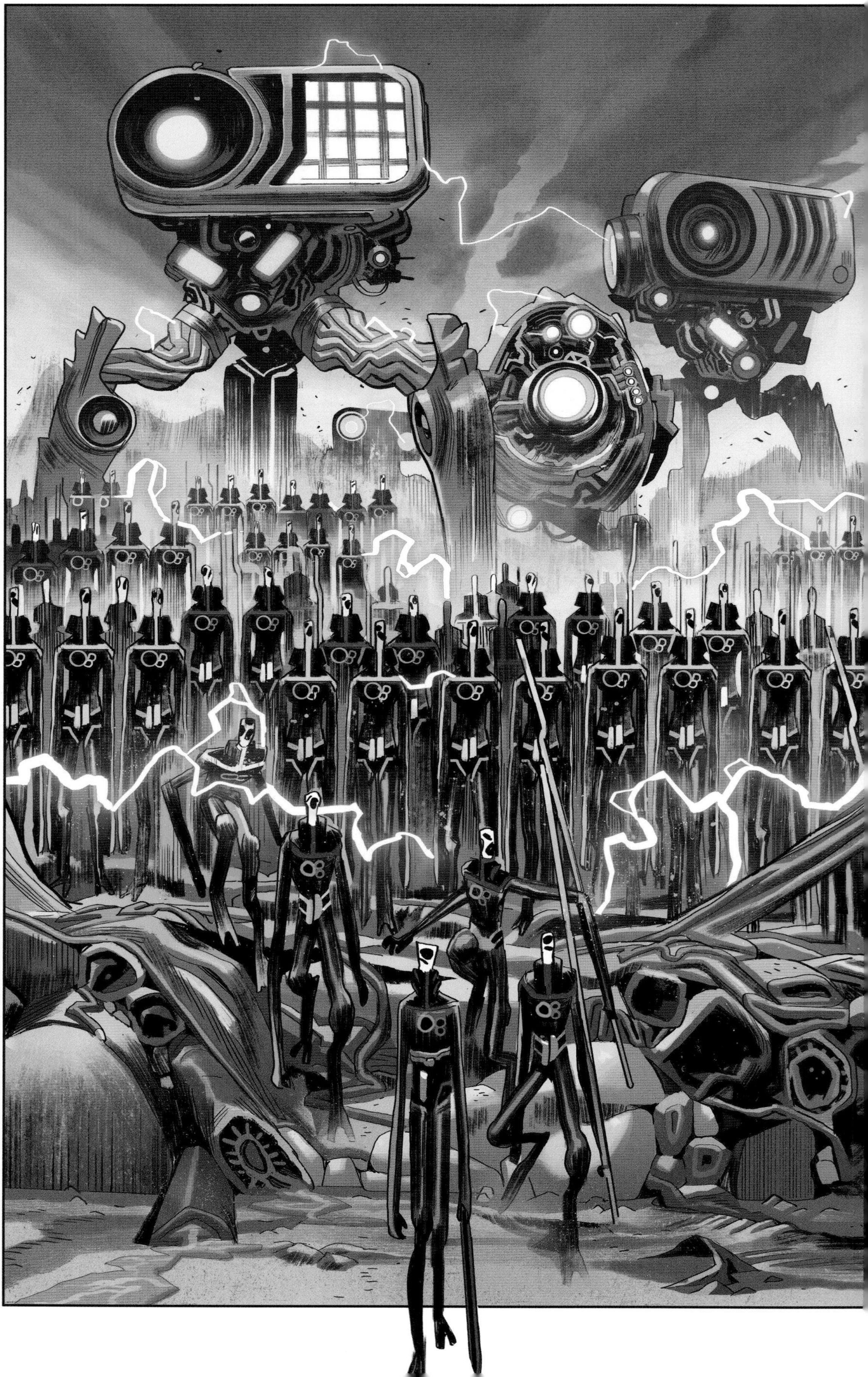

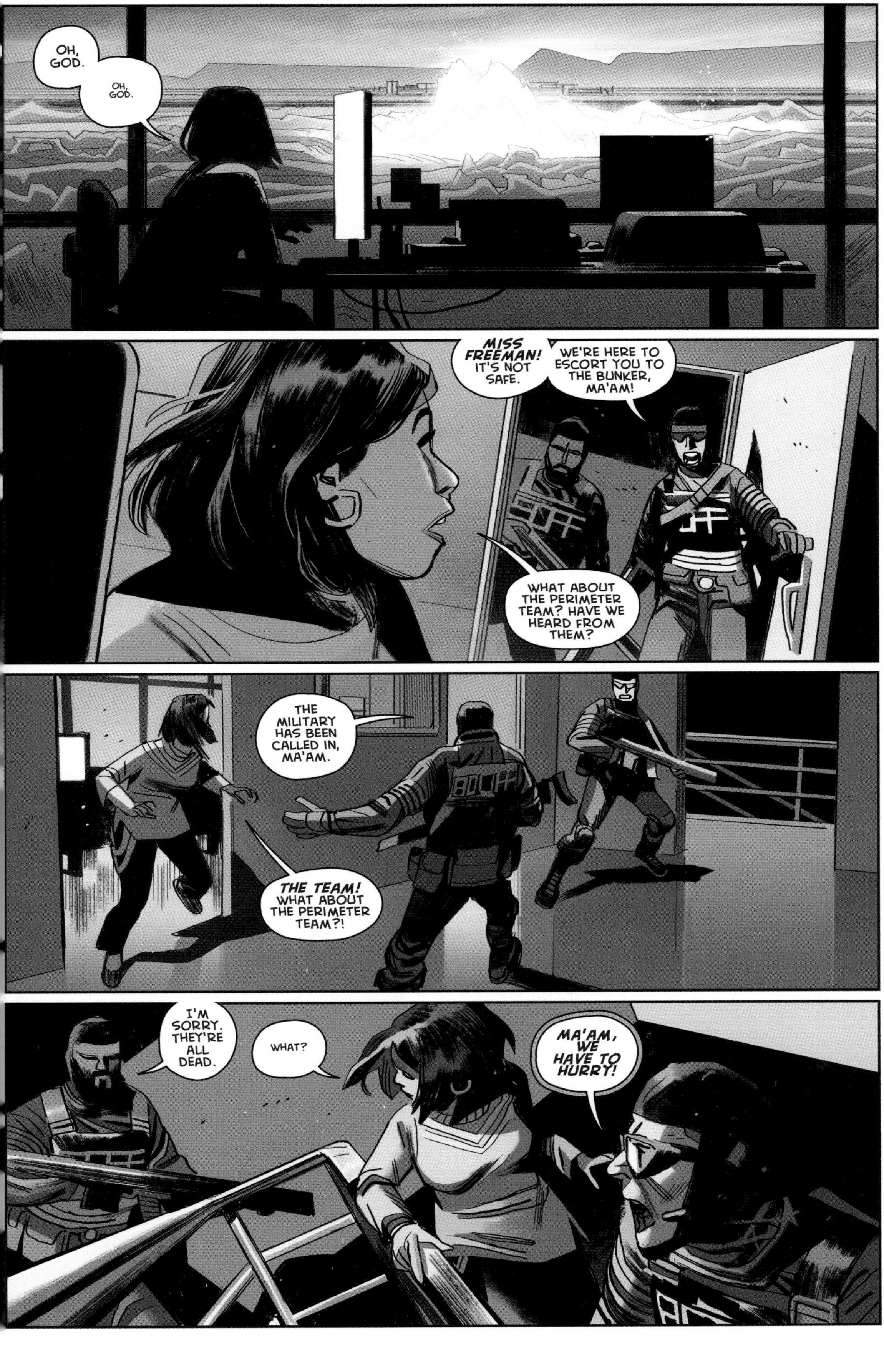
OH, GOD.
OH, GOD.
MISS FREEMAN! IT'S NOT SAFE.
WE'RE HERE TO ESCORT YOU TO THE BUNKER, MA'AM!
WHAT ABOUT THE PERIMETER TEAM? HAVE WE HEARD FROM THEM?
THE MILITARY HAS BEEN CALLED IN, MA'AM.
THE TEAM! WHAT ABOUT THE PERIMETER TEAM?!
I'M SORRY. THEY'RE ALL DEAD.
WHAT?
MA'AM, WE HAVE TO HURRY!

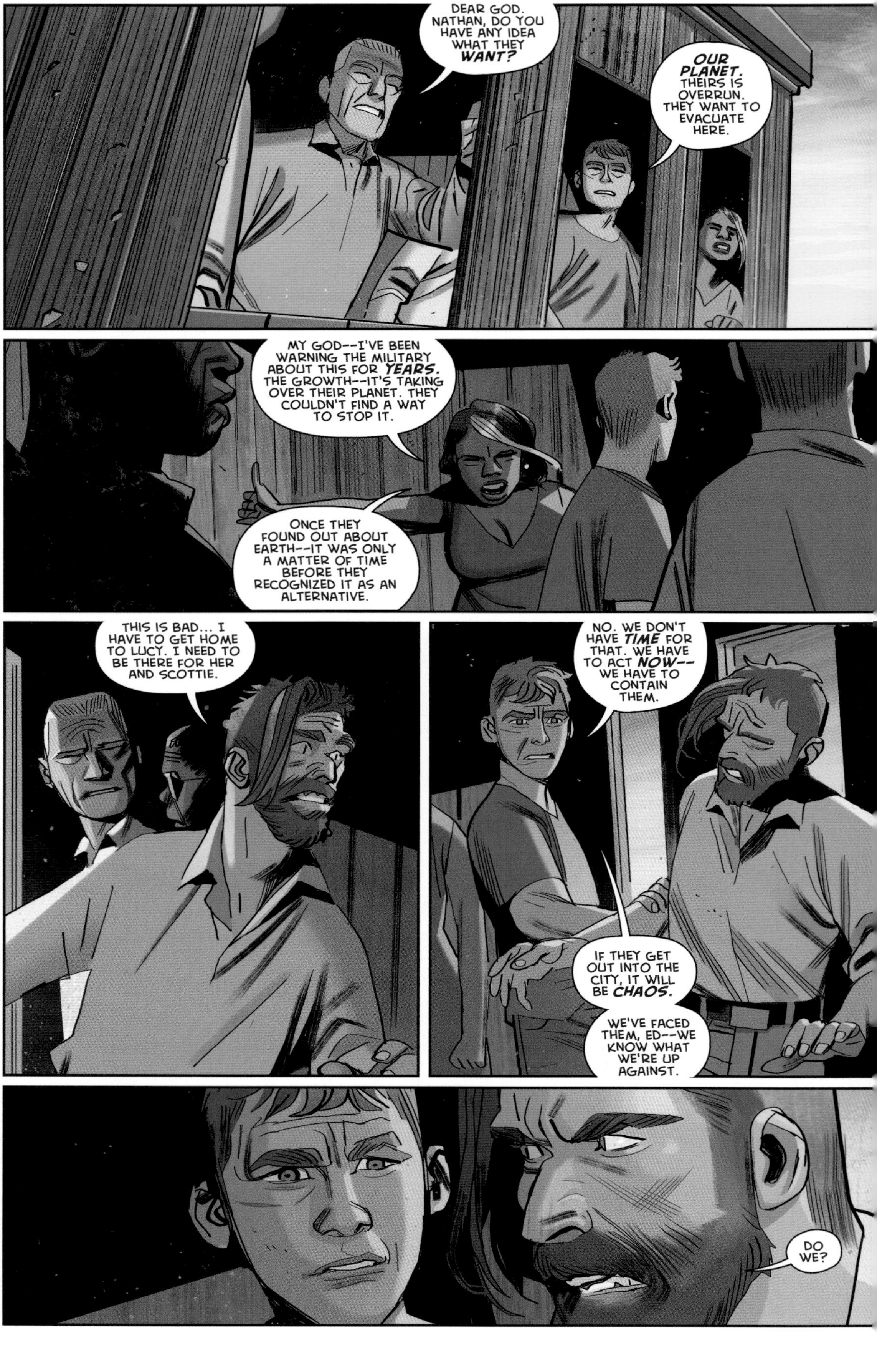
DEAR GOD. NATHAN, DO YOU HAVE ANY IDEA WHAT THEY WANT?
OUR PLANET. THEIRS IS OVERRUN. THEY WANT TO EVACUATE HERE.
MY GOD--I'VE BEEN WARNING THE MILITARY ABOUT THIS FOR YEARS. THE GROWTH--IT'S TAKING OVER THEIR PLANET. THEY COULDN'T FIND A WAY TO STOP IT.
ONCE THEY FOUND OUT ABOUT EARTH--IT WAS ONLY A MATTER OF TIME BEFORE THEY RECOGNIZED IT AS AN ALTERNATIVE.
THIS IS BAD... I HAVE TO GET HOME TO LUCY. I NEED TO BE THERE FOR HER AND SCOTTIE.
NO. WE DON'T HAVE TIME FOR THAT. WE HAVE TO ACT NOW--WE HAVE TO CONTAIN THEM.
IF THEY GET OUT INTO THE CITY, IT WILL BE CHAOS.
WE'VE FACED THEM, ED--WE KNOW WHAT WE'RE UP AGAINST.
DO WE?

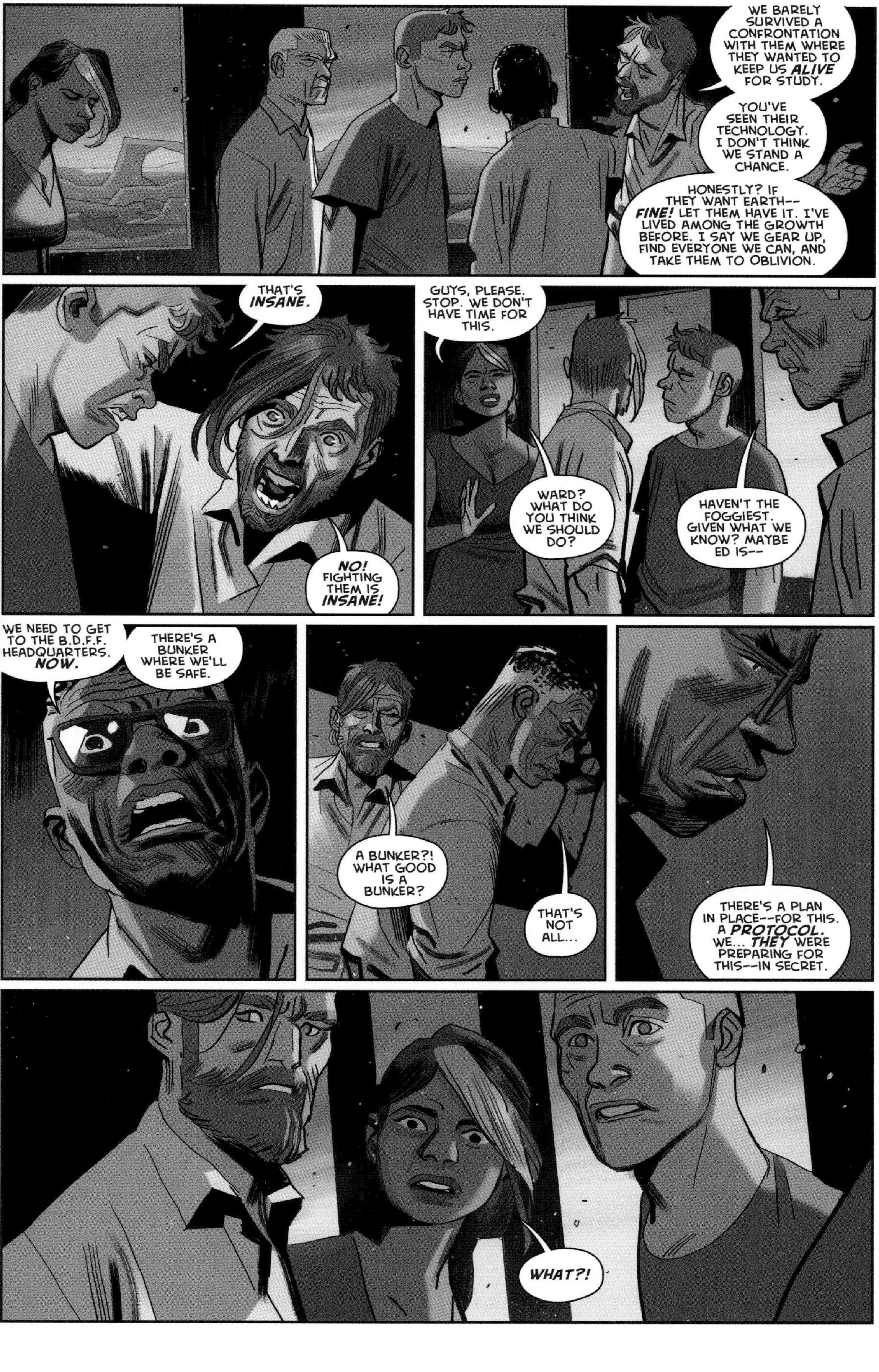
WE BARELY SURVIVED A CONFRONTATION WITH THEM WHERE THEY WANTED TO KEEP US ALIVE FOR STUDY.
YOU'VE SEEN THEIR TECHNOLOGY. I DON'T THINK WE STAND A CHANCE.
HONESTLY? IF THEY WANT EARTH-- FINE! LET THEM HAVE IT. I'VE LIVED AMONG THE GROWTH BEFORE. I SAY WE GEAR UP, FIND EVERYONE WE CAN, AND TAKE THEM TO OBLIVION.
THAT'S INSANE.
NO! FIGHTING THEM IS INSANE!
GUYS, PLEASE. STOP. WE DON'T HAVE TIME FOR THIS.
WARD? WHAT DO YOU THINK WE SHOULD DO?
HAVEN'T THE FOGGIEST. GIVEN WHAT WE KNOW? MAYBE ED IS--
WE NEED TO GET TO THE B.D.F.F. HEADQUARTERS. NOW.
THERE'S A BUNKER WHERE WE'LL BE SAFE.
A BUNKER?! WHAT GOOD IS A BUNKER?
THAT'S NOT ALL...
THERE'S A PLAN IN PLACE--FOR THIS. A PROTOCOL. WE... THEY WERE PREPARING FOR THIS--IN SECRET.
WHAT?!

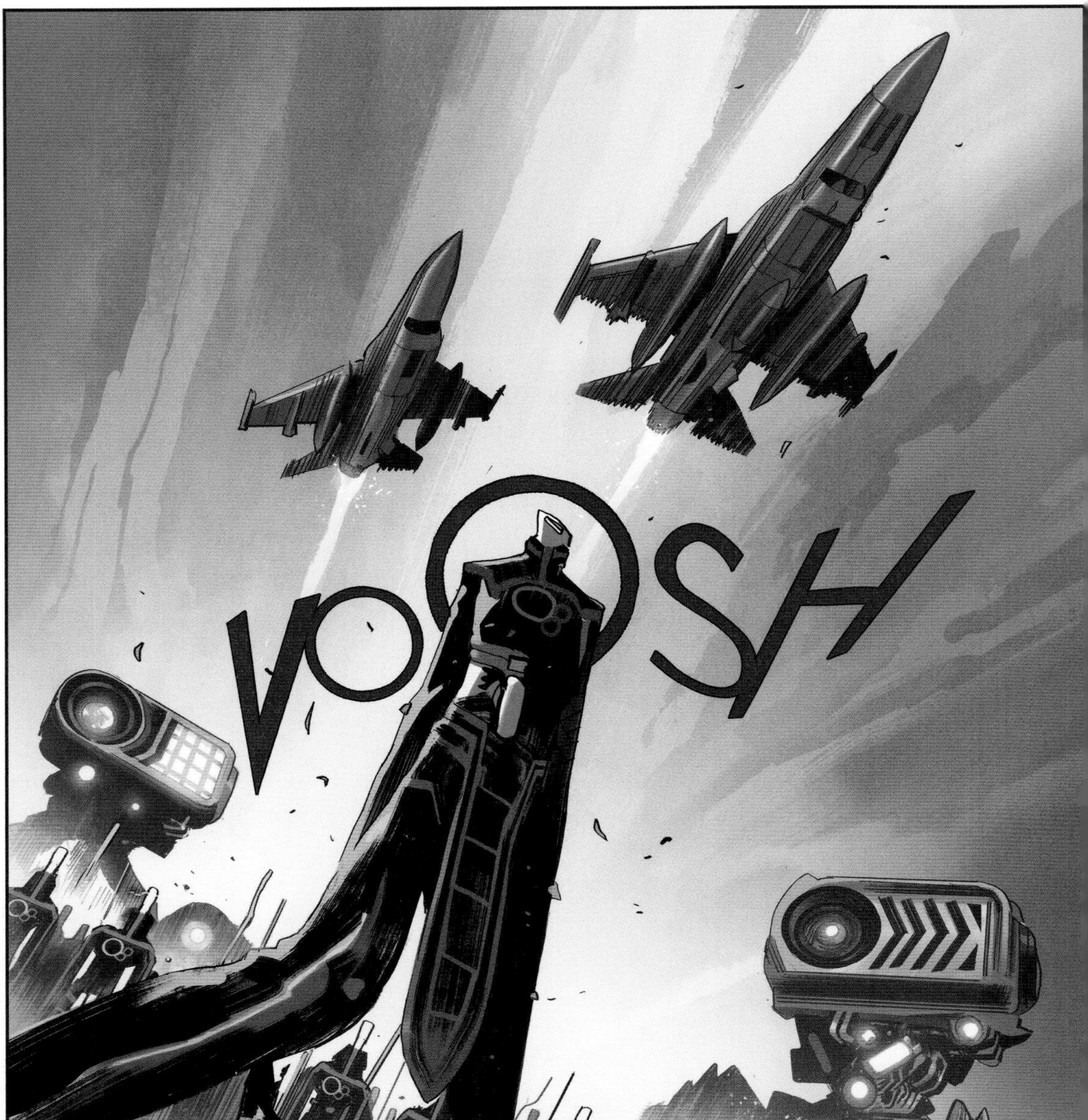
VOOSH

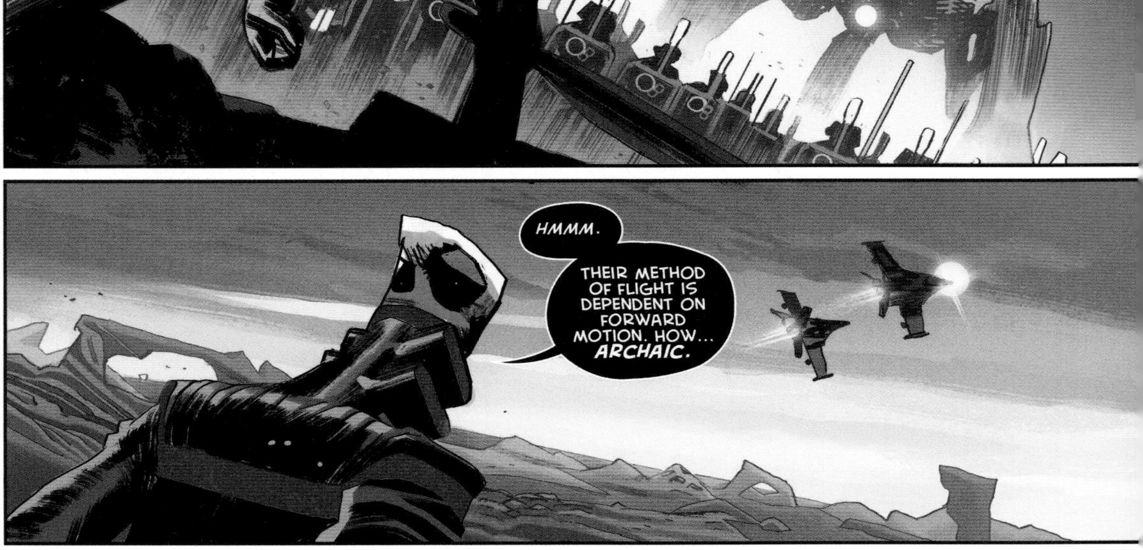
HMMM.
THEIR METHOD OF FLIGHT IS DEPENDENT ON FORWARD MOTION. HOW... ARCHAIC.

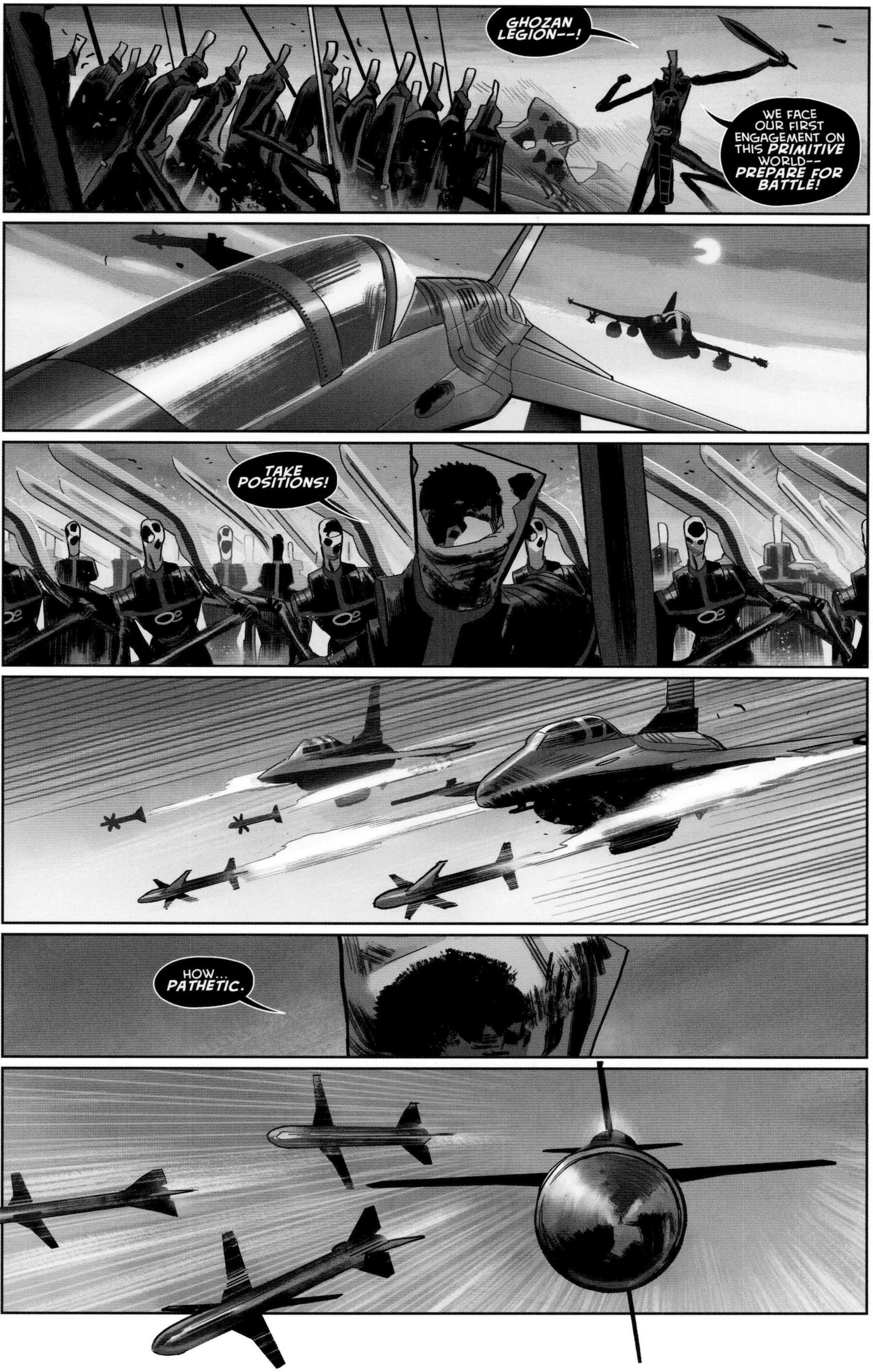
GHOZAN LEGION--!
WE FACE OUR FIRST ENGAGEMENT ON THIS PRIMITIVE WORLD-- PREPARE FOR BATTLE!
TAKE POSITIONS!
HOW... PATHETIC.

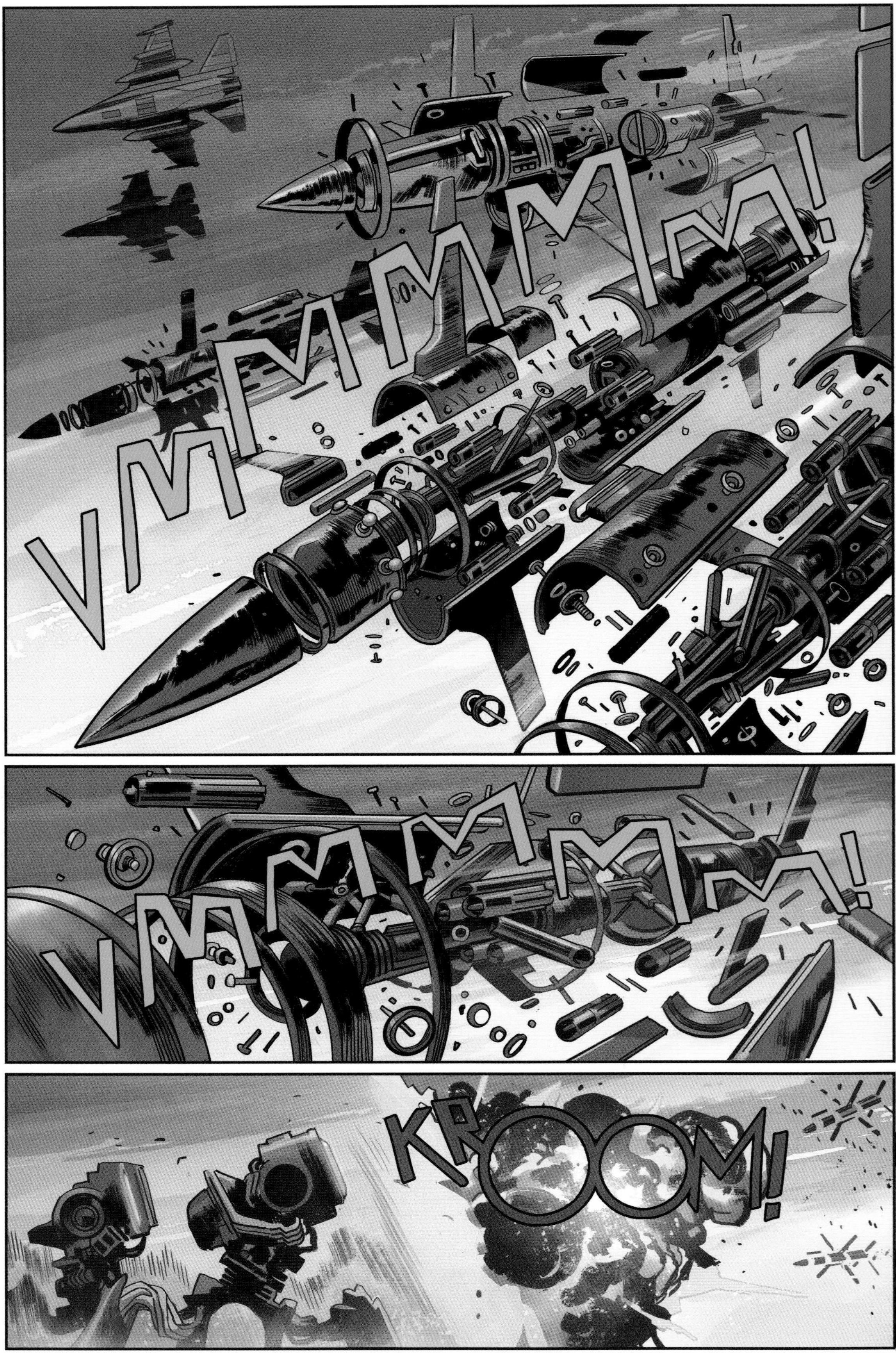
VMMMMMM!
VMMMMMM!
KROOOM!

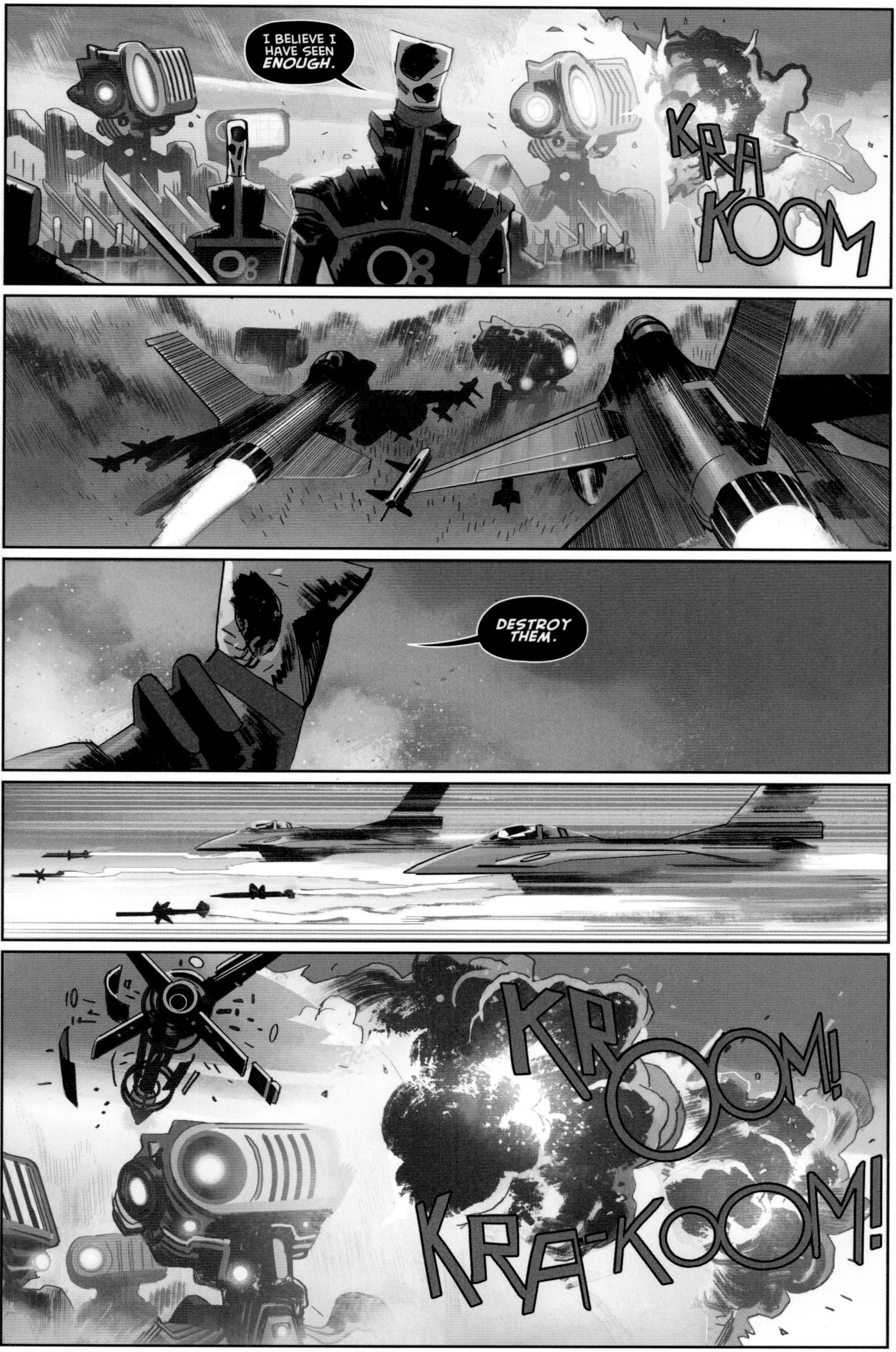
I BELIEVE I HAVE SEEN ENOUGH.
KRA KOOM
DESTROY THEM.
KROOM!!
KRA-KOOOM!

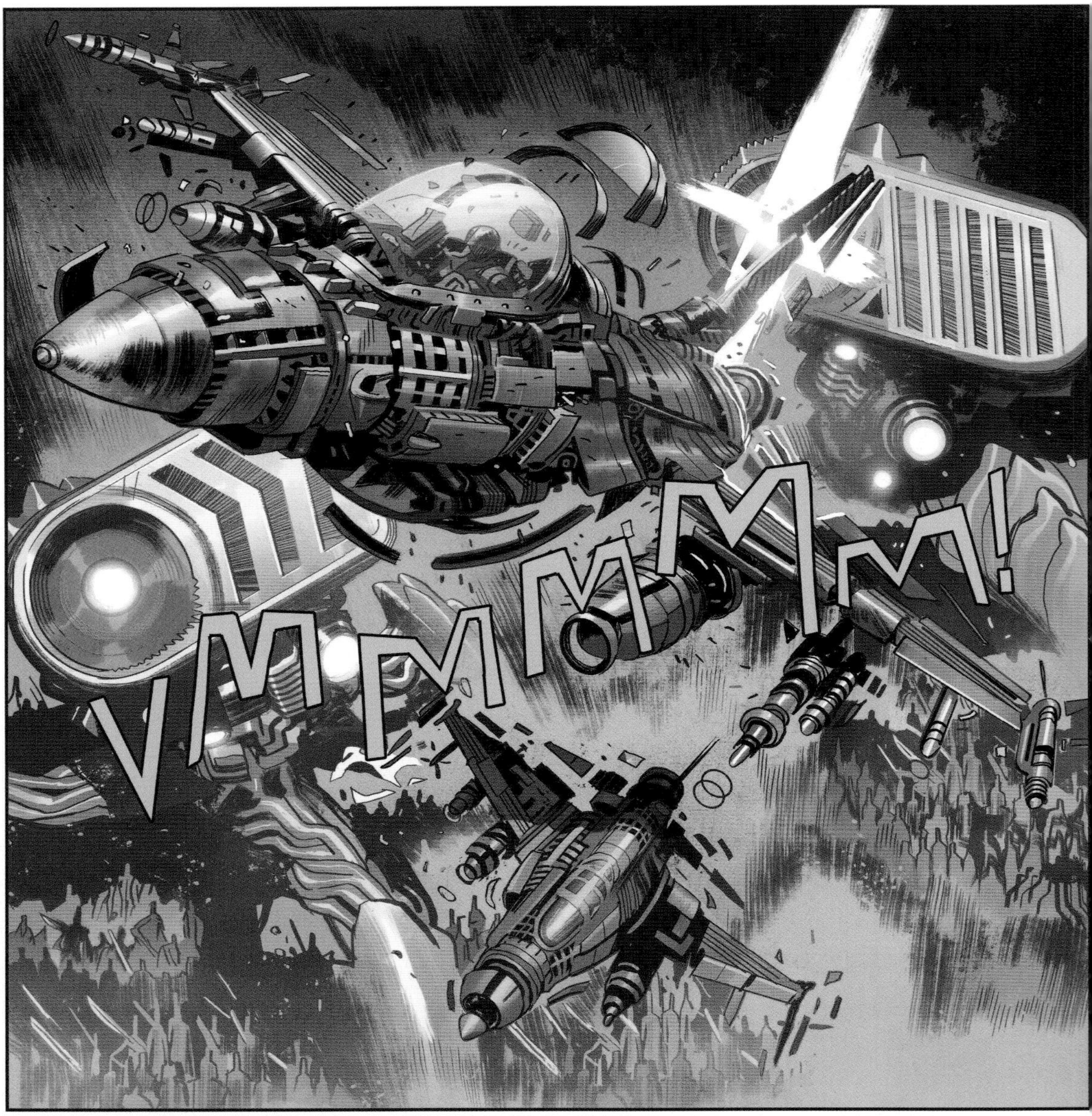
VMMMMMM!

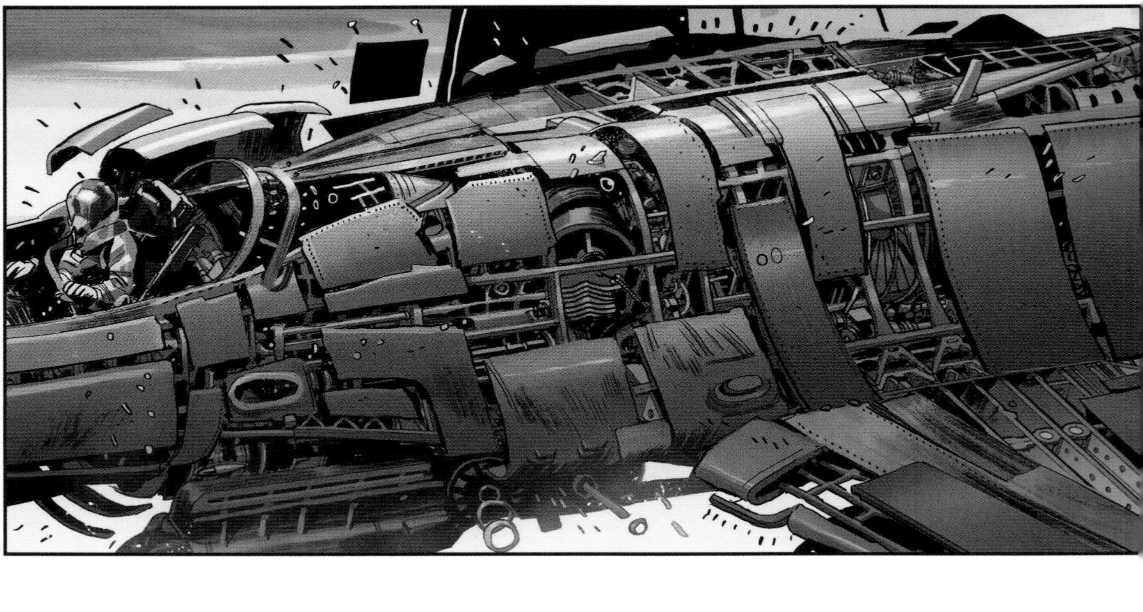

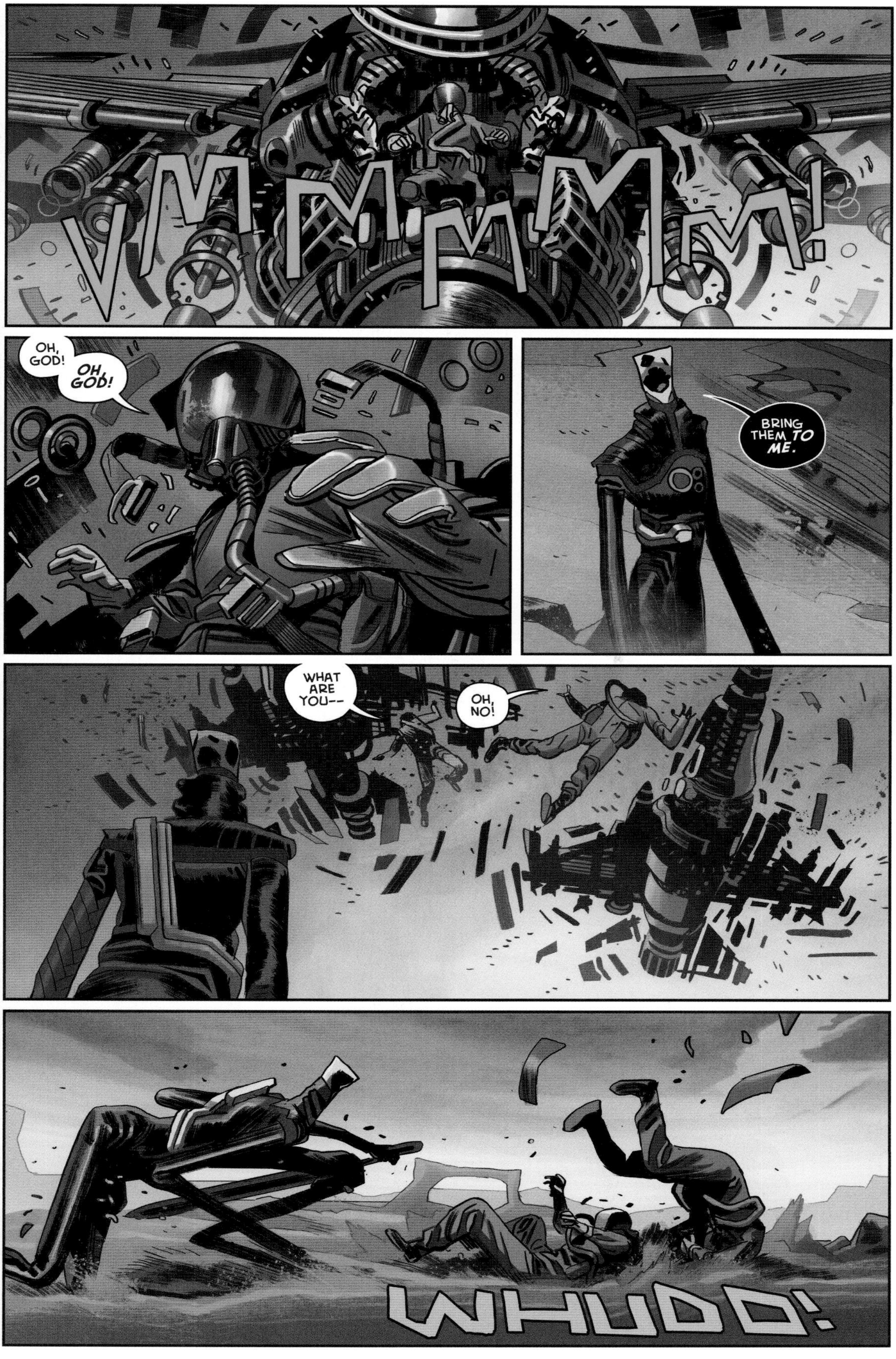
VMMMMMMM!
OH, GOD!
OH GOD!
BRING THEM TO ME.
WHAT ARE YOU--
OH, NO!
WHUDD!

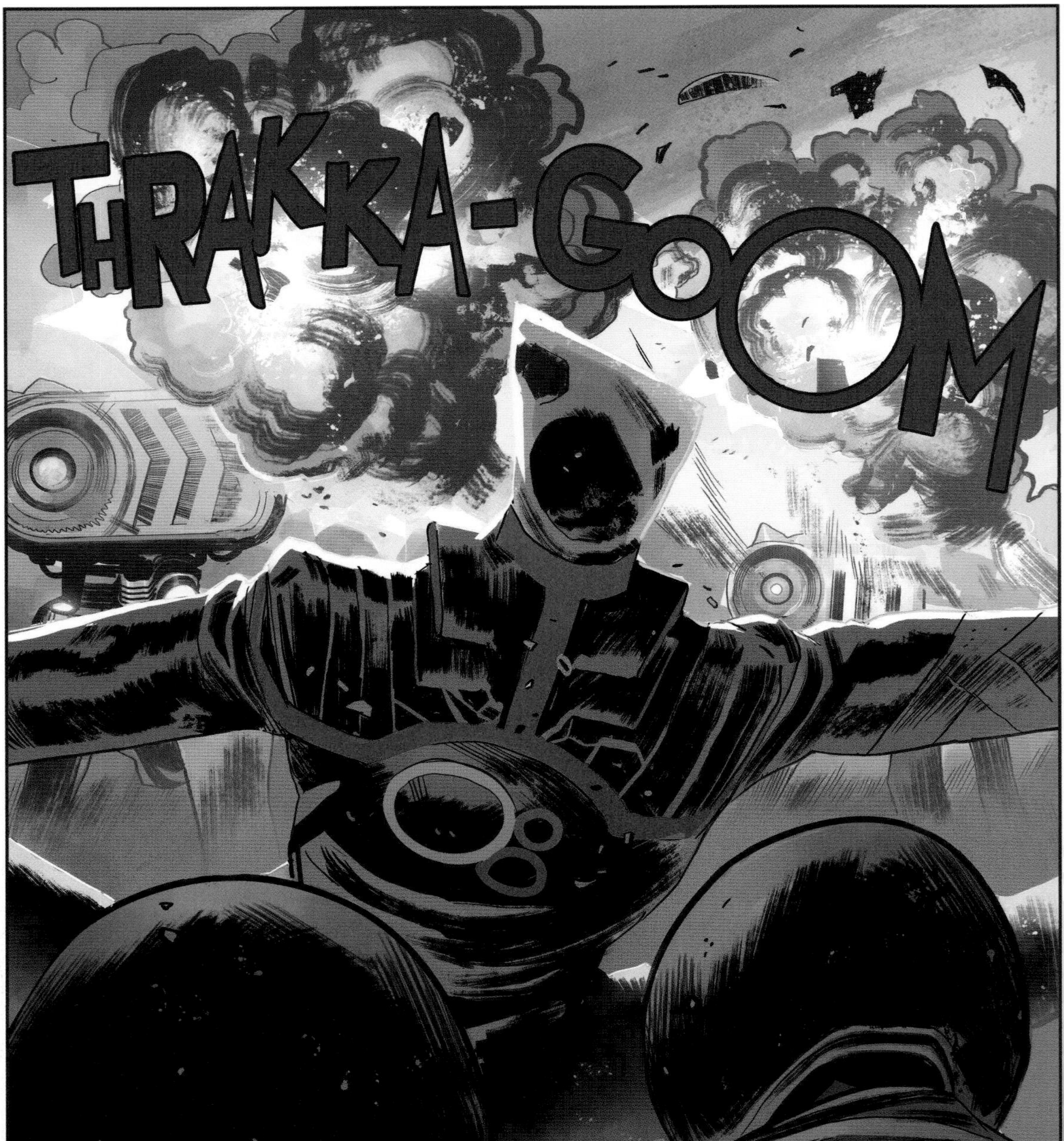
THRAKKA-GOOOM

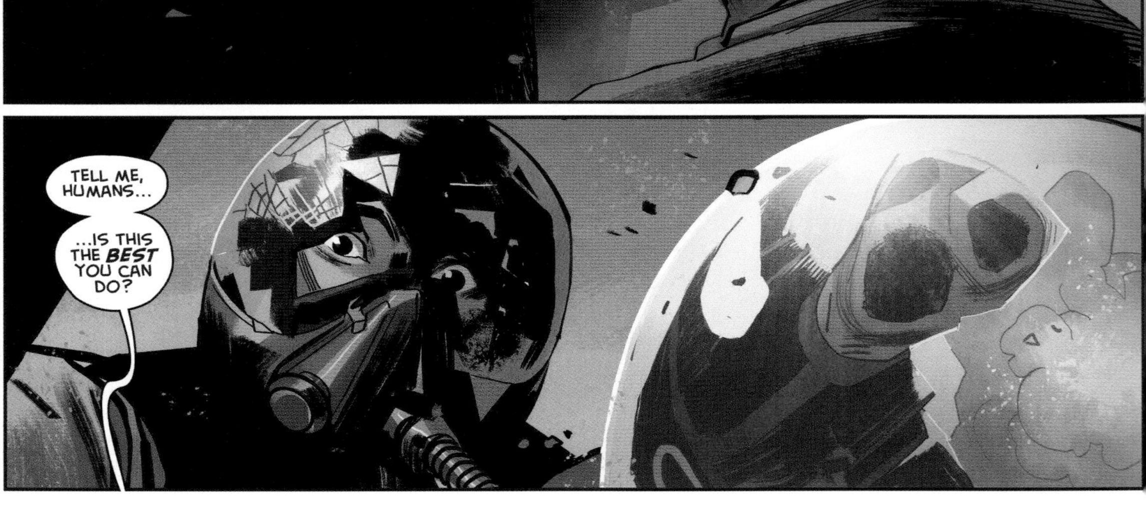
TELL ME, HUMANS...
...IS THIS THE **BEST** YOU CAN DO?

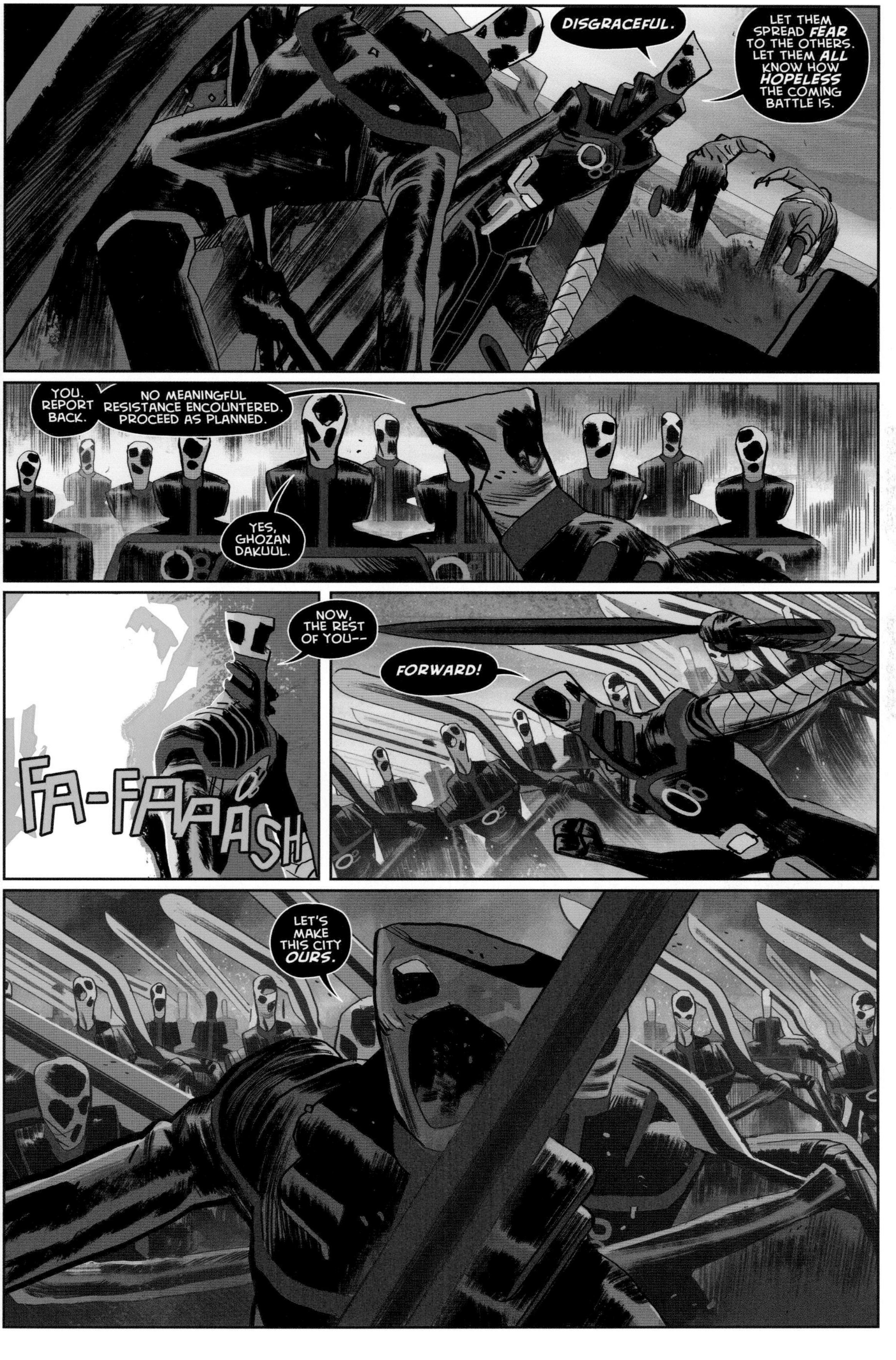
DISGRACEFUL.
LET THEM SPREAD FEAR TO THE OTHERS. LET THEM ALL KNOW HOW HOPELESS THE COMING BATTLE IS.
YOU. REPORT BACK.
NO MEANINGFUL RESISTANCE ENCOUNTERED. PROCEED AS PLANNED.
YES, GHOZAN DAKUUL.
NOW, THE REST OF YOU--
FA-FAAAASH
FORWARD!
LET'S MAKE THIS CITY OURS.

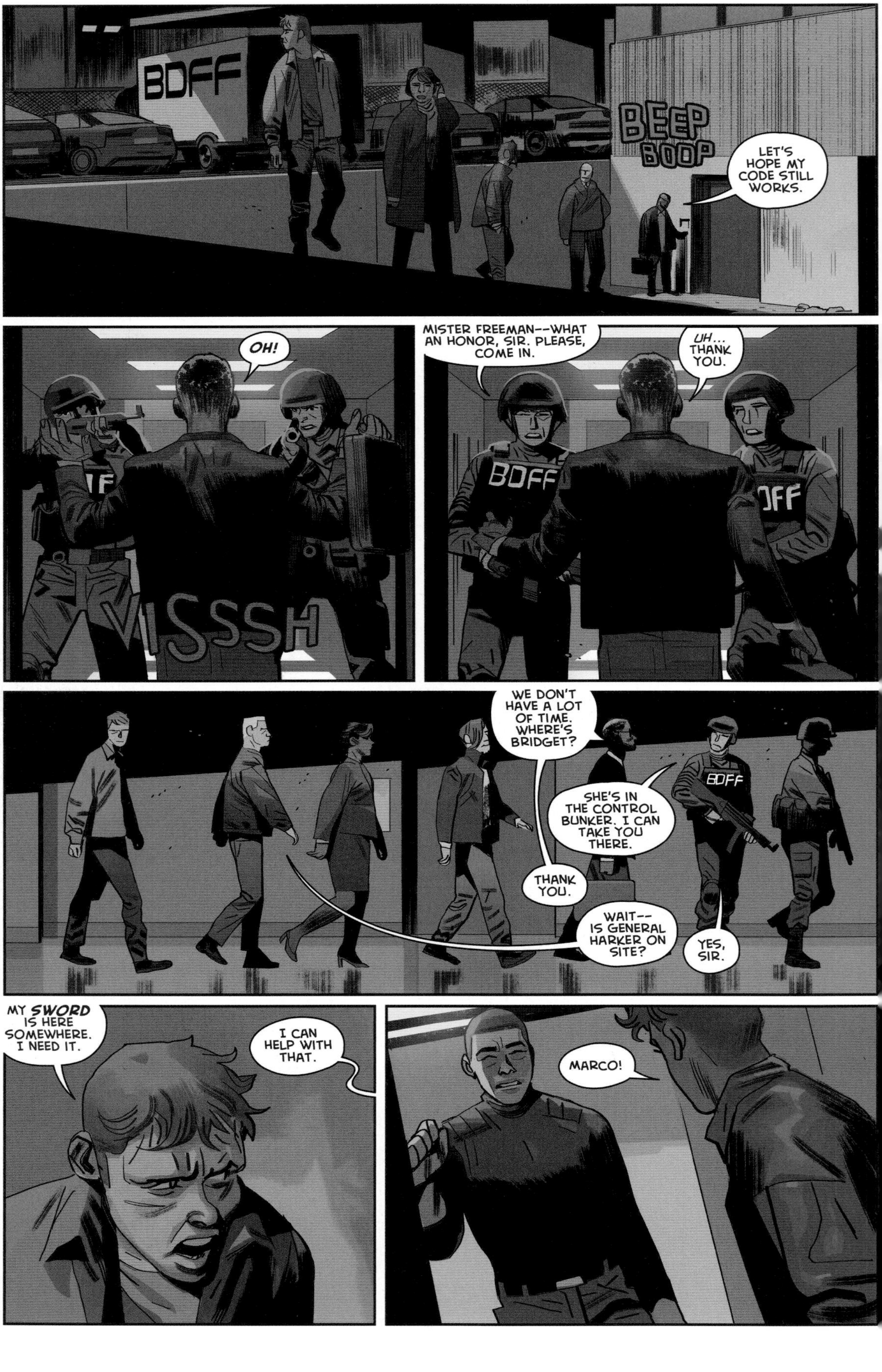
BEEP
BOOP
LET'S HOPE MY CODE STILL WORKS.
OH!
VISSSH
MISTER FREEMAN--WHAT AN HONOR, SIR. PLEASE, COME IN.
UH... THANK YOU.
WE DON'T HAVE A LOT OF TIME. WHERE'S BRIDGET?
SHE'S IN THE CONTROL BUNKER. I CAN TAKE YOU THERE.
THANK YOU.
WAIT-- IS GENERAL HARKER ON SITE?
YES, SIR.
MY SWORD IS HERE SOMEWHERE. I NEED IT.
I CAN HELP WITH THAT.
MARCO!

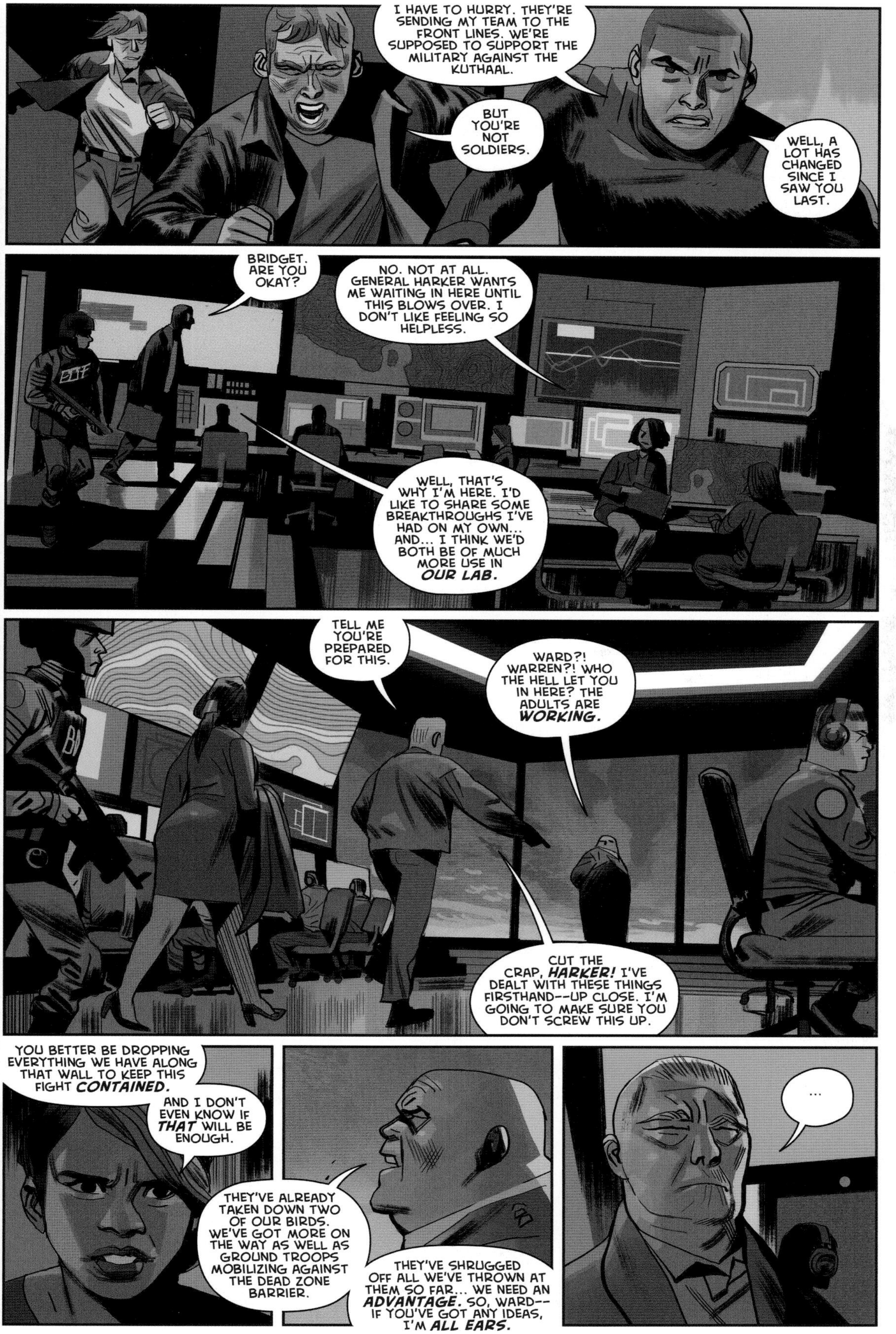
I HAVE TO HURRY. THEY'RE SENDING MY TEAM TO THE FRONT LINES. WE'RE SUPPOSED TO SUPPORT THE MILITARY AGAINST THE KUTHAAL.
BUT YOU'RE NOT SOLDIERS.
WELL, A LOT HAS CHANGED SINCE I SAW YOU LAST.
BRIDGET. ARE YOU OKAY?
NO. NOT AT ALL. GENERAL HARKER WANTS ME WAITING IN HERE UNTIL THIS BLOWS OVER. I DON'T LIKE FEELING SO HELPLESS.
WELL, THAT'S WHY I'M HERE. I'D LIKE TO SHARE SOME BREAKTHROUGHS I'VE HAD ON MY OWN... AND... I THINK WE'D BOTH BE OF MUCH MORE USE IN OUR LAB.
TELL ME YOU'RE PREPARED FOR THIS.
WARD?! WARREN?! WHO THE HELL LET YOU IN HERE? THE ADULTS ARE WORKING.
CUT THE CRAP, HARKER! I'VE DEALT WITH THESE THINGS FIRSTHAND--UP CLOSE. I'M GOING TO MAKE SURE YOU DON'T SCREW THIS UP.
YOU BETTER BE DROPPING EVERYTHING WE HAVE ALONG THAT WALL TO KEEP THIS FIGHT CONTAINED.
AND I DON'T EVEN KNOW IF THAT WILL BE ENOUGH.
THEY'VE ALREADY TAKEN DOWN TWO OF OUR BIRDS. WE'VE GOT MORE ON THE WAY AS WELL AS GROUND TROOPS MOBILIZING AGAINST THE DEAD ZONE BARRIER.
THEY'VE SHRUGGED OFF ALL WE'VE THROWN AT THEM SO FAR... WE NEED AN ADVANTAGE. SO, WARD-- IF YOU'VE GOT ANY IDEAS, I'M ALL EARS.
...

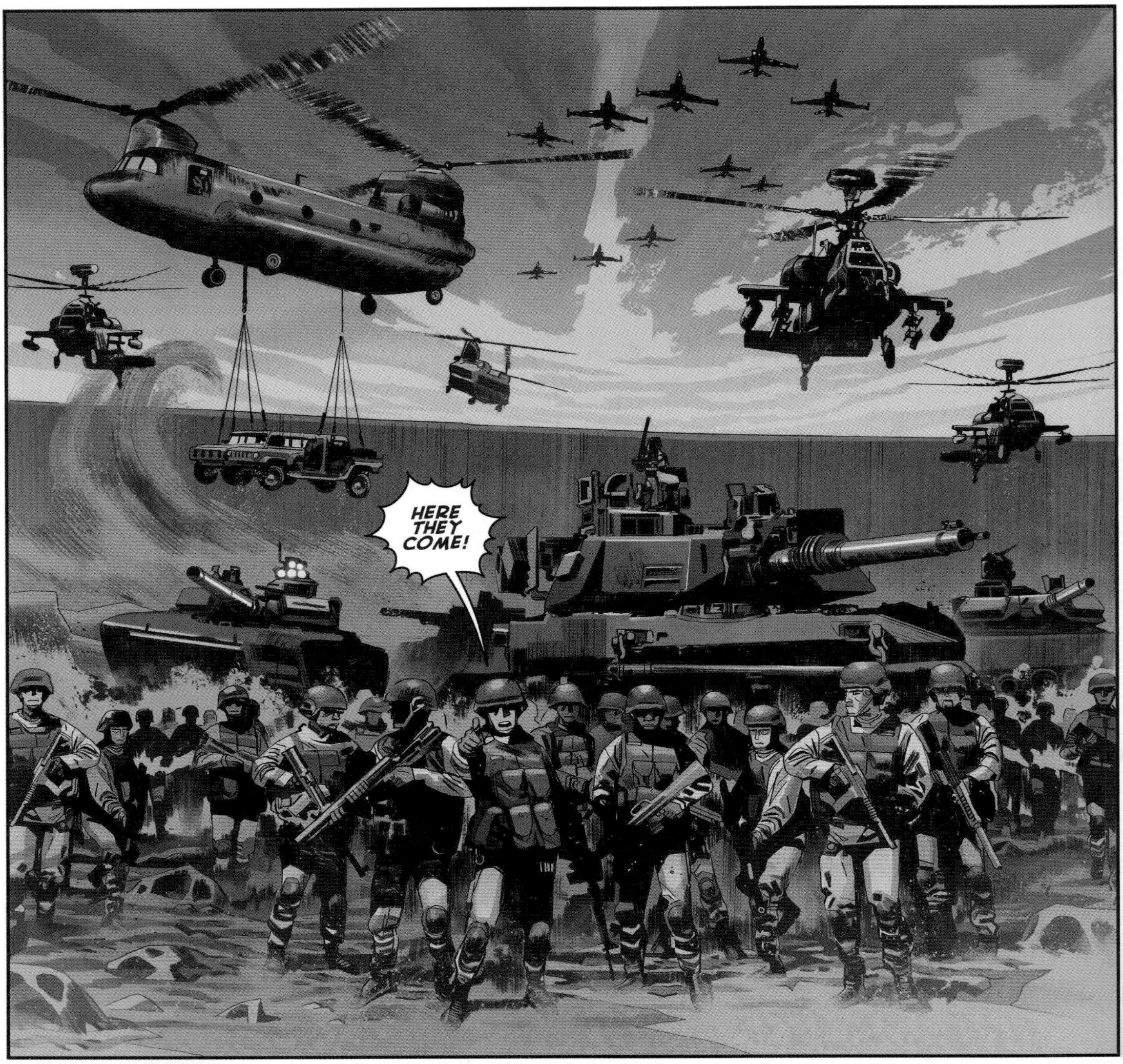
HERE THEY COME!

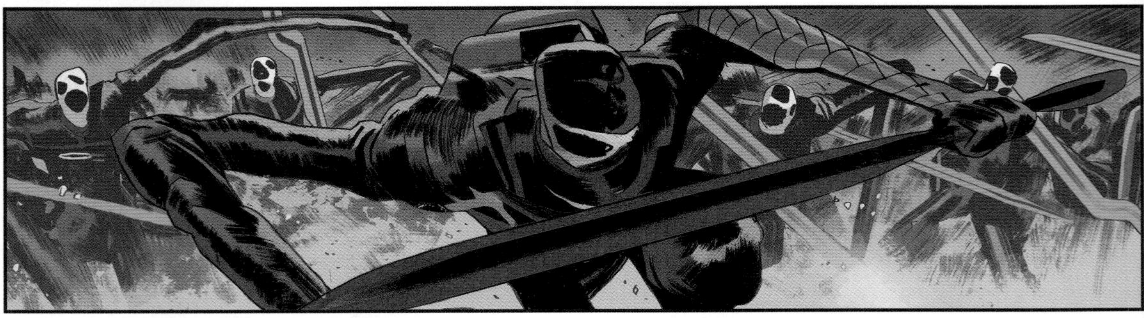

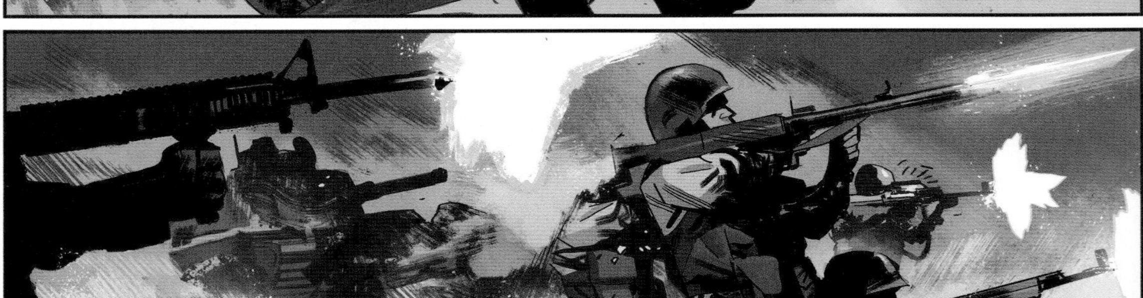

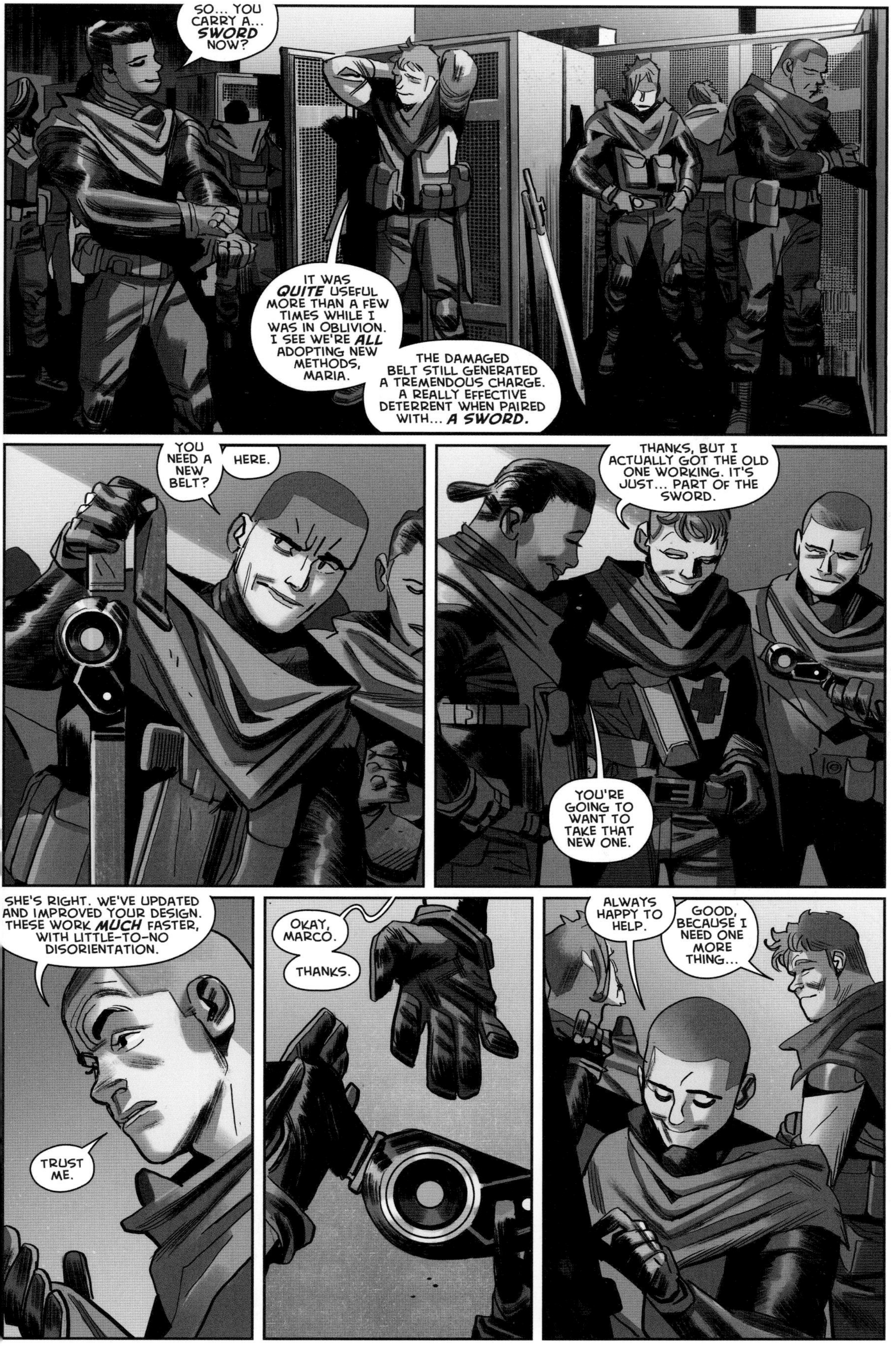
SO... YOU CARRY A... SWORD NOW?
IT WAS QUITE USEFUL MORE THAN A FEW TIMES WHILE I WAS IN OBLIVION. I SEE WE'RE ALL ADOPTING NEW METHODS, MARIA.
THE DAMAGED BELT STILL GENERATED A TREMENDOUS CHARGE. A REALLY EFFECTIVE DETERRENT WHEN PAIRED WITH... A SWORD.
YOU NEED A NEW BELT?
HERE.
THANKS, BUT I ACTUALLY GOT THE OLD ONE WORKING. IT'S JUST... PART OF THE SWORD.
YOU'RE GOING TO WANT TO TAKE THAT NEW ONE.
SHE'S RIGHT. WE'VE UPDATED AND IMPROVED YOUR DESIGN. THESE WORK MUCH FASTER, WITH LITTLE-TO-NO DISORIENTATION.
TRUST ME.
OKAY, MARCO.
THANKS.
ALWAYS HAPPY TO HELP.
GOOD, BECAUSE I NEED ONE MORE THING...

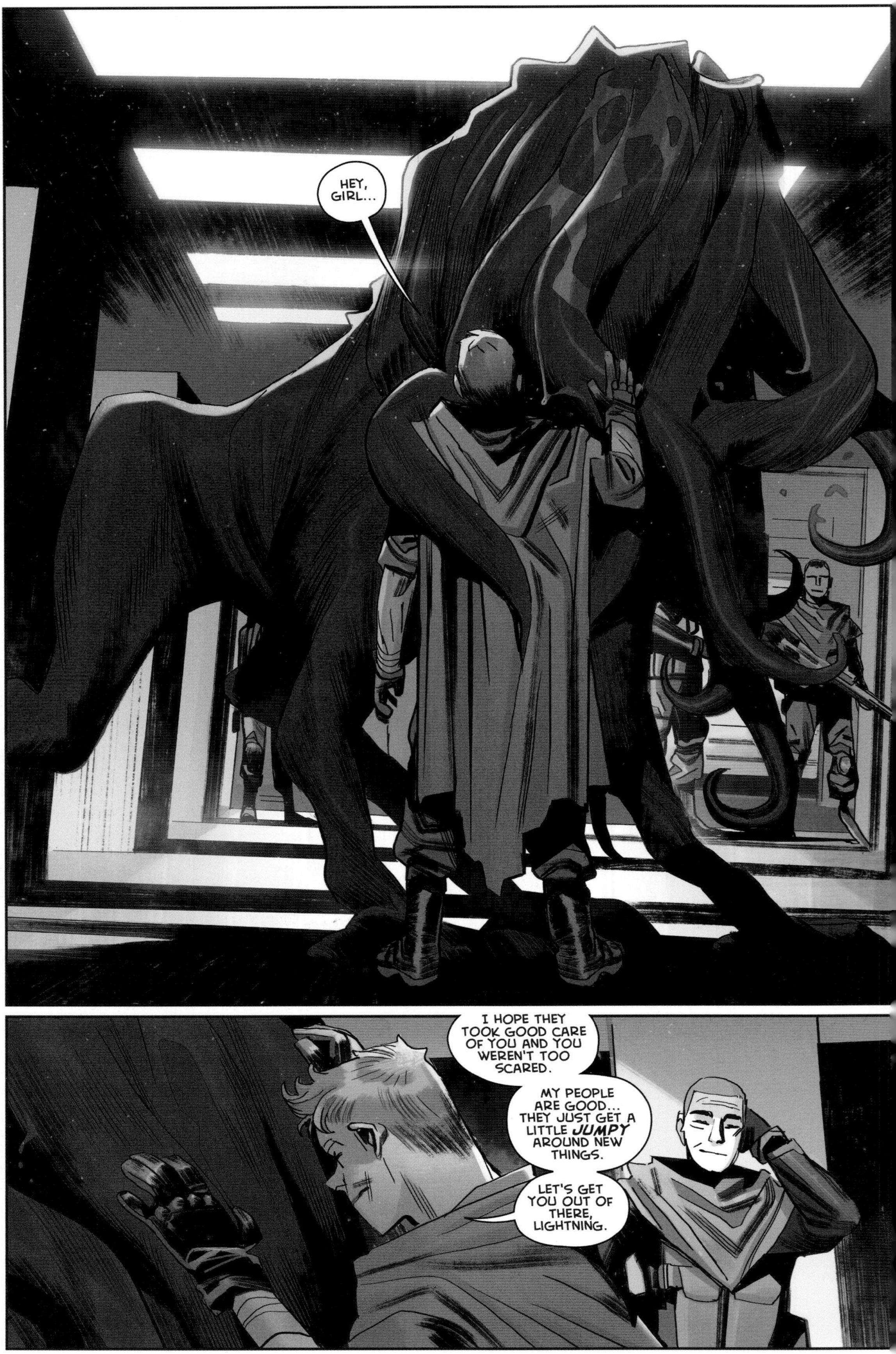
HEY, GIRL...
I HOPE THEY TOOK GOOD CARE OF YOU AND YOU WEREN'T TOO SCARED.
MY PEOPLE ARE GOOD... THEY JUST GET A LITTLE *JUMPY* AROUND NEW THINGS.
LET'S GET YOU OUT OF THERE, LIGHTNING.

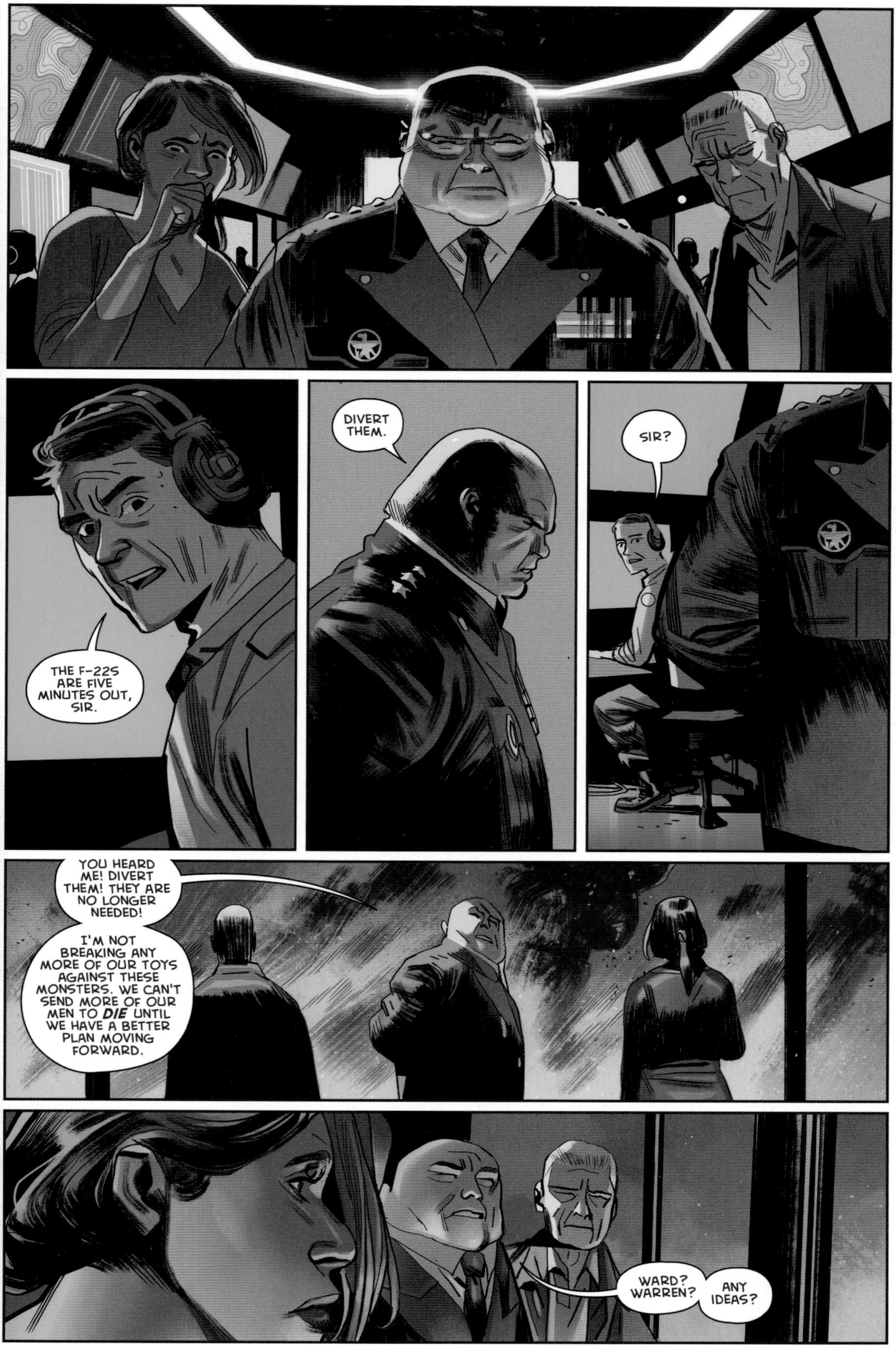
THE F-22S ARE FIVE MINUTES OUT, SIR.
DIVERT THEM.
SIR?
YOU HEARD ME! DIVERT THEM! THEY ARE NO LONGER NEEDED!
I'M NOT BREAKING ANY MORE OF OUR TOYS AGAINST THESE MONSTERS. WE CAN'T SEND MORE OF OUR MEN TO DIE UNTIL WE HAVE A BETTER PLAN MOVING FORWARD.
WARD? WARREN?
ANY IDEAS?

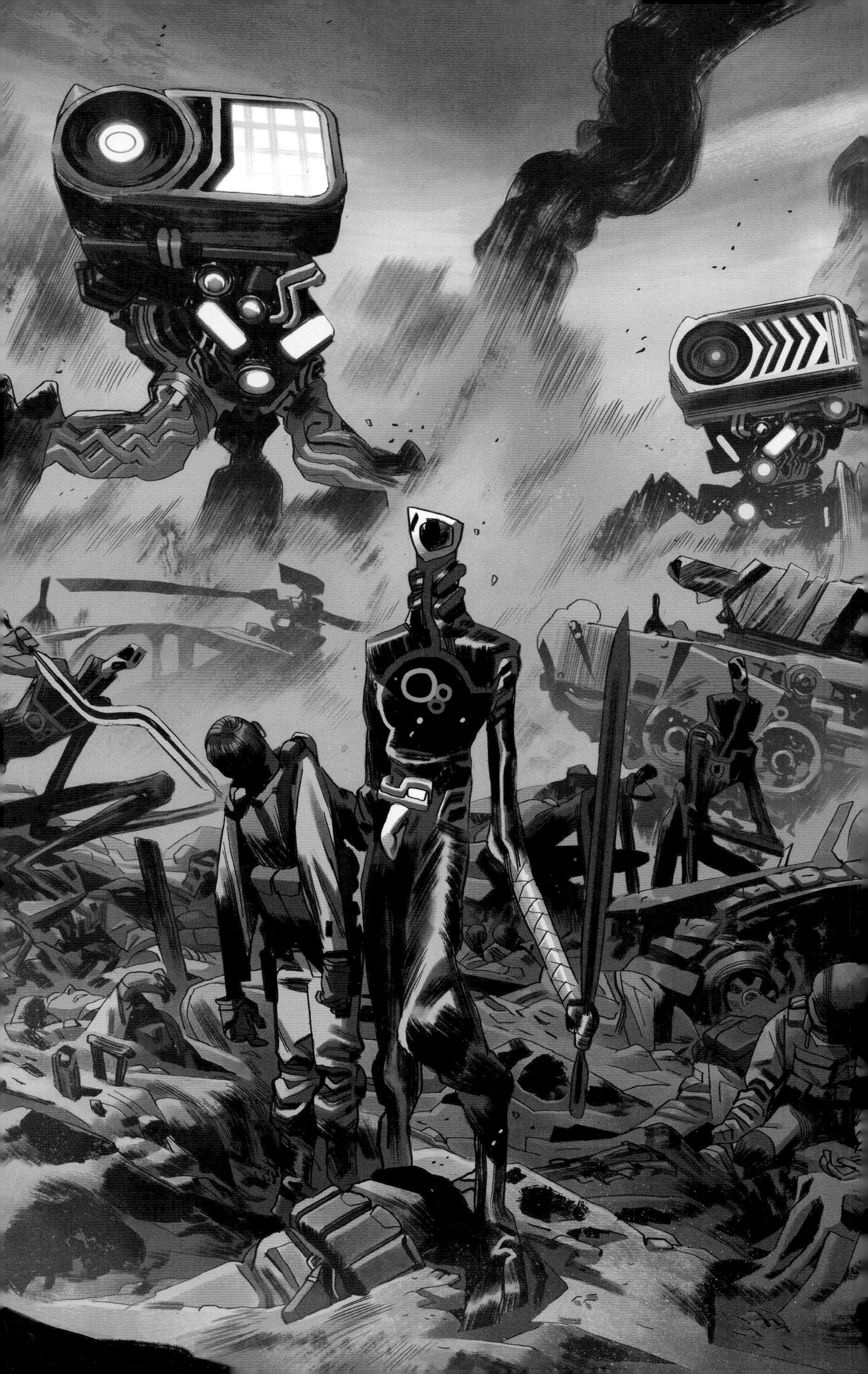

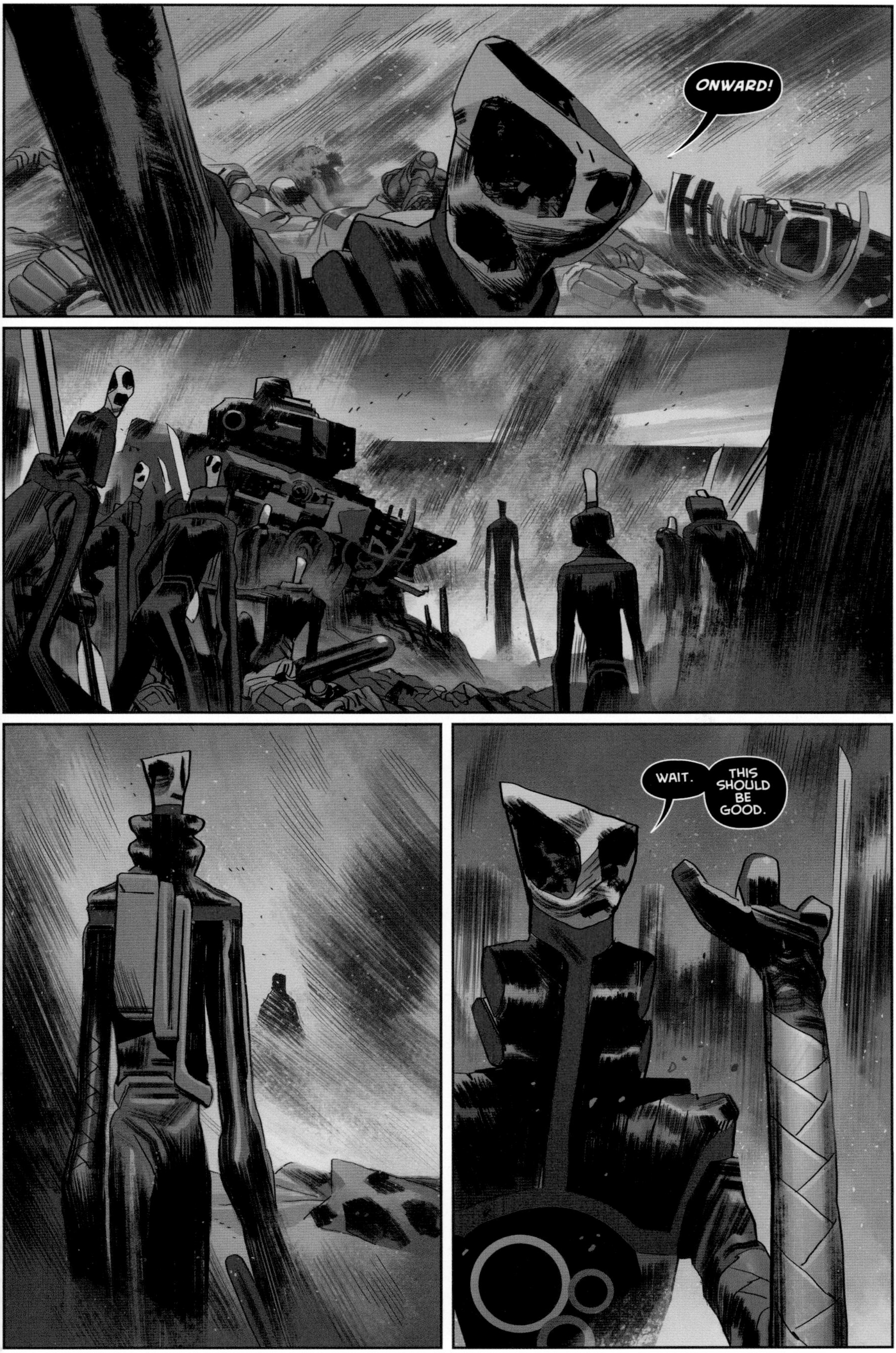
ONWARD!
WAIT.
THIS SHOULD BE GOOD.

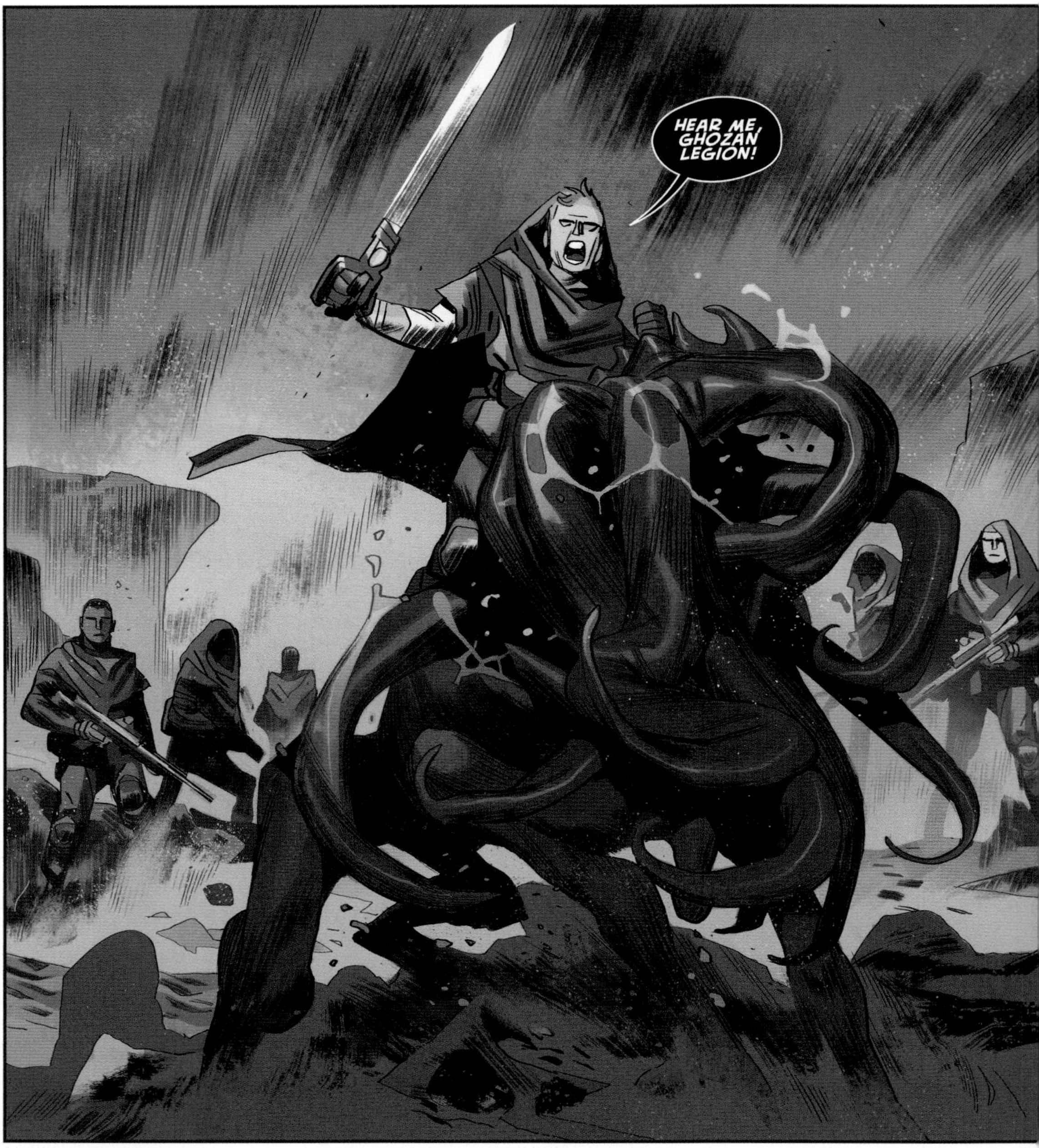
HEAR ME, GHOZAN LEGION!

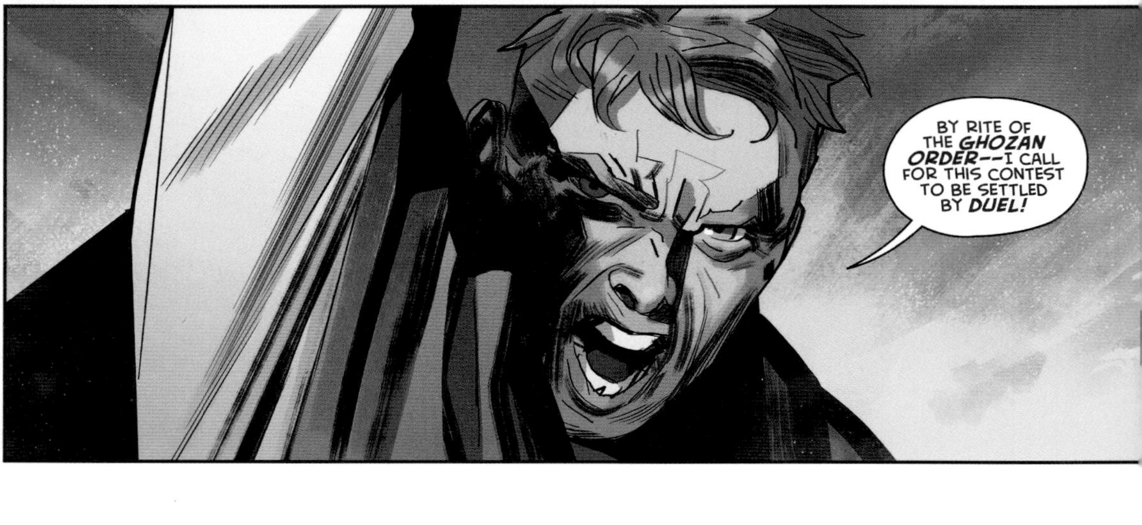
BY RITE OF THE GHOZAN ORDER--I CALL FOR THIS CONTEST TO BE SETTLED BY DUEL!

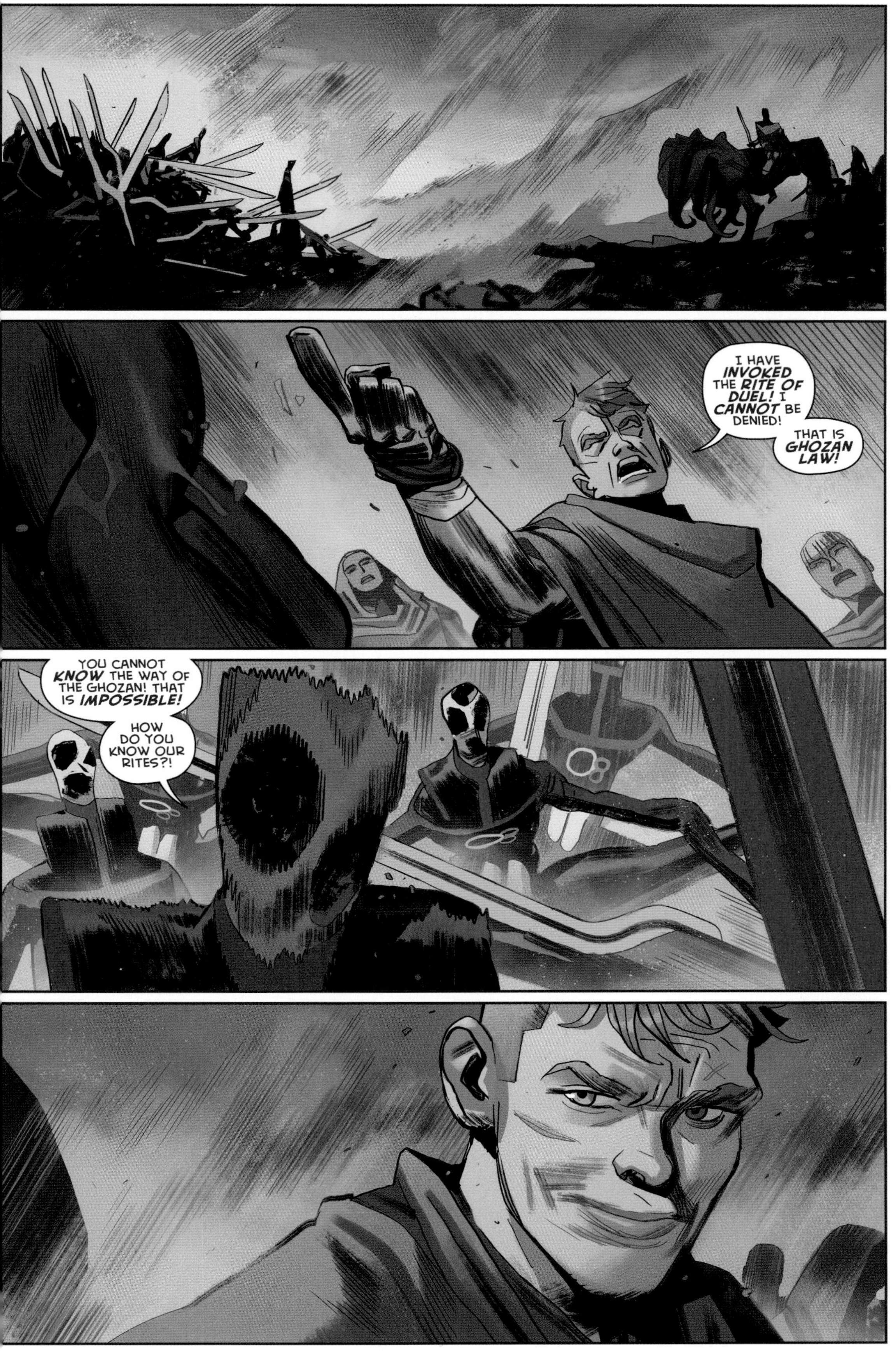
I HAVE *INVOKED* THE *RITE OF DUEL!* I *CANNOT* BE DENIED!
THAT IS *GHOZAN LAW!*
YOU CANNOT *KNOW* THE WAY OF THE GHOZAN! THAT IS *IMPOSSIBLE!*
HOW DO YOU KNOW OUR RITES?!

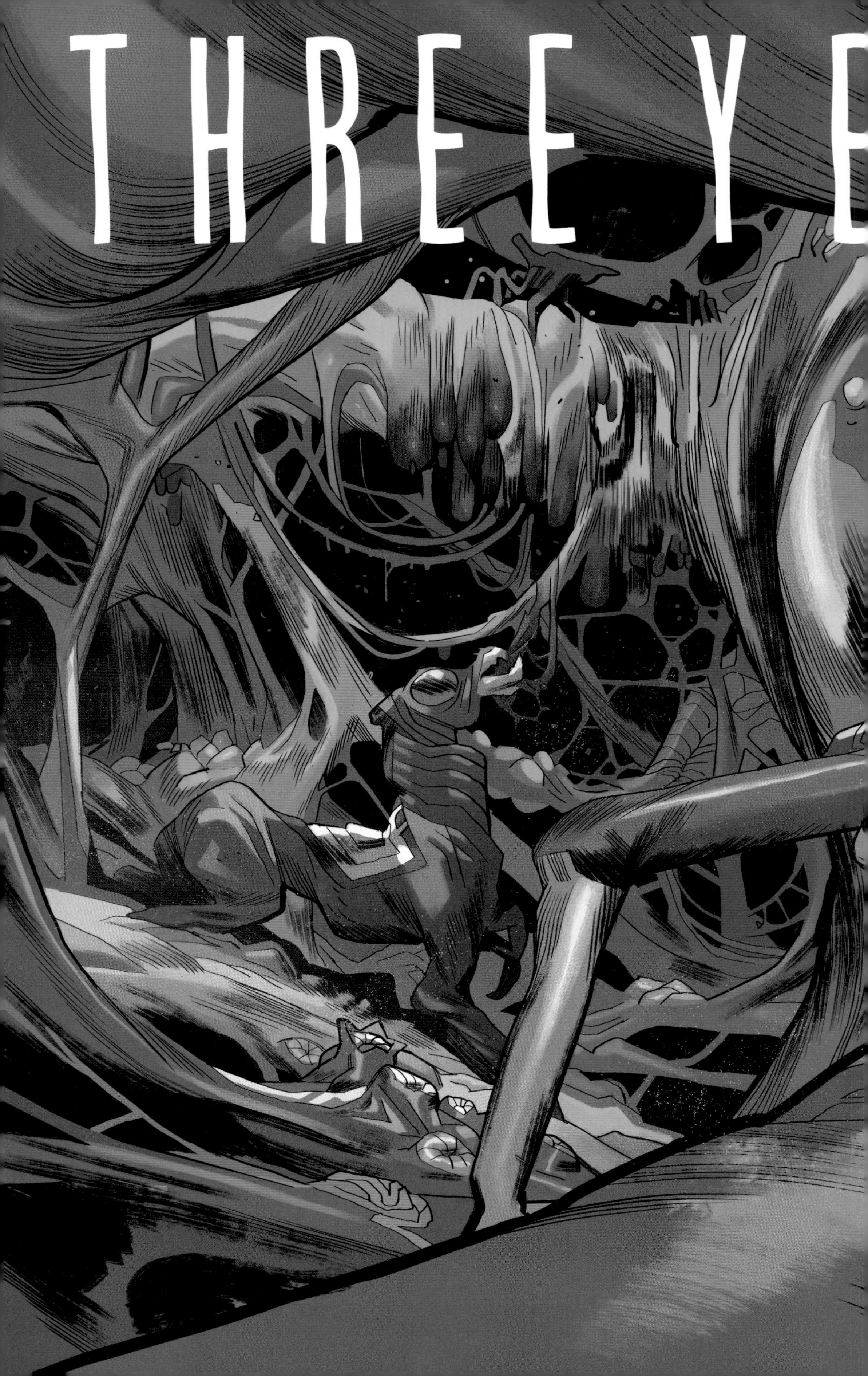
THREE YE

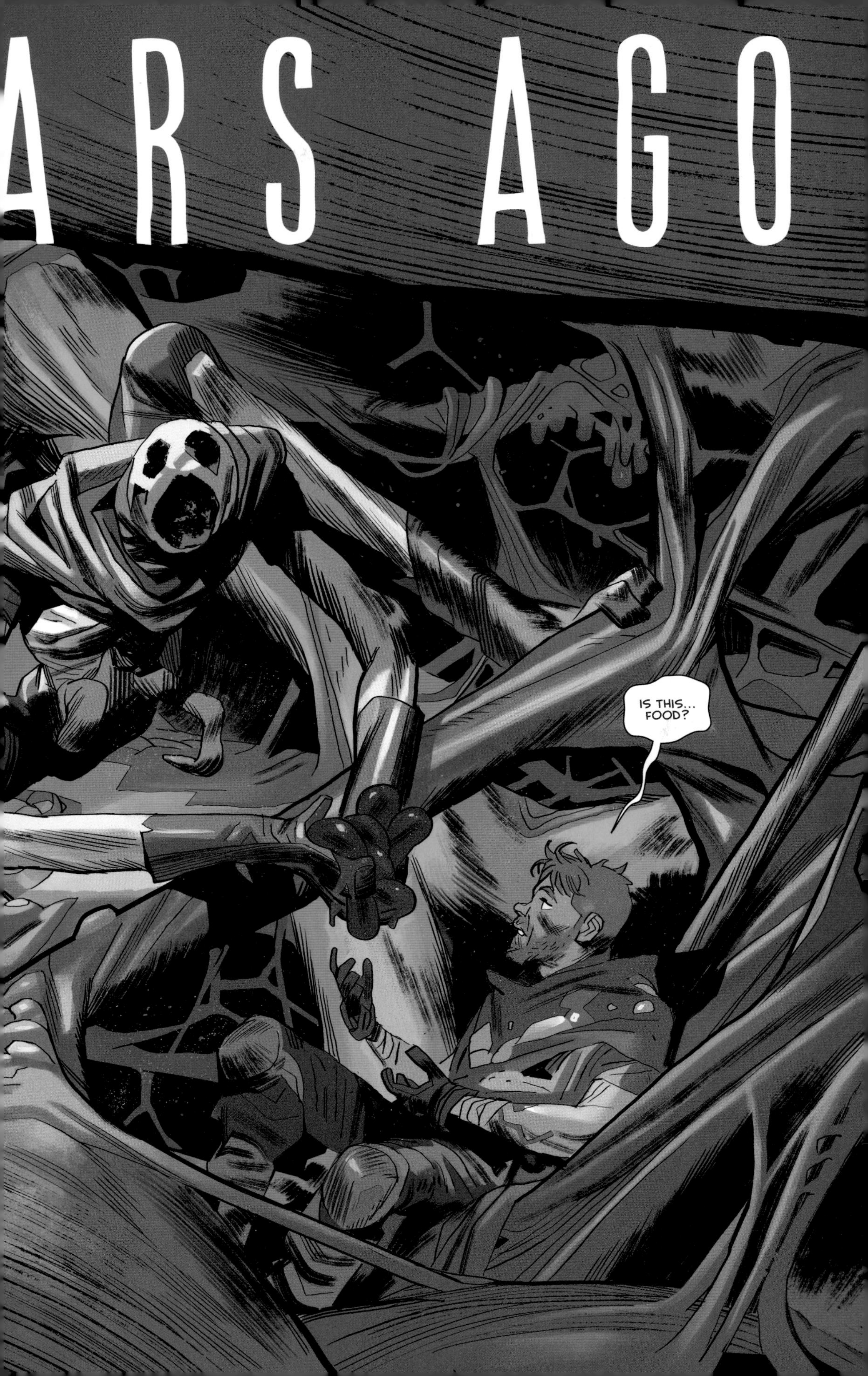
ARS AGO
IS THIS...
FOOD?

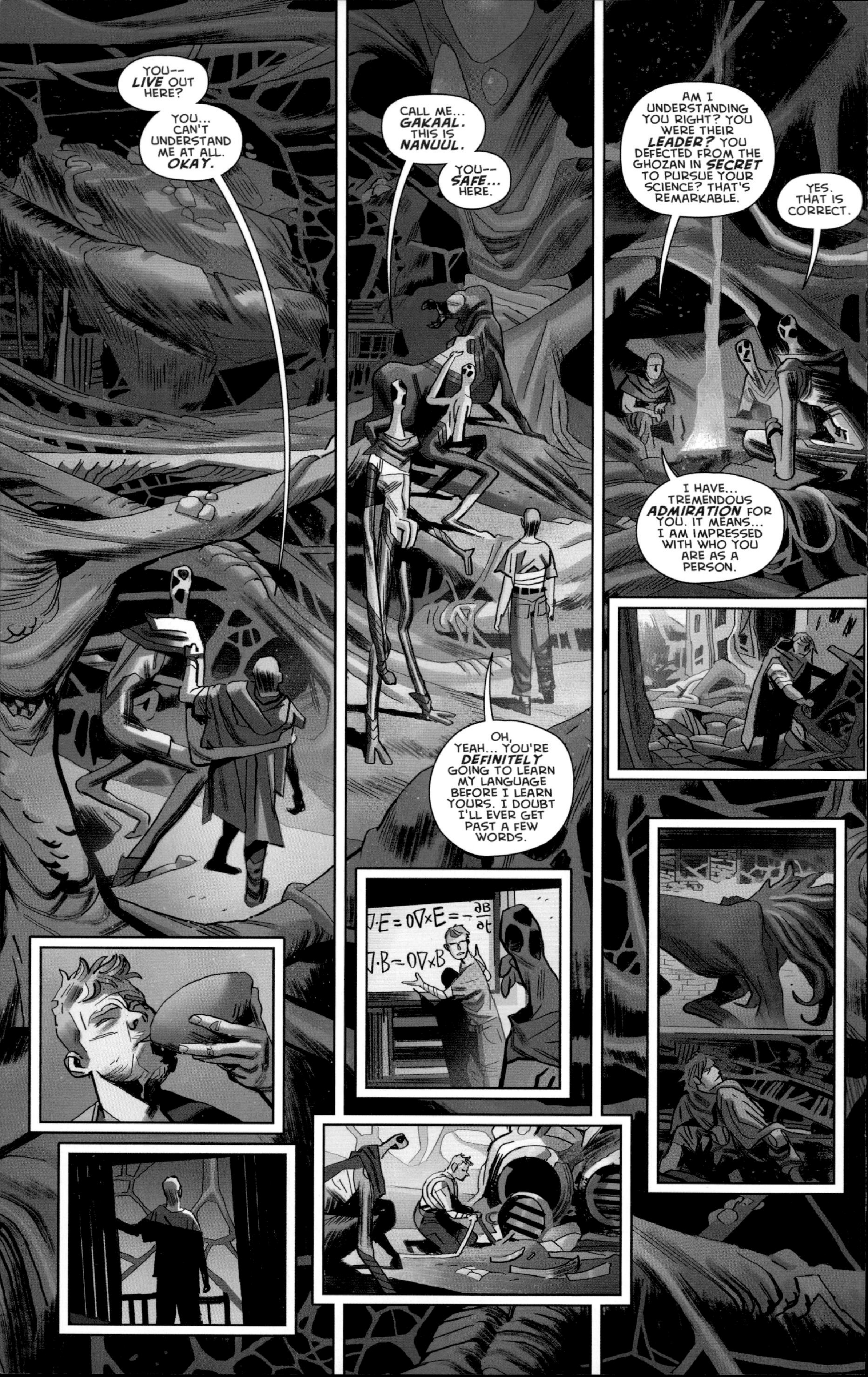

YOU-- LIVE OUT HERE?
YOU... CAN'T UNDERSTAND ME AT ALL. OKAY.
CALL ME... GAKAAL. THIS IS NANUUL.
YOU-- SAFE... HERE.
OH, YEAH... YOU'RE DEFINITELY GOING TO LEARN MY LANGUAGE BEFORE I LEARN YOURS. I DOUBT I'LL EVER GET PAST A FEW WORDS.
AM I UNDERSTANDING YOU RIGHT? YOU WERE THEIR LEADER? YOU DEFECTED FROM THE GHOZAN IN SECRET TO PURSUE YOUR SCIENCE? THAT'S REMARKABLE.
YES. THAT IS CORRECT.
I HAVE... TREMENDOUS ADMIRATION FOR YOU. IT MEANS... I AM IMPRESSED WITH WHO YOU ARE AS A PERSON.

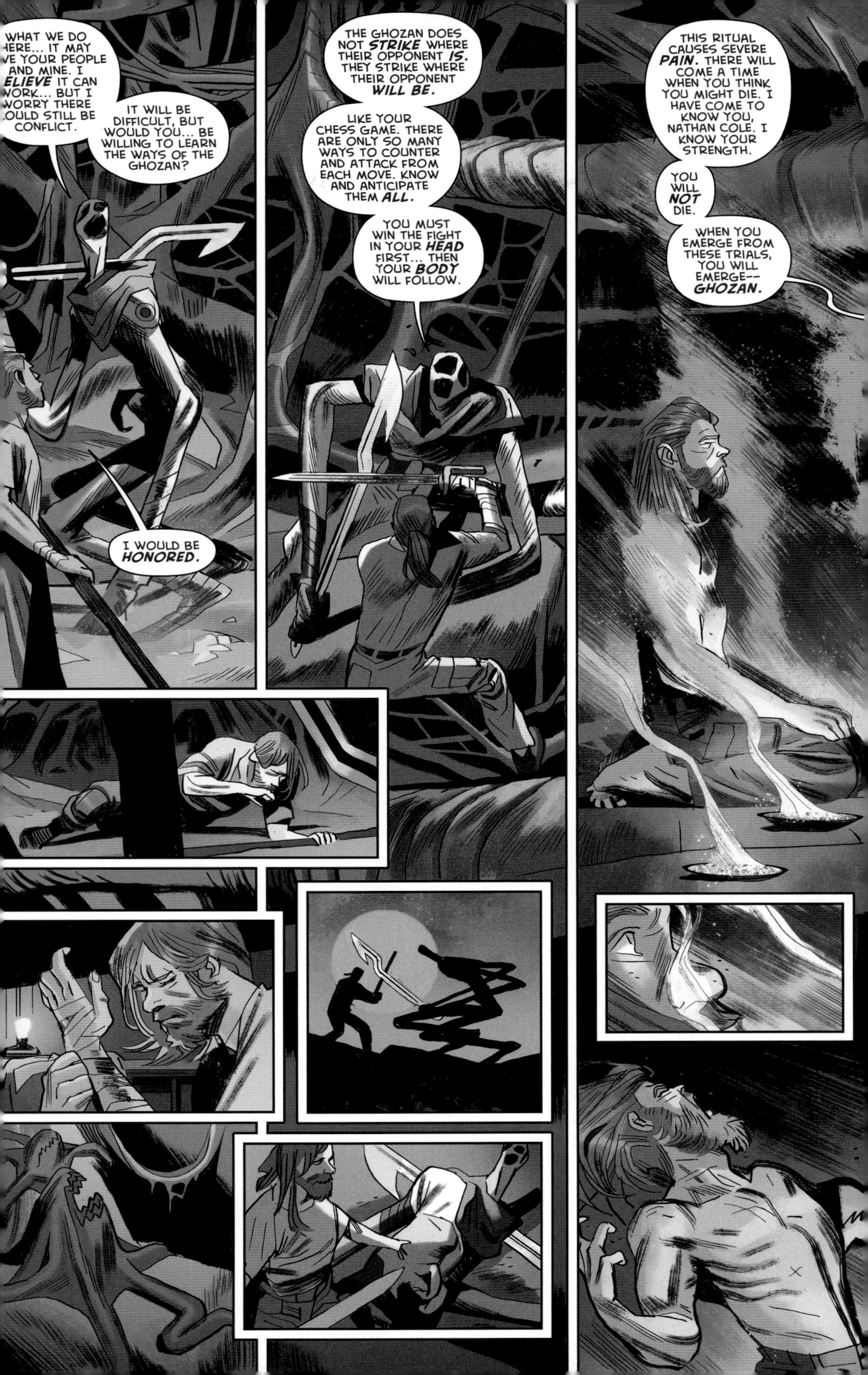
WHAT WE DO HERE... IT MAY VE YOUR PEOPLE AND MINE. I ELIEVE IT CAN WORK... BUT I WORRY THERE OULD STILL BE CONFLICT.
IT WILL BE DIFFICULT, BUT WOULD YOU... BE WILLING TO LEARN THE WAYS OF THE GHOZAN?
I WOULD BE HONORED.
THE GHOZAN DOES NOT STRIKE WHERE THEIR OPPONENT IS. THEY STRIKE WHERE THEIR OPPONENT WILL BE.
LIKE YOUR CHESS GAME. THERE ARE ONLY SO MANY WAYS TO COUNTER AND ATTACK FROM EACH MOVE. KNOW AND ANTICIPATE THEM ALL.
YOU MUST WIN THE FIGHT IN YOUR HEAD FIRST... THEN YOUR BODY WILL FOLLOW.
THIS RITUAL CAUSES SEVERE PAIN. THERE WILL COME A TIME WHEN YOU THINK YOU MIGHT DIE. I HAVE COME TO KNOW YOU, NATHAN COLE. I KNOW YOUR STRENGTH.
YOU WILL NOT DIE.
WHEN YOU EMERGE FROM THESE TRIALS, YOU WILL EMERGE-- GHOZAN.

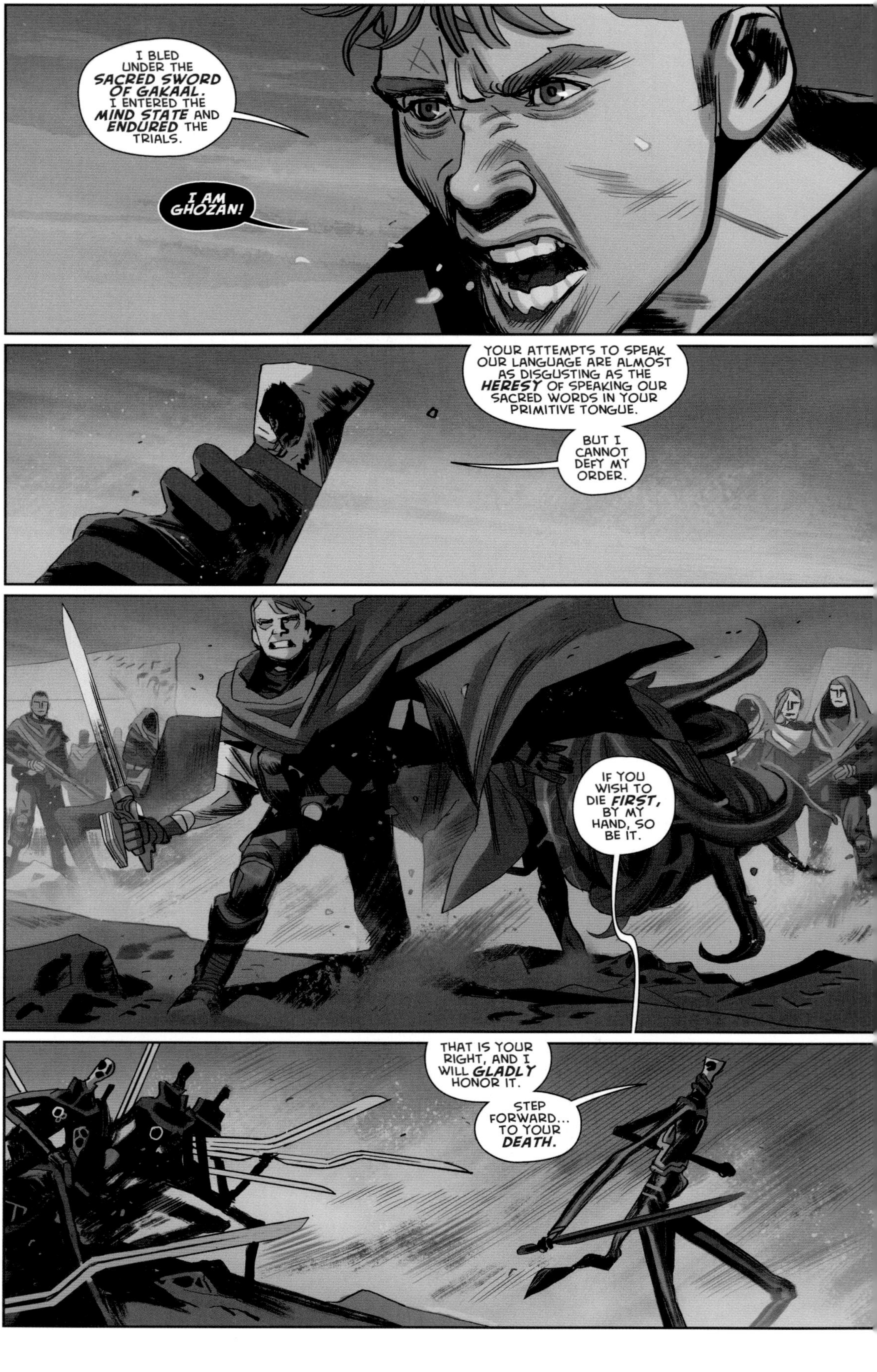
I BLED UNDER THE SACRED SWORD OF GAKAAL. I ENTERED THE MIND STATE AND ENDURED THE TRIALS.
I AM GHOZAN!
YOUR ATTEMPTS TO SPEAK OUR LANGUAGE ARE ALMOST AS DISGUSTING AS THE HERESY OF SPEAKING OUR SACRED WORDS IN YOUR PRIMITIVE TONGUE.
BUT I CANNOT DEFY MY ORDER.
IF YOU WISH TO DIE FIRST, BY MY HAND, SO BE IT.
THAT IS YOUR RIGHT, AND I WILL GLADLY HONOR IT.
STEP FORWARD... TO YOUR DEATH.

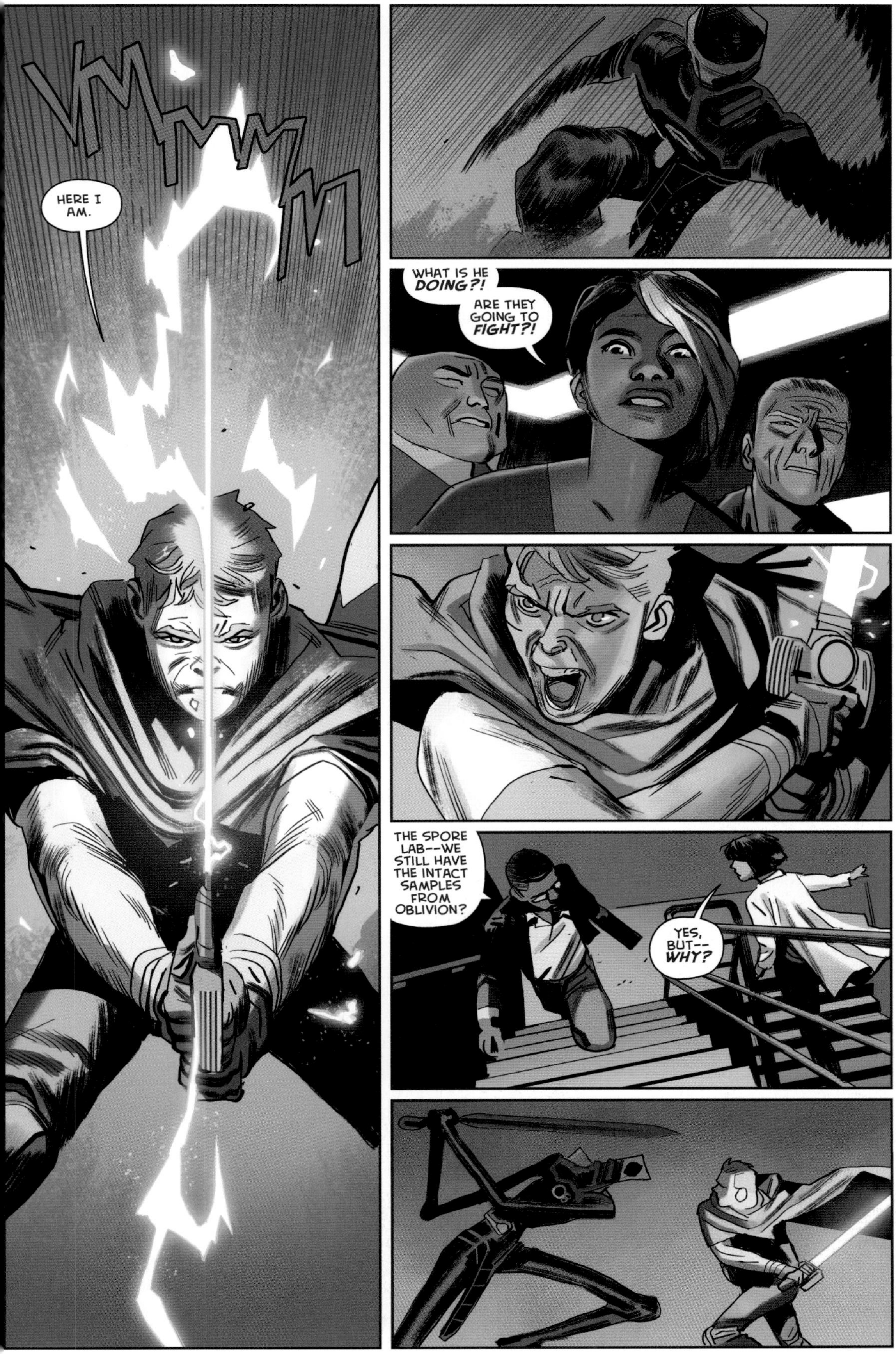
VMMMMMM
HERE I AM.
WHAT IS HE DOING?!
ARE THEY GOING TO FIGHT?!
THE SPORE LAB--WE STILL HAVE THE INTACT SAMPLES FROM OBLIVION?
YES, BUT-- WHY?

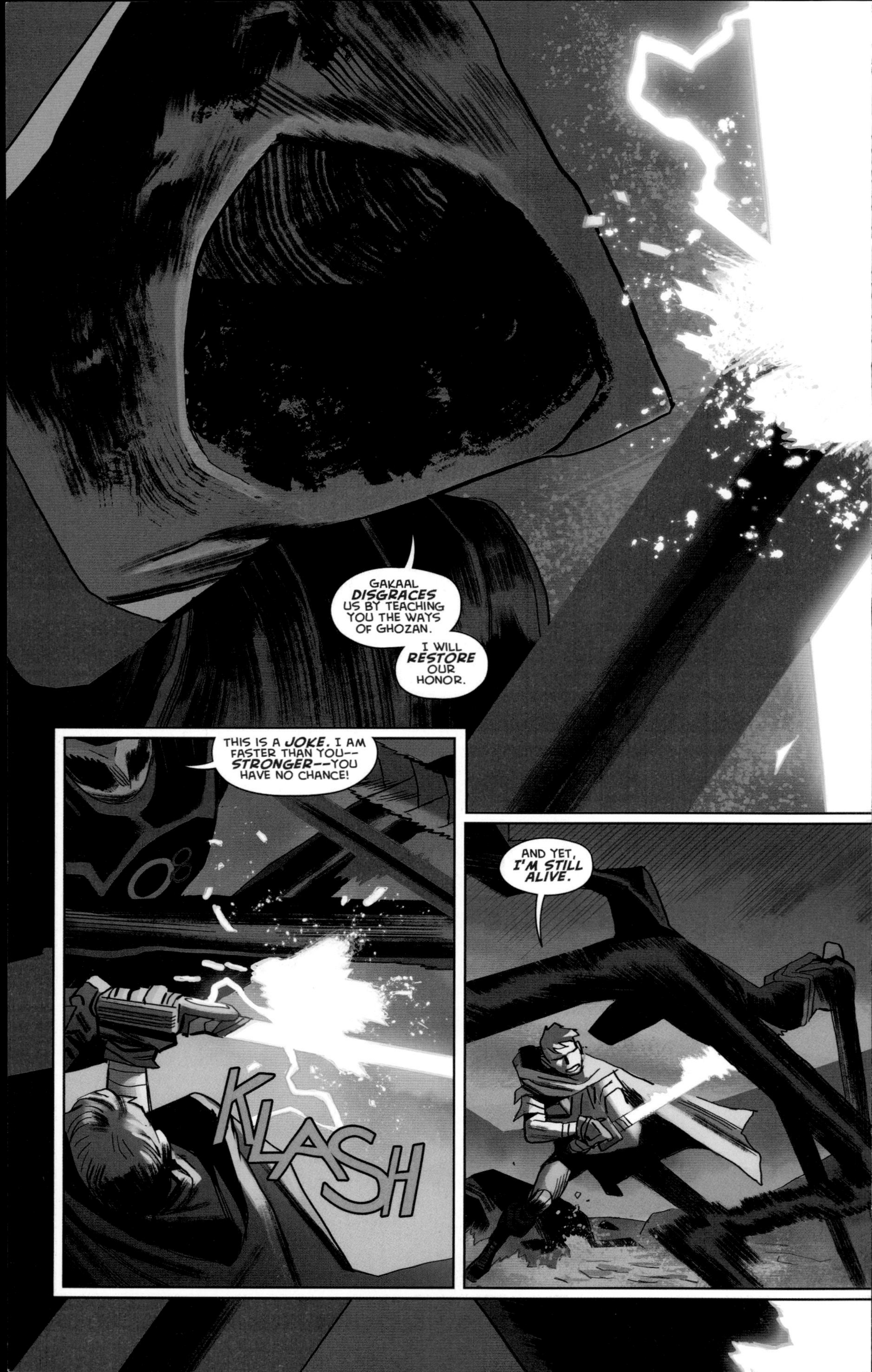
GAKAAL DISGRACES US BY TEACHING YOU THE WAYS OF GHOZAN.
I WILL RESTORE OUR HONOR.
THIS IS A JOKE. I AM FASTER THAN YOU-- STRONGER--YOU HAVE NO CHANCE!
KLASH
AND YET, I'M STILL ALIVE.

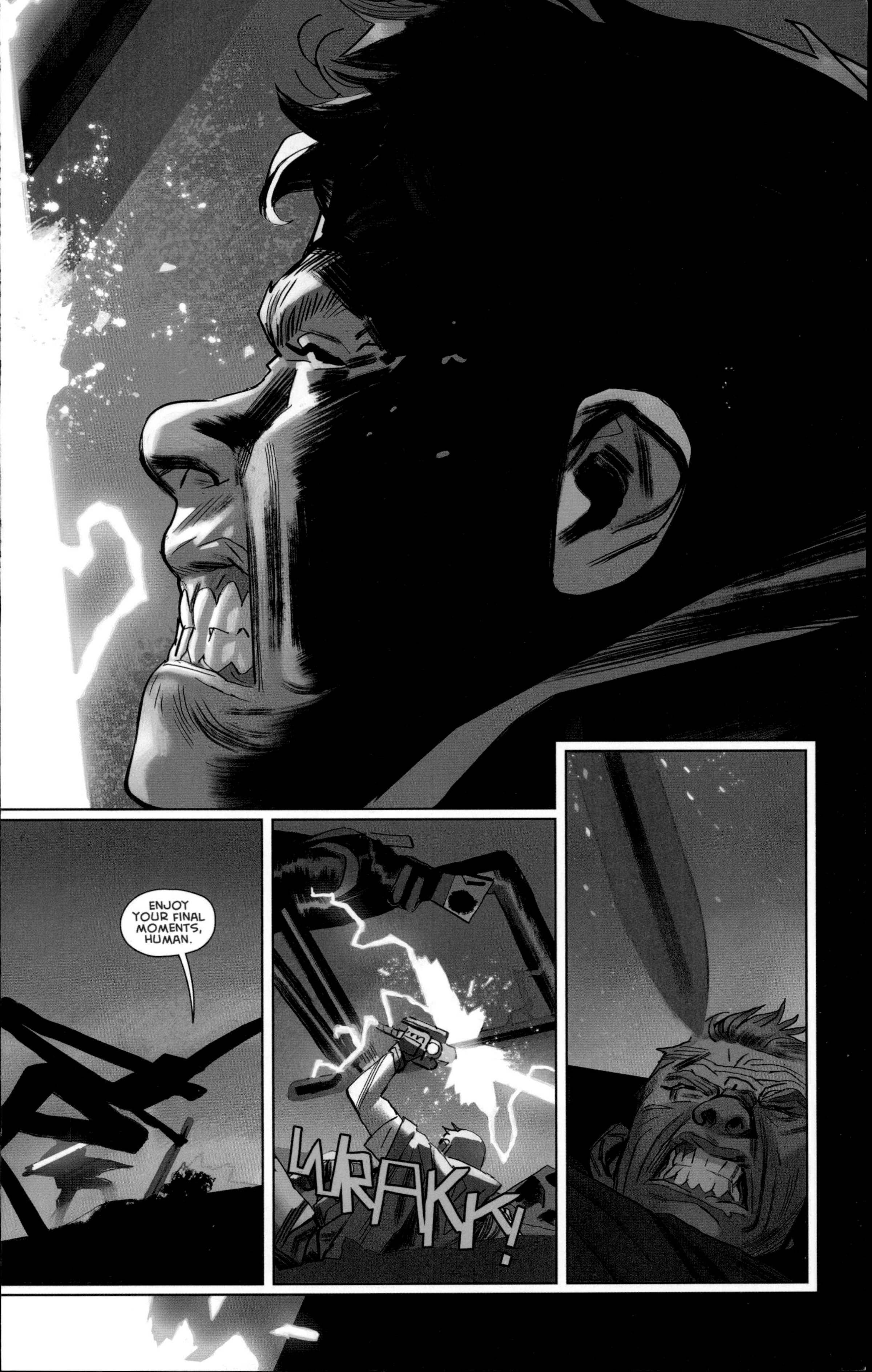
ENJOY YOUR FINAL MOMENTS, HUMAN.
WRAKK!

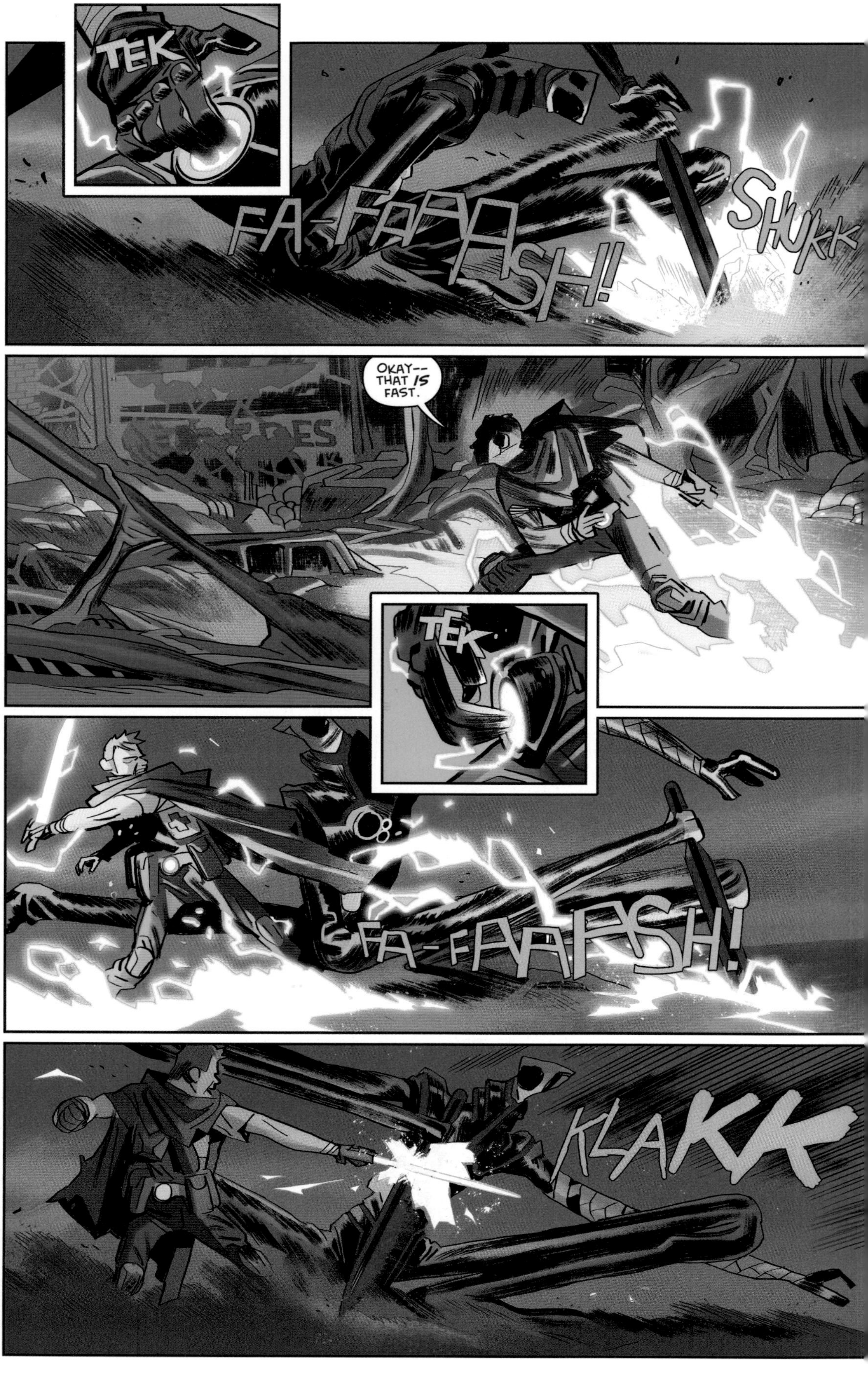
TEK
FA-FAAAASH!
SHUKK
OKAY-- THAT IS FAST.
TEK
FA-FAAASH!
KLAKK

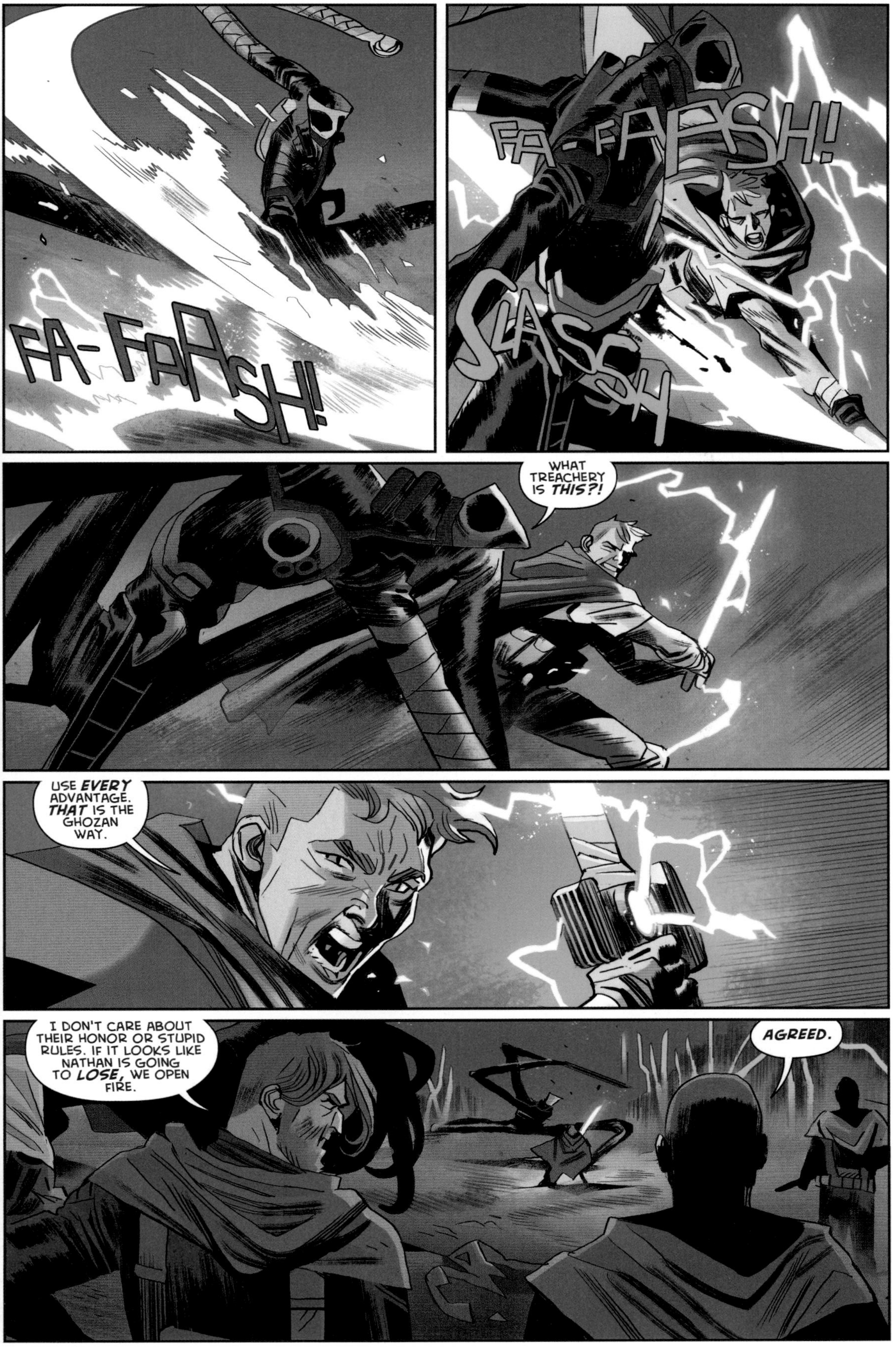
FA-FAASH!
FA-FAASH!
SLASSSH
WHAT TREACHERY IS *THIS?!*
USE *EVERY* ADVANTAGE. *THAT* IS THE GHOZAN WAY.
I DON'T CARE ABOUT THEIR HONOR OR STUPID RULES. IF IT LOOKS LIKE NATHAN IS GOING TO *LOSE,* WE OPEN FIRE.
AGREED.

WHAT BREAK-THROUGHS? WHAT ARE WE **DOING** HERE, DUNCAN?

HOLD ON--IT'S... GOOD TO BE BACK IN THIS LAB, **TOGETHER**.

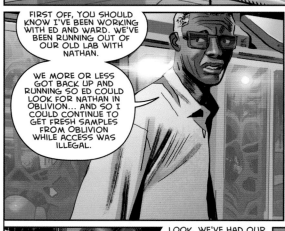

FIRST OFF, YOU SHOULD KNOW I'VE BEEN WORKING WITH ED AND WARD. WE'VE BEEN RUNNING OUT OF OUR OLD LAB WITH NATHAN.

WE MORE OR LESS GOT BACK UP AND RUNNING SO ED COULD LOOK FOR NATHAN IN OBLIVION... AND SO I COULD CONTINUE TO GET FRESH SAMPLES FROM OBLIVION WHILE ACCESS WAS ILLEGAL.

I KNOW.

YOU DID?

LOOK, WE'VE HAD OUR DIFFERENCES IN THE PAST, BUT I THINK WE BOTH AGREE NO ONE KNOWS US BETTER THAN WE KNOW EACH OTHER.

THE TIMING OF YOUR EXIT WAS PRETTY **OBVIOUS**, DUNCAN.

I GUESS IT WAS.

OKAY, I'M PULLING THE DATA FROM MY RECENT STUDIES OFF THE CLOUD.

I SPOKE TO NATHAN, HE SPENT **YEARS** IN OBLIVION WORKING WITH A KUTHAAL SCIENTIST TRYING TO **STOP** THE GROWTH OVERTAKING THEIR WORLD.

APPARENTLY, THERE WAS A TWO-TRACK PLAN. OPTION ONE WAS STOP THE GROWTH. OPTION TWO WAS INVADE EARTH. THEY GAINED THE MEANS TO INVADE FIRST-- HENCE WHERE WE CURRENTLY ARE.

SO THEY DON'T NECESSARILY **WANT** TO INVADE...

EXACTLY.

THEY'RE SIMPLY TRYING TO ESCAPE. WE TAKE AWAY THE **NEED** FOR ESCAPE-- **INVASION OVER.**

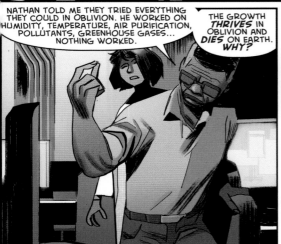

NATHAN TOLD ME THEY TRIED EVERYTHING THEY COULD IN OBLIVION. HE WORKED ON HUMIDITY, TEMPERATURE, AIR PURIFICATION, POLLUTANTS, GREENHOUSE GASES... NOTHING WORKED.

THE GROWTH **THRIVES** IN OBLIVION AND **DIES** ON EARTH. **WHY?**

NATHAN HAD TO **CREATE** ASPECTS OF EARTH'S ENVIRONMENTS IN OBLIVION... ALL WE HAVE TO DO IS... **BLOCK THEM** UNTIL WE FIND THE RIGHT ONE.

YES!

AND WE HAVE **LIVING SAMPLES** HERE IN THE LAB! SO WHATEVER IT IS THAT KEEPS THEM ALIVE... WE'RE **ALREADY DOING IT.**

WE'RE FACING A SUPERIOR MILITARY FORCE THAT WE HAVE **NO HOPE** OF DEFEATING.

YOU AND ME, WE'RE THE ONLY ONES WHO CAN SOLVE THIS PROBLEM... AND SOLVING THIS PROBLEM IS THE ONLY WAY TO SAVE **EARTH.**

LET'S GET TO WORK.

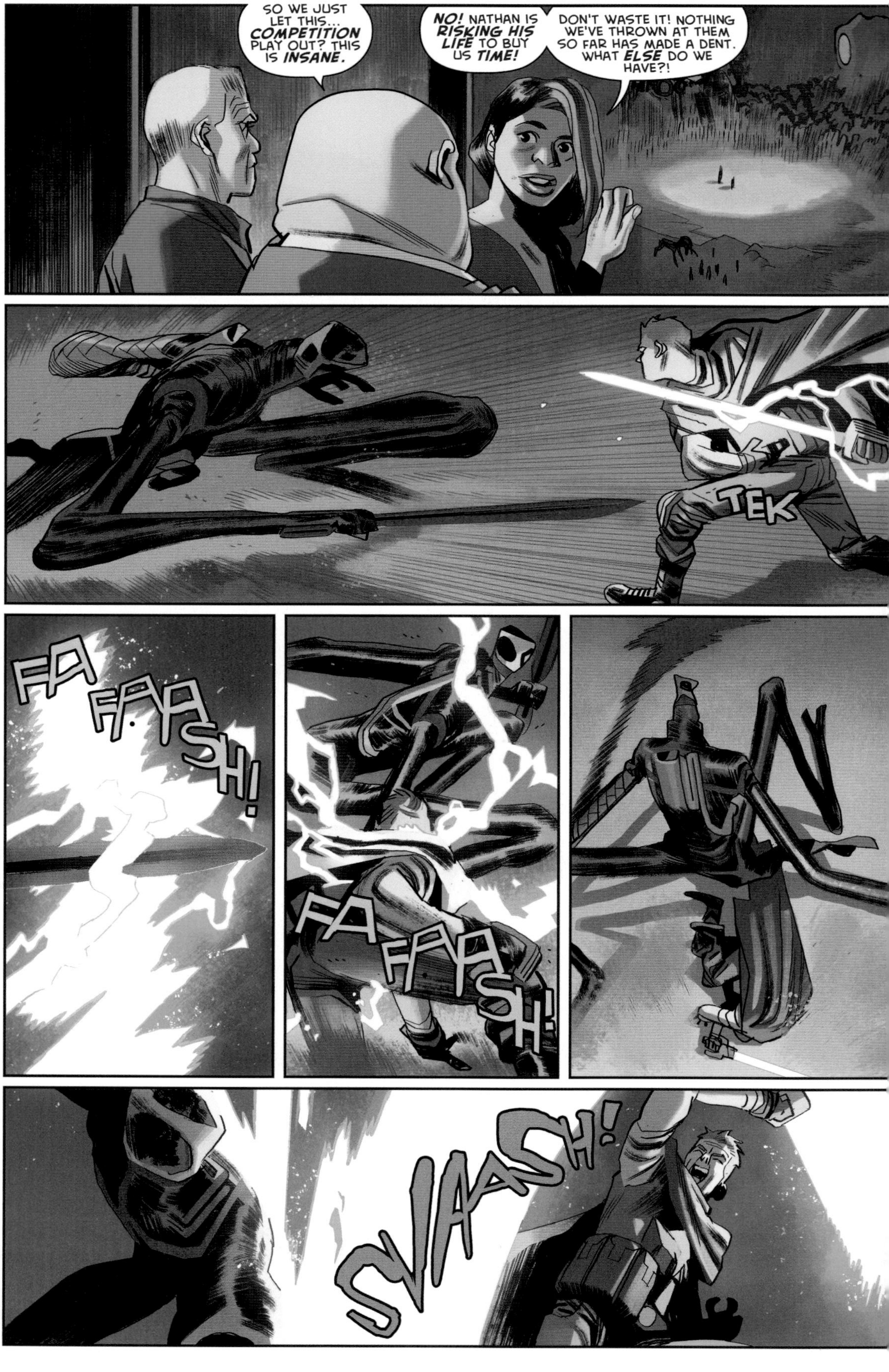
SO WE JUST LET THIS... COMPETITION PLAY OUT? THIS IS INSANE.
NO! NATHAN IS RISKING HIS LIFE TO BUY US TIME!
DON'T WASTE IT! NOTHING WE'VE THROWN AT THEM SO FAR HAS MADE A DENT. WHAT ELSE DO WE HAVE?!
TEK
FA FAAASH!
FA FAAASH!
SWAASH!

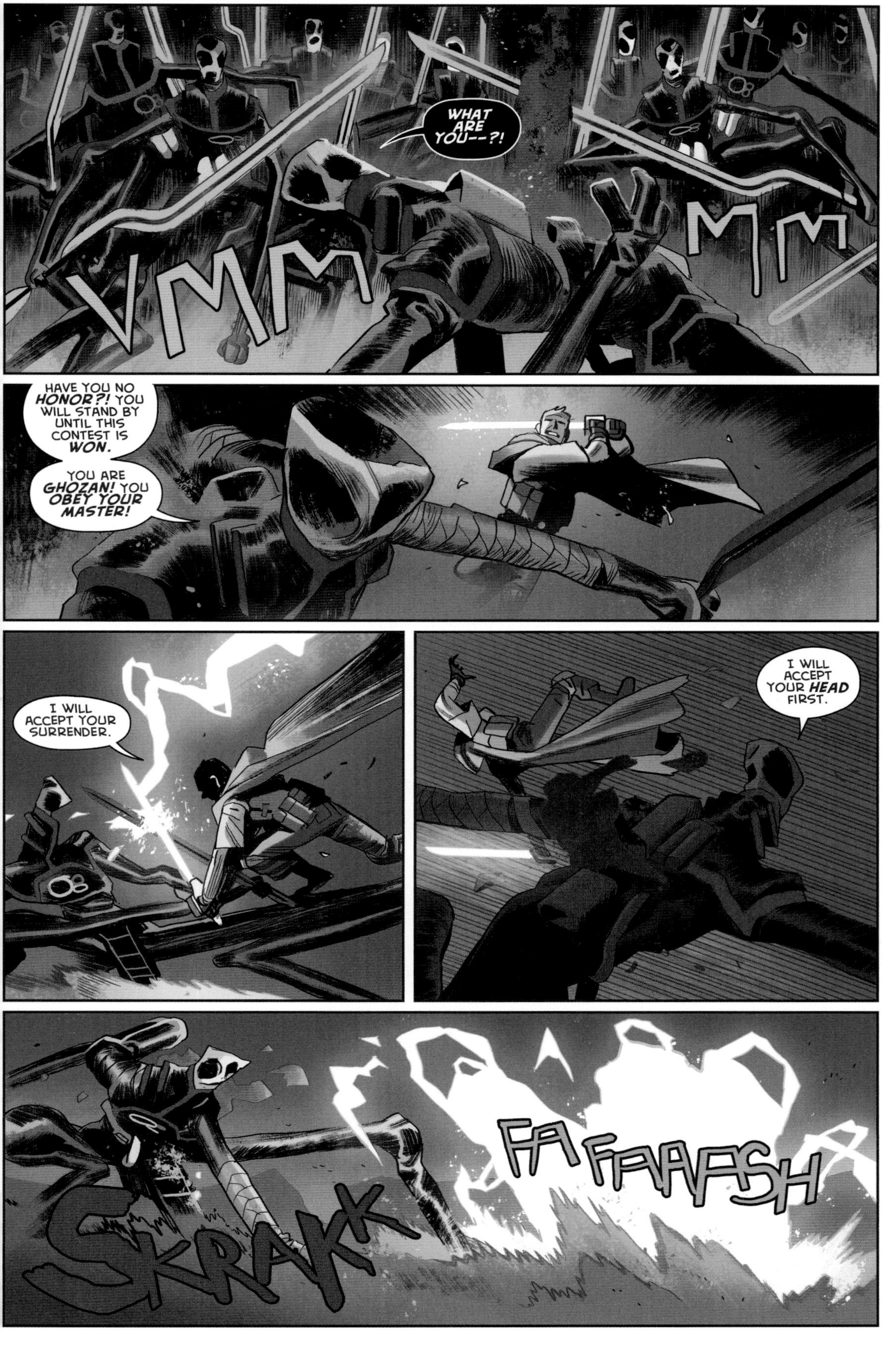
WHAT ARE YOU--?!
VMMM
MM
HAVE YOU NO HONOR?! YOU WILL STAND BY UNTIL THIS CONTEST IS WON.
YOU ARE GHOZAN! YOU OBEY YOUR MASTER!
I WILL ACCEPT YOUR SURRENDER.
I WILL ACCEPT YOUR HEAD FIRST.
SKRAKK
FA FAAASH

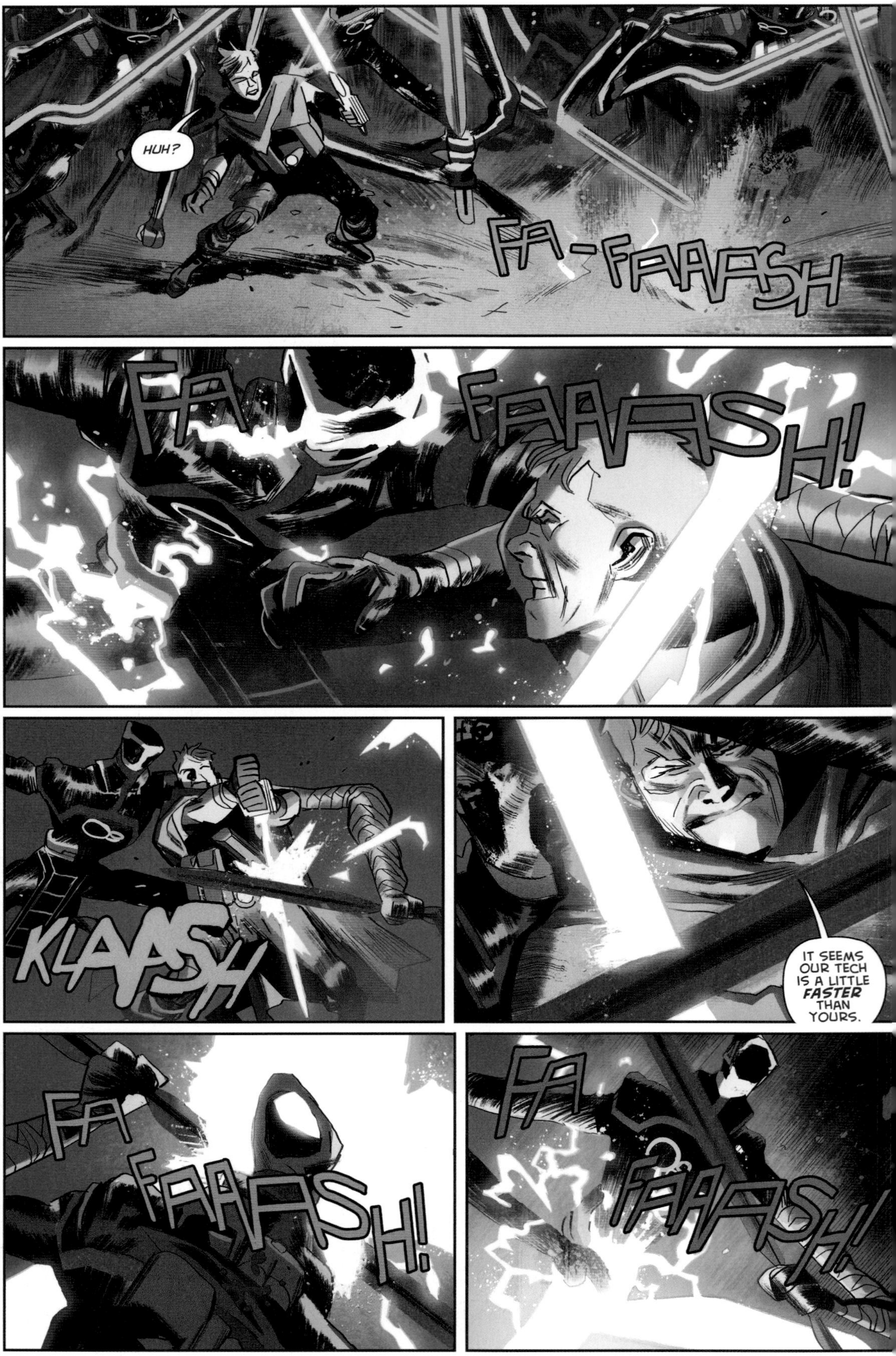
HUH?
FA-FAAASH
FA FAAASH!
KLAASH
IT SEEMS OUR TECH IS A LITTLE FASTER THAN YOURS.
FA FAAASH!
FA FAAASH!

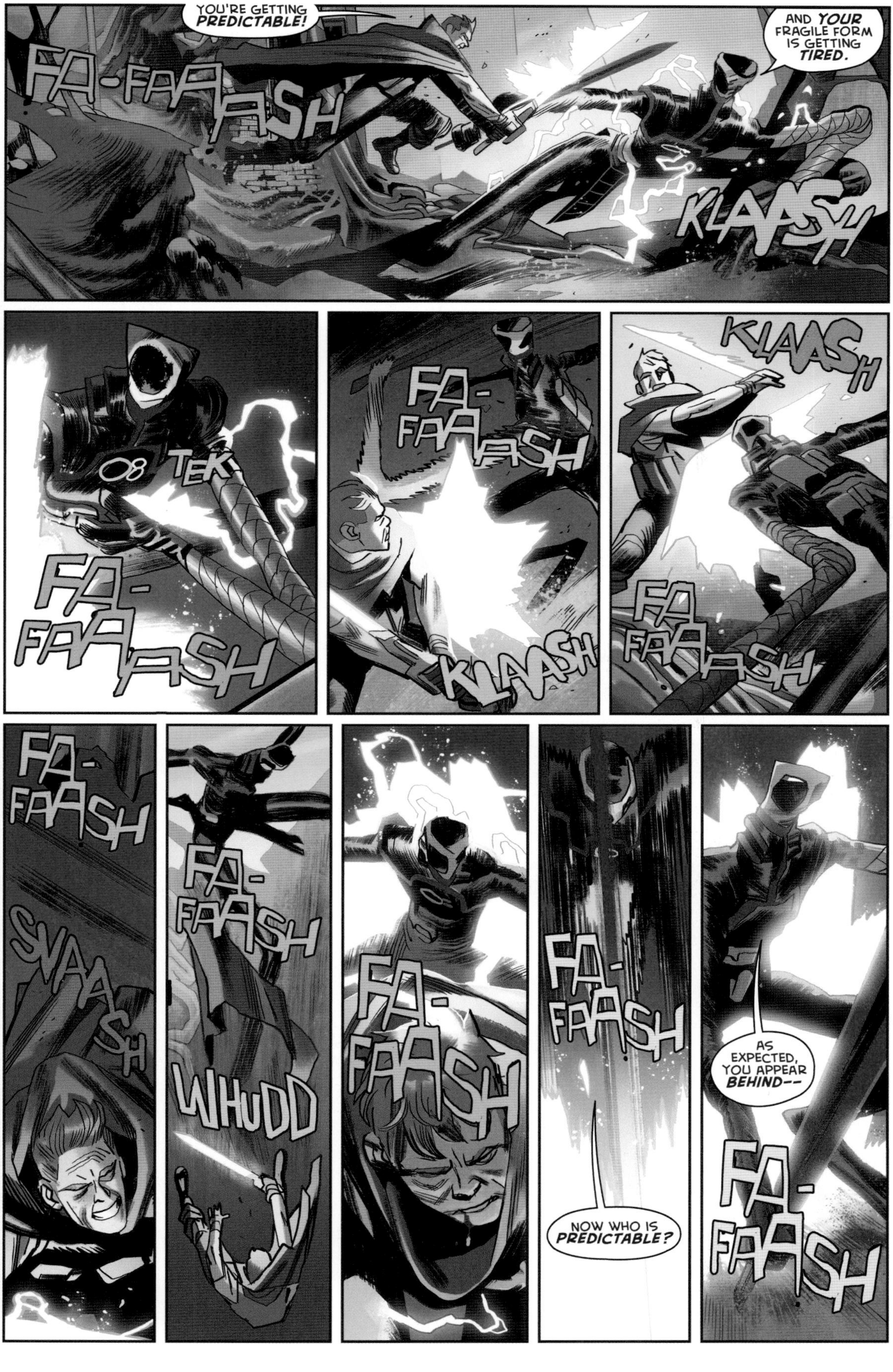
YOU'RE GETTING PREDICTABLE!
FA-FAAAASH
AND YOUR FRAGILE FORM IS GETTING TIRED.
KLAASH
TEK
FA-FAAAASH
FA-FAAAASH
KLAASH
KLAASH
FA-FAAAASH
FA-FAAASH
SNAASH
FA-FAAASH
WHUDD
FA-FAAASH
FA-FAAASH
NOW WHO IS PREDICTABLE?
AS EXPECTED, YOU APPEAR BEHIND--
FA-FAAASH

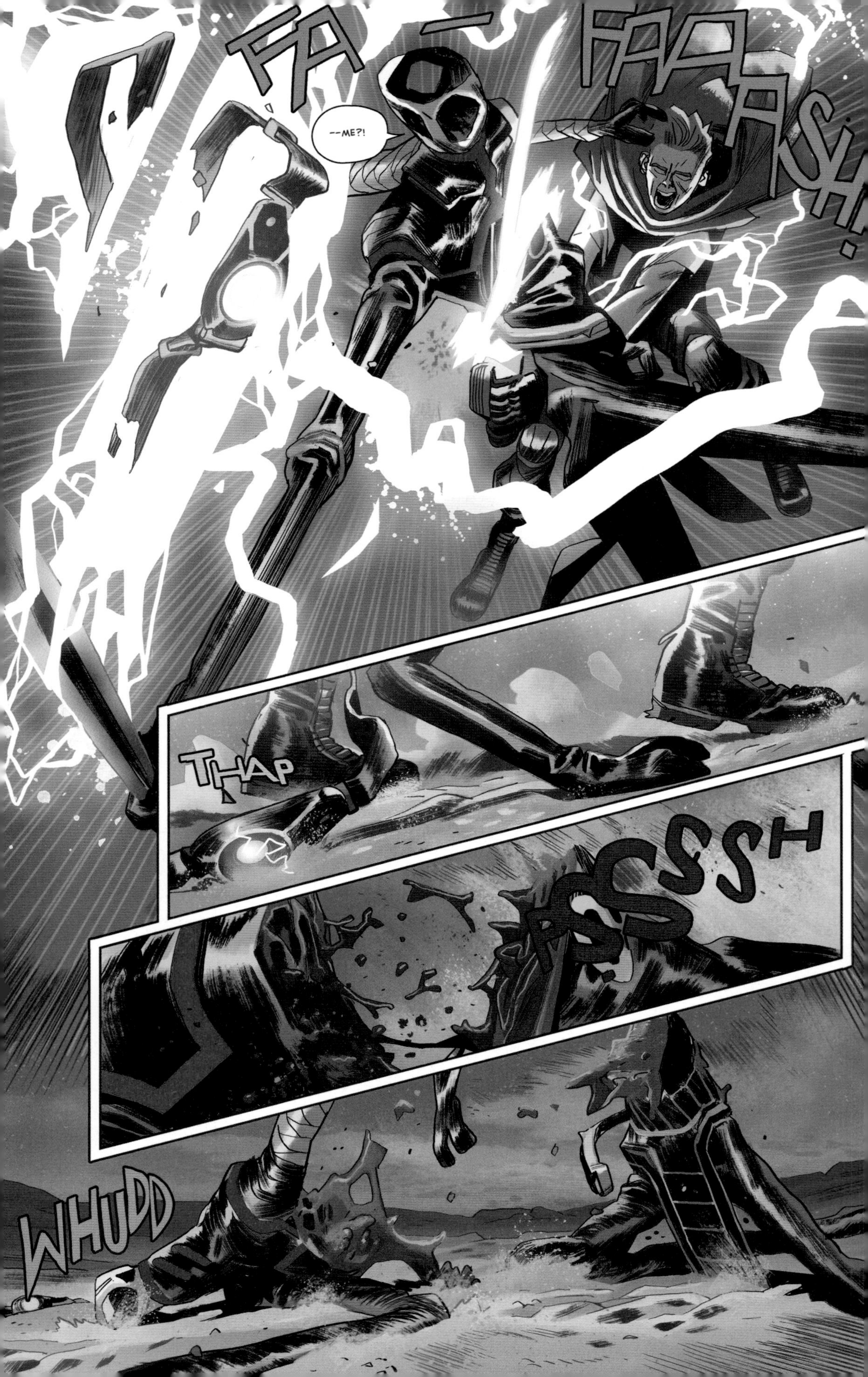
FA—
FAAASH!!
--ME?!
THAP
SSSH
WHUDD

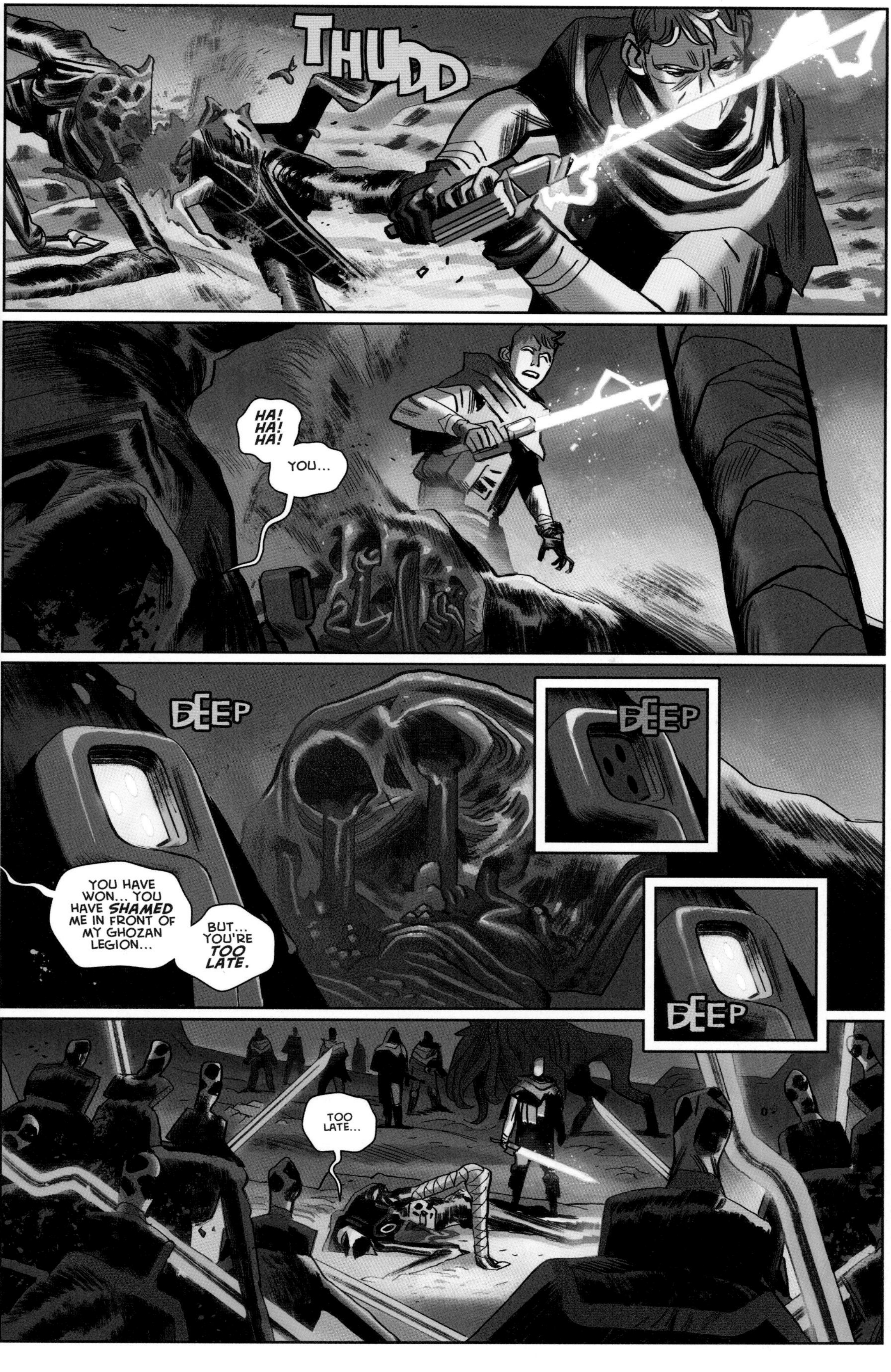
THUDD
HA! HA! HA!
YOU...
BEEP
BEEP
YOU HAVE WON... YOU HAVE SHAMED ME IN FRONT OF MY GHOZAN LEGION...
BUT... YOU'RE TOO LATE.
BEEP
TOO LATE...

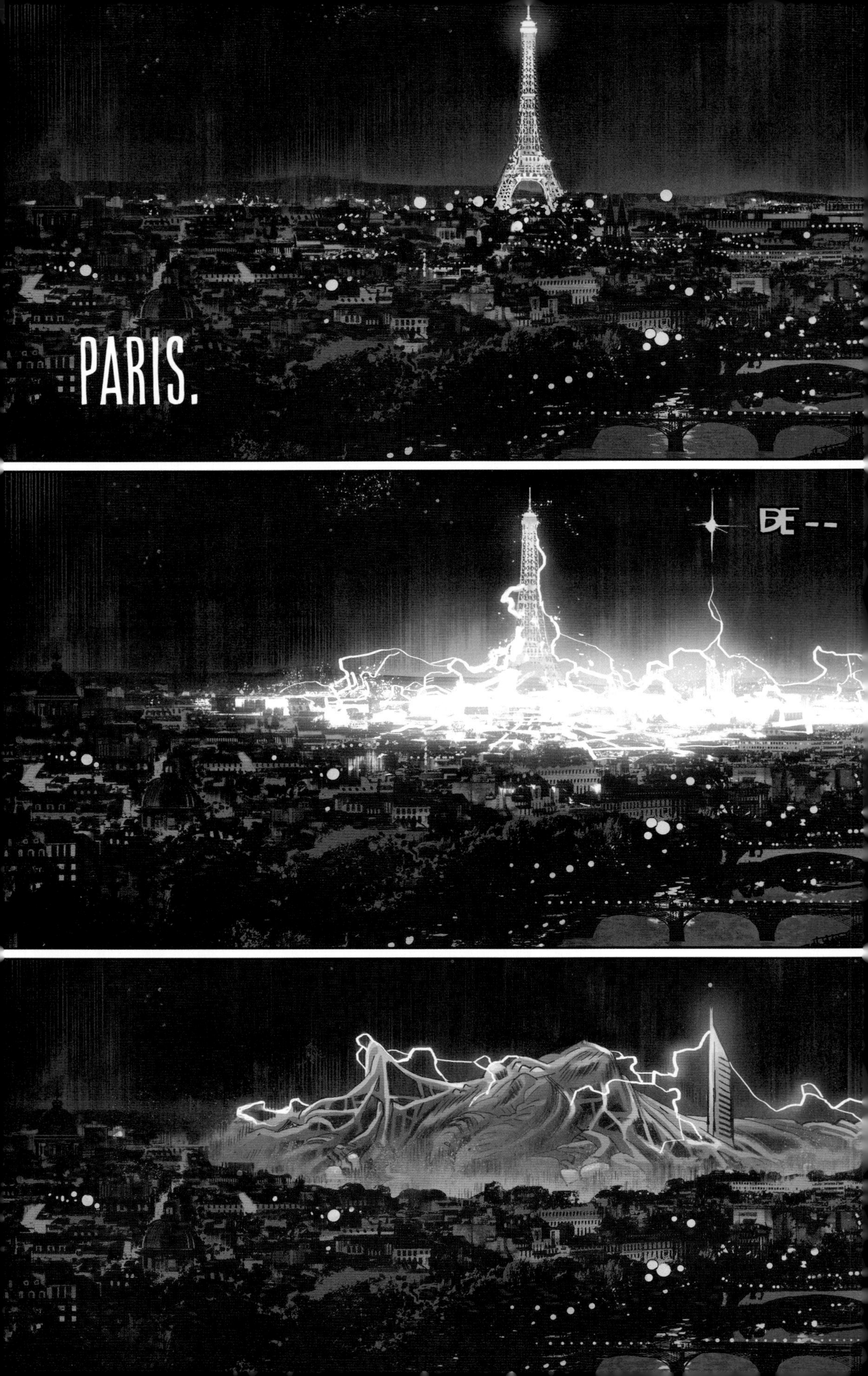
PARIS.
BE--

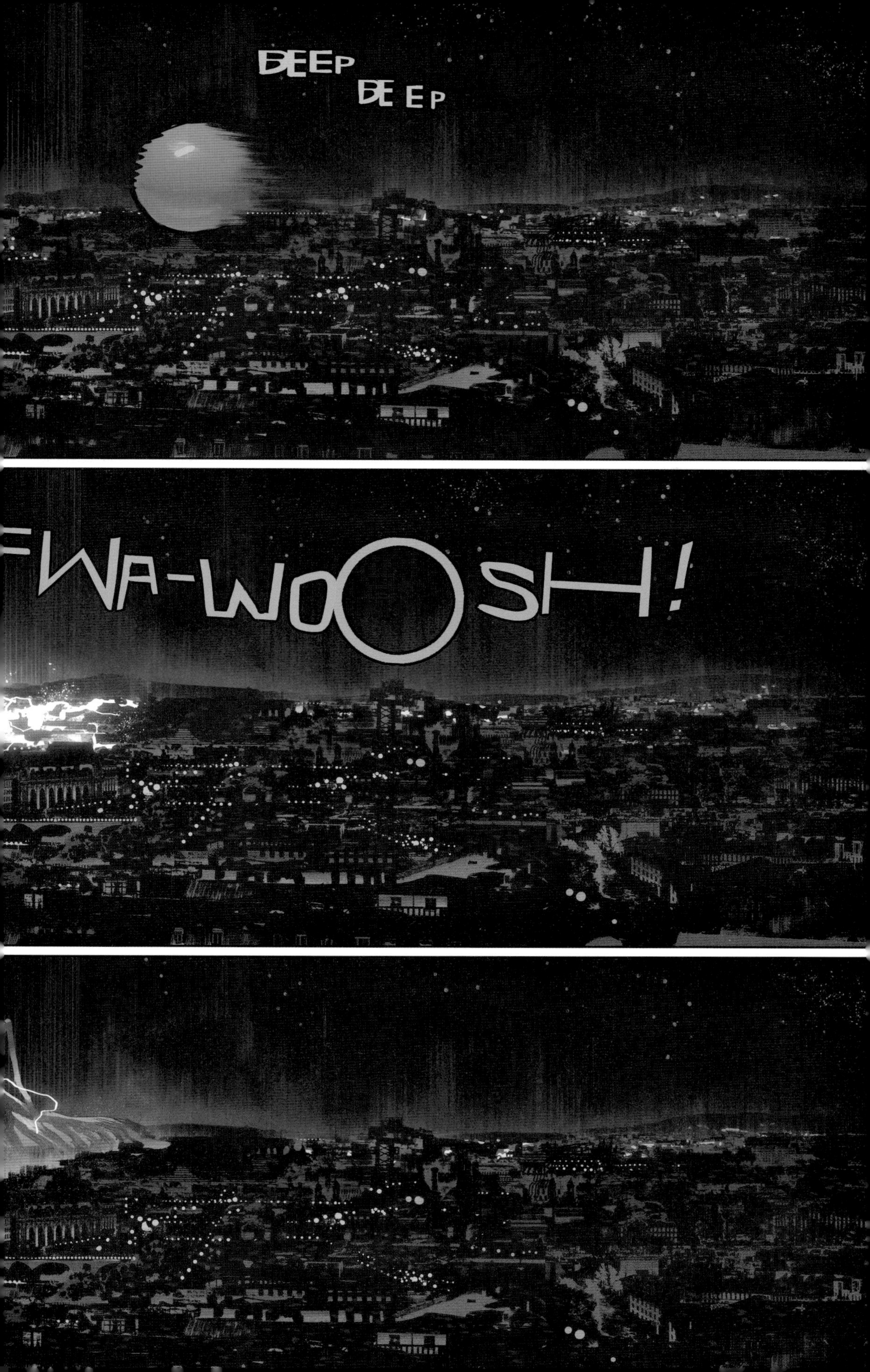
BEEP
BEEP
FWA-WOOOSH!

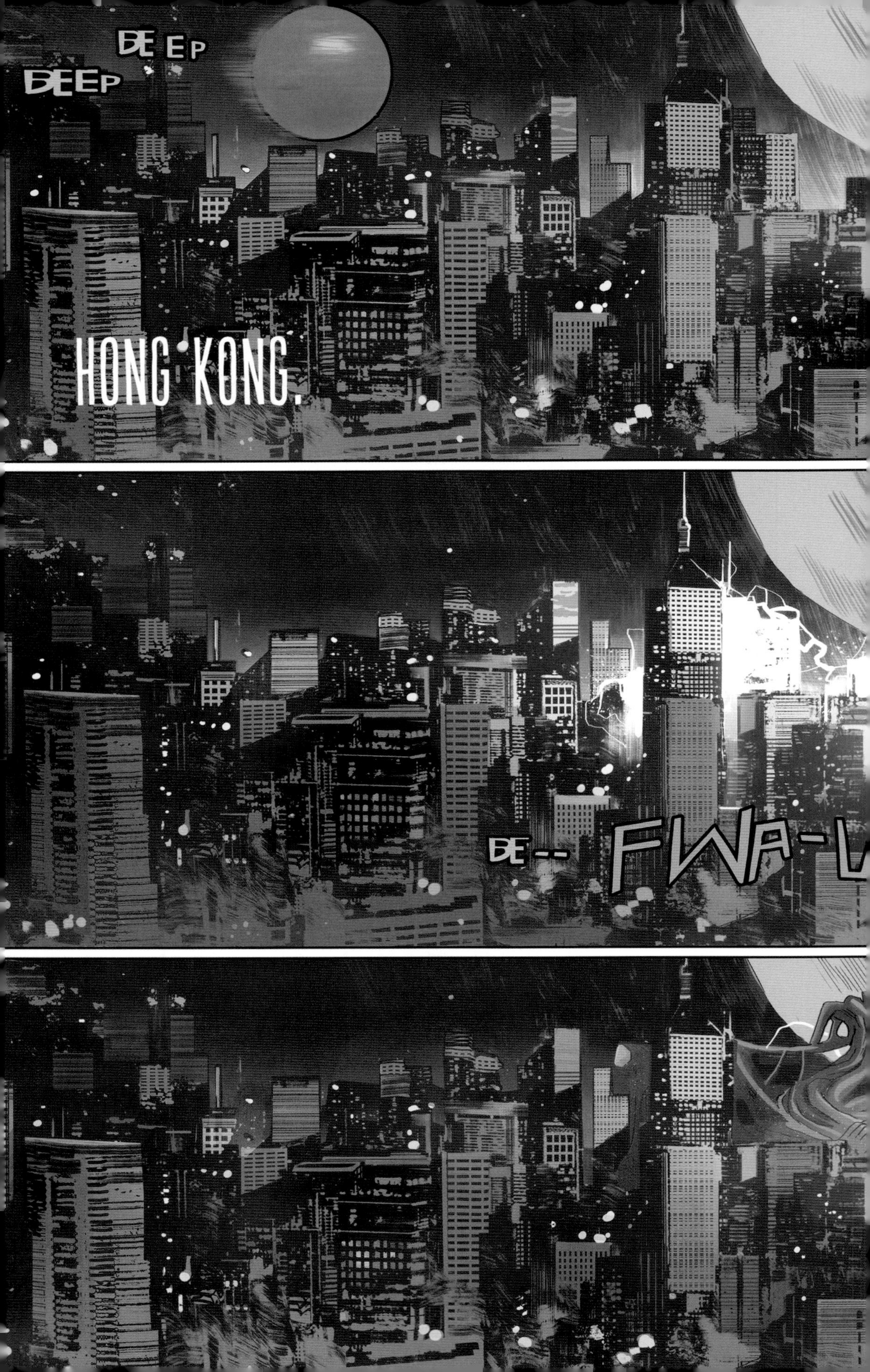
BEEP
BEEP
HONG KONG.
BE--
FWA-

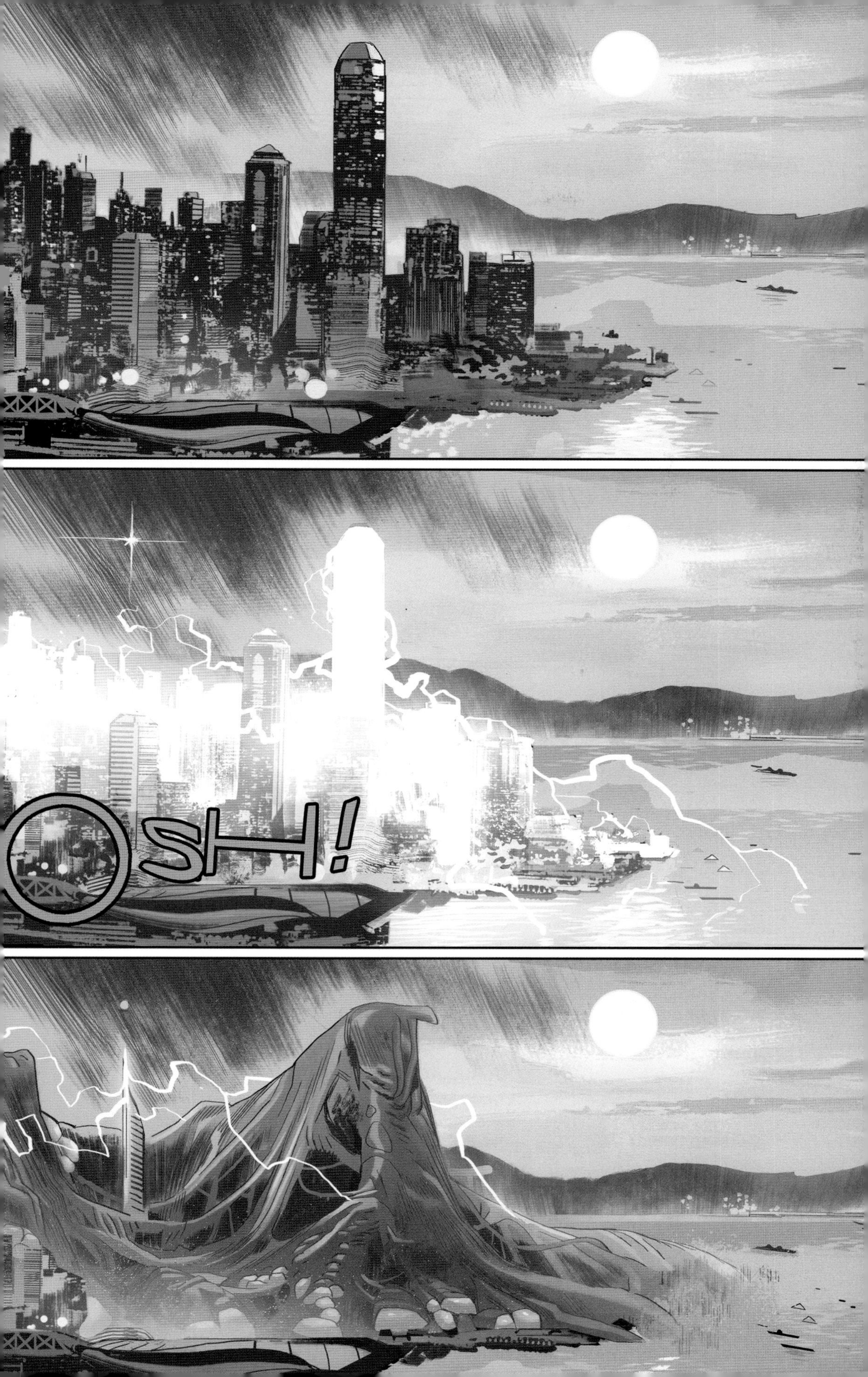
OSH!

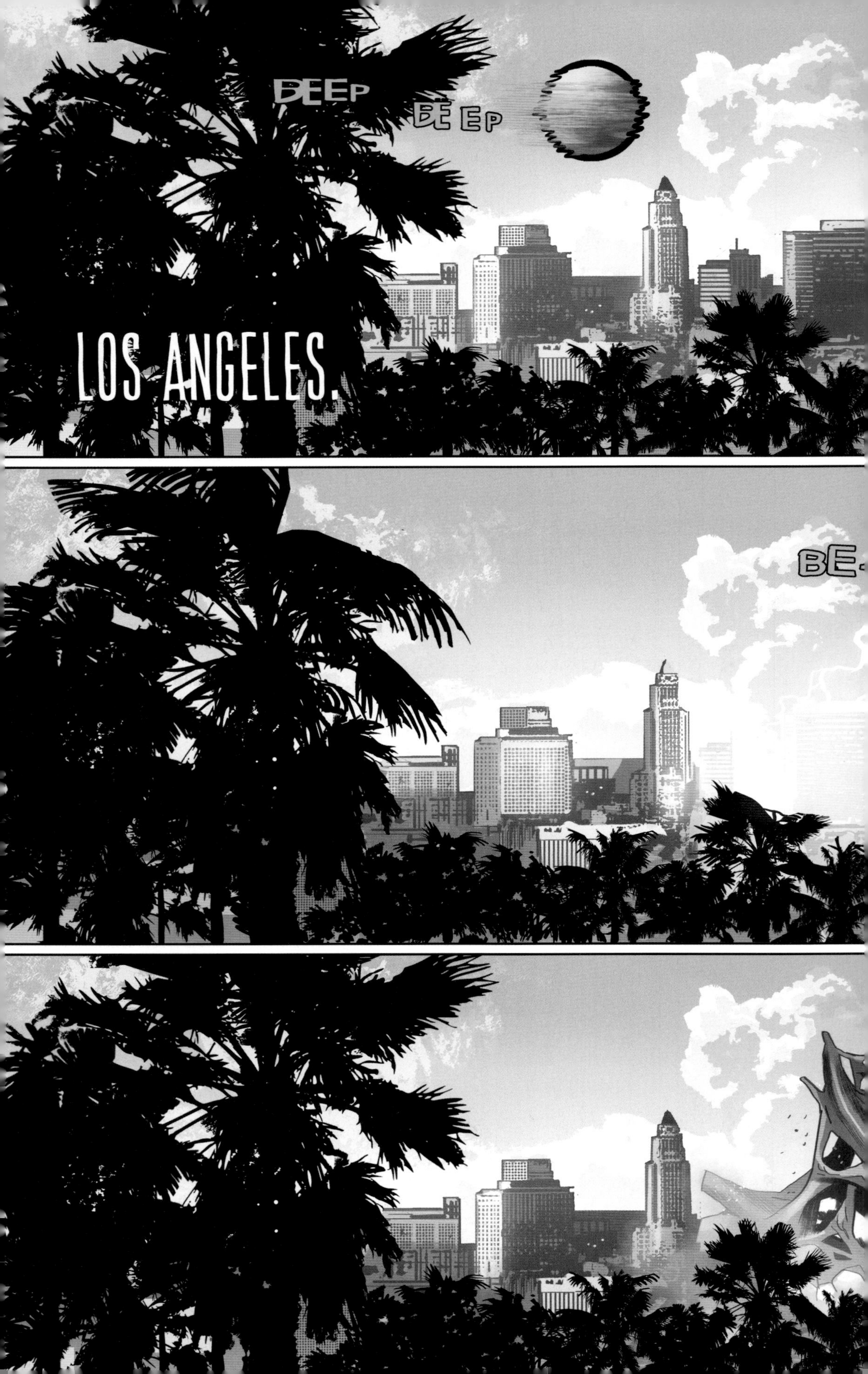
BEEP
BEEP
LOS ANGELES.
BE-

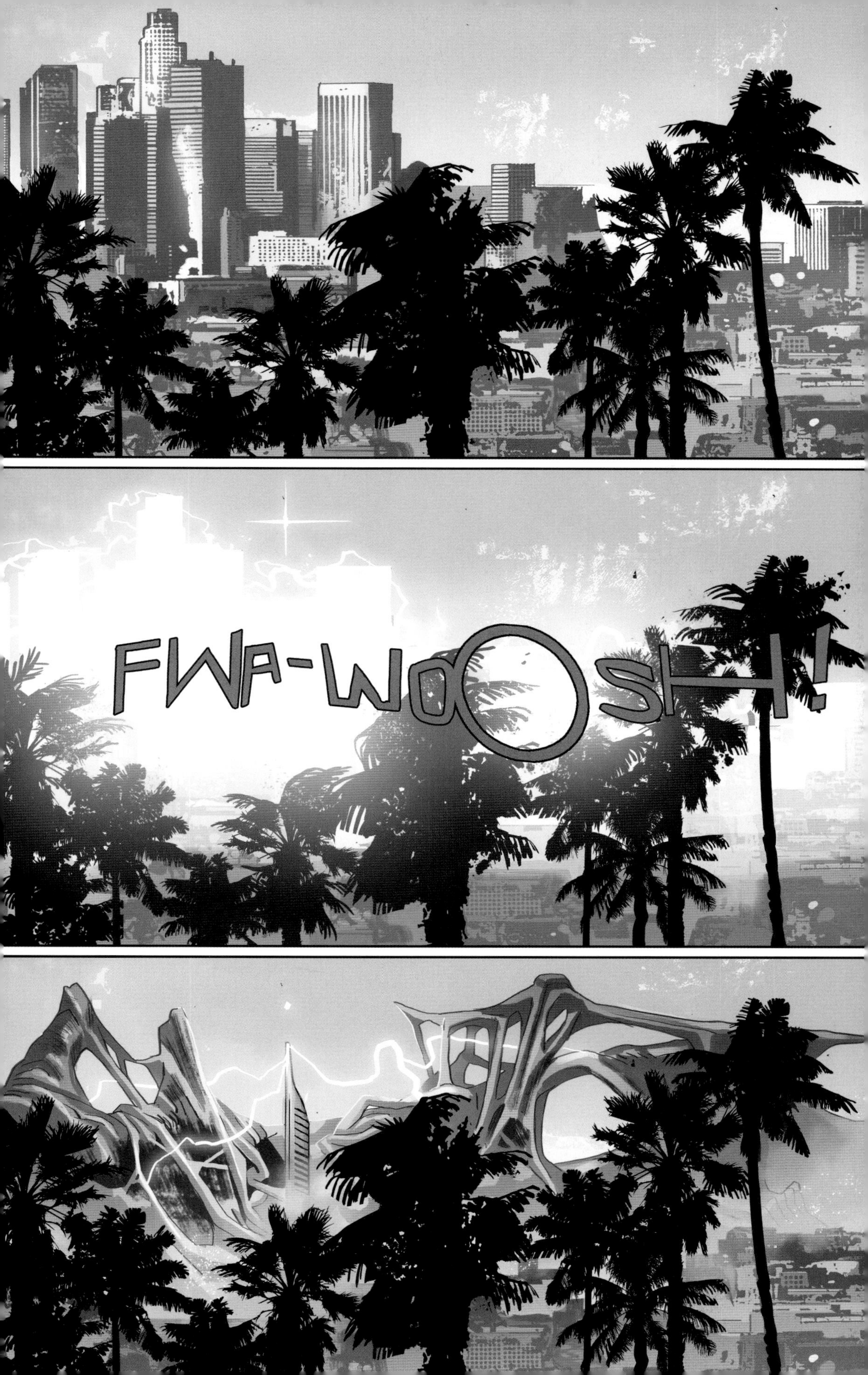
FWA-WOOOSH!

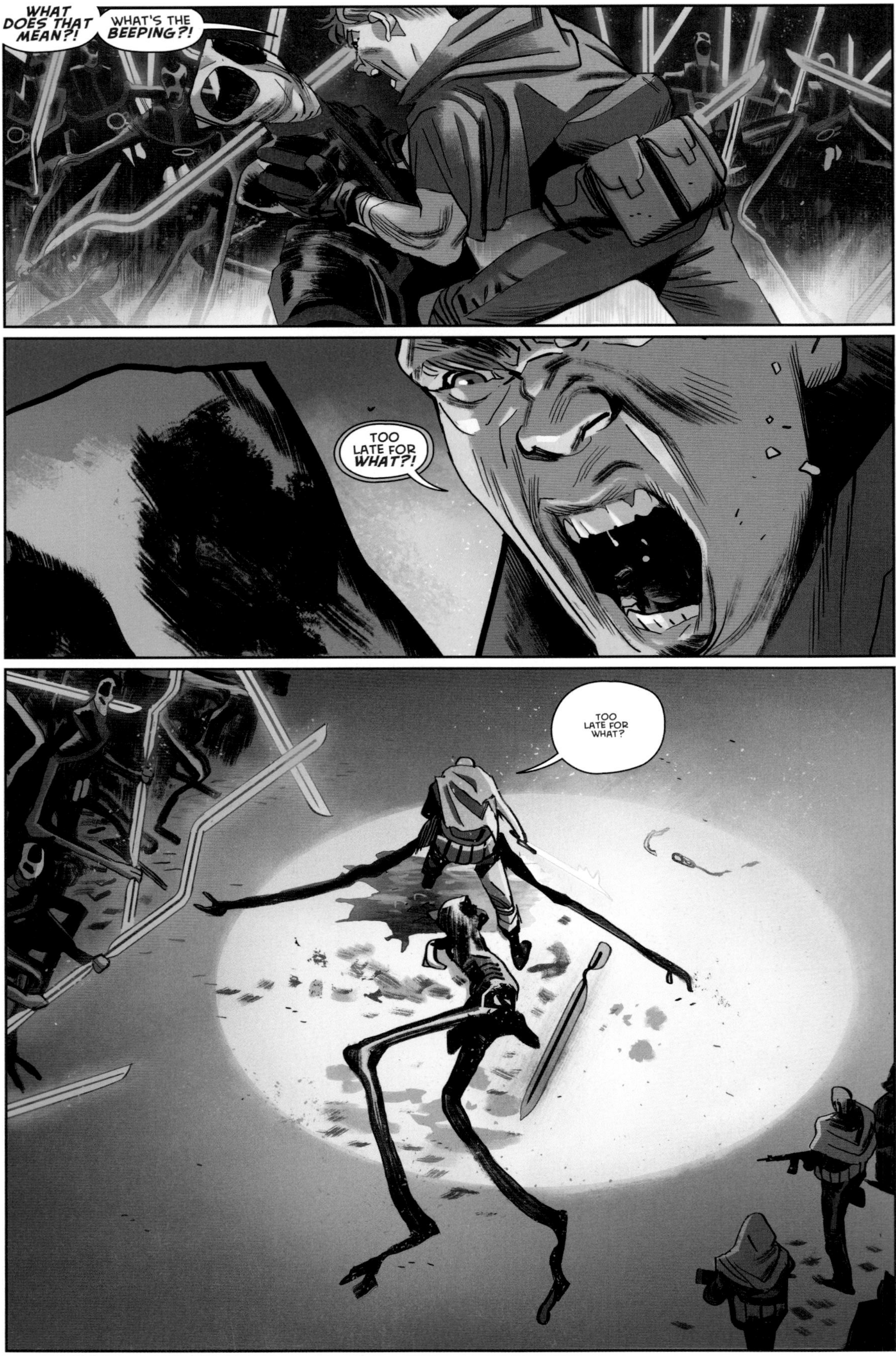
WHAT DOES THAT MEAN?!
WHAT'S THE BEEPING?!
TOO LATE FOR WHAT?!
TOO LATE FOR WHAT?

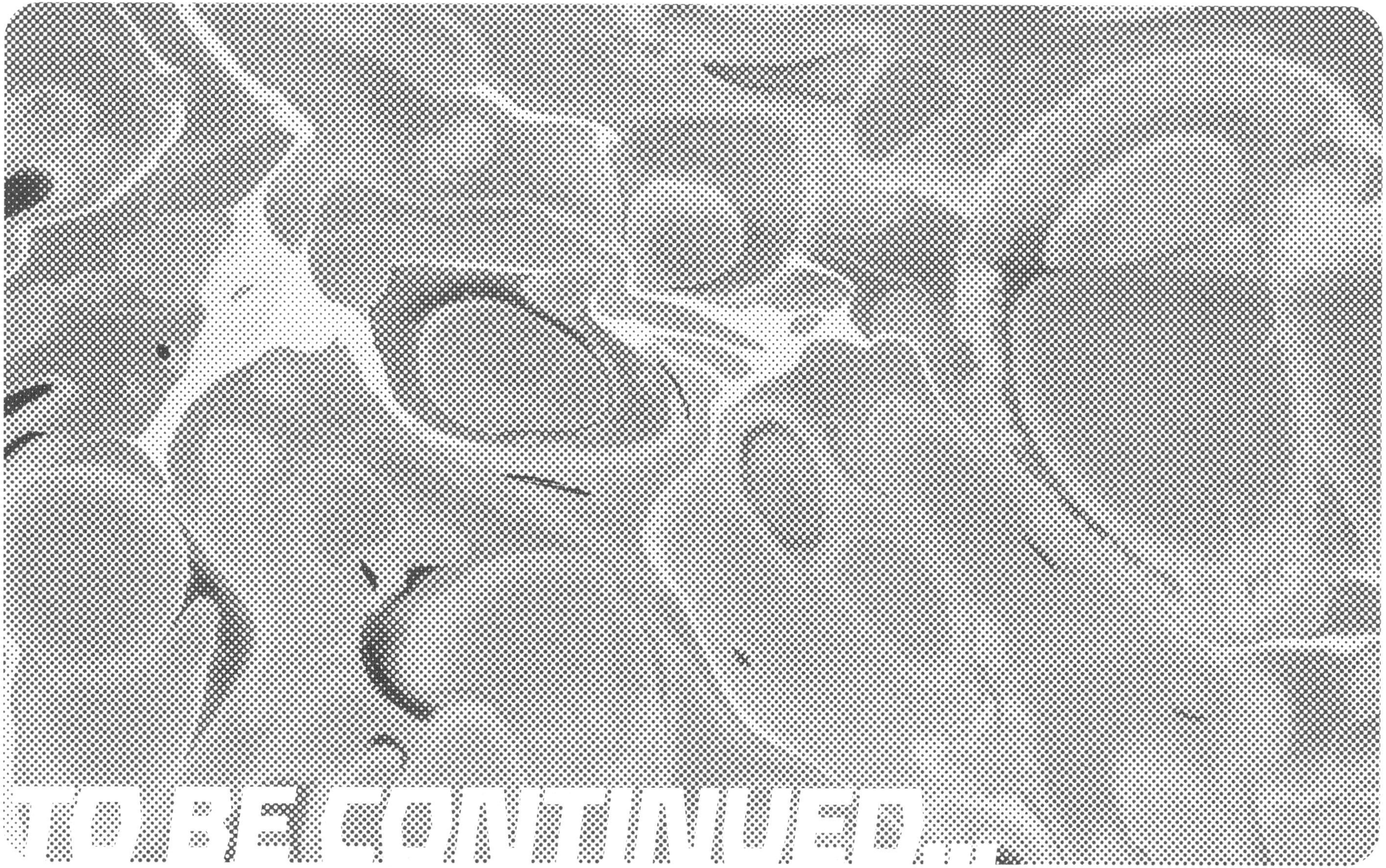
TO BE CONTINUED...

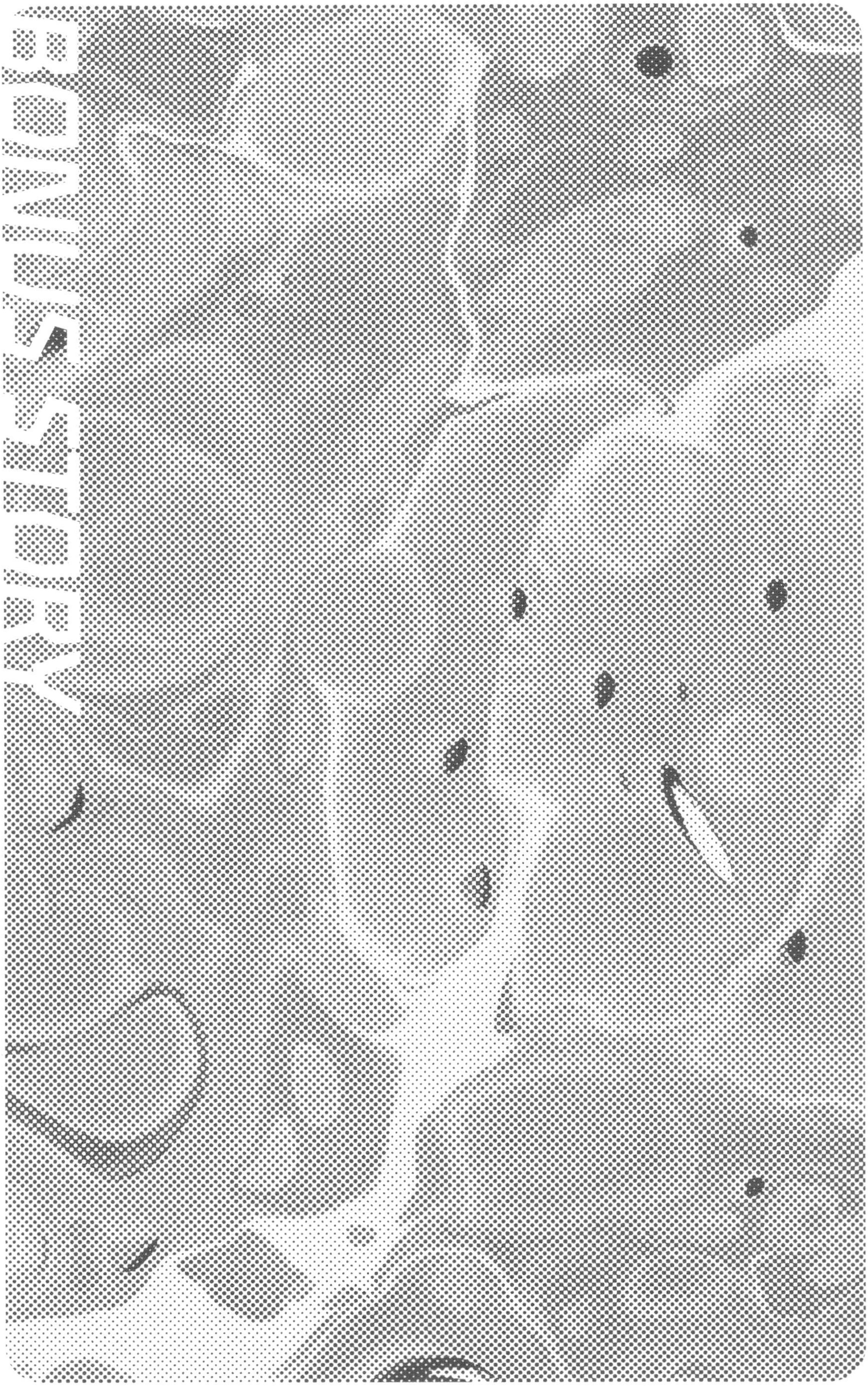
BONUS STORY

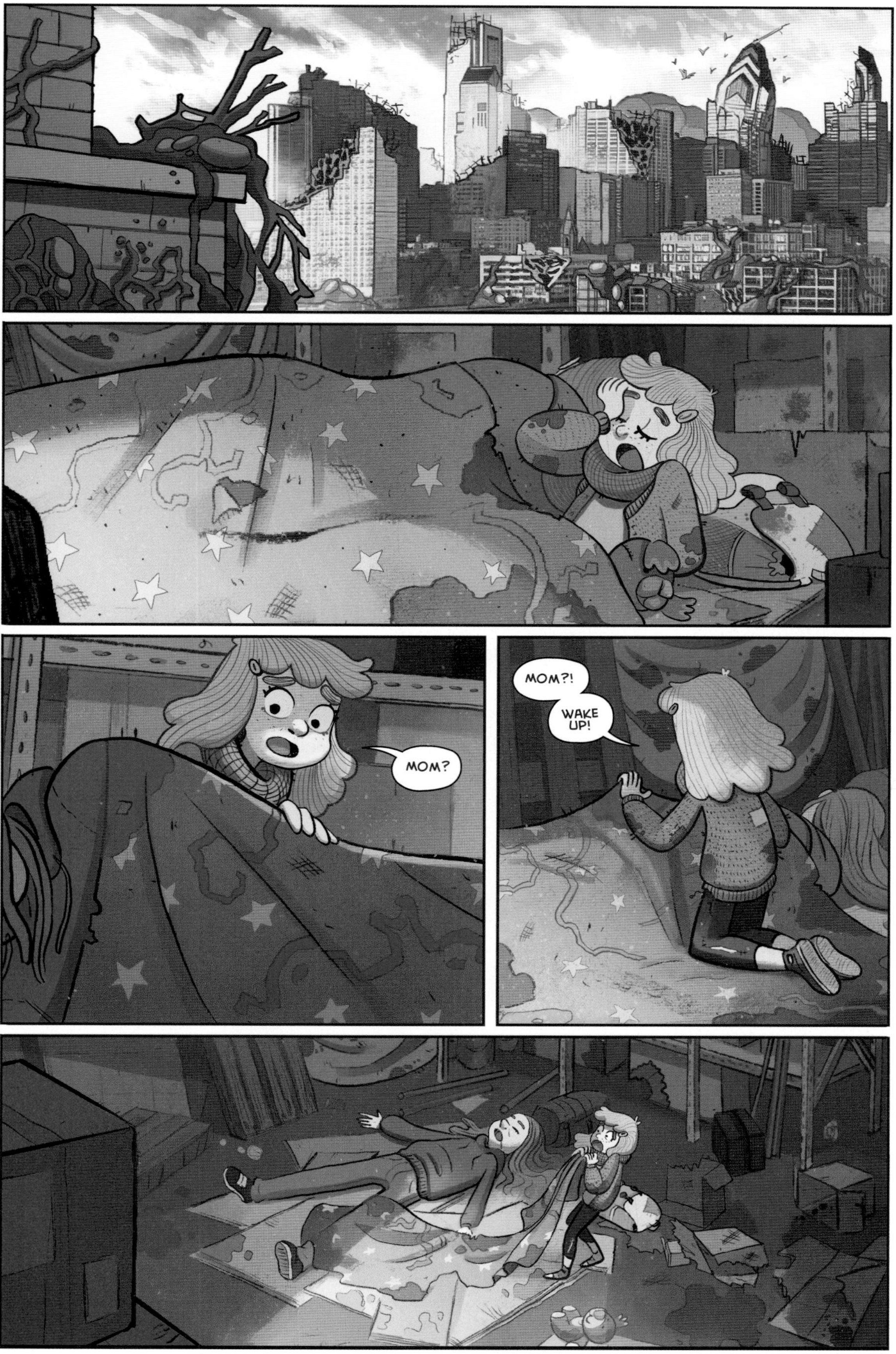
MOM?
MOM?!
WAKE UP!

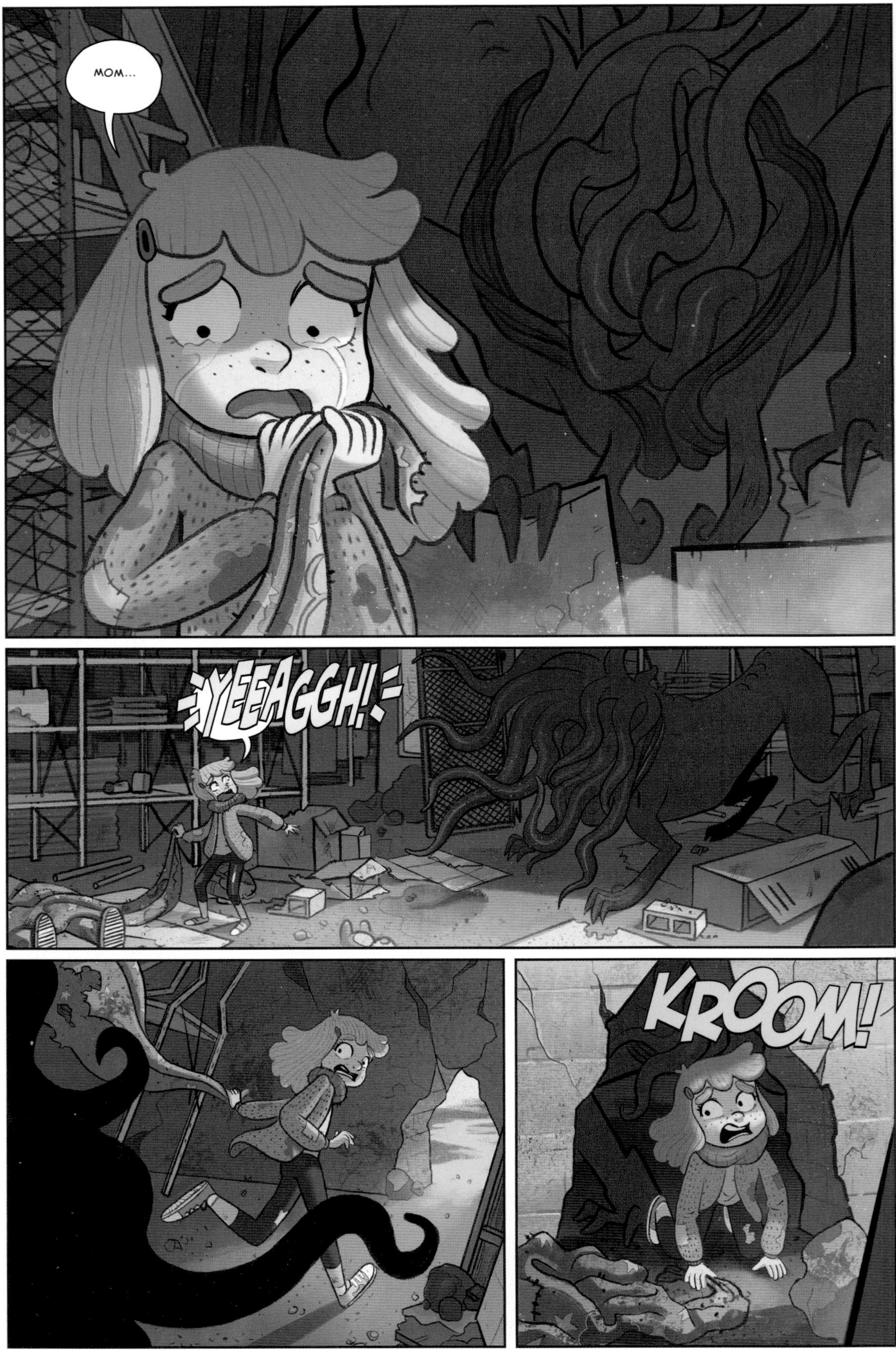
MOM...
YEEAGGH!
KROOM!

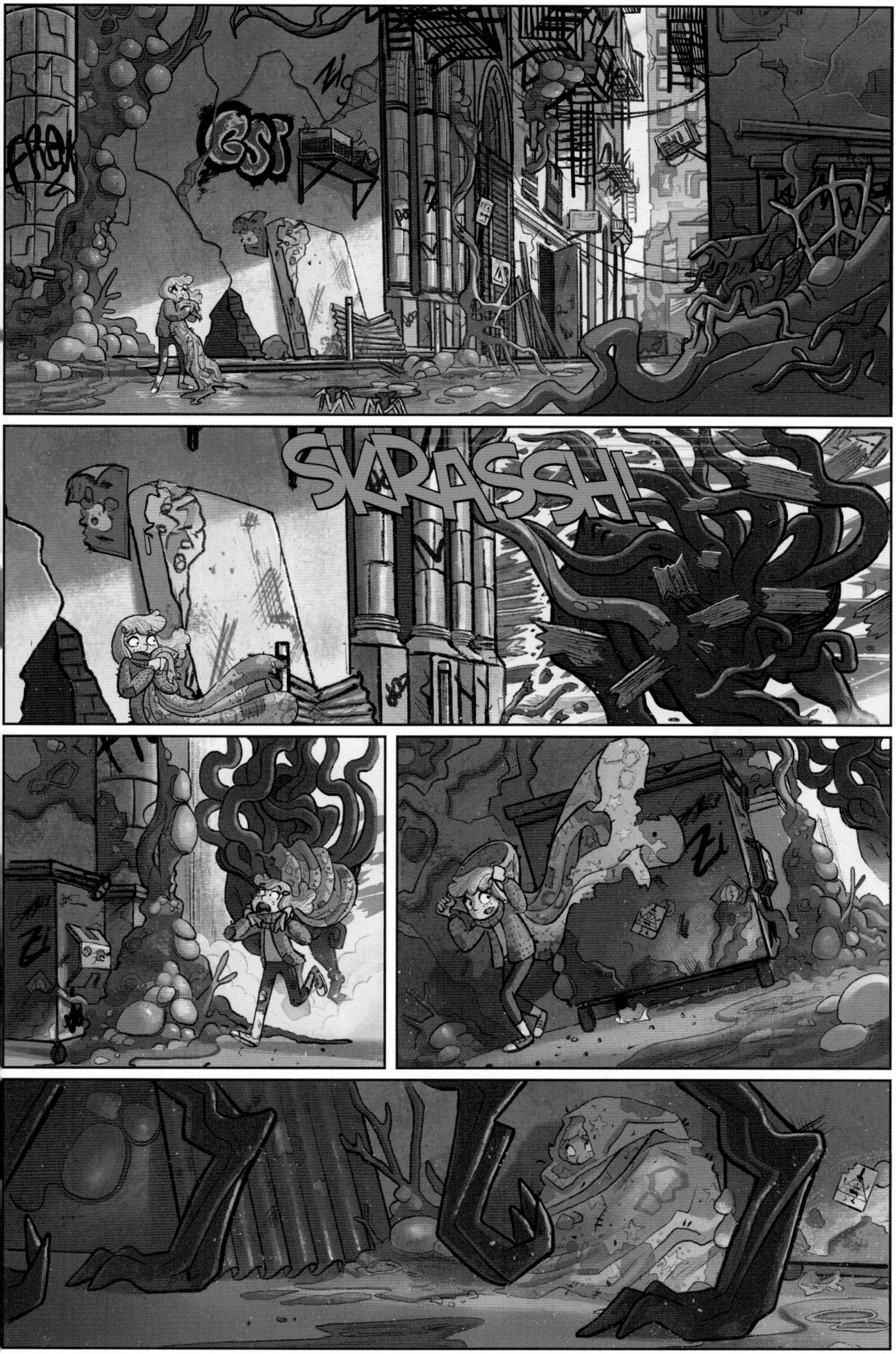
SKRASSH!

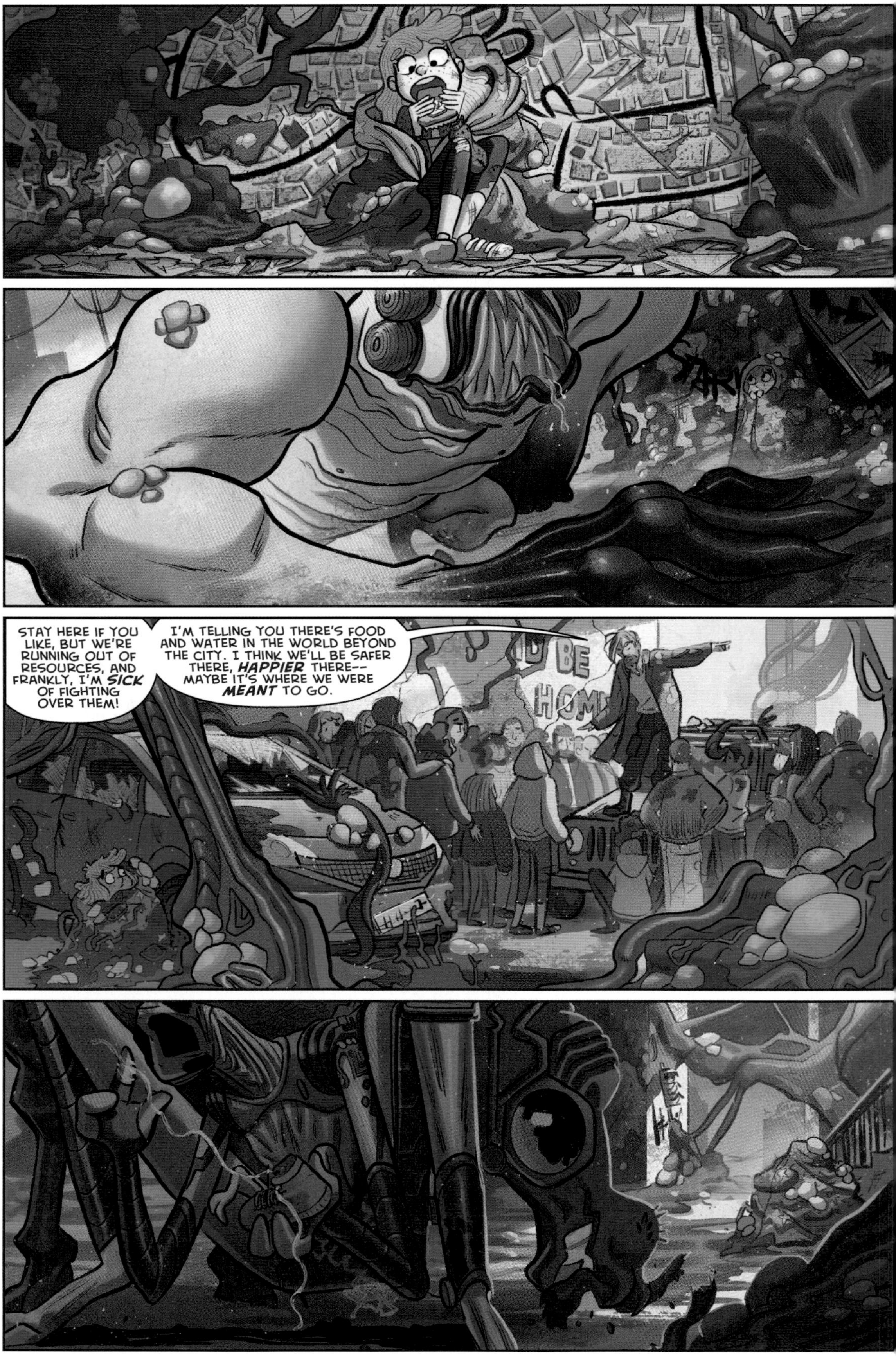
STAY HERE IF YOU LIKE, BUT WE'RE RUNNING OUT OF RESOURCES, AND FRANKLY, I'M *SICK* OF FIGHTING OVER THEM!
I'M TELLING YOU THERE'S FOOD AND WATER IN THE WORLD BEYOND THE CITY. I THINK WE'LL BE SAFER THERE, *HAPPIER* THERE-- MAYBE IT'S WHERE WE WERE *MEANT* TO GO.

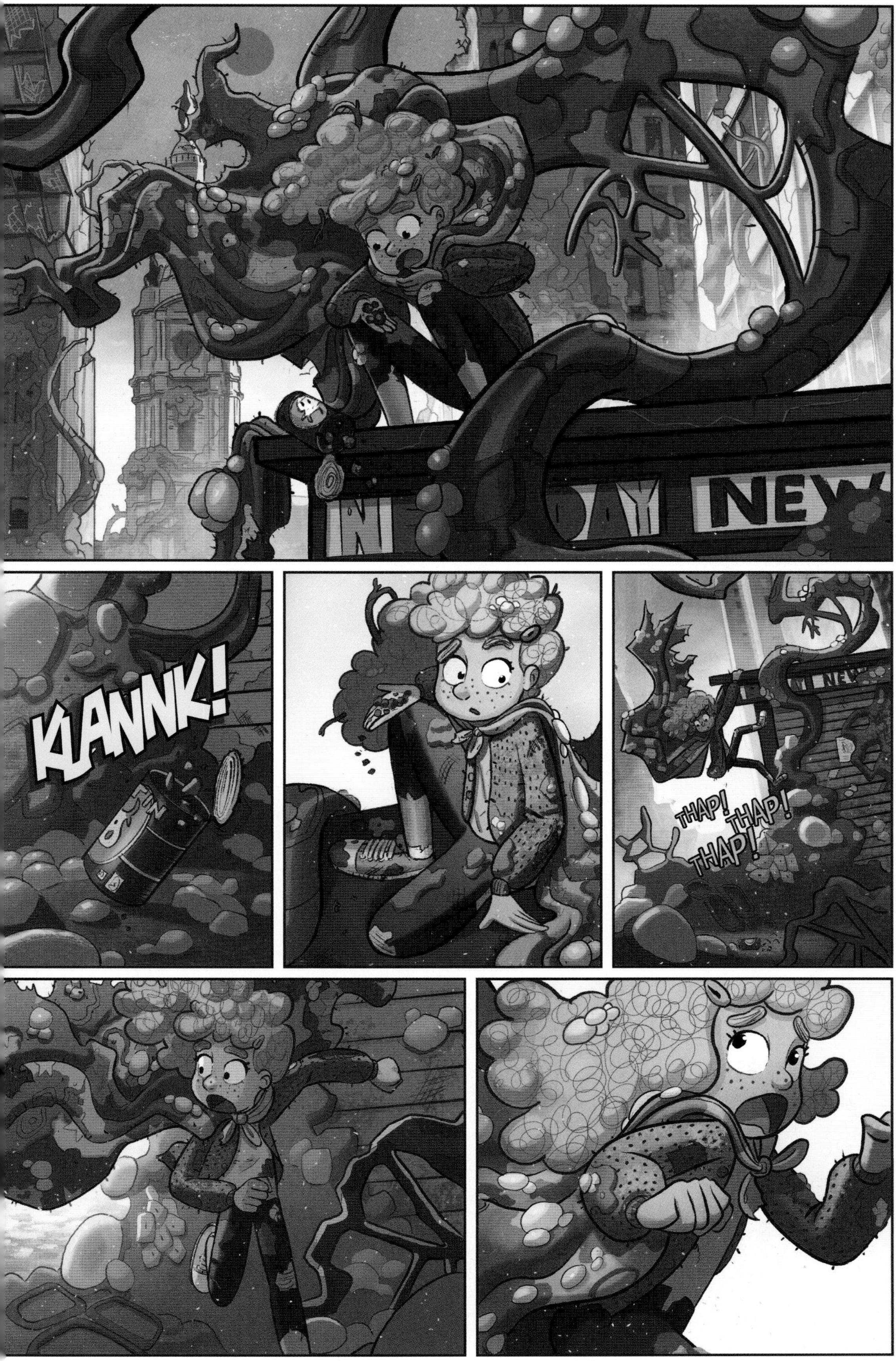
DAY NEW
KLANNK!
THAP! THAP! THAP!

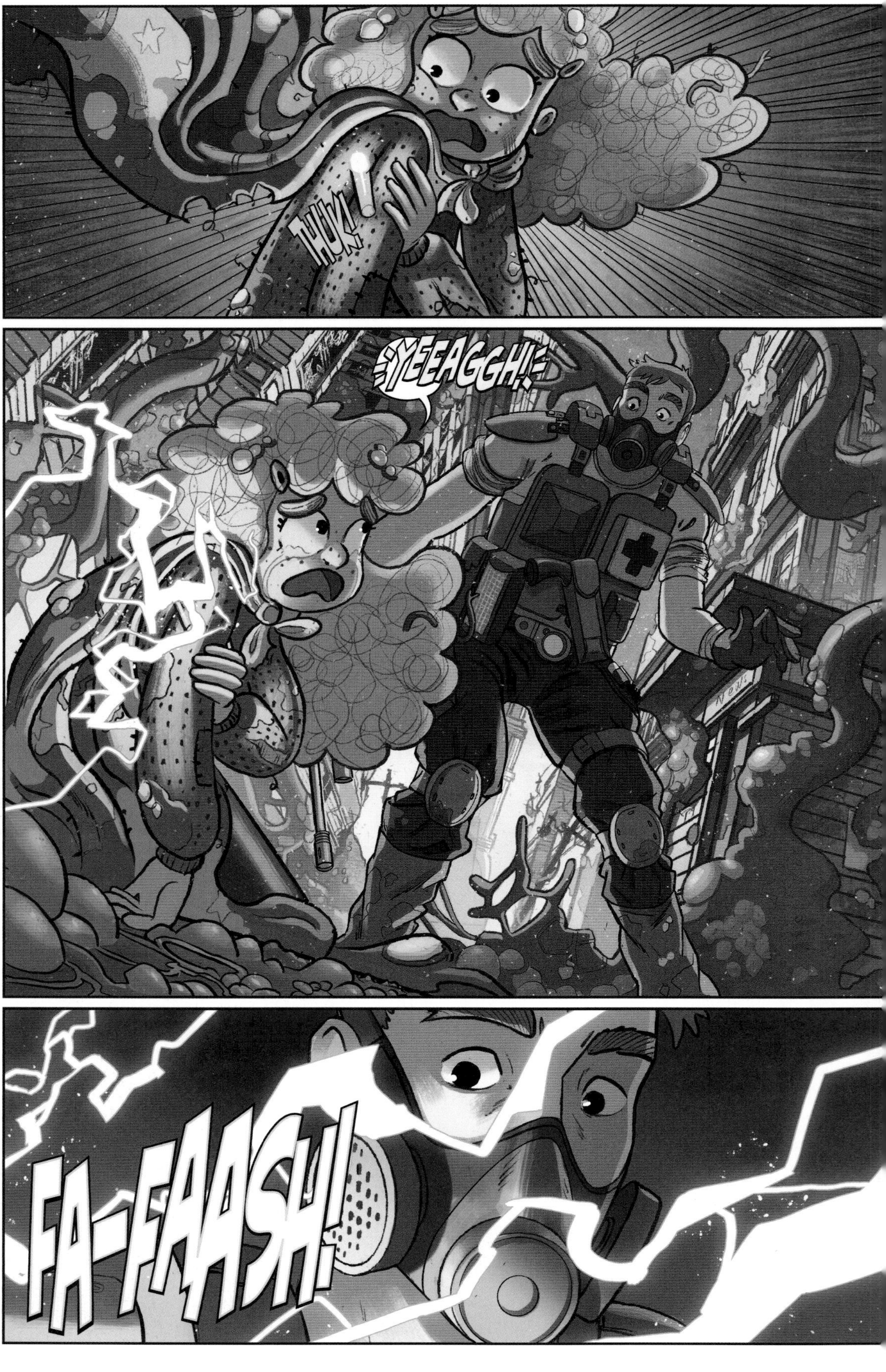
THUK!
YEEAGGH!
FA-FAASH!

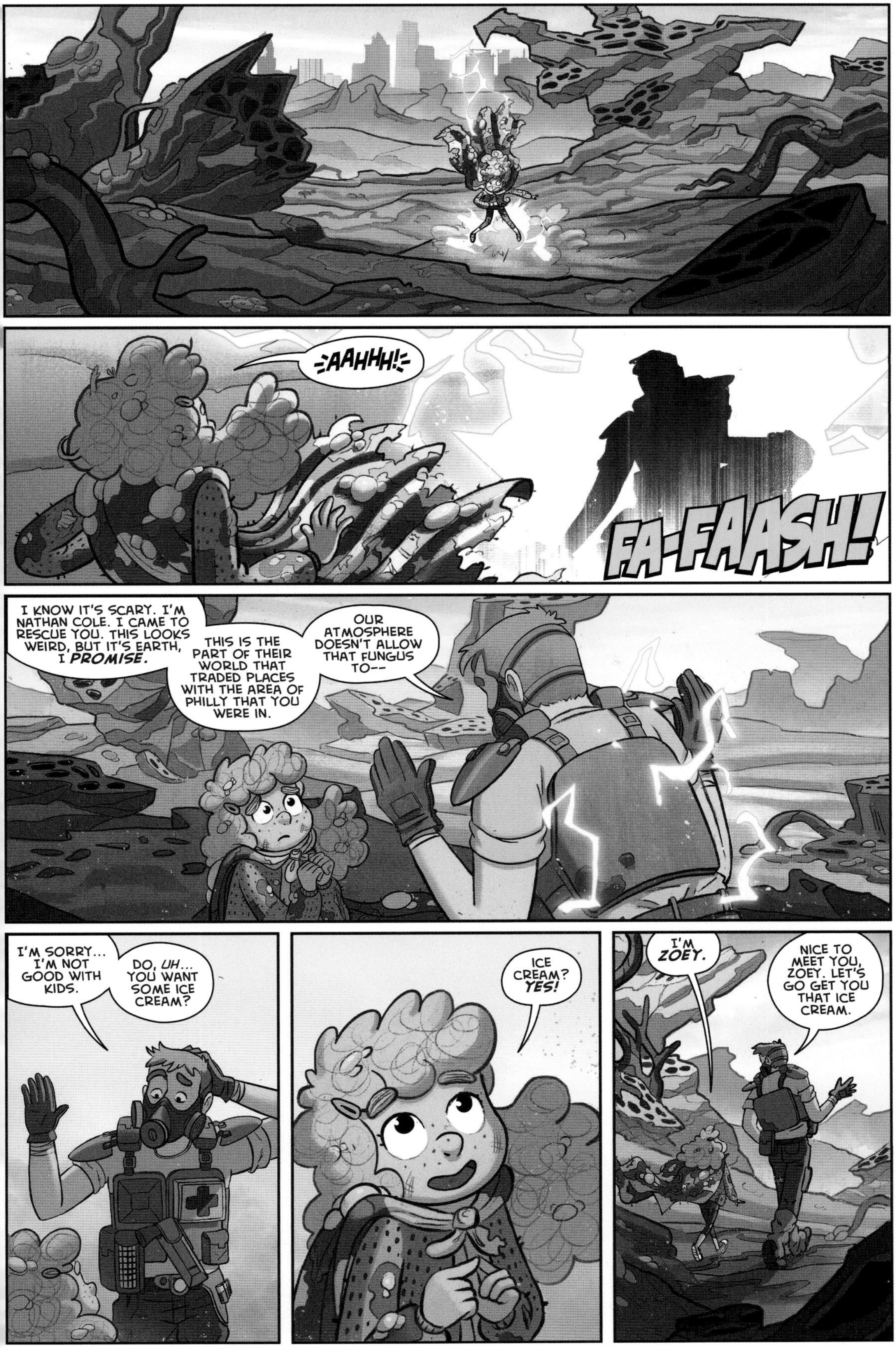
AAHHH!
FA-FAASH!
I KNOW IT'S SCARY. I'M NATHAN COLE. I CAME TO RESCUE YOU. THIS LOOKS WEIRD, BUT IT'S EARTH, I PROMISE.
THIS IS THE PART OF THEIR WORLD THAT TRADED PLACES WITH THE AREA OF PHILLY THAT YOU WERE IN.
OUR ATMOSPHERE DOESN'T ALLOW THAT FUNGUS TO--
I'M SORRY... I'M NOT GOOD WITH KIDS.
DO, UH... YOU WANT SOME ICE CREAM?
ICE CREAM? YES!
I'M ZOEY.
NICE TO MEET YOU, ZOEY. LET'S GO GET YOU THAT ICE CREAM.

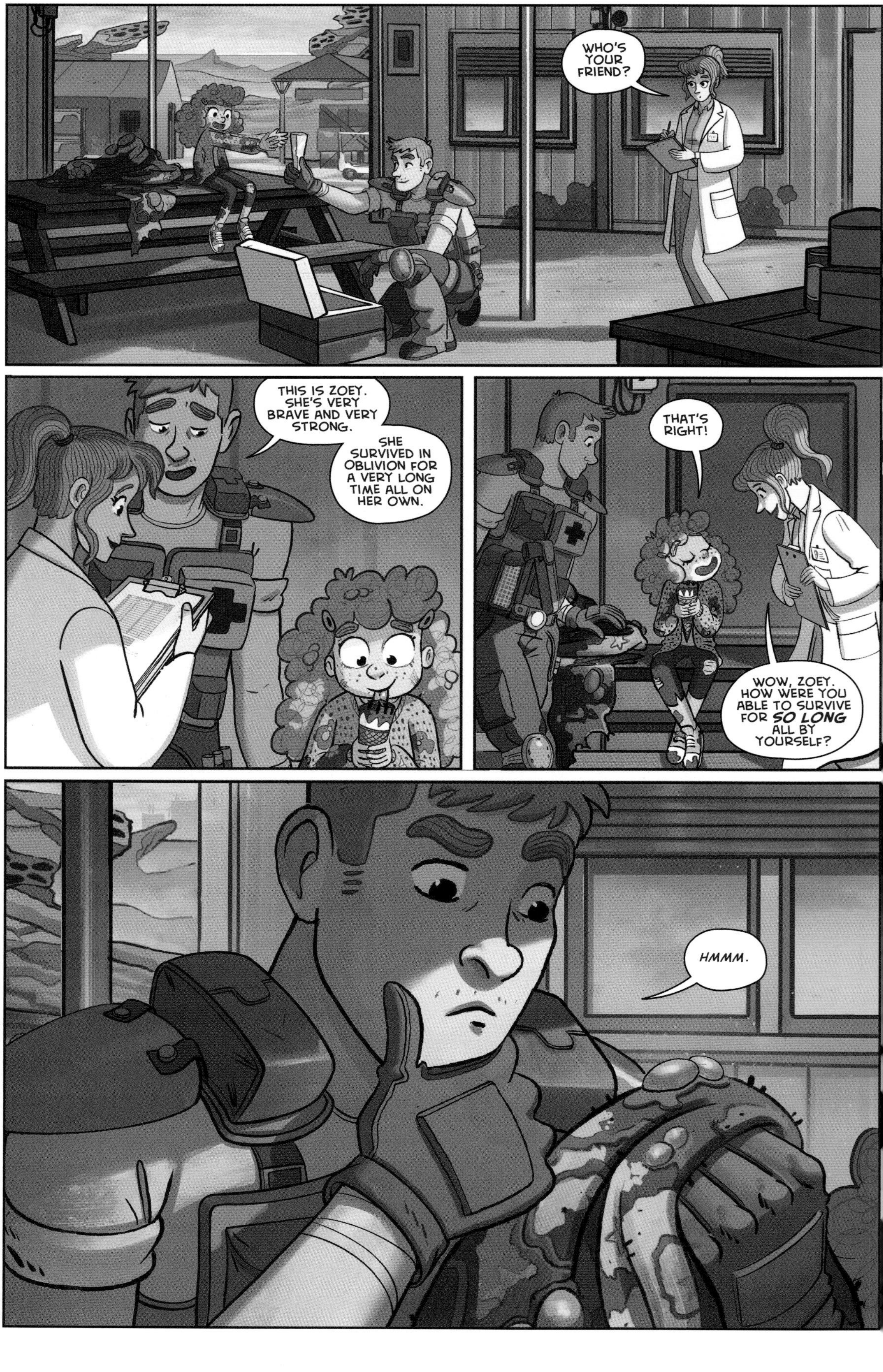
WHO'S YOUR FRIEND?
THIS IS ZOEY. SHE'S VERY BRAVE AND VERY STRONG.
SHE SURVIVED IN OBLIVION FOR A VERY LONG TIME ALL ON HER OWN.
THAT'S RIGHT!
WOW, ZOEY. HOW WERE YOU ABLE TO SURVIVE FOR SO LONG ALL BY YOURSELF?
HMMM.

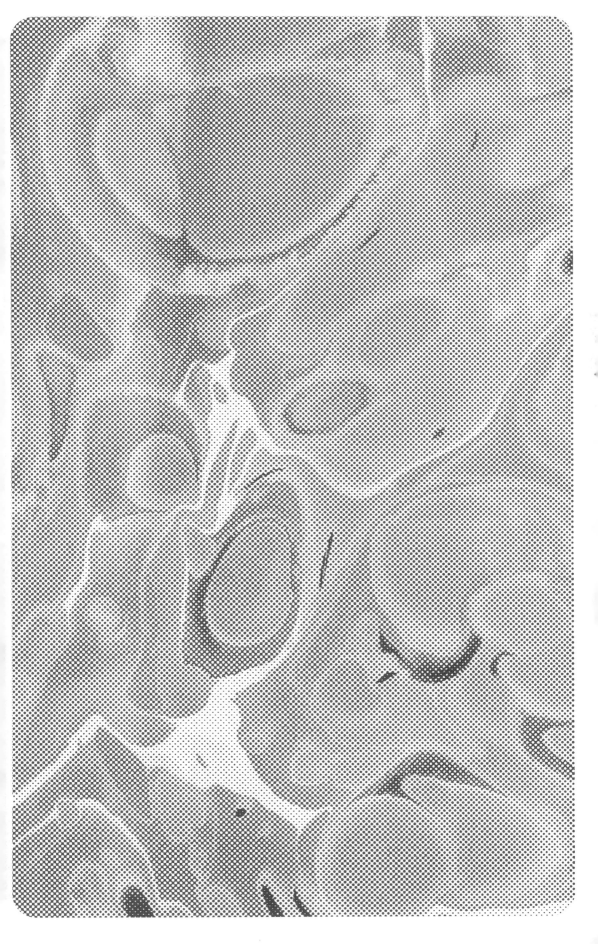

FOR MORE TALES FROM ROBERT KIRKMAN AND SKYBOUND

THE WALKING DEAD

ROBERT KIRKMAN CHARLIE ADLARD STEFANO GAUDIANO CLIFF RATHBURN

VOLUME 32
REST IN PEACE